THE MASS OF MEN

Rachel K. Wentz

AUTHOR'S NOTE: The training
sequences in this book are based on actual
events. The storyline is a work of fiction.

ISBN-13: 978-1492107545
ISBN-10: 1-492107549

THE MASS OF MEN

Other books by Rachel K. Wentz

Chasing Bones:
An Archaeologist's Pursuit of Skeletons

Life and Death at Windover:
Excavations of a 7,000-Year-Old Pond Cemetery

Let Burn:
The Making and Breaking of a Firefighter/Paramedic

A Bioarchaeological Assessment of Health from Florida's Archaic

Searching Sand and Surf: The Origins of Archaeology in Florida

The Body Blog: Explorations in Science and Culture

For Kirsten,
who taught me so much,
and my sister Leah,
for always believing.

I

She stood in line, the lone female among thirty-four cadets, an interloper, branded by a lack of testosterone. The cadets braced at attention, feet planted shoulder-width apart, fists knotted at the base of their spines as the instructors made their way across the polished wood floor, their footsteps echoing off the high walls of the gymnasium.

The heat in the gym was palpable, although the instructors seemed immune, their uniforms crisp, impeccable. The cadets sweated freely, their shorts and tee shirts, emblazoned with the academy logo, clung to their torsos as the vast space was infused with the odor of anxious flesh.

Samantha stood erect, lengthening her spine in a futile attempt to gain an extra inch, flexing the muscles of her back to appear bigger and stronger than her hundred and forty pounds. She stared straight ahead as the instructors worked their way down the line, examining the cadets with slow, critical eyes. They moved deliberately, shoulders back, stomachs in, remembering with nostalgia what it was like to be young, naive, and scared shitless.

Sam winced as they looked her over. She wasn't femininely beautiful, she sported the fresh-scrubbed looks that belonged in a J. Crew catalog, more innate than obvious. She had inherited her mother's lovely legs, her father's strong white teeth and hardheaded determination. Her hazel eyes were handed down from some distant German relative, as was her blond hair, which she had cropped boy short. Sam could feel the instructors taking in her shape, their eyes sliding down the length of her legs. For the first time since her struggles through puberty and braces, Sam was embarrassed by her looks.

As two instructors circulated in front, a third stood off to the side, taking the students in from a distance, sizing them up from afar. The instructors were seasoned officers, well-versed in the world of firefighting. They relished their role of breaking new recruits.

The students ranged in age from teenage boys fresh out of high school to men who had ventured down various career paths, some as professional athletes, others in the military. The older cadets were less intimidated. It showed in the way they carried themselves – erect stance, eyes forward. The eyes of the younger men danced in their heads. Somehow, they had all ended up together, grappling with their insecurities, waiting for the instructors to complete their excruciating inspection.

The taller of the officers reached for his clipboard, which had been placed with precision on a nearby chair. A whistle lay neatly beside it, its cord bundled in a tight coil. The officer maintained perfect posture, even while bending forward. He snapped back to attention as his eyes slid down the list of names, his booming voice sending a nervous ripple through the line of cadets.

"When you hear your name, respond with a 'check.' Ables! Adams! Bradford! Chancellor…"

Each name elicited a resounding "Check!" When he called out the name Peterson, a sarcastic "Yes, sir!" emanated from a big lug near the middle of the line. The officer paused as the second instructor swooped in.

"*Did you not hear the instructions, or are we now admittin' retards?*" shouted the burly officer in a southern slur, nose-to-nose with the reckless cadet.

"Y-yes," the lug stammered, "I mean, no."

"You better tack a 'sir' onto that or you'll be kissin' my fuckin' boots!" the officer barked, as the student shriveled with indignity.

"Kissing the boots" was code for pushups. Twenty pushups were the academy's standard reprimand, the paramilitary equivalent of a ruler to the back of the hand. For egregious errors, the whole group would perform.

Peterson dropped his eyes before muttering, "Yes, sir."

The officer backed away as roll call continued.

The instructor made it to the end of the alphabet. "Smith!"

"Check," Sam responded in a deep voice, a vain attempt to disguise her femininity.

Three more names were called, and roll was complete. The officer swung his clipboard behind his back, locking it between powerful hands as he braced before the cadets.

"Welcome to Class #64 of the Central Florida Fire Academy. I'm Officer Michaels," he said in a stilted tone meant to convey the seriousness of the situation. Sam noted his shaved head on which she could just make out a faint ring of auburn hair. He wore a brand-new baseball cap with the academy's logo; scant protection against the Florida sun that had intensified the rash of freckles covering his face and arms. A bushy handlebar mustache of darker auburn covered his mouth and stood in relief against a powerful jaw. His body was athletic, every inch of it tense, ready to spring.

"This is Officer Tanner," Michaels continued, with a quick jab of his clipboard.

Less polished but just as powerful, Tanner sported a dark shock of hair contrasting eyes of brilliant blue. He dangled his thumbs from his belt loops as he slowly raked the line. His thick frame disguised a dense layer of muscle underneath and a worn toothpick appeared permanently lodged in the corner of his mouth. He cocked his head as he fingered the pick, rolling it against the faint callous on his lower lip as he eyed the cadets.

Tanner stepped forward, removing the toothpick to mark the gravity of the moment. He threw back his shoulders as his deep drawl ricocheted off the gymnasium walls. "You're ours for the next three months. During that time, we'll lose a third of you, especially the heavy kid and the girl," he bellowed, his blue eyes skipping over Sam as if she had already been dismissed. He tossed a nod to Michaels and then plunked the toothpick back into his mouth, chewing for a moment before maneuvering it back in place.

Sam froze, embarrassed to be singled out so early in the process, furious at being deemed unworthy. She felt the old familial anger rise, an attribute passed from father to daughter, triggered whenever anyone dare challenge her resolve. She kept her eyes forward, all the while imagining ramming the toothpick through Tanner's fleshy jowl, yelling, *"Fuck you, sir!"* as she snapped a rigid salute.

She swallowed her anger, instead focusing guilt-ridden relief on the overweight kid who had decided, against all better judgment, to try to make it as a firefighter. Sam knew he might deflect attention from her, that his lack of physical strength might draw the wrath of the instructors, and that his inadequacies might make her transition easier. She stole a glance down the line and could just make out his trembling belly protruding among the row of washboard abs.

The third instructor, the one standing off to the side, glided slowly into her field of vision. Sam's spine stiffened as he took his place before the group. He was well built, lean, and appeared to be in his mid-forties. He had sandy hair cropped short and piercing grey eyes that sailed up and down the line before locking onto hers for a brief second. A matching mustache hid most of his mouth – a faint slit cut into the sharp contours of his face. Sam noticed he was handsome, but the coldness of his eyes overrode his good looks. She tried to imagine him smiling. He stood before them, shoulders squared, hands locked behind his back, examining his new class of cadets.

"This is Commander Daniels," Michaels announced reverently before ducking his chin and backing away.

"I welcome each of you," Daniels said in an even, quiet tone as his grey eyes slid up and down the line. "I hope you've come prepared to work. The officers are here to assist you through your training, so if you have a problem, let them know. If there's something you can't do, let them know. If you decide you've made a mistake by being here, let them know. Don't waste our time and we won't waste yours."

With a glance he turned the floor back to Michaels and resumed his position on the periphery of the room. Sam continued to brace as Michaels rifled the pages on his clipboard and laid out the day's schedule.

~

Commander Daniels watched her from the side of the gym. He had been watching her ever since she had taken her place in line. He tried not to, but the sense of familiarity was consuming. It settled in a portion of his brain where calm and pleasure once resided.

Perhaps it was the blond hair, the intensity of her eyes. Or perhaps it was the determination in her face that caused his mind to turn back on itself. Daniels forced his eyes forward, keeping the girl in his periphery as he tried to focus.

As Michaels wrapped up the overview, Daniels stole another glance and was startled by Tanner's barking order, "Take five and get back in line!" The words jolted the commander back to the present as his reverie disintegrated. With one last glimpse, he turned and marched slowly from the gymnasium.

~

After the break, the students filed back into the gym for the fitness assessment, which would gauge their strength and endurance. Here they would prove they possessed the stamina to enter a burning building wearing the sixty pounds of gear that would protect them from extreme temperatures and falling debris.

Once the cadets were lined up in formation, they were shuffled outside for a two-mile run. Three more instructors emerged from the gym, their faces hidden beneath ball caps and sunglasses, black tee shirts stretched taut across their muscled chests. They fell in behind the cadets and unleashed their fury.

"*At this pace we'll be here all goddamn day!*" one of them yelled as the officers pursued the cadets like a pack of jackals, hell-bent on culling the herd.

"*Pick up your fuckin' feet!*" another screamed as the officers infiltrated the group, darting among the students, disorienting them with their swiftness.

Sam stayed with the front of the pack, having trained for the last six months as she completed her paramedic certification. The officers exploited her strength, using her as an anvil to crush the weaker cadets.

"*The girl's kicking your asses!*" an officer yelled at the cadets bringing up the rear. "*Pick it up, you bunch of pussies!*" he screamed, dashing among the stragglers, his verbal assault aimed directly at their ears. A startled cadet stumbled and went sprawling to the pavement. The officer screeched to a halt, his stopwatch gripped in a sweaty fist.

"Since you can't keep up with the group, you fuckin' turtle, you can kiss my goddamn boots!" he barked as the cadet rolled into position and began hammering out pushups.

Sam knew the academy would be grueling; she wasn't about to show up unprepared. The heavy kid hadn't planned as well. He was huffing and puffing his way to the finish line as Tanner kicked gravel from the sideline, his clipboard flapping at his side like a broken wing as he shouted, "*Get your big ass movin'!*"

With the run completed, the students staggered back to the gym for the rest of the assessment. They jockeyed into formation as they struggled to catch their breath.

"Give us as many pushups as you can. The max score is 50. Start on my count," Michaels announced as the cadets broke from formation and spread out within the gym.

Sam dropped into position, noting the faint smell of socks

permeating the wood floors, listening to the grunts of the men nearby. The cadets braced in plank position as the instructors stood by, relishing each painful minute before finally blowing their whistles. By then, the weaker individuals were tiring, their backs slowly drooping, bellies kissing the floor. Sam focused on a far spot on the wall and pumped out fifty with little trouble.

Sit-ups were next. They had ninety seconds to perform. Sam hammered out eighty as one of the bigger cadets watched, straining to match her pace. But he had a massive upper body to contend with, Sam, the advantage of a lighter frame. The stronger cadets did well. The weaker ones wobbled from side to side, grimacing. Sam watched as the chubby kid squeaked out twenty. The instructors took note of her efforts. Tanner even managed a brief smile when he grumbled, "Nice job."

Following sit-ups, the students fanned out, arms and legs spread-eagle as a team of assessors tackled them with a vicious metal clasp. They measured the students' body fat by pinching the flesh along the backs of their arms, their waists, and the insides of their thighs. Sam noted the unsteady hand of the assessor as he placed the clasp against her leg. She stifled a grin as he scowled down at his clipboard, scribbling furiously.

Sam turned her attention to the heavy kid who stood nearby, still panting from the run, sweat rolling down his pink face as the calipers strained to accommodate his layers.

"Better set 'em to maximum!" the big lug from roll call snarled as those nearby snickered.

Michaels was on him in a flash. He braced before the cadet, his green eyes blazing. "I see I'm going to have to make you my special project, Peterson," he whispered irately, their faces close. "You can start by kissing my boots."

Peterson's shoulders slumped and he exhaled loudly, then dropped into position in front of the officer. Michaels pivoted; the toes of his boots positioned directly beneath Peterson's face. As the cadet pumped out twenty pushups, his forehead tapping the officer's boots with each downward stroke, Michaels took the opportunity to address the students.

"The academy is a paramilitary institution. You are expected to adhere to our code of conduct at all times," he proclaimed from a Superman stance as the cadet bobbed at his feet.

Peterson finished his pushups and sprang upright with a grunt. He brushed his hands off on his shorts and grudgingly resumed his place among the students. Michaels eyed the group and moved off.

When the pinching was done, each cadet thoroughly welted, they were made to squeeze a metal-handled contraption to assess their grip strength. The more macho in the bunch used the opportunity to show off, bearing down on the handle as they maxed out the gauge. The cadets watched closely as Sam squeezed out a modest score. Peterson shot her a belittling snort.

The heavy kid stepped up, glancing nervously at the group before setting his face and straining against the handle. As he gripped with all he had, bending forward to force his energy into that miserable contraption, a loud, whining fart escaped, sending the rest of the group into nervous fits of laughter. The instructors quieted them with quick shouts. Sam turned away, smiling despite herself.

With the assessment completed, the cadets were hustled to the showers. The men moved in a sweaty pack, swearing softly so as not to be overheard by the instructors. Sam broke from the group, relieved to be out from under the instructors' scrutiny, relishing the silence and isolation of the women's locker room, which was immaculate from lack of use. She stripped out of her damp clothes, jumped under a cold stream, washed with lightning speed, and ran a towel over her body before wrestling her way into a tight sports bra. She appraised her flattened chest with a quick sweep of her hands. She then donned a crisp, new uniform – black lace-up boots, matching fatigues, a blue academy tee shirt, and a heather-blue dress shirt, starched to perfection. The uniform felt foreign, her reflection in the mirror that of a stranger. Her short hair only added to her boyish appearance.

The cadets emerged as newly minted clones. Their dress shirts sported the academy patch on one sleeve, an EMT or paramedic patch, if certified, on the other. Their chests boasted silver name tags, last name only, as if their lowly rank afforded only partial identification. Their badges would be distributed upon graduation. Thus, began their first day at the academy.

~

The students sat bolt upright at their desks, speaking only when spoken to, writing frantically as Michaels outlined their curriculum. He braced in front of the class, broad shoulders flexed, his hands gripping the podium as if it might take flight. His bicep bulged as he flipped to the next page.

Tanner stood off to the side, leaning his large frame against the wall, eyeballing the cadets as he chewed on his pick. Commander Daniels moved silently throughout the room, gazing down on the students' notes, pulling papers from their desktops at random to gauge attention spans, notetaking skills. He stopped for a moment beside Sam's desk. Sam could smell the leather from his belt intermingled with an earthy soap smell. She stole a sideways glance and could make out the blond hairs that stood out on his forearm, which was tanned and corded. His hands were locked behind his back and Sam wondered if the man ever relaxed. She glanced up just as he turned away. Daniels sailed to the back of the room and disappeared.

Back in his office, the commander rifled through paperwork before leaning back in his chair, hitching a boot up on the open drawer, and gazing out his window. It seemed like a solid bunch. Most would pass. A few wouldn't make it. He had developed a keen eye for those who would succeed, those who would fail. He was rarely wrong. The evidence was on their desks.

Daniels could gauge a student's potential by the way they took notes. He recognized the frantic scribbling of those determined to stay on top. Then there were the others, those who scrawled pictures and geometric designs as they watched the minute hand perform its slow creep.

He was curious how the girl would do. He had seen the intensity in her face, but would that translate? She wasn't the first female to come through, though they certainly weren't common. Daniels ran a strict academy. His reputation for breaking recruits was well deserved. If a student wanted an easier path, they could always travel to the next county over for a watered-down version of his curriculum. Few women graced his door.

Her notes impressed him. They were neat and clearly written, each of her sections labeled and underlined; an attention to detail Daniels appreciated. He had noticed her hands, the right of which continued to work despite his presence, the left splayed out on her notebook, stabilizing it as she wrote. Her fingernails were trimmed short, no polish. Not the painted daggers of the last female, who ranted when told they would have to go. This one was prepared to work and, most importantly, blend in.

~

"You have thirty minutes for lunch," Tanner announced as he erased the whiteboard and swung his bulk to face the students. "Be back by thirteen hundred or your ass is mine." He grinned before yelling, "Break!"

The students scrambled from their desks and headed to the cafeteria in a noisy herd. Lunch finally afforded them a chance to talk. Sam slid into the seat next to Johnny Simms, a paramedic she knew from the months spent completing her clinicals. Johnny smiled before turning his attention to a pile of wilted greens.

"So, when did you decide to give up the ambulance for firefighting?" Sam asked as she plowed into her lunch, grimacing at the blandness of the vegetables. She dropped her fork in disgust and bit off a hunk of dry biscuit, chasing it with a gulp of water.

"When I realized it was the only way to build a pension," Johnny replied with a wry grin.

Johnny's easy demeanor camouflaged a laser focus. He had a methodical approach to patient care and Sam considered him one of the most talented medics in the county. She glanced at the long scar that ran along the left side of his face. As she did, two cadets took seats on either side of the table. The taller of the two spoke up as he vigorously shook a carton of milk, his voice modulating with the jerking of his arm.

"I'm Lance, this is Trey," he said, indicating with a jut of his chin the leaner, sandy haired individual next to Johnny.

Sam noticed the dichotomy of their appearance: Lance was dark haired, lanky, with giant hands and feet, and a bushy mustache that clashed with his baby face. He cracked open the carton and took a deep swig, his Adam's apple bobbing with each swallow. Trey was lightly built, subdued and serious. He gave a stiff nod as he meticulously sliced his turkey. Where Lance's movements were awkward and erratic, Trey's were restrained, systematic. They seemed to play off each other, like an old married couple. Sam watched as Lance eyed Johnny's scar.

"That's quite a scar you got there," Lance mumbled in between bites as he continued to stare at Johnny's face, oblivious to his discomfort.

"How'd you get that? Bar fight?" He grinned over a mouthful.

"Car wreck," Johnny muttered before dropping his eyes to his tray. Sam knew he would say no more. Johnny guarded the story of his wreck. All Sam managed to get out of him during her tenure on the ambulance was that it happened when he was a teen and he had gone into cardiac arrest. That made him a miracle, in Sam's eyes. Trauma arrests rarely came back.

"Where did you guys come from?" Johnny asked as a means of diverting attention from his face.

"Michigan," Lance replied, taking another deep chug from his milk. He swiped a quick finger over his mustache. "We were sick of freezing our asses off, so we applied and relocated. Just arrived two days ago. Trey's piece-a-shit Honda barely made it." He eyed Trey and paused to gulp a few more bites. Trey took up the story.

"We had a bit of trouble getting to class this morning," he added gravely, bracing his fork and knife against his plate as he recounted how his car had sputtered to a halt three blocks from the academy.

Lance took over, leaning into the conversation, working his arms for effect. His knife and fork hung in midair. "So, I'm standing in the intersection, trying to shove the car to the side of the road," he began, shifting his eyes conspiratorially. "Trey's screaming at me to push, cars are *whizzing* by us, no one will stop to help, and some guy leans out the window and yells, 'Hey assholes, go back to Michigan!'

Here Lance paused, wide-eyed. "Is that any way to treat a fella?" he whined before tucking back into his lunch.

"Don't sweat it," Johnny replied, grinning. "This isn't the best area to be looking for help." Johnny would know. He had worked the west side for years and was familiar with the brutality of the territory.

As they returned to their meals, a young cadet quietly took up the seat across from Sam. He smiled shyly as he flipped open his napkin. "I'm Tyler Williams, but I go by Ty," he murmured, cutting his eyes to his tray.

"I'm Sam," she replied, noting that his shyness was enhanced by the beauty of his face, the perfection of his bones. Ty was graced with exquisite coloring; the soft brown of his hair, the deep tint of his skin, and dark hazel eyes, which Sam could barely appreciate because of his dodging glance. After some coaxing, Ty told her about growing up in Ocala, and how it was assumed he would be taking over the family's sprawling farm.

"Why did you leave?" Sam asked after Ty fell silent.

"My father," he replied, eyes on his tray.

Sam noted the strain that played across his features and was struck with the urge to touch his face.

Sam had the alphabetical good fortune to be positioned between Johnny and Ty when they stood in formation. The heavy kid hadn't been as lucky. His first name, "Tate," had quickly been transformed by the officers to "Tater" on account of his spud-like physique, and his last name of Patterson put him elbow-to-elbow with the smartass, Peterson. He was doubly cursed. He sat in isolation, hunched over his tray.

Like Lance and Trey, Shane and Bo had also signed up together. They were young, both sons of Orlando firefighters, and both attempting the academy for the second time. The seriousness of their situation sapped any excitement they may have felt. The pressure, most likely doled out by their fathers, was plastered across their young faces.

Aaron Peterson sidled up to Sam's table with an exaggerated swagger, his belt loaded down with an array of tools and a knife big enough to take down a good-sized hog. His large head sported a fleshy face, and his narrow eyes hovered above a cocky grin. Sam watched as he plunked down his tray and cut his beady gaze to Ty. He settled into his lunch, continuing to analyze Ty, while scooping large forkfuls of mashed potatoes into his face, which didn't keep him from blurting out his thoughts on the academy.

"This is going to be a bitch!" he exclaimed as he worked a piece of bread around his plate, smacking his lips with gusto. "Had a cousin who went through a year ago, said Daniels is one cold motherfucker. Pluck you out just for lookin' at him wrong. And Michaels ain't much better," he continued in between gulps to no one in particular. "Got an ass so tight he can whistle Dixie."

When no one responded, Aaron took it as an insult and scanned the table for a victim. His gaze landed back on Ty.

Ty eyed him before returning to his tray. Aaron glanced from Ty to Sam. "Well, it looks like we got two pretty girls in class," Aaron announced, grinning and leaning back in his seat. "I only noticed the one this mornin'." He swiped at his mouth with a meaty hand.

Ty ignored him and stabbed at a hunk of broccoli. Sam glared down the table at Aaron as if examining a large turd, and then slowly swung her eyes to Ty. Her gesture only encouraged the lug.

"Hey, Pete," Aaron shouted at the lanky kid across the table, apparently a comrade from the sticks. "Which one's prettier? Hard for me to decide."

Pete forced a grin and kept eating, eyes on his plate. He was used to Peterson's blathering, having attended the same EMT course. He knew to smile and nod; the only way to avoid falling victim to Aaron's cruelty.

"Hey! Pretty-boy!" Aaron called down to Ty. "You sure you're in the right place? I think the fuckin' home-ec class is down the hall!" He laughed loudly despite a mouthful of peas.

Sam glanced over at Ty and saw the brown skin of his neck flush. She could see the anger rise in his face, but he maintained control and kept his eyes down. Although Ty was not tall, he had the build of someone used to the physical work of a farm. But he seemed disinclined to fight. Sam admired his restraint. Her mind was churning out ways to verbally pummel Peterson, but she knew a response in Ty's defense would only encourage Aaron's antagonism. Instead, she leaned in and whispered across the table, "Jealous asshole," bringing a warm smile to Ty's lips.

Aaron grunted his disapproval at their communal lack of humor and returned to his potatoes.

~

The "cigar sessions" had become a ritual. At the end of the first day, Michaels and Tanner congregated in Daniels' office to discuss the new group of cadets and go over class logistics. They gathered in the soft leather chairs, an arrangement Daniels implemented when he took over as commander of the academy, so that he could converse with his team without the barrier of a desk.

The cigars were a secret the officers shared. Prior to lighting up, Daniels would issue a quick nod and Tanner would spring from his seat and quietly close the door, since tobacco was forbidden at the academy. It was their singular guilty pleasure. They earned it.

The only person privy to their ritual was Miss Davis, Daniels' Administrative Assistant. Nothing got by Maggie. She knew everything that went on at the academy, no matter how covert the operation. To harass the officers, she always waited until she smelled the telltale smoke emanating from beneath the office door before poking her head inside. As soon as she appeared, the men dropped their hands in an attempt to conceal their contraband.

"I'm leaving, Commander, if there's nothing else you need," she said sweetly, forcing a straight face and batting crinkled, knowing eyes. Her plump frame was hidden behind the door and her round face seemed to float in midair.

"We're fine, Miss Davis," Daniels replied gruffly with a guilty wave of his empty hand. In the nine years Maggie had worked for him, he had never referred to her as anything other than Miss Davis. Intimacy, even in the slightest degree, did not come naturally to the commander.

Once the door was securely closed, Daniels relaxed in his chair and eyed his officers. "So, what do you think?" he began, drawing on his cigar and leveling an icy stare. The sessions always started with the same five words.

Michaels sat bolt upright, frozen at attention. Even in the comfort of the office, Michaels' posture remained impeccable. He flipped through his clipboard, which he kept perpetually at his side, attached by some invisible umbilicus. "A strong bunch," he replied as he scanned his notes. "A few weak ones, but they should be gone in no time. One smartass, but overall a stable group. I think they'll do well." As he spoke, he held a protective hand over his clipboard to guard it from falling ashes. He eyed Tanner for input.

Tanner was leaning back, puffing leisurely on his fat cigar, his toothpick temporarily dislodged and sticking out from his breast pocket. He relished the meetings in the commander's office. They were a reminder of how far he'd come since his days as a green cadet. He took one more savory puff before commenting.

"Pretty sharp group," he began, eyeing the burning end of his cigar. "Peterson's gonna be a handful, but nothin' we can't tamp down with a little pressure. Good lookin' chick," he added with a wink. It'd been a while since they'd had a female at the academy.

Then Tanner remembered.

Daniels forbade the instructors to comment on female cadets. Tanner was reminded by the razor look Daniels shot him as he reached for the ashtray. To cover the blunder, Tanner continued in a formal tone, parroting Michaels.

"I think they'll do well," he said, his twang barely audible as he stiffened in his seat. He looked to Michaels for a reprieve, but Daniels pushed through so as not to dampen the air.

"We've got some young ones in the group," Daniels continued, flicking his ashes. "Shane and Bo are back, so keep an eye on them and see they don't get in trouble." Daniels knew from experience that the difficult males, especially those hell-bent on proving themselves, tended to prey on the youngest. It always happened when men converged, as if the training weren't enough to prove their prowess. The young ones were often crushed in the process.

Daniels went over the schedule, assigning adjunct instructors for the days spent on the training ground. Safety regulations dictated one instructor per six students; training with live fire required an even higher ratio. Lining up the adequate number of adjuncts was a constant in Daniels' daily routine. He relied on Michaels to stay on top of it.

With their cigars smoked down to stubs and the schedule set, the meeting wound down and Michaels and Tanner rose to leave. Tanner popped his toothpick back into his mouth and grabbed the ashtray on his way out. It would be returned by morning, emptied and clean. It was just something he did, a form of tribute for being included.

With the office to himself, Daniels returned to his desk and scanned the list of cadets. His eyes slid down the names, settling near the end. *Smith, Samantha,* he read, thinking back to her appearance in lineup, berating himself for remembering. He rose from his chair, tossed the list onto his desk, ran a hand through his bristled hair, flipped the lights off, and left.

II

The Central Florida Fire Academy was one of three primary programs at The Institute, a technical college that opened its doors in 1972. The Institute was divided into three wings that jutted out from the main administration building like spokes of a wheel. The medical programs took up the north wing where students trained in the fields of radiography, respiratory therapy, and surgery. They stuck to their wing and had little interaction with fire or police. The cadets would spot them occasionally. The med students stood out in their frosty white scrubs, most having exchanged their backpacks for rolling suitcases in which they toted their reference books between car and classroom.

The Police Academy occupied the middle wing. Fire and police would pass each other throughout the day as their respective cadets moved between classrooms and training fields. The police were a serious bunch, what with the weight of social stability resting on their broad shoulders. They rarely laughed.

The Fire Academy made up the south wing. The surrounding grounds were divided between fire and police, each with their designated training fields. A dense line of pines formed the periphery of campus, divided by a thick barrier of foliage that separated the two fields. The police cadets had their own training tower where they practiced forcible entry by bashing in doors while screaming at the tops of their lungs. Throughout the day, they could be seen rushing toward the building, climbing like a swarm of combat-ready ants through every orifice of the structure, apprehending their suspects, and dragging them out onto the tarmac. The remainder of their field contained elaborate obstacles constructed for man and beast: one for the officers, the other for their dogs, since the academy also served as the state's primary canine center.

Commander Daniels was in charge of fire. He had fled a life and career in San Diego almost ten years ago, starting over at the academy. The position was the perfect salve for his exodus. Here, he combined his love of training with the construction of new firefighters and each class contained his success stories. Although not all the students passed, in fact at least a quarter of each class failed, he knew the ones who made it had worked hard and given their best, and that he had played a role in their success.

He had an excellent crew of instructors he relied on and trusted. Most had been handpicked upon his arrival as he expanded the role of the academy beyond the minting of new cadets. Michaels and Tanner oversaw the academy training; Taylor and Adams led the special ops program, where teams from larger departments were certified in high angle, trench rescue, and urban search and rescue. The teams came from throughout the southeast for the week-long courses. A large-print calendar lined the wall of Daniels' office, colored lines delineating the specialized courses. If the calendar was not marred in bright colors, Daniels wasn't happy.

Daniels also directed a corps of highly trained adjuncts. The academy was now one of the top training facilities in the southeast; an achievement he savored, especially on those low days. His instructors were some of the best, and they depended on him for his cool head and leadership. Although he oversaw the operations at the academy and was responsible for the masses of paperwork that accompanied his position, Daniels made it a practice to maintain a presence on the training ground. He enjoyed it. He liked seeing the cadets advance through their training, learning new skills, becoming proficient on the fire ground. He took pride in their achievements, took part in any issues that arose, and enjoyed working alongside his instructors.

The officers didn't mind his oversight. Initially, they interpreted it as micromanagement and were insulted by his constant attention. But Daniels' unobtrusive manner, and the ease with which he relinquished control on the training ground, eventually won them over. They came to rely on his quiet presence.

~

Sam arrived early on the second day as the sun emerged through the trees beyond the training towers, casting oblong shadows across the expansive grounds. She parked beneath the limbs of a giant oak and read through the previous day's notes, scanning ahead to the next chapter. As she flipped through her text, sipping a cup of steaming coffee, she glanced out over the training field and could make out the rigid shapes of Michaels and Daniels running laps around the field. They kept perfect pace, their bodies mirror images of each other.

"Maniacs," she muttered, shaking her head.

Today would establish the routine of their training, which would stretch from September to December. Sam could stand anything for three months. She may have been challenged when it came to size, but growing up the daughter of a naval officer, regularly torn from the security and stability of each temporary home, had made her a chameleon. She could adjust to any situation, any group in which she was placed.

She grew up an only child. Her mother died of breast cancer when she was barely six and resided in the far recesses of her memory, surfacing only on rare occasions. Sam couldn't remember much: delicate hands, pale blue eyes, and the timbre of her mother's voice resonating through her chest as she rocked Sam in her lap. The rest had been lost.

Her father raised her, his greatest gift her introduction to books. He was a learned man with a voracious love of literature. A captain in the Navy, they were tethered to the ocean, constantly on the move up and down the east coast. Sam still maintained a close affinity with water. She associated his memory with the smell of the sea, the sun on her face. She remembered the dark outline of the rooster tattooed on his left calf: a sailor's talisman against drowning. He was gone now, the victim of a weak heart.

Sam grew up in the company of men. Her father would frequently take her to the port, where the ships sat like monstrous grey beasts. She remembered the thick smell of oil and diesel fuel, how the diamond plating shone in high relief beneath the lights of the bridge. She remembered her first tour of a submarine, the polite sailor lifting her small frame through each of the oval doorways connecting the compartments. As they walked the inner length of the vessel, her father provided a running monologue on the mechanisms that kept it watertight as it descended into the depths.

As she got older, Sam became aware of the subtle shift that occurred when she and her father entered the company of his men. Sam was never sure if it was her father's rank or her sex that caused the men to halt their conversations, stand a bit straighter. It seemed they paid deference to both. She watched the way the men interacted with her father, grew familiar with the silent acquiescence that surrounds men of rank. Sam learned to gauge a man's worth by the number of gold bars on his shoulders, the weight of his uniform in full regalia.

Like all military lives, theirs was a transient existence. Sam grew accustomed to the feel of walking into a new classroom, all eyes on her as she scanned the room, searching out the empty seat. She was used to being the odd man out, the outsider entering unfamiliar turf, relying on her ability to encase herself in a bubble of self-confidence, needing nothing and no one to provide security, a sense of place. The years of grade school were lessons in isolation, the slow construction of a tough outer shell.

The fire academy would force her back into that shell, from which she would peer out at the surrounding landscape, etched with the scrutiny and judgment of those whose turf was being infiltrated by one who didn't belong; one whose sex defined her as unfit for the world in which they moved. Sam would depend on her life lessons to see her through this passage.

~

Each day at the academy began with an hour of physical training: a mile-and-a-half run, calisthenics in the gym, endless pushups and sit-ups, and a barrage of verbal abuse. Following morning drills, they would either head to the classroom or out to the training field, depending on the day's curriculum.

PT would bring the group together, forge the bonds that would enhance their camaraderie on the training field. They fed off each other with words of encouragement. As they ran, they formed a tight group, moving in steady cadence. They would grow accustomed to this forced contiguity over the next three months. The tight confines of drills would instill a sense of familiarity among them as their identities coalesced.

On the second day, their gear was distributed. The cadets filed into the gym where piles of worn, yellow turnout gear had been dumped in the center of the room. A whistle blew somewhere in the gym, and the students broke ranks and combed through the piles, searching for coats, pants, and gloves that fit. Boots were scattered along the periphery of the gym, the size printed in bright yellow marker on the heel of each boot.

The gear smelled as if it had been stored in a damp attic and seen many a long, wet season, the inner linings perpetually stained with the perspiration of anxious students. Sam finally located gear that fit, cinching down her waist and adjusting her suspenders so they formed a tight curve over her shoulders. Helmets were distributed last, most of which were heavily scarred from years of abuse, the result of being thrown to the concrete by frustrated students.

Peterson paraded around in helmet and boots, clowning loudly to his cronies before marching over to Sam and Ty. Ty was sprawled on the floor, retying his shoes after securing a pair of boots. Sam stood beside him, gathering her gear.

"I see ya found the girl's pile," Aaron shot at Ty. Ty ignored him, concentrating on his laces, while Sam's anger bubbled to the surface. She cut her eyes to Aaron as she folded her coat across her arm. "So how much extra tuition did it cost you to special-order that helmet?" she said, eyeing him as she reached down for her boots.

The whiff of dissension immediately drew a small crowd. Ty scrambled to his feet as the students looked on anxiously, awaiting Peterson's response. Aaron froze, his cocky grin fading into the depths of his jowls as he was instantly transported back to grade school, standing on the playground as the other kids taunted him with, "*There goes Pumpkin-headed Peterson!*"

He shot Sam an angry look, then ripped the helmet from his head. "At least I belong here, bitch!" he snarled, emphasizing the slur with a thrust of his helmet. All eyes shifted to Sam.

"Think so, dumbass?" Sam replied evenly, cocking her head. "Good thing IQ tests aren't required, you fucking troglodyte."

The students hooted at Sam's bravado as Aaron grappled for a response, stymied by the alien vocabulary. Sam turned to walk away and felt him lurch toward her; could smell the combined stench of his cologne and sweat as it wafted over her shoulders. As she whirled around, Michaels' voice boomed across the gym.

"*Peterson, get the fuck over here!*" he yelled, jabbing at the ground with his clipboard.

Aaron glared at Sam, repeating, "Bitch," under his breath as he stomped off across the gym. The small crowd dismantled and returned to their gear.

Ty turned to Sam. "You better watch him," he said, his eyes following Aaron across the gym.

"I'll try to hold my tongue next time," Sam replied, nudging him with an elbow.

With another shriek of the whistle, the students were ordered to don their gear and line up in formation. They squirmed as they braced in line, adjusting to the feel of the thick material scratching their necks, the unfamiliar weight of their helmets. It was an adult version of dress-up; green cadets masquerading as trained professionals. It was thrilling, yet humbling. The students were reminded of the hostile environments in which they would perform, where their lives depended on the protection of their bodies. Their gear would keep the fire from scorching their skin, the deadly temperatures from boiling their blood.

With their gear stowed in their lockers, the cadets hit the showers and met up in the classroom. They would spend the remainder of the week going over fire ground safety: how to lift properly, how to report an accident, and how to avoid becoming a training ground casualty. They would then move on to fire behavior, familiarizing themselves with the "fire triangle" and its counterpart, the "tetrahedron."

Michaels drove the point home as he paced in front of the class. "The most vital skill for a firefighter is recognizing the different stages through which a fire evolves and being alert for the rapid deterioration of conditions that can lead to catastrophe."

Monday would be their first day on the training field. There, they would be oriented to the two massive structures in which they would spend most of their time. The first was the "tower," a grey four-story building made of concrete blocks, with inner and outer stairwells and large, glass-free windows. The tower was used for basic drills: throwing ladders, advancing hoselines, implementing highrise gear, and raising and lowering tools.

The second structure was the "burn building," a hulking, charred chasm of dense brick plumbed with natural gas lines. The gas fueled the controlled burns. To produce the blinding smoke characteristic of real fires, the building would be stuffed with wooden pallets and bundles of hay, which would be lit off during drills. The more fuel, the thicker the smoke. The walls were treated with burn resistant material so that the fires could be relit without fear of structural degradation. Routine training fires would burn around three hundred degrees near the floor; temperatures at the ceiling could reach six hundred. Their first lesson in firefighting: "Stay low."

The week passed uneventfully, although the first round of exams stripped two from their class. Their gaping lockers stood as bleak reminders. Today would mark their first day on the training field. Days on the training ground still began with PT. The cadets were hustled through their workout, skipping the showers and heading straight to the tower; anxious to be free from the classroom. They lumbered across the field, perspiring freely from the run, their arms weighted down with gear and helmets. Tanner jogged stealthily up from behind before deploying a verbal ambush.

"You guys out for a fuckin' stroll? Get your asses in formation and

line up on deck!" he screamed as the students broke into a trot.

They arrived at the base of the tower winded, then quickly assembled their gear in alphabetical order, mirroring their placement in formation. They snapped to attention as Michaels emerged from the tower.

The instructors had multiplied; now there were six, each anxious to shout the cadets into submission. They were decked out in all black: tee shirts, fatigues, and combat boots. They barked orders as Michaels silently surveyed the scene, since he ran the show when Daniels was not around. Once the cadets were lined up, Tanner laid out the schedule for the day, working off his own battered clipboard. For a moment, Sam thought Michaels had relinquished control of his, but it magically appeared at his side as he moved down the line.

"Today we're gonna do airpack drills," Tanner announced as he paced before the line, his toothpick wagging as he spoke. "First, you'll have thirty seconds to don your gear, minus the pack. Once you got that down, you'll be given another thirty seconds to have the whole assemblage donned, breathin' off your tanks, ready for entry. Fuck it up and you do it again. And we've got all day." He grinned, gave a short chirp of his whistle, which he accomplished with toothpick in place, and the cadets fell out of formation.

They gathered their gear and Sam followed Johnny into the dark interior of the tower. The cadets blinked like sheep as their eyes adjusted to the dim light. Their airpacks were strewn neatly across the concrete floor. They consisted of lightweight composite tanks attached to metal harnesses, with heat-resistant straps that fit over the shoulders. When in place, the tank rode like a backpack, the control knob at its base. A high-pressure metal hose ran from the base of the tank to a regulator that controlled the air pressure as it exited the tank. A gauge that hung over the shoulder indicated the level of air in the tank, which was to be monitored at all times. When the air pressure dropped below a certain level, a bell would go off indicating the firefighter had only minutes to exit the building or change out their tank.

After stepping into their bunker pants and donning their hoods and coats, the cadets dropped to their knees before their packs. Sam followed Johnny's lead, a habit she acquired while completing her clinicals under his watchful gaze. She laid out her gloves and helmet neatly alongside as Johnny shot her an approving glance. Sam settled back on her haunches and waited for the order to begin.

Tanner lowered his bulk to ground level and knelt before his pack. The packs were positioned upside down, so they could be thrown overhead, then slid into place.

"To don your pack, grab the tank with both hands, throw it over your head, and then cinch down your straps," he announced loudly, his twang reverberating against the barren walls. "You want them tight, but leave enough room so you can move your arms." He slung the pack over his head and had it in place with lightning speed, his beefy hands giving quick yanks to the shoulder straps. He then clicked his waist buckle and threw the strap of his facemask over his neck. "Voila!" he exclaimed with a grin.

"Once you got it on, then secure your mask," he continued. He swiveled his head, spit his toothpick onto the concrete, and brought the mask up to his face. He slid the rubber network of straps, known as the "spider," over the back of his head, then gave quick pulls on the spider's straps, securing the mask tightly to his face.

"Then attach your regulator," he yelled, his voice muffled by the mask. He gripped the regulator and with a quick twist, snapped it onto his mask while simultaneously cranking open his tank with his free hand. A smooth hiss issued forth as he took a deep breath. He swung his head side to side to show off the setup, then slid his Nomex hood over his head and plunked his helmet in place. He tightened his chin strap, slipped on his gloves, and then clapped his hands together, indicating he was done.

"That's all there is to it," he yelled from behind his mask. He quickly reversed the order, dropping his gloves to the ground, stripping off his helmet and hood, pulling his mask off and turning off his tank, his hands working robotically with smooth efficiency. He then lumbered to his feet and slid out of his coat. He dropped it in a pile next to his abandoned pack, thrust a fist into his pocket, and rooted around before withdrawing a fresh pick and tossing into his mouth.

"You got sixty seconds to don your gear. That includes bunker pants and boots, coat, hood, helmet, and gloves. You'll get an extra thirty seconds when we add the airpacks. You'll do it 'til it's automatic. What we call muscle memory. Once you guys are released into the real world, haulin' ass to a call under lights and sirens, you won't have time to think about donnin' your shit. It's gotta be instinctual, so go to it!" he barked as he ran sausage-like fingers through his thick hair.

The tower erupted in the noise of the drill: the grunting of students, the clanking of metal against concrete, and the constant shouts from the instructors. An hour into it, Sam's head was splitting and the muscles in her shoulders trembled from repeatedly lifting her pack.

The tower was stifling. She used her hood to mop the sweat from her eyes as she watched with envy as the larger cadets threw their tanks with ease, the packs feather light in their muscled grips. The students had ninety seconds to be fully "bunkered out" and breathing off their tanks. That meant every bit of their gear correctly fastened, gloves on, airpack in place and turned on, ready to make entry. Any oversight was cause for failure. If all their clasps were not fastened, they did it again. If they forgot to secure their collar flap, they did it again. If their spider wasn't secure – and the instructors checked this by grabbing hold of their mask and yanking side-to-side – they did it again. Their day was consumed with the timed drills.

Late in the afternoon, when they felt somewhat proficient, Daniels materialized on the tarmac. Tanner barked, "Hit the deck!" and the cadets scrambled into formation.

This time, Daniels did the honors. He started at the beginning of the line, slowly examining each cadet's gear for loose clasps, unsecured hooks. The students were soaked through from the stifling heat of the tower; the relentless autumn sun beat a steady rhythm across their shoulders. Standing in full gear, having Daniels eyeballing them, only added to their tension. They were sweating buckets.

As the commander found errors, he would quietly identify the discrepancy in short sentences directed at each cadet.

"Loose strap."

"Tighten your chin."

"Cinch your left shoulder."

In response, the cadet would quickly rectify the oversight and Daniels would move on.

As he approached the end of the line, Sam could barely stand still. Her shoulders ached from donning her pack, the muscles along her spine were knotted coils. Amidst the heat and fatigue, she had forgotten to secure the Velcro of her collar. It was now caught under her left shoulder strap but had been overlooked by Tanner.

Daniels slid into position in front of her. Sam could feel his eyes travel the length of her body and waited for him to move on, unaware of her mistake. She took the opportunity to look closely at his face.

His skin was smooth and darkened from the sun. The soft brown of his lashes emphasized the clarity of his piercing grey eyes. Silver flecks adorned his mustache and Sam felt a visceral tug as she imagined running her tongue along its bristled border.

Daniels avoided her gaze as he inspected her gear. He locked onto her strap like a laser.

He didn't say anything. Instead, he reached up with both hands, gently pulled her collar flap free and secured it neatly beneath her chin. He then moved on to the next cadet.

Sam held her breath, embarrassed by the oversight, furious at being coddled. Michaels and Tanner exchanged questioning looks. Sam bit her lip to keep from speaking out, her fury quickly giving way to frustration, the exhaustion sapping her anger and strength. She wanted off the field, away from the men, away from the intense heat.

Daniels completed the inspection and threw a nod to Michaels, who released the cadets with a shriek of his whistle. They climbed out of their gear, placed their packs inside the tower, and hauled their equipment across the training field.

"Fuckin' teacher's pet," Peterson muttered in Sam's direction as the students traversed the field. Sam's grip tightened around her gear and she avoided the eyes of the men.

~

Daniels lingered in the empty tower. He knew he had made a mistake. He had felt the stares of his instructors, yet he couldn't explain what came over him. When he stood in front of the girl and felt her eyes rake his face, words escaped him, and it was simply easier to act. Before he knew it, he was reaching for her gear.

Daniels pulled the tower door shut and twisted his key, cursing himself under his breath as he headed across the empty field. He would never make that mistake again. And yet his mind kept returning to the firm curve of her collarbone as his hand slid beneath her strap.

~

Ty had successfully battled his nerves throughout the week. The verbal abuse from the instructors was nothing compared to what he knew, having grown up in the shadow of a father whose idea of discipline was beating his son into submission.

Ty hated his father, hated his brutality. He had seen his mother's transformation over the years, the deep-set lines that now marred her fading beauty.

His family's spread was immense. His father owned a vast portion of Ocala, having obtained most of it via avaricious ancestors who arrived in the late 1800s. Ruthlessness was engrained in Ty's genes, yet the majority of his code seemed to come from his mother, much to his father's dismay. Ty certainly inherited her beauty. His father, sedate after a few drinks, would stare at his son, at that beautiful face that lacked any hint of his biological contribution, and that alone could set him off. At times, he simply wanted to knock those good looks from Ty's face.

Ty's saving grace, at least in his father's eyes, was his work ethic. The kid could work, which enraged his father all the more when Ty announced he was leaving. Those were some difficult days. His father assailed him, but Ty refused to give in. He just kept taking it, as if biding his time until his father's arm tired and he could escape, which he did two days later. Ty's mother wanted him to go, had encouraged him to flee. She had witnessed the abuse long enough to know it would never change. If she achieved anything in life, it would be the release of her son.

So, Ty fled. He came to Orlando, his spot already secured in the academy, and found a small apartment near downtown. The first days were filled with a strange, startling silence. No one yelling his name from across an open field, no flinching at the approach of heavy boots. For the first time in Ty's life, there was no one to fear.

III

Once the rhythm of the academy was established, the novel gave way to routine. Sam didn't know which was worse, the grueling days spent drenched on the field or the monotonous days in the classroom, where a wrong answer would send a student to the front of the class where they'd be forced to drop and pump out twenty pushups. Both realms were degrading, both meant to separate the serious from those who merely liked the way "firefighter" rolled off their tongues; who relied on that magical word to impress women at bars and increase their chance of getting laid.

The training grounds were a constant bustle of activity. The training divisions for the Orlando Fire Department and Orange County Fire and Rescue occupied portables at the back edge of the field. Crews from their departments were regulars on the field, utilizing the burn building and training tower when they were not being used by the cadets.

While the cadets learned the basics, the special ops program honed the skills of seasoned teams. At times, teams occupied the south corner of the field, where they practiced confined space rescues deep within the trenches. Other times, they would be running drills for urban search and rescue, their cadaver dogs bounding at their sides amidst jagged piles of rubble. The cadets would watch the high angle teams as they rappelled from the steel-girded tower, their bodies light as moths as they sailed down the ropes.

All the while, Daniels moved between the classes, eyes scanning the field for any hint of carelessness, the slightest safety discrepancy. He would stand, arms crossed, coffee mug in hand, intently watching the teams perform. When his eyes locked on a violation, he would emit a piercing whistle, his arm slowly rising as he pointed out the error. His instructors would snap to attention, correcting the mistake as the teams continued to work.

Each day of class meant new skills to master. As the weight of their gear grew familiar, the cadets learned to manipulate tools through the thickness of their gloves, to move and bend while maintaining their balance with the added weight of their packs. Even navigating the stairwells took practice. The bulk of their boots slowed them down. The weight of their gear worked in concert with gravity, making the upward climb an exhausting test of stamina.

The instructors drilled them relentlessly. An officer would brace at the base of the tower, clipboard in hand, screaming, *"Prepare for entry!"* To make matters worse, they would saddle each student with a fifty-foot section of hose folded accordion-style on their shoulder before barking, *"Make entry!"* The cadets would race into the tower, gasping for breath at each landing as they scrambled skyward before bursting onto the roof where another instructor waited, clutching his stopwatch like newly caught prey. The student would throw the hose to the concrete, rip off their helmet, and bend forward in an attempt to oxygenate their starved lungs.

"Are you kidding me?" the officer would bellow. "My fuckin' sister could run faster than that! Do it again!" The exhausted cadet would then gather their gear, trudge back downstairs, and grudgingly take their place again in line.

Sam bristled when she realized being compared to a girl was the ultimate of insults.

Aside from the relentless badgering, the adjuncts were high caliber professionals, well versed in the molding of green recruits. They worked the class hard and expected one hundred percent but were fair when it came to praise and acknowledgment of the students' efforts. They were honorable men, except for one: Officer Lee.

Lee was a high-angle specialist and led several of the special ops courses when he wasn't training cadets. He was renowned for his rope skills, a master at rappelling, but he lacked the balance and fairness of the other instructors. He was quick to criticize, relentless when it came to pushing the cadets. It was doubly so for females, who, according to his philosophy, belonged in the fire service like tits on a bull. He had been present when Daniels corrected Sam's gear and had overheard Aaron's "teacher's pet" remark. From that point on, Lee referred to Sam not as "Smith" but as "Pet," using it to get a rise out of her at every opportunity.

"Hey Pet, bring that piece of hose over to this side of the tower!" he would yell, always loud enough for those around to hear. Sam grew to despise him. Their communications were frequently preceded by a few seconds of malicious eye contact.

It was their first day working with ladders. The students had gone over lengths, applications, and proper handling procedures. Now they would be laddering the tower. Tanner lined the cadets along the deck as two of the adjuncts set up one of the extension ladders against the building. Tanner then positioned himself next to the ladder.

"A few quick reminders," he said, one hand resting on the side beam, one fingering his toothpick as he leaned his beefy torso casually against the frame. "The fly is the upper half of the ladder." He slapped his palm against an upper beam. "These are the dogs," he continued, indicating the metal hooks that catch on the rungs once the ladder has been raised to the desired height, "and you had better not forget to yell, 'Dogs locked!' once your raise is complete," he added, scanning the cadets to ensure they were listening. "If those dogs don't lock in place, the ladder can come down." He slapped the side of the ladder again for emphasis. "I assure you, that will ruin your whole day." He grinned and then turned his head to spit.

"Also," he continued, wiping his mouth with the back of his hand, "once the ladder is raised, grab the slack in the halyard." He pointed to the rope that ran the length of the ladder, used to hoist the fly section upward. "Tie it off behind the ladder so it's out of your way." Here he knotted the loose rope around one of the lower rungs and then rotated it to the backside of the ladder.

"Go to it," he said, and the students broke from formation.

They practiced in pairs, lifting and carrying the ladders using proper technique to minimize back injuries, cautiously performing their raises. Once the students had mastered the ladder in pairs, they practiced doing it on their own.

The twenty-four-foot ladder could be manipulated by one person with ease. The thirty-five-footer was a different beast. Because of its size and weight, the larger ladder required at least two people to handle. After several rounds of practice, the students broke for lunch.

The cadets were lounging in the grass, finishing up their lunch in the cool rectangular shade of the tower. The stifling heat of summer was slowly giving way to fall and the break in humidity was greeted with relief. Sam was huddled with her usual group: Ty, Johnny, Lance, and, of course, Trey, since where there was one, there was always the other. Tate had joined the group as of late. Moved by his isolation, Sam had invited him over on the second day of class. He had been a fixture ever since. He seemed to crave the company. Once Tater started talking, it was tough to get a word in. It was as if he had been stockpiling words, just waiting for the chance to unload. Tate had just finished one of his lunchtime ramblings and, as usual, Lance was sprawled out on his turnout coat, snoring loudly.

Aaron had acquired a small following: guys either too dimwitted or too scared to turn down his bid for friendship. It seemed their loyalties were born out of a sense of doom rather than desire. They were immersed in a discussion of their usual topics: NASCAR, drinking, and the latest issue of *Field and Stream*.

Officer Lee was reclining against the edge of the tower. Michaels and Tanner were having a private meeting over one of their clipboards and had their backs to the students. Sam noticed Lee eyeing her group. She nudged Trey beside her. "Asshole alert, twelve o'clock," she whispered, glaring at the officer as she stowed her trash.

"Hey, Pet!" Lee yelled from the sideline. "You and Draper throw that thirty-five-footer. Let's see whatcha' got!" He balled up the remnants of his lunch, his long-corded muscles flexing as he worked the bag to a wrinkled pulp. Like the rest of the instructors, he was decked out in all black, but on Lee, the dark clothing contrasted sharply with his pale skin, giving him an ominous pall. His clean shave only intensified the narrowness of his face, which was perpetually pinched against the glare of the sun.

As the group watched, Trey and Sam rose from their spot, grabbed their gloves and helmets, and walked to where the thirty-five-foot ladder lay off to the side. Once they had their gloves on and their helmets cinched down, they went through the motions, shouldering the massive ladder and carrying it over to the base of the tower. They strained in unison to position it upright. Trey pulled forcefully on the halyard to raise the fly as Sam braced her weight against the base to keep the ladder from slipping. After Trey called, "Dogs locked!" they lowered the ladder's tip against the building and checked the climbing angle. They rested for a moment, filling their hungry lungs before reversing the raise and returning the ladder to its original spot. They were heading back to the group when Lee spoke up.

"Do it again!" he shouted, cocking his head, his eyes shaded by his ball cap.

Sam and Trey exchanged annoyed glances as they worked to catch their breath. "Sorry," Sam whispered as she adjusted her helmet. She knew

Lee's wrath was directed at her and that Trey was caught up because he happened to be sitting next to her at lunch. Trey gave her a quick wink as he swiped at his brow.

They repeated the process, this time slowed from the exertion of the first round. They struggled on the walkup, but finally got the ladder upright. Sam strained against the weight of the fly, yanking the halyard hand-over-hand before yelling, "Dogs locked!" Trey gulped air as he steadied the ladder against the building. They grabbed a few moment's rest before carefully lowering it back to the ground. They staggered under its weight as they carried it back to the starting point, then ripped off their helmets and gloves before bending forward to catch their breath.

"Now let's see Pet do it on her own," Lee sneered, grinning from beneath the shade of his cap.

Trey swung his head and glared at the officer before glancing over at Sam. Sam remained bent over, her eyes on the ground, the sweat dripping from her face forming a small puddle on the tarmac as she hissed, "Motherfucker!"

"What should I do, Sam?" Trey whispered.

"Let her do it!" Lee yelled. His grin had vanished.

The other cadets had wandered over and formed a nervous huddle on the sideline. Ty stepped forward, his eyes on Sam. "Show that asshole," Trey whispered as Sam straightened her back and worked her hands back into her gloves. As she reached down for her helmet, her eyes locked on Ty. His mouth formed a tight line, his brow was furrowed in a knot. He gave her a slight nod of encouragement as Sam threw her helmet on and approached the ladder.

As Sam got into position, Michaels turned from his clipboard. He glanced at Lee before shifting his eyes to Sam. But before he could intervene, Sam went ahead with the raise.

Sam positioned herself at the center of the ladder and turned it onto its beam. She then planted her feet and stood up, carrying it in an extended carry, since there was no way she would be able to get it onto her shoulder. She butted the base of the ladder against the base of the tower, laid it flat, and walked to position herself at its top, her back to the tower. She stared out over the field, took two deep breaths as she squatted beside it, and stood up, bringing the ladder's tip up with her. She took a few quick breaths before pivoting beneath the tip, hoisting it above her head and fighting to extend her arms. She locked her elbows to prevent the ladder from crashing down on her head, then rung by rung, slowly walked her hands down the ladder. She could feel her back straining under its weight, her muscles flexing and over-arching as she tried to keep it steady above her head. She finally got it parallel to the tower and braced her body against it as she gasped for breath, the effort and humiliation burning in her cheeks.

Sam strained against the halyard, using the weight of her body to raise the fly. When she heard enough clicks of the dogs to ensure it was sufficiently high, she checked them and called, "Dogs locked!" She struggled to position the base of the ladder and then checked the climbing angle. She finished by knotting the halyard and then stood, hands on hips, panting as she waited for Lee to give the order to lower.

Her heart pounded; her gloves were soaked through. Sam could feel the stares of the men and fought the urge to turn her back to them. She kept her eyes down as she slowly stripped off her gloves.

Lee looked on nonchalantly as he rose from his chair. "Take it down," he said over his shoulder as he sauntered toward the trash can, tossing the remnants of his bag in with barely a glance. Michaels watched from the sidelines in stony silence.

~

Michaels wasn't sure what to do; rare for someone who prided himself on his decisiveness. His first notion was to kick Lee's ass. Michaels detested a superior attitude in an instructor. Yes, they had to be strict, but they didn't have to be assholes. Fortunately, Daniels usually chose instructors who didn't feel the need to chastise and belittle the cadets. It was especially dangerous with females. One whiff of sexual harassment and an instructor could be tossed out of the program; pack your shit, hit the road. Daniels had a no-tolerance policy and Michaels respected it.

Michaels considered discussing the matter with Daniels, but then flashed back to the incident with Smith's gear. He had never seen Daniels put a hand on a student, especially one of the females. When Daniels corrected her gear, it had thrown Michaels for a loop. Tanner had mentioned it the next morning but, out of loyalty, Michaels had brushed it aside.

Normally, Michaels would have yanked Lee aside, set him straight, and not given it another thought. Sometimes the instructors got a bit overzealous. It had happened before. But this situation was more complicated. Michaels feared he might be perceived as sticking his neck out for the female and wanted to avoid any hint of favoritism. At the same time, he couldn't just ignore Lee's behavior. But if Michaels brought up Lee's behavior, would it make Daniels self-conscious about his own treatment of Smith? *What a fucking conundrum.*

It was so much simpler when it was all guys. The minute you introduced a female, class dynamics turned to shit. Suddenly everyone had to be overcautious about what they said, what they did. It was easier when it was just a bunch of young peckerheads.

Michaels would keep his silence. After all, nothing had happened, no one got hurt. If Lee did it again, he'd rip him a new one. In the meantime, Michaels would wait.

IV

By the end of the second week, the class had settled into small social pockets and another student had dropped. When they were not divided by the instructors, Sam's group stuck together and began meeting upstairs in the library after class to study. After a few sessions, it became clear Tate was the most methodical of the bunch, so Sam recommended he take the lead. It was unanimous.

Tate took great pride in arranging the sessions. He would sit at the head of the table, books and notes spread before him in concise order, and a veil of seriousness would settle over his face, which usually remained flushed from the day's activities. He would then cough into his hand to wrangle the group's attention before announcing the topics for the evening. He assigned the material based on each member's strengths and the students would take turns leading group discussions, while Tate sat back, monitoring the clock, keeping them on topic.

The class was fairly cohesive. Aaron continued his monopoly as class dick, but most of the students got along well. There were two giants – Mark and Bill – who had both played football for Florida State. Mark had gone on to play for Tampa Bay, but had spent the entire year on the bench before being cut. Like Sam and Johnny, they were a few years older, and their friendly banter occasionally gave way to the low-level harassment they had acquired as football players. They usually targeted Shane and Bo.

Mark and Bill would swagger through the cafeteria, their trays laden with enough food to placate a troop of Boy Scouts, and they'd purposefully wait for the young cadets to get settled before sidling up to their table.

"Move on down, boys," Mark would grumble as Bill glared at them good naturedly.

Shane and Bo knew better than to argue. They would nod submissively, quickly reassemble their trays, and slide down to the opposite end of the table. The boys had bigger things to worry about. Shane was barely squeaking by with a seventy-one; Bo trailed several points behind. They were just two weeks in and already struggling.

Sam spent most of her time with Ty. When they realized they lived only a mile apart, they started carpooling to class, using the commute to study. Whoever happened to be in the passenger seat would throw out questions and the drive became a helpful supplement to their evening study sessions. It also gave them a chance to share stories.

Ty spoke frankly about his father, about the bullying and the abuse. He had come to accept his father's propensity for violence, had never really questioned it. It had become part of their existence, always there but never discussed. His father tried to compensate. An incident was always followed by some useless gift; always expensive, always pushed aside. The only gift Ty kept was the new Mustang he was given after a particularly bad week. It was the one gift that would aid his escape.

Sam shared the stories of her father, about their life overseas and their transient existence. It seemed Sam and Ty represented two ends of a spectrum. Ty had spent his entire life surrounded by the familiarity of hearth and home, growing up among lifelong friends, yet with a father he could never know because of the violence that lived between them. Sam grew up with no sense of place, an isolated, wandering existence, but with a loving father whom she adored. It was as if Sam and Ty's differences balanced them, binding them to each other.

~

The students soon learned that as firefighters, they would always be carrying something. Gear, tools, ladders, medical equipment – it seemed their hands were forever occupied. Today they would carry each other.

They assembled on the training field and lined up on deck, their gear neatly piled in front of them. They would begin with proper "carries" – techniques they would employ to remove victims, patients, and their fellow firefighters from danger. The first half of the day would be spent in turnout gear, perfecting their techniques; during the afternoon exercises, airpacks would be added and the drills would be performed fully "packed out" and breathing off their tanks.

The day started easily enough. Ty and Sam paired up, as did the rest of their group: Lance with Trey, Mark with Bill, and Johnny with Tate, although the dread of toting Tater was evident on Johnny's face. They started with the traditional firefighter carry – throwing their partners over their shoulders and walking an obstacle course made of cones. Ty and Sam were perfectly matched. Although Ty outweighed her by twenty pounds, they were the same height, which made him relatively easy for Sam to manipulate. Ty simply slung Sam over his shoulder like a sack of grain; no doubt a skill he had perfected on the farm. Ty may have lacked height, but he certainly didn't lack strength.

Johnny didn't fare as well. Tater's husky physique proved quite a burden, although Tate encouraged him with gentle coaxing as they moved through the exercise. "Smooth and steady, buddy," Tate murmured, his head dangling down Johnny's backside. "Distribute the weight across your shoulder and compensate by shifting to the other side."

"Thanks, Tater," Johnny wheezed through gritted teeth.

Trey and Lance appeared to have mastered the skill long ago. Bill and Mark breezed through. The cadets were decked out in their worn turnout gear, looking like a squad of over-ripe bananas as they hauled each other around the course while the instructors lounged against the tower, sipping coffee. Tanner warned them about the limitations of the carry.

"Now you all remember," he said as he moseyed among the cadets. "You won't be using this carry in an actual fire. The last thing you want to do is hoist your buddy's ass right up into the superheated gases." He grinned as he twirled his pick.

As the morning wore on, they moved on to various drags, using pieces of webbing as makeshift harnesses to haul each other through the tower. They then placed blankets on the floor, rolling their "victims" onto them and pulling the blankets to safety. Sam proved the effectiveness of the technique by dragging Tate with little trouble.

To prepare for the afternoon sessions, when they would be hauling each other in full gear, they practiced using the built-in device on the backs of their coats. Each bunker coat had a strap sewn in, just below the collar. A rescuer simply had to grab the handle of their downed partner and go, staying low to the ground as they pulled the victim to safety. An obstacle course was set up in the bottom floor of the tower. An old couch was placed in the middle of the floor and chairs were positioned strategically throughout the room so that the students would have to make their way around the obstacles while dragging their partners. There were colored markers on the walls at various locations around the room, which each rescuer was required to tag. Once they had tagged all the marks and dragged their partners out the door and onto the tarmac, the exercise was completed, and their time would stop.

It was a challenging course, even without their airpacks. On hands and knees, it was hard to build momentum, especially dragging the dead weight of their partner. It was tough on the rescuer, but it was no picnic for the victim, either. Since the exercise was timed, speed was of the essence, which meant a rough ride for the victim. Victims compensated by clutching their helmets low on their heads as their partners hauled ass through the course. Sam did well dragging Ty. Ty flew through the course since Sam's weight was of little consequence. Aaron took the opportunity to pounce.

Throughout the morning, Aaron had watched Sam and Ty handling each other with ease. He had partnered with one of his NASCAR buddies and although Aaron was big, he lacked grace. He had trouble manipulating the course, his bulky frame making it hard to negotiate the obstacles, and he vehemently blamed his victim, berating him for not staying tucked and slowing him down. When the class broke for lunch, he was still fuming.

Sam's group was reclining in their usual spot when Aaron and his brood wandered over. "Hey, pretty-boy! Ya had it pretty easy today, didn't ya?" Aaron exclaimed, flicking his head in Sam's direction. Ty sipped his water as he eyed the big cadet. Sam was sprawled out on the grass, her coat rolled into a makeshift pillow as she crunched on the remains of an apple.

She raised a hand to her brow to block out the sun.

"Don't you have someplace to be, Peterson?" Sam said coolly from her spot on the ground. "Like a tractor pull or a monster truck gala?" Mark, lying next to her, chuckled and smacked her shoulder. Sam polished off the apple with one final aggressive bite.

"Fuck you, Sam," Aaron griped, hands planted on his hips.

"In your dreams, fat ass," she mumbled, chucking the core and grinning as it bounced off the toe of his boot. Aaron kicked at the apple, but his large boot missed and merely stirred a cloud of dust. Sam gave a contented snort.

"Anyway," Aaron continued distractedly, turning his attention back to Ty. "I'd like to see ya run the course with some real weight behind you." Aaron cocked his hip, eyeing his friends for encouragement. They shuffled their boots, embarrassed to be caught up in his mischief.

"You want to go at it?" Ty replied, climbing to his feet and brushing off his backside. "I bet I can beat your time, even dragging your big ass through the course."

"Let's go!" Aaron shot and turned abruptly for the tower. Sam glanced up at Ty.

"What the hell?" she griped as she extended her hand. Ty yanked her to her feet, grinned, and then grabbed his gear and headed for the tower.

"You can drag me first. Then I bet I can beat your time dragging you," Ty explained to Aaron as they donned their helmets, coats, and gloves. The other cadets had flocked to the first-floor windows to watch the competition. They yelled words of encouragement as the men readied their gear.

Ty stretched out on the floor, cinched down his helmet, and folded his arms neatly across his chest. Aaron dropped to his knees with a grunt and swiped the sweat from his brow with a gloved hand before taking hold of Ty's strap. Tanner, not wanting to miss the action, had shoved his way through the crowd and was braced at the starting point, his trusty stopwatch in hand.

"You boys ready?" Tanner called, grinning as an anxious silence settled over the assemblage.

"You say when," Aaron grumbled, giving his helmet strap a yank. Sam stared down at Ty, perplexed. Ty had spent his entire childhood evading his father. Sam couldn't understand why he would voluntarily go up against Aaron's anger.

Tanner yelled, "Go!" and Aaron lurched forward. He dragged Ty with little effort, but his movements were clumsy and awkward; within seconds, his breath was coming in ragged gasps. He purposely bashed Ty into as many obstacles as possible, which only slowed his progress, but Ty kept his head tucked and arms crossed, and absorbed the impacts with ease. Aaron made it through the course, tagging the marks on the wall and finally hauling Ty through the doorway. Aaron bellowed victoriously as he deposited Ty onto the tarmac, then bent low to catch his breath before lobbing a gooey wad of grey phlegm onto the pavement. As he stood up, he swung a large boot at Ty's shoulder and snarled, "Beat that, pretty-boy!" Ty rolled onto his belly and then sprang to his feet. He brushed himself off and headed back to the starting point.

"A minute and twenty-eight seconds!" Tanner announced, holding his stopwatch in the air. Aaron lumbered back into the tower, panting and sweating. He knew he outweighed Ty by at least sixty pounds. He had this in the bag.

Ty coolly adjusted his helmet and gloves as Aaron flopped onto the floor, crossed his hands over his chest, and grinned. "Come and get me, sweetie!" Aaron sneered, his face flushed crimson. Ty glanced up at Sam as he dropped into position and gave her a wink. Sam stared back, bewildered.

"Ready? Go!" Tanner yelled and Ty was off. Even hauling Aaron's large frame, Ty moved quickly and gracefully through the course. It took him a few seconds to adjust to the added weight, especially after dragging Sam, but once he got moving, he worked the course smoothly. Ty tagged the wall at each turn and even managed to keep Aaron's big head from impacting the furniture. Aaron's expression was hard to read beneath the shadow of his helmet, but his smile had vanished once he realized how efficiently Ty moved.

As Ty tagged the last of the marks, he turned into the straightaway that led to the doorway. The students shouted through the windows, waving their arms, absorbed in the competition. Tanner held the stopwatch close to his face, pumping his thick arm back and forth, urging Ty on under his breath. He wanted nothing more than to see Peterson lose. But Ty had other plans.

As he passed the last window, Ty stopped suddenly, stood up over Aaron, grabbed the collar of Aaron's coat and hoisted his shoulders off the ground. The students gawked in silent disbelief.

Earlier in the day, Ty had noticed the large hooks strategically placed beneath each window, which served as anchor points for tying off ropes. In one smooth movement, Ty attached the escape handle on the back of Aaron's coat to the hook, leaving Aaron sprawled on his back, securely affixed to the wall. Ty bent down and whispered, *"Take that, you fat fuck!"* before turning casually and striding toward the door.

"What the hell?" Aaron squawked as he clambered for the hook. But his position on the ground prevented him from gaining enough leverage. He struggled like a turtle on its back, kicking his giant boots and screaming, *"Get me the fuck off this hook!"*

The class erupted. Sam stood with her mouth agape as Ty glided past, grinning. Aaron desperately looked to Tanner, who stood in the doorway, his toothpick elevated in a wide grin, but Tanner simply shook his head before moseying out the door. As Aaron's ranting continued, one of his minions finally stepped forward and unhitched him from the hook. Once released, Aaron scrambled to his feet and bolted from the room.

Ty had settled against the base of the tower and was polishing off a bottle of water. Aaron rushed toward him, seething, his large face flushed, soaked with perspiration. Just as he reached down to yank Ty to his feet, Tanner, who was standing nearby, calmly spoke up.

"Don't even think about it, Peterson, unless you plan to pack your shit."

Aaron froze, his hands clenched, veins bulging, leaning over Ty as Ty relaxed against the building.

"You're lucky he's here, asshole, or I'd beat the shit out of you!" Aaron screamed at Ty through a shower of spittle. Ty merely finished his water, his eyes on the training field.

"Get your gear together, Peterson," Tanner yelled before turning to the group. "The rest of you grab your shit and move your asses to the third floor!" The cadets gathered their equipment and headed upstairs. Sam reached a hand down to Ty and pulled him to his feet. They smiled at each other, grabbed their gear, and headed upstairs.

Aaron popped another top and cranked the radio up. After class, he had driven the short distance to the Shell station, bought a six-pack, and returned to campus. He was parked in the shadows of the back parking lot, hunched behind the wheel, guzzling beer, fuming. *Their goddamn study session's got to end sooner or later.* He didn't care if he had to wait all night. He was going to find out where that fucker lived so he could pay him a little visit.

By nine o'clock, he had finished off the beer, made two trips to the bushes to piss, and was on the verge of dozing when he saw the group head to their cars. He punched the radio off and watched as Ty and Sam pulled slowly out of campus. Aaron grinned through a satisfying belch, cranked his truck, and followed.

V

By week three, the class had been reduced by four. They were about to lose another. Today they would be initiated into the smoke maze. The maze served three purposes: it reinforced the skills of a blind search, it taught them how to move through confined spaces, and it pushed them to the limits of frustration.

The maze was constructed of plywood and ran throughout the second floor of the tower. It was composed of a long, winding tunnel consisting of erratic twists and turns. The cadets entered on hands and knees, fully packed out, breathing off their tanks, blind as bats. Their facemasks were covered with black felt and the timer started the moment the students crossed the black line. They would crawl as fast as they could, all the while feeling in front, along the sides, and above their heads. The floor's elevation changed constantly. One minute they would be climbing, the next minute, the floor would drop several feet. The corners were intentionally tight, forcing the cadets to contort their bodies in order to squeeze through its confines. The ceiling, like the floor, changed elevation, and if they weren't cautious, they would collide with the low spots. And then there were the obstacles.

The obstacles were specifically designed to entrap unsuspecting students. Ropes looped down from the ceiling to ensnare their packs, forcing them to slide sideways. Wires stuck out intentionally to snag their gear. But worst of all were the hidden cubbies.

The cubbies were small access points where the instructors could reach through the walls of the maze and make contact with the students. Through these points, the instructors could knock the students' helmets off, yank off their masks, and the most frightening trick of all, turn off their tanks. They usually waited until the exhausted cadets were squeezed into the tightest part of the maze, when they were turned on their sides trying to maneuver through a constriction. Suddenly, the students would take a breath and their masks would be sucked against their faces. *No air!*

Exhaustion, frustration, and the inability to see made for a lethal combination and the students who lacked the ability to rein in their anxiety quickly succumbed. They would try to reach behind to turn their tanks back on, but the narrow walls made it almost impossible to bend their elbows. Every second that passed meant another second without air. Their lungs would scream, the blood would pound in their heads, and their first instinct would be to kick out the sides of the maze to escape. Just when they thought they would pass out, they would manage to turn their knob just enough to release a faint trickle of air. The maze was a bitch.

As intimidating as it was, Sam enjoyed it, once she had mastered her first run. Being smaller gave her an edge and she relished the honor of having the fastest run of the day. She slid side to side easily and enjoyed the challenge of feeling her way through. She quickly realized the key was keeping your cool. The minute you started to panic, everything went to hell. If you got stuck, stop, take a deep breath, and think. If you were caught on something, work methodically to release yourself. If they turned off your air, work your arm behind you as efficiently as possible to turn your tank back on. Sam realized the instructors wanted the weaker students to panic; they wanted the claustrophobics to freak out so they could be weeded out of the program. The last thing the academy wanted was to produce firefighters who would be overwhelmed once they got inside a dark, smoky structure. The maze was there to do the weeding.

As the students awaited their turn, Tony, one of the less agile cadets, prepared for entry. He stood nervously in the doorway, adjusting and readjusting his gear. The instructor motioned him inside, checked his gear, and went over the instructions.

"Use proper technique, stay low, and feel your way. The timer starts when you cross the line."

Tony slowly got down on hands and knees. He checked his gloves one last time and gazed nervously through his mask at the instructor. The instructor slapped the covering over his mask, smacked his shoulder, and yelled, "Go!" Tony was off.

He didn't last long. He made it through the initial straightaway, but as soon as the walls started to tighten, Tony started to panic. As his breathing increased, he began emitting faint yelps, and as the maze got tighter, his yelps got louder. The darkness only intensified his claustrophobia, his mask, like a smothering hand. Each breath was an effort. He slid forward on his belly, clawing at the walls to pull himself along. But by using the walls, he forgot to check the floor and pulled himself headfirst into one of the drop-offs. Dizzy and disoriented, with pain shooting down his neck, he clambered to stand up, only to slam his helmet against the low ceiling. He panicked.

"Get me the fuck outta here!" he screamed as he beat blindly at the sides of the maze, fighting his regulator to catch his breath, his humiliation sidelined by the fear that overtook him. The instructors raced forward, snatching open one of the trap doors as Tony shoved his way past, ripping his helmet from his head, tearing his mask from his face, and stripping off his hood. He dropped to his knees, gasping for breath, keeping his back to the adjuncts, swiping at his face with a gloved hand. His chest heaved as he fought the panicked sob that rose in his throat.

Tanner approached slowly and placed a gentle hand on the boy's shoulder. "You wanna give it another shot, buddy?" he said quietly as the cadet wiped the snot from his face. Tony shook his head like a convulsive, reigniting the pain in his neck. "Can't do it," he mumbled through hiccupped breaths. Tanner reached down, grasped Tony by the arm, and pulled him to his feet.

"Grab your shit," Tanner said with a flick of his head. Tony gathered his helmet and hood and Tanner walked him down the stairs. No one spoke, there were no goodbyes. They marched solemnly across the field as the cadets returned to their drills.

~

Michaels knew something was up. Daniels hadn't been out to the training field in three days, the longest stretch Michaels could recall. He loitered outside the locker room, waiting for the students to clear the hallway and the other instructors to leave. He then walked slowly toward the commander's office.

He approached the open door to Daniel's office and stood for a moment before knocking. Daniels was reclined at his desk, a boot elevated, resting on an open drawer; a pose Michaels had seen on countless occasions. But usually Daniels had a book in his lap, voraciously devouring its contents. Today, he merely stared out the large window that overlooked the back of campus.

Daniels loved the view. From his desk he could gaze out at the thick line of pines sheltering the training field and lose himself among the trees. At those moments, California and its lingering echo of grief seemed lightyears away. In the winter, as the afternoon sun slipped toward the horizon, the pines threw off elongated shadows across the grounds. Daniels gauged the season by the length of their dark fingers.

A soft knock brought him back to his desk. "Sir," Michaels murmured as he entered the room. Daniels gestured for him to sit down. They looked at each other for a moment, no words passing between them. Daniels was always amazed by Michaels' ability to gauge his mood. Michaels was one of those rare individuals who could read a room within a split second of entering. He knew when to speak, when to remain silent. He waited for Daniels to break the silence.

"How are things going?" Daniels finally asked, lowering his boot and pivoting to face the officer.

"Very well. The training is coming along nicely, although we lost another to the maze. A minor incident at the tower, but things have calmed down."

"What incident?" Daniels' brow furrowed.

"That asshole, Peterson. Williams made him look bad so now he's out for blood. I think Tanner set him straight, but we'll keep an eye out."

Silence settled on the room again. Michaels stood up reluctantly and smoothed his uniform. "Will we see you on the field tomorrow?" He shoved his hands deep into his pockets.

"Sure, I'll be out," Daniels replied after a moment. "What's on the agenda?"

"Search and rescue," Michaels responded, perplexed. Daniels always knew what was on the agenda; he usually had the entire schedule memorized.

"I'll be there," Daniels said wistfully as his gaze floated back to the window. Michaels marched from the room, paused for a moment outside the doorway, and then walked on.

~

The morning was cool, one of the first of the season. The students were assembled at the tower where they would be taken through the basics of search and rescue. Michaels stood before them, his hands braced rigidly behind his back, clutching his clipboard.

"One of the most important skills you'll master is searching a building," he announced, eyeing the cadets. "It can mean the difference between rescuing a victim versus stumbling across their charred remains during overhaul. Technique is key!" He emphasized his words with a thrust of his clipboard.

The students were instructed to perform a right-handed search. Crawling on hands and knees, they would enter the search room and make contact with the wall on their right. Moving quickly along the wall, they would use their right hands to follow the contours of the room, their left to sweep out toward the center of the room to locate victims. Their reach would be extended by using a tool, such as a Halligan or pike pole, sweeping the tool in large arcs across the floor. By following the right-hand wall, they could search the entire room and end up back where they started. If there were doorways leading off the room, they were to enter each doorway and continue the pattern: right hand along the wall, left hand sweeping the floor. Eventually they would make it through the entire structure. If they located a victim, which were heavy, man-sized dummies filled with sand, they would do an about face and drag the victim back along the wall, retracing their steps.

The two-man searches would use the same technique, only one

person would remain along the wall as the other stretched out into the center of the room. Their bodies would become extensions of each other: one would guide the search, the other would perform the sweep. Two-man searches would be utilized in large, open areas.

The cadets would perform a one-man search and then pair up to practice the two-man technique. Later in the morning, they would be timed and graded. Their masks would be blacked out; they would rely solely on their sense of touch. To add a dose of reality, the room would be filled with smoke. The smoke was a harmless product, pumped into the room from a small generator. It hung heavier than wood smoke and had a faintly sweet odor, reminiscent of burning fruit. It was safe to breathe, although it tended to cause headaches, forcing the instructors to don airpacks when working within the search room. The smoke was meant to raise the stress levels of the students. Even though they were blindfolded, just knowing it was there was enough to cause jitters.

Sam's solo run went smoothly, and she made good time scrambling easily throughout the room. She had stripped off her mask and was trying to catch her breath when Tanner approached and turned to address the group.

"Pretty fast time, huh Smith?" Tanner ignored Sam and eyed the cadets.

"Yes, sir," Sam replied, panting and smiling as she removed her helmet.

"What's the purpose of a search, Smith?" Tanner said loudly, cocking his head and scanning the students.

"To locate and remove victims," Sam replied apprehensively, sensing a classic Tanner ambush.

"Beg pardon?" he added sarcastically, a hand cocked to his ear.

Sam snapped to attention. "To locate and remove victims, *Sir!*"

Tanner suddenly pivoted, jabbing a finger toward the room and yelling into her face, *"If that's the case then why the fuck did you leave Grandma to roast on the couch?"* His toothpick was dangerously close to poking Sam in the nose.

Sam cut her eyes to the interior of the room and could just make out the dummy reclined on the couch through the light smoke. It wore a tattered bra and a ratty grey wig. Sam had checked behind the furniture but forgot to run her hands along the cushions.

"Grandma was missed because I forgot to check the couch, sir!" Sam exclaimed, unconsciously leaning away from the dancing pick.

Tanner downshifted to a soothing twang. "Too late now. She's a crispy critter, thanks to your incompetence." He glared at her with a twinkling eye, then spun on his heel and ambled away.

Sam eyed the grinning cadets. "Won't happen again, Officer Tanner," she called after him, trying to keep a straight face.

Later that morning, Sam and Ty readied their gear for the two-man drill. Ty would lead the search by hugging the wall, Sam would sweep the floor. If they located a victim, they would work together to remove it while reversing their search.

"You've already killed one today, Smith, so get your head out of your ass and concentrate!" Tanner barked from the side of the room. Sam gave a silent nod as she pulled on her mask.

Sam and Ty crouched together near the doorway. The smoke wafted from the room as the instructor swung open the door, using his boot to jam it open. Once they were breathing off their tanks, the instructor covered their masks with the black felt, swatted their shoulders, and yelled, "Go!"

Ty located the inner wall and began crawling. In her left hand, Sam held a three-foot Halligan. As they moved forward, Sam kept her hand near Ty's boot as she swept the tool in wide arcs toward the center of the room. Ty moved steadily, not waiting for Sam, relying on her to keep them together. As they worked, Sam could feel the movement of Ty's body. Unable to see where they were going, the feel of him provided comfort; the proximity of his body reassured her. She pictured his face as they went deeper into the room.

In the open areas, where her tool swept cleanly, Sam stretched her body away from Ty's, maintaining contact via her right boot to his left. Occasionally she would feel him reach out and grab her leg, assuring himself she was still there. When they had made their way deep into the room, Sam's tool struck something soft. She slapped Ty's leg to indicate she was leaning out. Ty kept his right foot on the wall and stretched his body toward her. Sam reached into the blackness and felt the object, recognizing the contours of the dummy as she slid her hand over its surface.

"We have a victim," Sam yelled and pushed her tool toward Ty so he could use it to maintain contact with the wall. The dummy lacked a strap, so they were forced to take turns dragging it by its arms while maintaining contact with the wall on their left. The work was awkward, but they eventually found their way back to the doorway. They kicked open the door and stood upright before each grabbing an arm and dragging the dummy across the threshold.

"At least no one died this time," Tanner grumbled from the doorway as Sam and Ty headed downstairs.

The morning ticked away, and the students completed their practice rotations. Now they would be timed. Sam volunteered to go first, if only to redeem herself. The instructor opened the door to the room and Sam positioned herself on her knees, just outside the doorway. The search room was pitch-black, the smoke swirled in a thick haze.

As she secured her mask and tightened her spider, she glanced into the room. The faint light coming from the hallway caught something high up on the wall. Sam peered through the smoke, trying to catch the reflection when she noticed a dark form against the wall. The smoke parted momentarily, and she could just make out someone standing inside the room, leaning casually against the wall, his gloved hands resting on the belt of his airpack. He had one leg bent against the wall, the other supporting his frame. He was fully packed out, his gear completely black. His face was hidden behind his mask, but with a slight movement of his head, Sam could read the reflective letters on the side of his helmet: D-A-N-I-E-L-S. Sam could feel his eyes on her. The reflectors on his gear shown as her eyes adjusted to the darkness and her last glimpse was the commander's outline looming above her.

In one quick swoop, the instructor threw the covering over her mask and yelled, "Go!" With a nervous flip of her stomach, Sam raced forward. She worked quickly. Her right hand swept the wall in rapid, forward thrusts while her tool alternately scraped the concrete in wide arcs across the floor. She worked her way deep into the room. Although she couldn't hear him, Sam knew Daniels was following her. The only noise was the rhythmic hiss of her regulator and the occasional shout from the instructor, but she could sense him moving along the wall, gauging her progress. Her thoughts returned to the inspection: the way those grey eyes had moved over her, the intensity in his face. She almost missed the dummy, her mind caught up with where he was within the room, and the way the black gear magnified his body. Rattled, she set down her tool, grabbed the dummy by the arms, and yanked it in the opposite direction, following the wall back the way she had come.

She finally reached the doorway, dumped the dummy in a pile on the floor, and was given a slap on the shoulder indicating she was done. "Nice job, Smith," the instructor said, ripping the felt from her mask. Sam removed her helmet and pulled the mask from her face. She was still on her knees when she looked back into the room. As she stood up to leave, she could see Daniels settling back against the wall. All Sam could hear was the whisper of his respirator as the door swung closed behind her.

VI

As the third week drew to a close, Sam faced a new nemesis: hormones. Her cycle ran like clockwork. Sam could predict moods and emotions based on the calendar: the days when she would be edgy and irritable, when a careless driver in the next lane would set her screaming, or the times when her emotions simmered right at the surface and even a commercial for life insurance could make her eyes brim. And then there were "those days," when ovulation peaked, and her senses became razor-sharp. Her eyes grew more alert, smells more intense, and everything around her took on a subtle sexual undertone. Sam usually dealt with it like she dealt with the other crazy effects of her cycle, but the academy would force her onto new terrain.

The day started benignly enough. The cadets congregated on the training ground and began their morning run. The air was clear, and a copper sun was just emerging on the horizon, bathing the pines in an orangey glow. They started easy, loosening their joints. As the run progressed, Sam found herself in the center of the pack. Suddenly, she became aware of the men around her. She could hear them breathing, see the sweat forming on the backs of their necks. Their shoulders flexed as their arms pumped in rhythm with the run. Sam took a deep breath and focused on the tree line. Back in the gymnasium, they worked through their exercises, hammering out pushups and sit-ups as the men grunted around her. Sam stared at the ceiling and tried to concentrate.

They spent the morning working with various diameter hose, practicing the different types of rolls in which they were stored. It was mundane work, but Sam welcomed the monotony. She didn't have to focus, she simply moved through the motions and kept her thoughts to herself. They broke for lunch and headed for the grass.

The group had shifted from the shade of the tower to a small clump of trees on the southern edge of the tarmac. Sunlight filtered through the thin branches, providing the perfect balance of sun and shade. They wore bunker pants and boots; most days were spent in turnout gear and the cadets had become accustomed to its bulk. They now moved with ease and familiarity within their gear, their boots felt natural on the training ground.

The group had spread out in the shade, using their coats as makeshift picnic blankets. They had dropped their suspenders, which hung in loops at their hips. One by one, the men peeled off their shirts, laying them aside to dry. Sam was sitting in the grass, elbows on bent knees, clutching her water bottle and occasionally rubbing it along her forehead, enjoying its cool wetness. Through the corner of her eye, she scanned the men around her as they reclined on their coats, their arms stretched above their heads. Her eyes slowly took each of them in: Lance's long legs, which looked that much longer in bunker pants and boots; Johnny's quiet smile, as he held up a hand to blot out the sun; Ty's stunning face, which Sam thought she had grown accustomed to, but today struck her with an intensity that made it hard to look away. Even Tate appeared transformed. He had struggled the first two weeks of class but was slowly improving. He was now able to keep up during the runs and had lost a bit of his outer layer. Today, Sam couldn't help noticing the smoothness of his skin and the dimples that stood out when he grinned. She took another pass at her face with the bottle.

They spent the afternoon assembling and disassembling fifty-foot-sections of hose. It was late in the day and the shadows were slowly making their way across the field. Sam was exhausted and about to jump out of her skin from being in such proximity to the men. The cadets were cleaning up as Ty and Sam headed for the last two sections of hose lying on the tarmac.

Ty reached down and snatched the end of the first section from the pavement. He straddled the hose, clutching the coupling between gloved hands, the section of hose disappearing between his legs. Sam picked up the end of the next section and approached him, feeling the blood rise in her face as she brought her coupling in line with his. She stole a glance from beneath her helmet.

Ty's brown arms were flexed, they tapered into his gloves. His helmet shaded the top half of his face, leaving his soft mouth exposed to the sun. Sam struggled to line up the threads, screwing, then unscrewing the couplings as the threads crossed and locked. As she fought with the couplings, Ty grinned.

"God damn it!" Sam grumbled under her breath.

"What's going on over there?" Ty smirked. Sam eyed him anxiously. The shade from his helmet only intensified the green in his eyes, his teeth flashed as he smiled. There was a line of sweat on his upper lip and Sam's pulse galloped as she imagined licking it off. *How can anyone be THAT good looking?* Ty put a hand out to steady her wrist, giving it a light squeeze, and suddenly Sam envisioned throwing him to the tarmac and tearing him out of his gear.

"I need some water," she muttered, yanking her coupling free and dropping it to the pavement with a clatter. Ty looked on as Sam stomped off toward the tower.

The day finally ended, and the cadets headed back across the field. "Everyone's heading out for Friday night burgers. You coming?" Ty asked as they dragged their gear toward the locker rooms.

"I think I'll pass," Sam replied, hitching her helmet over her shoulder. "I just want to do some reading and have an early night. You guys go ahead. Johnny can give you a ride home, can't he?" They stopped in front of Sam's locker room.

"Yeah," Ty replied as he shifted his gear to his other arm. "So I'll call you tomorrow?"

"Sounds great. You guys have fun and stay out of trouble," Sam called over her shoulder as she pulled the locker room door open. Ty watched her disappear and then headed down the hall.

Sam stripped down and stood under a cold shower as the day's grime slowly slid from her body. After toweling off, she threw on sweats, stopped by the cafeteria for a snack, and then headed across campus to the library. She took a small table on the first floor, in the back corner where she could focus, and reviewed the week's material, scanning ahead to the next chapter.

By eight, she was exhausted and her back ached. She stretched her arms high above her head, then tucked her head on the table and closed her eyes. She immediately flashed back to the men's bodies scattered around her on the grass. Behind the black of her lids flashed tanned skin sprinkled in beads of sweat. She could smell the men, feel the heat of the sun. She gave her head a quick shake as she sat up to gather her books. There he stood in front of her: Commander Daniels.

The man moves like a ghost. Her mind flashed back to the search room of the tower: the dark outline of his body, his face hidden behind his mask, smoke swirling between his legs as he reclined against the wall. Sam could feel the blood rise in her chest.

"You're here late, Samantha," Daniels said in an even tone. Sam didn't know if it was his sudden appearance or the fact that he called her by name, but it took her a few seconds to formulate a response.

"I was just heading out," she stammered, gathering her books and trying not to notice the perfect lines of his uniform, the sharp angle of his shoulders.

Daniels pulled out a chair and sat down. Sam stiffened in her seat.

"How's your training coming?" he said, folding his hands neatly in front.

"It's going well," Sam replied as she quickly gathered her paperwork, shoving it into her notebook.

"I'm glad. Any problems?"

"No. I like being on the field, much more so than the classroom. I always prefer being outside, if given the choice," Sam prattled, trying to fill the space between them with words.

"Well, let us know if there's anything you need. I'm sure it's tough, being stuck among all those men." Daniels' face warmed to almost a smile, transforming his features, softening his beautiful angles. Sam felt herself staring and quickly dropped her eyes.

She took a deep breath and tried to relax. She glanced at his hands, perfectly folded. His forearms were smooth, and she remembered the first day of class when he had stood next to her desk; the closeness of his body, the faint smell of leather. Sam forced herself to look into his face, which was relaxed, yet maintained its usual intensity. The calm grey of his eyes never left hers. It was as if he was looking through her, his gaze fixed and penetrating. Sam spoke without thinking.

"Do you miss San Diego?" she asked, immediately berating herself. The last thing Sam wanted was to shift onto personal terrain, but it seemed something within her was directing the conversation. She held her breath, curious if the commander would wade in.

Daniels paused for a moment as a shadow crossed his face; his eyes tightened before he answered. "Sometimes," he replied, his voice quieter than before.

"Chief of Training, Special Ops Commander; an impressive background," Sam said as she felt the flush rise to her face.

"How do you know about all that?" Daniels cocked his head slightly as his eyes ratcheted down to an even keener focus.

"When I was applying to the academy, I reviewed the credentials of the staff," Sam replied, trying to match his eye contact. "I read your bio. Was it hard to adjust to the east, after being in California?" Having spent her life moving around the country, Sam knew what it was like entering new territory, having to adjust to a new way of life. She felt her brain calming and regained a bit of her composure.

"No, I like it here. When I left California, I needed a change." Daniels dropped his eyes for the first time and peered down at his hands, his face hardening.

"Why are you here so late?" Sam asked, forcing her eyes from his hands.

"I come here a lot in the evenings. I'm researching an article and I'd rather be here when there are fewer people around. I like the silence." Daniels eyes were riveted once again.

"I do, too," Sam replied. "That's the hardest part of the academy: being forced into a group. I'm used to time alone, and that's hard to come by around here."

Daniels smiled faintly then dropped his eyes to his hands again. They sat in silence and then looked at each other as if on cue, realizing it was time to go. They stood up and Sam gathered her books, shoving them into her backpack. Daniels picked up the last of her books and handed it to her across the table. Sam noticed his forearm flex under its weight and once again felt the flush in her chest. She imagined grabbing hold of his arm, yanking him onto the table, and working her way down every inch of that beautiful body. She forced a smile as she crammed the book into her backpack.

They walked out of the library and down the empty hall. Sam was aware of the soft tread of their boots on the polished floor. They arrived in front of the lobby to Daniels' office and paused. The commander turned to her.

"Well, goodnight, Samantha," Daniels said with a wan smile, turning toward the door.

"Sam," she announced as Daniels turned back. "Everyone calls me Sam; nobody calls me Samantha."

He stared at her. "That's a shame. It's a nice name."

"So is Mathew," Sam replied, catching the hint of surprise in the commander's face at hearing his name spoken by a cadet.

"I tell you what," Sam added, cutting her eyes to him. "When there's no one around, you can call me Samantha."

Daniels smiled and dropped his eyes. "All right." He spoke to the floor before hitting her one last time with that grey intensity. "Good night, Samantha."

Sam's smile faltered. "Good night, Commander."

With her words, they were whisked back to the confines of their rank structure and reminded of the barrier that existed between them. While Daniels was her commander, Sam would be relocated to subordinate. The familiarity of their conversation was transient, ephemeral. It faded the moment they were reminded of their positions within the system.

Sam turned on her heel and strode away. She could feel Daniels' eyes following her.

VII

The next morning, Sam's phone rang before dawn.

"You up for a run?" Ty blurted as soon as Sam picked up.

They had started meeting early in the morning on weekends, taking long runs through downtown and ending up at a small café for breakfast. Sam tried to clear her head as she flashed back to her hormone-infused dreams.

"Um, how about tomorrow morning? I had kind of a rough night and I've got some things to catch up on." She rubbed her eyes with a balled fist.

"You OK?"

"I'm fine," Sam mumbled, yawning into the phone. "How about six tomorrow?"

"Great. I'll see you then, but don't forget Johnny's tomorrow night!"

"Sounds good. See you in the morning." She hung up and curled herself back beneath the covers. Sam purposely ignored her backpack and spent the morning catching up on laundry. She was ahead on her studies, so she simply enjoyed the solitude of the balcony, sipping hot coffee, flipping through the paper.

She had bought her condo with a portion of the money her father had left her. It was fifteen floors up and bordered the heavily treed historic district in downtown. It faced north, which meant Sam could watch the sun rise and set during the warmer months before it slid south for the winter. The view looked out over a small lake and Sam loved watching the summer storms skirt the horizon, their grey tails filled with lightning.

The next morning, Ty rapped on her door before dawn and they headed out on their usual course, winding their way through the darkened, bricked streets. Ty would run a mile or two before showing up at Sam's to satisfy his need for distance. After forty minutes, Sam's legs began to tire.

"All right," she gasped in between breaths as she grabbed his arm. "Enough."

"Come on!" Ty protested. "How about one more mile?" He wiped his brow with the back of his hand as they slowed to a walk. The one concession his father had made while Ty was in high school was allowing him to run track. Training with the track team was the only time Ty was allowed to be absent from the farm; the only freedom he was permitted. He lost himself among the miles.

"You go ahead," Sam replied grudgingly, giving him a nudge with her elbow. "But I'll be having coffee without you."

"All right," Ty griped. "I guess that's all I can expect from a girl." He grinned and waited for Sam's response. Ty quickly learned that teasing Sam usually resulted in her touching him in retaliation. He looked for any excuse to provoke her.

Sam reached over and grabbed his neck. Ty flinched but did not pull away.

"What have I told you about those remarks!" she grumbled through gritted teeth, unable to stifle her laughter.

"Sorry, sorry!" he feigned as they headed for the café. Sam glanced over at him as they walked. When she thought about how shy Ty had been on the first day of the academy, it was hard to believe he was the same person. He had opened up completely; not just with her, but in general. It was like the escape from his father had permitted the release of his personality. It was an amazing thing to watch.

At the café, they bought coffee and muffins. Ty grabbed the sack and followed Sam outside. "Let's go across the street to the lake," she said over her shoulder, making a beeline for the water. "It's too nice to be inside."

They settled in the shade and devoured their muffins, chasing them with the hot coffee. When they were done, they laid back in the grass, side by side, enjoying the looseness of their muscles, the cool of the morning. Sam sat up and glanced down at Ty. He squinted skyward as the flowing branches painted shadows over his body.

"Can I ask you something personal?" Sam said quietly.

Ty eyed her, grinning. "How can one man be so smart *and* handsome?"

"I'll give you the handsome part," Sam griped. "Seriously, though…"

"Anything," Ty replied, shielding his eyes with a raised hand.

"The situation with your father," Sam began tentatively. "How is it you managed to get through those experiences and still end up the way you are? I mean, it amazes me that you are as gentle a person as you are considering what you went through."

Sam spent long hours thinking about Ty. Her mind seemed to drift to him whenever she spent time alone with her thoughts. Sam marveled at the complexity of Ty's personality, how he had survived the violence of his childhood with such gentleness intact. But Sam also marveled at the changes Ty provoked in her. Ty aroused Sam's sense of protection, a deep nurturing she had reserved solely for her father. When he died, Sam banished the instinct, retreating to the bitter safety of her isolation, the cool comfort of seclusion. Ty stirred the old feelings, as if tossing a pebble into the still waters of her soul. Sam felt increasingly connected to him as the delicate folds of their friendship unfurled.

"I don't know," Ty replied, pulling himself into a sitting position, their shoulders touching. His eyes settled on a spot across the lake. "I used to blame myself. I'd try to figure out what I was doing wrong. But then I realized no matter what I did, he'd come after me." Sam stared at Ty in profile, at the perfect lines that defined his face. "I just don't understand how anyone could strike you, Ty," she whispered, surprised to feel the emotions rise in her throat. Sam steadied her breathing, her gaze drifting across the lake.

Ty looked at her. "I'm OK," he added simply, nudging her shoulder. Sam's eyes moved slowly over his face. She placed her hand on the back of his head and drew him to her. Ty's head fell naturally to her shoulder and they sat for a few silent minutes before taking up their coffee. Sam gave his neck a quick squeeze before releasing him. They lay back in the grass as she found his hand.

They drove to Johnny's under a late afternoon sun. The small house stood on the north side of town and held a shaded backyard perfect for grilling out. Lance, Trey, and Tate were already there, as were Shane and Bo, who had recently joined the study group in hopes of improving their grades. Mark and Bill, the two burly football players, thundered through the front door. Bill snatched a bottle from the bag Mark carried and the evening quickly devolved into a drinking competition. Bill prided himself on his ability to consume vast quantities of alcohol. He was anxious to show off his gift.

"You guys are going to be sorry, come tomorrow," Sam warned as Bill set up a line of shots. He placed an empty glass in the center of the table.

"Thanks for the warning, Mom," Bill replied sarcastically. "Here's the rules." He leaned his bulk against the counter as he addressed the men. He then held up a quarter between two thick fingers. "Bounce the quarter into the glass. If you make it, everyone else has to take a shot. If you miss, *you* have to take the shot. Who's up first?" He scanned the group as Mark reclined on the far counter, draining a beer in record time.

"Shouldn't we wash that quarter first?" Tate griped, eyeing the coin with disdain.

"Sure thing, Tater, right after you change your tampon. Who's first?"

"I'll go!" Ty exclaimed, grinning at Sam as he stepped forward. Sam shook her head, grabbed a beer from the sink, and drifted into the living room.

As the game wore on and the noise level in the kitchen became unbearable, Mark joined Sam on the couch. Johnny was busy patrolling the mess as the men worked their way through the tequila before moving on to a case of beer. Mark spread out beside her, his massive frame enveloping half the couch as Sam shifted to make room. He leaned in close as he told her about his short stint in professional football.

"Had you always thought of becoming a firefighter?" Sam asked over the noise wafting in from the kitchen.

"No," he replied loudly into her ear, "I was supposed to follow my father into the Special Forces, but I had a small mishap when it came to jumping out of a fucking plane." He fingered the label on his bottle.

"What happened?" Sam asked, wishing they had a quieter spot in which to talk.

"My father took me skydiving for my eighteenth birthday. You know, to give me a taste of what it would be like once I joined up." Here, Mark paused, staring at his bottle as he replayed the incident in his head: his father waking him before dawn, ordering him to get dressed, that he had a special gift in store. They had driven to the small airstrip in silence, been among the first group to go up, but when the time came for Mark to jump, he had been so overcome with fear, even his tandem instructor couldn't get him to budge from the bench. Mark's refusal to jump had meant the end of his father's dreams of Special Forces. Their relationship had never recovered.

"I thought by making it in pro football he would look at me differently, maybe take pride in what I was doing. But then I got cut. I don't know what I'll do if I can't make it as a firefighter."

"Anyhow," he continued, taking a quick sip of beer. "What's your story?"

"I grew up in the military too. My father was a captain in the Navy."

"No shit? Where were you stationed?"

Realizing they had both spent time in the Philippines, they compared stories about their childhoods, the places they had lived. The drinking went on and after a few hours, the men were trashed. Johnny and Sam shoved the furniture from the center of the room, throwing blankets and pillows down so nobody would be tempted to drive home. A DUI was cause for dismissal from the academy and even in their inebriated states, the cadets knew better than to risk it. Johnny helped Sam fold Ty into the car.

Sam drove through the quiet streets of downtown as Ty, head back, eyes closed, rambled incoherently. One minute he would be laughing, then suddenly turn serious, all the while talking a blue streak. They arrived at Ty's and Sam pulled him from the car. Sam fumbled for Ty's keys at the front door while Ty placed a steadying hand against the wall. His head drooped heavily between his shoulders. Once Sam had the door open, she wound his arm around her shoulder and guided him to his room. She lowered him onto the bed with a grunt, then went to the kitchen and poured a glass of water. When she came back, Ty had stumbled into the bathroom and was sitting on the floor against the wall, his head in his hands.

"Are you all right?" Sam knelt beside him and placed a gentle palm to his forehead.

"I'm sick," Ty mumbled. Sam reached for the waste basket and placed it between his feet. Ty's arms drooped over his knees and his head fell back against the wall. Sam could see the slow rhythm of his pulse in the arteries along his neck. She got up and found a washcloth, soaked it in cold water, and placed it on his forehead. Ty began mumbling again, but the only words Sam could make out were "father" and "home." He seemed to be arguing with himself and Sam wondered if the demons from childhood were surfacing.

Sam thought back to their conversation by the lake and once again, she tried to imagine someone striking him. How had Ty survived the violent encounters with his father without becoming hardened and hateful? It amazed her that Ty could remain peaceful when he had never known peace. Perhaps Ty's mother had passed down some inherent strength. Surely, she had witnessed the brutality between father and son. She had encouraged Ty to escape and Sam wondered how he dealt with leaving her behind.

Ty had quieted and appeared to be dozing. Sam moved the trashcan away and helped him to his feet. She slung his arm around her shoulder again and guided him into his room. He sat down heavily on the bed, then slowly collapsed backward. Sam removed his shoes, tossing them off to the side, and then worked his shirt over his head. She pulled the covers down and slowly guided him into bed.

Sam sat down beside him. Her hand rose instinctively to his head and she traced the hair that outlined his face. Ty fumbled for her hand. He clutched it to his chest, his eyes securely closed. As Sam rose from the bed, Ty spoke.

"Love you, Sam," he mumbled through his inebriation. Sam stared down at him, then bent down and kissed his forehead. He was asleep instantly, breathing deeply through parted lips. Sam returned to the bathroom and flipped off the light. She pulled the front door shut, making sure it locked behind her, and drove off into the night.

Sam arrived early the next morning. Ty wore his academy shorts and clutched a boot in one hand as he wandered through the house in search of its partner. "How's the head?" Sam grinned as she took a seat on the arm of the couch.

"What the hell happened last night?" Ty grumbled as he lurched forward, stumbling over the missing boot. He snatched it up and crammed it into his duffel bag. "The last thing I remember is Bill lining up shots. God, I feel like shit." He rubbed at his temples, then pulled a crinkled tee shirt from his bag. He wrestled it over his head as Sam grabbed his backpack.

"Well, I'm glad to see you're alive. Now grab the rest of your stuff and let's go. I have a feeling it's going to be a hard run."

Johnny and Sam were the only ones from their group who had made it through the night unscathed. Ty stumbled around the track on unsteady legs. Lance and Trey were holding their own, but Tater was sidelined near the shrubs, dry-heaving. Mark and Bill, veterans of the all-nighter, were able to run, but they grumbled their way around the track, cursing under their breath. Shane and Bo were in horrendous shape. After begging Tanner to excuse him from the run, Shane was ordered to stand on the sidelines for jumping jacks. He flapped his arms half-heartedly, stopping every so often to lean over and spit.

"You'll learn one day, boy," Tanner exclaimed, grinning and chomping his pick.

Their group wasn't the only ones sick that morning. Tanner had searched out Michaels in his office when he'd not shown up on the field.

"What's goin' on, brother?" Tanner asked from the doorway to the office. He polished off his cup of coffee, crumbled the paper cup in his fist, and chucked it into the garbage can across the room. Michaels was hunched at his desk, his eyes rimmed in red, blowing his nose into a paper towel.

"Can you lead today?" Michaels croaked. "I'm not going to make it out." He folded the paper towel meticulously and took a swipe at his nose.

"Sure," Tanner replied. "I've got Lee comin' out. We're just doin' ropes and knots. Should be a piece of cake." Tanner checked his watch before turning for the door.

But the mention of Lee's name set Michaels on edge. He flashed back to the incident with Smith and the ladder. If Tanner were busy with one half of the class, there would be no one to keep Lee in line. Michaels was about to tell Tanner to be sure to work with Smith, but caught himself, worried he'd appear overprotective. Tanner gathered his clipboard and stopwatch and headed out the door. Michaels braced his head in his hands and stared at his desk.

On his way out, Michaels stopped in Daniels' office. Daniels was buried in paperwork and barely glanced up when he knocked.

"I'm heading home, Commander. I feel like hell. Tanner's going to run the class. He's got Lee coming out."

"You all right?" Daniels reached for his mug and took a quick sip, scanning the officer over the rim of his cup.

"I'll be fine. Will you do me a favor though?" Michaels asked as he took a step into the office. "Will you check on the class, make sure everything runs smoothly?"

Daniels could read the concern in Michaels' tone. "Something up?" Daniels leaned back in his chair and placed his mug on the desk. He folded his hands across his belly.

"No, I just want to make sure everything's covered," Michaels replied, dropping his eyes, and fumbling with his paper towel.

"I'll stop in. Don't worry. Go home and get some rest. You look like hammered shit."

Michaels waved goodbye with his paper towel and headed out of the office. He had an uneasy feeling in his gut but was too miserable to give it further thought. *I'm sure everything will be fine,* he told himself as he left the academy.

~

The cadets were lined up on deck. The men had recovered from PT, but their hangovers were apparent. They stood listlessly in front of their gear. Tanner was unlocking the heavy wooden doors to the tower, but there was still no sign of Michaels. Sam glanced across the tarmac to see Lee crossing the field.

"Shit," she mumbled under her breath. "Not that asshole." Ty looked on, his face set.

Lee marched over and braced off to the side. Tanner paced up and down the line as he laid out the plans for the day. "We'll be goin' over ropes and knots today, so I hope you've been practicin' your shit," he barked as he scanned the cadets. "We'll split ya'll up and go through the formations." Here he glanced down at his clipboard. Sam held her breath.

Suddenly, Lee stepped forward. "I'll take the bottom half of the alphabet," he announced, grinning at Sam. He then strode over to the tower to retrieve the bag of rope. Sam shot a pleading look to Tanner.

"Fine by me," Tanner added, his eyes still on his clipboard. "You heard the man. Top half with me. Grab your shit and let's go." He turned abruptly for the tower, the top half of the class following on his heels. The rest of the class stood in a silent huddle, waiting for Lee's return. Sam chewed nervously on her lip.

Lee brought out the bag of rope and distributed the ten-foot sections by throwing them forcefully at each cadet. The students fanned out in a circle and practiced their knots as Lee sat with his legs astride a backward metal chair, his ball cap pulled low over his forehead. When the cadets had worked through their knots, Lee stood up, hitched up his belt, and sauntered over.

"OK girls, it's time to show me what you know."

One by one, Lee had them stand in front of the group and perform. When the cadets made mistakes, he'd snatch the rope from their hands and construct the knot himself.

"I thought you guys were supposed to be practicing," he exclaimed in disgust, throwing the rope back at Tate. He turned to Sam. "All right, Pet. How about a figure eight?"

Sam stepped forward, took a deep breath, and focused on the rope. She worked the rope slowly, nervous fingers fumbling, and could feel Lee growing impatient. He shifted in his boots, planted his hands angrily on his hips, and exhaled audibly. Sam pulled the knot taut and held it out, hoping he wouldn't notice her trembling palm. Lee yanked it from her hand, gave it a quick inspection, and threw it back at her.

"Now show me a figure eight on a bight," he continued with a smirk as he scanned the group, anticipating their confusion. The students had been instructed in the basics but had yet to move on to the more complex knots.

"I don't know that knot," Sam muttered, her eyes on the ground.

"Well, I guess you can drop and give me twenty."

Sam's head shot up. Lee stood with his head cocked, grinning. When Sam didn't move, the grin slid from his face. He took a menacing step forward. "I said give me twenty," Lee repeated louder, a long finger pointing at the ground.

Sam handed her rope to Johnny and dropped into position. She pumped out twenty pushups and then stood up, brushing the dust from her palms, her eyes fixed on the ground.

Lee snatched the rope from Johnny and threw it back at her. "How about a figure eight follow through," he continued as Sam fumbled for control of the rope.

Sam clenched and unclenched her fists. "I don't know that knot," she repeated, her jaw tightening.

"Well, you know what that means," Lee replied in a sing-song before hardening his tone. "This time give me thirty."

Sam could hear the men around her shifting in their boots. She glanced over at Ty, who stood glaring at Lee, his rope wound around a clenched fist. Sam handed her rope back to Johnny, who caught her eye, silently urging her on. She dropped into position and pumped out thirty pushups as Lee counted aloud in a mocking tone. When she was done, Sam climbed to her feet, working to catch her breath.

"One last chance to redeem yourself, Pet. Show me a figure eight bend." Lee stuffed his hands into his pockets, his legs spread in a defiant stance.

"I don't know that knot," Sam repeated for the third time. She fought to keep her frustration in check, knowing it would just fuel his antagonism.

"I tell you what," Lee replied, congenially. "You and me are gonna' have a private session. Follow me." He turned abruptly and walked toward the far side of the tower. When he didn't hear Sam follow, he turned and yelled, "Over here, now!"

Sam kept her eyes on the ground. She was afraid if she looked at Ty or Johnny, she would tear up. Sam dug her fingernails into her palms to stave off the emotion and followed Officer Lee around the side of the tower.

~

The morning had gotten away from him. Daniels glanced at his watch, realizing the paperwork had kept him at his desk for two hours. He remembered Michaels' request to check on the class. Michaels wouldn't have asked had he not had good reason. Daniels grabbed his coffee cup, topped it off on the way out of the office, and headed out to the training ground.

As Daniels crossed the field, he could see Tanner on one side of the tower, working through knots with his group. The rest of the students were standing in a huddle in front of the tower. They watched the commander approach, a mix of worry and relief on their faces.

As he approached the group, Daniels noticed two things immediately. First, there was no instructor. Second, he couldn't locate Samantha anywhere on the field. His grip on his cup tightened. "Where's Officer Lee?" he barked.

"He's on the side of the tower," Johnny replied, flicking his head in the direction Lee had taken Sam.

Without a word, Daniels headed for the side of the tower. He could feel the anger rising in his throat. There was no reason for an instructor to leave students unattended or to segregate a student, especially a female. As Daniels came around the tower, he could see Samantha standing in front of Lee, her eyes on a length of rope in her hands as she worked it into a knot. He could read her fury. She was red-faced, sweating, and out of breath. Lee stood with his back to Daniels.

"No good!" Lee yelled, snatching the rope from her hands, and throwing it to the ground. "Drop!"

Daniels opened his mouth to yell but froze, his eyes locking on Samantha as she dropped into position. Sam paused to catch her breath before beginning.

Her arms were rigid, the pushups perfectly formed, despite her exhaustion. Sam continued with her back straight, her body a fine line. She finished and slowly stood up, panting. Lee bent down to pick up the rope. As he did, Sam glanced up, locking eyes with Daniels. She shot him a look, shaking her head ever so slightly.

"I think we're done here," Lee muttered angrily. He threw the rope at her again and turned to march back to the group. Sam gathered the rope in her hands. When she looked up, Daniels had disappeared. She slowly followed Lee back to the front of the tower.

As Lee approached the cadets, he lifted a hand to his face and rubbed at his jaw. "Sometimes you just gotta school a woman," he said, grinning.

Ty could feel the rage building; a rage he'd not felt since home. Johnny looked up as Sam came around the side of the tower, trying to read her face. Johnny knew Lee wouldn't actually harm her, but Sam's humiliation was apparent.

Sam rejoined the group, her eyes glued to the ground as she worked to catch her breath. Her face was flushed and covered in a sweaty sheen. Lee shot her a look and then headed for the door of the tower to retrieve more equipment. The group stood with ropes in hand, no one willing to break the silence until Tate finally muttered, "You OK, Sam?" Sam gave a silent nod as she swiped at her face.

As Lee entered the darkness of the tower, he stood for a moment to let his eyes adjust to the dim light. The hands were on him in an instant. They gripped the front of his shirt, throwing him against the inner wall. Suddenly, Daniels face loomed close. Lee could smell the coffee on his breath as the commander pinned him against the wall.

"If you ever mishandle a cadet, I'll see you never teach again! I'll make it my personal quest to ride your ass right out of this state!" Daniels exclaimed in a fierce whisper, envisioning grabbing the officer by the throat with one hand while running a consoling hand over Samantha's delicate skull. He shoved Lee one last time before storming from the tower.

Lee straightened his uniform and leaned back against the wall. He knew Daniels had a temper and could be a cold son-of-a-bitch, but he had never seen him so furious. After all, Lee hadn't been that far out of line. Sure, he pushed the cadets, even danced on the line separating discipline from abuse, but it was his job to push these assholes. He was here to make them firefighters, not coddle the little fucks.

Daniels had seen him get tough with students before. What was different about today, other than it happened to be a female? It's not like he laid a hand on her. If he were going to cop a feel, he'd wait for an opportunity when he had her in the tower. He wasn't stupid enough to do it in broad daylight.

Lee shook off the incident, grabbed the equipment, and headed back out to the group.

Lunch was a solemn affair. The group ate in silence, staring at the ground as they quietly munched their sandwiches. Ty sat next to Sam; his body close. He leaned into her and she forced a smile before returning to her thoughts. The group stayed close to the tower. The skies were growing heavy, the academy flag snapped in the wind. They picked at their lunches while Tate made small talk. After a few meager attempts at conversation, he gave up and the group slipped back into silence.

Aaron and two of his sidekicks wandered over. "How'd your training go this morning, Sam?" He smirked as he twirled a piece of rope. "I heard you had a private lesson. Wanna' give us some details?" He flicked the rope at one of his buddies as the two at his side exchanged idiotic grins.

Sam studied Aaron as he stood over her in bunker pants and helmet, his belt loaded down with redneck paraphernalia. Suddenly, her anger at all things male boiled over. She imagined issuing a swift kick of her boot to his balls, dropping him to the tarmac like a lead weight. Instead, she replied evenly, "You'd think with a head that big, you'd know when to shut the fuck up." Aaron's friends stifled their laughter as the rope in Aaron's fist went limp.

As the cadets snickered, Aaron scanned the group, grappling for a response. But it was always harder arguing with a female. His mind seemed to go blank, his sarcasm sputtered. Desperate, he turned to what he knew; the only way to deal with a woman who couldn't hold her tongue. He leaned over, jabbing a thick finger in Sam's face.

"You better watch your fuckin' mouth, Sam, or I'll take you behind the tower and set you straight myself!"

Ty leapt to his feet, causing a chain reaction as the group sprang into action. Ty grabbed hold of Aaron's tee shirt as the group quickly closed in, shoving and shouting. As the men clashed, Sam scrambled out from beneath the fray, scanning the field in search of Tanner. Lee looked on with disinterest as he reclined beneath the shade of the tower. Sam watched with relief as Tanner came rushing over, his large boots kicking up dust. He made it just in time, before fists flew.

"Throw a punch and pack your shit!" Tanner yelled as he grabbed hold of Aaron and Ty, wrenching them apart. "Get to the other side of the tower, Peterson!" he shouted, shoving Aaron aside. Aaron muttered under his breath as he stomped off, his friends following close behind. Ty adjusted his shirt and scanned the crowd for Sam.

Tanner turned for the tower, swiping at his forehead as he marched past Lee.

"*Do your job!*" Tanner fired at him as Lee dropped his eyes and picked at his fingernails.

~

Daniels spent the afternoon trying to lose himself in paperwork, his anger still simmering from his encounter with Lee. The door to his office remained closed, a sign for Miss Davis to hold his calls. The paperwork was piled up, awaiting his attention. He would stay late to wade through the mess.

Just after five, a light knock on his door roused him from his work. Miss Davis poked her head in. "I'm heading out, Commander. Is there anything else?" she said, aware of his dark mood. Miss Davis could read the commander as well as Michaels could. She knew the signs of his low days.

"No, I'm fine. Thank you," Daniels replied dully, his grey eyes strained.

"There's coffee left. Shall I keep it on?"

"That would be fine. I was just going to check. Have a good evening," he added, returning to his paperwork.

"Shall I leave this open?" she asked, her hand on the doorknob.

"That's fine," Daniels replied without looking up.

As the quiet settled over the office, Daniels stretched in his chair, then stood up to get the blood flowing in his legs. He looked out the large window, across the empty training ground and could see that the door to the tower stood open. He glanced at his watch before returning to his desk, searching for his coffee cup.

He wandered through the office, checking the usual spots. Then he remembered the incident with Lee. He had set the mug down inside the tower just before their confrontation. Daniels returned to his window, scanned the field again, and then glanced up at the darkening sky. The clouds were heavy and low; the rain would be here in no time. Faint thunder rumbled in the distance and a small dusty cyclone danced across the tarmac. The tower door stood gaping. Daniels grabbed his uniform jacket and headed out of the office.

As Daniels crossed the field, a hard wind bent the pines and the hedgerow separating the fields danced erratically. He buried his hands in the pockets of his jacket, bracing against the wind as he made his way toward the tower. The light in the sky was fading as evening approached. The dark interior of the tower formed a black rectangle in the wall.

The floor of the tower was inhabited by shadows, the air laced with the familiar scent of burnt wood. Daniels loved the smell of the tower. It was engrained in his brain, linked to everything he was. It could immediately put him at ease, its familiarity a solace.

He scanned the empty floor. Why had Tanner left the door open? *God, he hated it when Michaels wasn't around.* Daniels located his mug and was turning to leave when he heard a noise from the upper floor. He stood still, listening intently, not sure if he had actually heard something or if it was merely the wind finding its way into the structure. At least Tanner had the foresight to shutter the building against the approaching rain.

Daniels moved slowly toward the stairwell, placing his mug back on the table, the rubber soles of his boots silent against the concrete floor. The noise sounded again. It was soft; not its volume, but the noise itself: cloth on cloth. He took the stairs noiselessly, listening as he climbed. It seemed to be coming from the third floor. His hand slid silently up the metal railing.

Daniels arrived on the third floor and stood in the open doorway. It was dark, but one of the back lights burned dimly. Samantha stood in the center of the room holding a section of rope, working it through her hands, frustration marring her face. As she manipulated the rope, it gently slapped against her bunker pants, emitting the sound Daniels had heard from the first floor. Her book lay open on the floor beside her. Sam glanced down at the page and tried the knot again. When it failed to work, she balled up the rope and threw it angrily across the room. As the rope sailed, its tail caught her above the lip. Her head snapped back in response.

The rope ends were sealed with a thick coating of wax to prevent fraying; they became sharp over time. The heft of the rope produced just enough force to break a fine line above her mouth. It bled instantly. Sam stripped off her gloves and threw them to the concrete. She then walked to the side wall and slid down onto the floor. She sat with her legs bent, elbows on her knees, swiping at her face as the blood smeared across her cheek.

Sam glanced up and saw him. She didn't move; she was too tired to go through the motions of protocol. It had been a shitty day and she wished now she had simply gone to the library with the others. The incident with Lee had made her leery of anyone in uniform. Seeing the commander rekindled her humiliation.

Daniels crossed the room slowly. He could sense her tension. He approached her as one approached a startled animal: with slow, cautious movements. As he did, Sam ducked her face beneath her fingertips.

"I was wondering why the tower was open. What are you doing here, Samantha?" Daniels said quietly.

Sam looked up at him, her face still bleeding, her eyes bloodshot. "Just practicing," she replied, indicating the rope on the floor with a slight jerk of her head. Her eyes dropped to her hands, which were now streaked with blood. She examined her palms and then took another swipe at the wound.

Daniels strode over to the table near the window. A stack of paper towels sat near a column of paper cups. He pulled a few from the stack and crossed the room to her. Sam eyed him cautiously, reflexively tensing as he approached. She started to rise, but before she could, Daniels squatted down in front of her, his bent knees almost touching hers. He held out the paper towels and Sam slowly raised her bloodied hands to accept them. She tried wiping the blood, but it had started to dry, staining her hands a dark crimson. Her bleeding had slowed to a faint trickle.

Daniels rose quickly and returned to the table. A large jug of water was mounted nearby; each floor was equipped so that students could stay hydrated throughout the day. He grabbed a few more paper towels and wet them under the small faucet, then returned to her.

Sam surveyed his movements, the fluid grace of his limbs. Daniels knelt in front of her and tore the soaked towels in two, one half of which he handed her to use on her hands. The other, he folded into soft curves and carefully placed against the wound on her face. Sam's head jerked slightly under his touch. She put her head back against the wall and watched him as he dabbed at the wound. Daniels folded the towel again, using the clean side to wipe the smeared blood from her face. He held her jaw gently as he worked, her fine bones like those of a bird: fragile, built for flight. He then sat back on his haunches, knees to the floor, clutching the bloodied paper towels.

Daniels tried to remember the last time he had treated a patient. His mind raced backward, to his days as a young medic on one of San Diego's busiest Rescues. But that was years in the past. The feel of his hands on another had become strange, inappropriate.

Sam felt the urge to flee, but part of her was transfixed by Daniels actions. It was confounding seeing him render care instead of giving orders, and the lightness of his touch contradicted his stony exterior. Daniels seemed equally at a loss. He stared down at the bloody towels as if they contained the essence of her; he imagined the cells coursing through her veins. He pressed his thumb into their warmth before finally rising.

They needed to leave.

Being at the tower after hours, alone with a female cadet, could have serious implications. Daniels flashed back to the threats he had made to Lee. He reached down, unconcerned with the dried blood on her hands. Sam accepted his hand and he pulled her up. Sam stood with her back against the wall as she wiped her hands. Daniels broke from her and returned to the table, wet a few more paper towels, and then handed them to her. When her hands were finally clear, she tossed the towels into the nearby trash and gathered her rope and gloves. As they turned to leave, Daniels halted.

"Which knot were you having trouble with?"

"The double overhand safety on a figure eight."

"Show me," he said, eyeing the rope in her hand.

Sam stood before him reluctantly. She dropped her gloves to the concrete and started constructing the knot, but when she was halfway through, her fingers became confused.

"Every time!" she griped, dropping her hands. The rope slapped gently against her bunker pants.

Daniels lifted the rope from her hand and untangled the knot. He then constructed the knot using slow, steady motions until he gave each end a firm tug and a perfect figure eight lay across his palm.

"Try it again," he urged, untangling the knot, and handing it back to her.

Sam began again, but as she faltered, Daniels placed his hands on hers, guiding them in the proper direction. Their hands moved in unison, working the soft fabric of the rope, winding it against itself until the knot was perfectly formed. Sam pulled it tight and then smiled, the cut above her lip bright red against her teeth.

Daniels stared at her, aware of the minutes ticking by. They had to leave.

Sam reached down, picked up her gloves and book, and they headed for the stairwell. They descended to the first floor and Daniels grabbed his mug. The wind still blew, and the rain was falling in heavy sheets. They stood for a moment in the doorway, looking out over the training field as its distant edges disappeared in the downpour.

Sam wore bunker pants and a tee shirt, her suspenders looped loosely at her sides. Averting his eyes from her frame, Daniels slipped off his jacket and carefully placed it over her shoulders. Sam's hand floated to his arm.

"Thank you. Not just for tonight, but for not interfering with Lee."

Daniels stared at her, remembering her appearance as Lee worked her, her face set in anger and frustration, and how different she looked now, away from the others.

He gave a quick nod, pulled the door closed behind them, and locked it. They headed across the field as the wind blew the rain against their faces.

~

Now this is an interesting turn of events, he thought to himself as he watched Sam and the commander leave the tower. He watched from his vehicle, his anger from earlier still fresh. He had been about to leave campus when he noticed Smith heading out to the tower. He wasn't sure why until now. And all this time he assumed she was fucking that pretty-boy,

Williams. Perhaps she wanted to add some rank to the mix.

He smiled smugly to himself as he pulled out of campus.

~

Ty waited for Sam to show up at the library. When an hour passed, he grew restless, rechecking his watch as he glanced downstairs at the entryway. She finally appeared just as the group was packing up. Her hair was wet, and she stood at the end of the table, distracted.

Ty pulled out a chair. "You want to sit?"

Sam shook her head, her eyes moving over the table.

They drove home in silence in a light rain. Sam sat with her head back, eyes closed. Ty glanced at the cut above her lip. "We missed you at study session," he said, his eyes back on the road.

"How'd it go?" Sam asked without opening her eyes. She adjusted in her seat and turned her face toward the window.

"Fine," Ty mumbled as the wipers beat a steady rhythm.

It had been their worst day yet at the academy. The incident with Lee had embarrassed the whole group; no one more than Sam. The run-in with Peterson only added to the day's frustrations. Ty's grip on the steering wheel tightened when he thought about Lee's smugness, Peterson's threat.

"You feel like talking?"

"No, I'm good," Sam replied quietly.

When they arrived at her building, Ty turned off the engine. Sam opened her eyes and glanced at him before pulling her backpack from the floorboard.

"Can I come up for a minute?" Ty asked, his hand still gripping the ignition switch.

"Sure," Sam replied after the briefest hesitation.

When they arrived upstairs, Sam dropped her backpack in the front hallway and hauled her gear bag to her room. Ty took a seat on the couch. The faint light from the hallway threw soft shadows across the living room and Sam moved in silhouette. She sat down next to him, sliding down so that her head was reclined against the back of the couch. Ty could smell the shampoo from her hair, the soap from her skin. The light carved her profile in the darkness and she stared straight ahead, seeming lost in thought.

"What did you do to your lip?" Ty finally asked, gently touching the area near her wound.

"I smacked myself with a rope. Its fine," Sam replied before returning to her silence.

Ty watched her. "Look, I can tell you're tired. Let me let you get to bed." The silence was becoming uncomfortable. He quickly rose from the couch.

Sam was too tired to argue. She pulled herself up from the couch and followed Ty to the door. As they paused beneath the light of the hallway, Ty suddenly turned to her and slipped his arms around her. He drew Sam to him and simply held on.

Sam slowly brought her arms around him, burying her head against his neck. Ty's warmth broke through the frustration of the day and she melted against him.

There was nothing sexual in the act. It was the simplest form of affection, the purest act of friendship. Sam could feel the softness of his skin against her face. The throbbing of her cut subsided, and she became aware of nothing but the feel of Ty's body.

Ty looked at her once more before turning and walking out. Sam closed the door behind him, clicked off the light, and stood in the silence of the darkened hall.

VIII

The next few days came as a welcome relief. The cadets spent the first two days in the classroom, which gave everyone a needed break from the training ground. The days passed uneventfully and by the end of the week, they had two milestones before them. Friday would mark the end of the fourth week of training, which meant they were a third of the way through. It would also be their first day with live fire.

For days, Tanner had rambled on about fire suppression, going over the different types of extinguishing methods in excruciating detail. Now the cadets would have the opportunity to test the various methods on actual fires, which would be lit off on the training field in large, circular burn pans.

Michaels was back, to the relief of everyone involved. He slid back into his role as class leader, which Tanner gratefully relinquished. It had been a tough few days on the field. He had barely made it in time to intervene in the altercation between Williams and Peterson. And there were whispers about an incident between Lee and the girl. But Tanner hated dealing with the bullshit between students. He just wanted to train.

On Friday morning the cadets rushed through PT, anxious for the live burns to begin. The run went smoothly, everyone seemed more relaxed, and even Peterson was quieter than usual. He sneered at Sam as she entered the gym, but Sam simply flipped him a dainty bird and kept walking.

The cadets assembled at the tower, nervously checking and rechecking their gear. Four instructors were on hand for the burns and Sam was relieved to see that Lee was not among them. The instructors huddled on the sideline, readying their gear. They slid into their bunker pants as the cadets anxiously looked on.

The students donned their turnout gear and spent the morning practicing with extinguishers. The instructors allowed them to break into their usual groups, which suited everyone. The days when they were divided alphabetically were never as enjoyable, since it split Sam's group in half. The only saving grace was that Peterson was relocated to the upper half with Mark and Bill. Aside from the instructors, Mark and Bill were the only ones who could keep Aaron's behavior in check. One glance from either of them and Aaron quickly shut his trap.

The students broke for lunch, gulping their sandwiches and chugging water so that the fire training could get underway. As they assembled their gear, Daniels marched across the field. He wore black bunker pants and boots and had stripped down to a black tee shirt. Like the students, the instructors were clones, only much better dressed. Sam watched his easy stride, the way his eyes scanned the field, always checking, always alert. He joined the group of instructors, bracing on the periphery of the huddle, as Michaels laid out the plans for the afternoon.

The cadets were split into teams. Each student would operate an extinguisher first. Once each of them had mastered the skill, the teams would move on to handlines. The day would end with flammable liquids fires, which would be fought using high-expansion foam.

The rotations began. The fire was lit in the smaller of the two pans, which were shallow metal containers shaped like giant plates. The smaller pan was the size of a kiddy pool; the larger, the size of a Volkswagen. Tanner hoisted one of the extinguishers and approached the burning pan.

"Now, you all remember the acronym, P-A-S-S," he announced loudly over the hiss of the fire, his muscular arm flexing under the weight of the extinguisher. "Pull the pin, aim the nozzle, squeeze the handle, and sweep the nozzle to and fro," he continued, miming the instructions. He then eyed the group. "Who's first?"

The cadets exchanged nervous glances as Tate quickly stepped forward. "I'll go," he exclaimed, thrusting a hand skyward like a trophy. Emboldened by his role as study group leader, Tate was anxious to exercise his newfound confidence.

"Good man," Tanner replied as he spit his toothpick onto the tarmac and popped a fresh one in his mouth. He then turned back to the group; the toothpick clenched between his molars. "Now you all watch old Tater here to see how it's done. Tater," he added, cutting a grin at the cadet, "don't fuck it up."

Tate gave a quick nod, then slipped on his gloves and adjusted the strap of his helmet. He took a few deep breaths before stepping forward. Tanner handed him the extinguisher and he jostled it into place, dangling the tank in his left hand and gripping the small nozzle in his right.

"Verbalize the commands," Tanner yelled over his shoulder as he moseyed over to Michaels, who was engrossed in his clipboard. Tate turned to address the group.

"I pull the pin," he began as he wrenched the pin from its holding and dropped it to the tarmac with a metallic clink. "I aim the nozzle," he continued, extending his arm as if he were feeding a hungry lion, "and I squeeze the handle." He bore down on the handle, but nothing happened. He stared at the nozzle with dismay.

"What the fuck, Tater?" Tanner barked, his large hands planted on his hips. "Squeeze the sumbitch with a little gusto!"

"Need a hand, Nancy?" Aaron jeered, elbowing the cadet next to him with a sharp blow to the ribs.

Mark eyed Aaron and took a step forward. "You want my boot up your ass, shit-for-brains?" he snarled as Bill grunted in agreement.

"Zip it, gentlemen!" Michaels shouted, without looking up from his clipboard.

Tate gave a grateful nod to Mark and then slowly squeezed the handle again, waiting for the inevitable rush of discharge, when suddenly the nozzle exploded in a white plume. The jolt sent him careening in a tight circle, dousing the surrounding cadets in CO_2. The students erupted in laughter as Tate brought the nozzle under control and finally managed to snuff the flame.

"Sorry about that, Officer Tanner," Tate muttered as he placed the extinguisher reverently at Tanner's feet. He then removed his helmet and brushed it clean using one of his gloves.

"Better luck next time, Tater," Tanner chuckled. He planted a friendly slap on Tate's back, almost knocking him into the group of snickering cadets.

When the students had rotated through using the extinguisher, they prepared for the hoseline exercise. Here, they would work in teams of two. One person would operate the nozzle, the other would back up the nozzle man by keeping an arm fully extended with his hand against the nozzle man's back. The person operating the nozzle would brace himself against his partner while using both hands to direct the stream.

The students were partnered as usual: Sam and Ty, Lance and Trey, Johnny and Tate, and Mark and Bill. Their lighter frames put Sam and Ty at a disadvantage, but Johnny and Tate had an even rougher time. Tate, encouraged by a successful second attempt at the extinguisher, served as backup man for Johnny and was so gung-ho, he almost maneuvered the cadet right into the pan.

"What the fuck are you doing, Tater?" screamed Tanner over the noise of the engine. "Don't scorch him!" he added, grinning, his toothpick dancing as he watched the two men scuffle. Johnny struggled to restrain Tate's movements while behind him, Tate plunged forward. Even Daniels was amused, his mustache bent in a wry smile.

But the real fun came when the foam began to flow. Tanner set up the operation, dumping the concentrated mixture into the engine's tank to aerate it before it was launched onto the fire. As Tanner worked on the engine, Michaels addressed the students.

"Remember," he shouted over the noise of the pump. "You want to launch the foam so that it rains down on the fire. That's the only way it will effectively blanket and smother the flames."

The large pan was lit off and they watched as the flames rose higher, deep red against the pale autumn sky. The students unconsciously formed a circle around the pan, mesmerized by the fire's proximity. The burning liquid morphed into various shades of blue and danced against a crimson backdrop. The cadets stared at the pan as if hypnotized, entranced by its primal lure. Sam stole a glance at Daniels, who stood off to the side, his arms crossed in front as he stared into the flames. A blissful calm had settled on his face, softening his angular features. Aware of Sam's stare, his grey eyes darted over, holding her gaze before slowly sliding back to the fire. Sam followed his lead and tried to focus.

They worked in teams as the foam shot forth, covering those who failed to get out of the way and snuffing the flames with such efficiency that Tanner was soon griping about the relights. The instructors wandered among them, shouting orders, and directing the rotations. Everyone was relaxed, enjoying the fun.

"Let us take another shot at it, sir!" Lance yelled over to Tanner as Trey strapped on his helmet. By this time, the surrounding field was blanketed in a dense layer of foam, as if a blizzard had suddenly descended upon the training grounds. Tanner grinned and the pan was lit off. Lance was on the nozzle; Trey stood behind him, guiding the line, and pushing Lance forward. But as they made their approach, Lance lost his footing and went sprawling, disappearing beneath the thick blanket. He flailed his arms and legs as Trey tried to pull him to his feet. But as Trey tugged on Lance, he lost his footing and quickly disappeared.

Suddenly, it was a free-for-all. The cadets plunged in, trying to wrestle the nozzle from Lance, who hung on for dear life. Tate had taken a diving plunge and emerged as a grinning snowman. Ty pulled Sam in and they were both consumed. Bill and Mark looked enormous, their bodies resembling snow covered mountains. Even Shane and Bo had managed to relax long enough to take a dive into the mass.

The instructors indulged the students, flashing back to their first experience with foam, how it always seemed to evoke the bubble baths of their youth. Even Michaels joined in the festivities, his clipboard momentarily abandoned on the tailboard of the engine. Tanner finally shut down the operation and switched over to a normal stream, spraying the students down as if he were breaking up a riot. The class was reduced to a soaking mass, the perfect ending to a hellish month.

IX

The cadets were back in the classroom the next two days. Friday's session seemed to rejuvenate everyone, and they started the week refreshed. On Wednesday they reported to the tower and spent the day running "evolutions" – staged attacks on mock fires. The instructors would lay out the scenario, describing which part of the tower was "involved," or burning, and the cadets were to respond from an engine staged on the tarmac, advance the appropriate size hose, and simulate attacking the fire.

They spent the day pulling hoses, advancing them into the tower, and flowing water to simulate the attack. They would then break down the sections and load them back onto the engine. Their day turned into one long evolution: pull, advance, spray, break it down, and reload. By the end of the day, they were spent. That is when the instructors made their announcement. The students knew it was coming. On Friday, they would be put through their first confidence test: they would be jumping into the air bag.

The confidence tests were designed to challenge the student's ability to overcome fear; the tests forced them to perform. Confidence tests primed the cadets for the chaotic situations in which they might find themselves and were a means of testing their resolve. The air bag would be placed at the base of the tower beneath the windows. The students would begin by jumping from the third-floor window. If they made it through their first jump, they would then jump from the fourth floor.

Once Michaels released the students, Sam ran back up to the third floor to track down her gloves. When she arrived on the floor, she found Mark standing at the window, his large frame blotting out the light as he stared out onto the tarmac.

"What are you doing up here? Thinking of ending it all?" Sam asked sarcastically as she crossed the room, snatching her gloves from the nearby table.

"I'm not going to be able to do it," Mark mumbled, his eyes locked on the distant field as he mentally thumbed through his rolodex of failures.

"What aren't you going to be able to do?" Sam stuffed her gloves in the pocket of her bunker pants and eyed him. It was hard to picture Mark not being able to do anything he set his mind to. The guy was a monster. Then she remembered their conversation at the party: the skydiving incident and the fear that had overcome him. The same fear that had reshaped his future and kept him from pursuing a career in the Special Forces.

"There's no way I'll be able to jump from this or any other window," he muttered, shaking his head. "I'm standing here looking down and I know there's no fucking way it's going to happen. What the hell do I do now?" First the military, then pro football. If he flunked out of the academy, his father would simply write him off.

Sam leaned against the wall adjacent to the window. "Mark, this is nothing like jumping out of an airplane. You can't even compare the two. We'll be standing down there, cheering you on. I'm sure it won't be as bad as you think." Sam was amazed that someone as physically imposing as Mark could let the fear of a forty-foot drop make him contemplate quitting. She marveled at the frailties each of them fostered.

"Why don't you talk to Michaels about it?" she added, brightening. "Maybe he can work with you on it, let you climb the ladder truck to get used to the height. I'm sure if you did that a few times the jump would seem like nothing."

"The jump's not even the worst of it; what about the fucking church raise?" he replied, his voice rising as the thought of the second confidence test crystalized in his mind.

The church raise would be their final test and would be performed during the last week of class. A thirty-five-foot ladder would be fixed with four ropes from its top. The ladder would be raised in the center of the training field and the ropes would serve as anchors. A person would be placed on the end of each rope and the individuals would spread out to provide stability at four corners. When in place, the ladder would appear anchored to the ground like the center pole in a tent. The students were required to climb up one side of the ladder – a difficult task with the ladder fully vertical – put one leg over the top, hook it through the top rungs to lock themselves in, and then let go and lean back. They would spread their arms to full extension, all the while hovering three stories up. They would then climb over the top of the ladder and down the other side. The instability of the ladder caused it to sway and the men on anchor would have to work to keep it steady. It would be an unnerving experience, even for those comfortable with heights.

"Besides, I can't talk to Michaels about it," Mark griped, finally turning to her. "All the guy talks about is football. I can't own up to being such a pussy," he added before catching himself. "Sorry," he muttered, dropping his eyes.

"Do you want me to say something to him? I could tell him we're both uncomfortable and ask him if we could do some extra training to prepare."

"I can't ask you to do that. I know it's tough for you here as it is. Not that you can't handle it," he stammered with a raised hand.

"Really, I don't mind. It won't be as big a deal if we both do it." Sam pushed from the wall. "I just want to see you get through. There's no way that asshole Peterson's going to pass and not you. You're the only one we have who can shut him up," she added, smiling. "Let me talk to Michaels." Sam slapped his gargantuan shoulder and they headed downstairs.

After class, Sam waited for the group to head to the library before stopping by Michaels' office. He was standing at his desk, rummaging through a stack of papers, an intense scowl crinkling his features. She knocked lightly on the doorframe and waited.

Michaels glanced up, expecting one of the men. When he saw it was Sam, he did a double take and snapped to attention, a wad of papers clutched in his hand.

"Can I speak to you a minute, sir?" Sam took a tentative step into the office.

Michaels faltered, caught between whether he should sit or stand. He lurched forward, stopped, thought better of it, and then pointed for Sam to sit down. He settled stiffly behind his desk, all the while still clutching the ball of paperwork in a clenched fist. Sam stifled a grin as she took her seat. By now, she was well versed in Michaels' formalities. He was a rigid perfectionist. Like Daniels on steroids. But where Daniels was icy calm, Michaels was tight as piano wire. One pluck could send him humming.

Michaels released the papers and smoothed them out on his desk. He then folded his hands, cleared his throat, and looked her in the eye.

"What can I do for you, Smith?" he announced officially. But before Sam could speak, Daniels came striding in, his eyes glued to an open folder in his hands.

"Scott, did you finish the preliminary. . ." was all Daniels got out before grinding to a halt when he saw Sam. He glanced at Michaels and Sam watched as the two men tried to work through the situation via the eye contact they normally relied on, only it seemed having a female in the room was jamming their signal.

Sam camouflaged her smirk by scratching at her face. There was something satisfying about seeing such polished men squirm.

"Smith just came in to talk to me about… well, we haven't got that far yet," Michaels said, his eyes darting between Sam and the commander.

"Don't let me interrupt," Daniels replied, doing an about face.

"It's no problem, Commander," Sam interjected as she rose from her seat. Daniels slowly turned back to her. "I was just going to ask Officer Michaels if it would be possible to do some practice drills to prepare for the airbag jump. Mark and I would feel more comfortable if we could do some work on the ladder truck prior to the confidence test." Here, Sam paused, waiting for a reply. When neither spoke, she continued. "Is that possible?" She glanced from one to the other.

"I don't see a problem, if Michaels has the time," Daniels replied, eyeing Michaels, and immediately regretting answering for him. Daniels always tried to give his instructors free rein to run the class, especially Michaels, who was used to being at the helm. The blunder raised a subtle blush on the commander's face.

"That's not a problem," Michaels responded in a staccato. "We could do some training after class. We've done it before. We usually let the students come to us instead of offering up the extra work. That way we can focus on the ones who take the initiative to ask for help," he prattled in an endless stream; the most words Sam had ever heard the officer utter at one sitting.

"Thank you," Sam replied, looking from Michaels to Daniels, then back to Michaels. "When can we start?"

The men stared at each other. Michaels took Daniels' silence as a go-ahead.

"We'll be on the field tomorrow, so let's do it after class."

Sam turned to leave, which set off a nervous chain reaction between the men. Michaels stood up abruptly, almost knocking over a cold cup of coffee on his desk. Daniels tried to sidestep out of Sam's way, almost spilling his paperwork in the process. Sam thanked them both and quickly left the office, snorting a chuckle as she pulled the door closed behind her.

The next morning at PT, Sam pulled Mark aside. "We're all set for this afternoon," she whispered as Mark's face tightened. "One thing at a time," she added, soothingly.

~

Michaels stopped in Daniels' office on his way out to the training field. He braced in the doorway until the commander looked up from his work, then stepped inside the office. "Would you be available after class, while I run through the drill with Smith and Harris?"

Daniels leaned back in his chair and reached for his mug. "Sure, no problem," he replied, smiling, and taking a deep drag of coffee. "I'll see you then." He replaced his mug and returned to his paperwork.

Michaels nodded stiffly and left the office. As he headed down the hallway, his face broke into a grin. The ladder truck was Daniels' pride and joy; he used any excuse to be around when it was in operation. Michaels knew if he hadn't extended the invitation, Daniels would have shown up anyway, feigning some excuse to visit the tower. Daniels would never admit it. He knew he had more important responsibilities to attend to, but given the chance, he couldn't help himself.

The invite was two-fold: Michaels knew Daniels loved working the ladder, but Michaels also liked watching him at the controls. Like their morning runs, it was one of the few times Daniels actually enjoyed himself.

That evening, when class wrapped up, Mark stuck around the tower to assist Michaels in setting up the truck. Sam headed for the locker rooms. "Come on," Ty griped as he followed her down the hallway. "We're going for burgers." At least once a week, the group headed to a dilapidated burger joint a few miles from campus to gorge themselves on greasy burgers and fries. Sam was glad to have a reason to pass.

"No, I think I'll head to the library and do some reading. You guys go ahead," she replied, avoiding his gaze, and fiddling with her gear. Ty looked at her for a moment before shrugging and walking away.

"Sure I can't change your mind?" he added, turning back to her and grinning.

"Next time," Sam replied, smiling. She turned and walked to her locker room. Ty stood watching her for a few seconds, then headed down the hall.

Sam changed into a fresh tee shirt, washed her face to remove some of the day's grime, grabbed her gloves and helmet, and left the locker room. As she came down the hallway, Daniels emerged from his office. He tucked his gloves into his helmet as he waited for her to catch up. Sam glanced at his gear, perplexed.

"Are you ready?" Daniels asked, swinging his helmet onto his shoulder like a purse.

Sam gave a nervous nod and they continued down the hallway. They exited the back of the building and crossed the training field. Michaels and Mark waited on the backside of the tower, the ladder truck already in position, out of view of the main buildings. Daniels and Michaels donned their helmets and gloves. Mark and Sam followed suit. Daniels then climbed up into the cab, started the truck, and began the elaborate setup.

Once the truck was idling smoothly, he climbed down from the cab and stood before the panel on the driver's side. The panel housed numerous levers that controlled the discharges for water and a separate set of controls for the "stick," the extension ladder mounted on top of the truck. The ladder lay down the center of the truck like an enormous metallic spine.

Daniels worked the controls with familiar ease. His hands moved lightly over the panel, his eyes shifting between the gauges and the body of the truck, checking its progress and position. With one smooth motion, two panels on each side of the truck opened up and thick metal jacks extended out to the side, settling onto the tarmac: two toward the front, two near the back. He activated another set of levers and the truck rose off its wheels where it settled, suspended about a foot off the ground by the massive jacks. When the jacks were set, he walked around the truck, sliding giant metal pins into the slots located on each of the jacks to prevent them from collapsing should the hydraulics fail. He then returned to the panel and began positioning the ladder for climbing.

As Daniels worked the lever, the tip of the ladder rose slowly from its bed. He did not extend the ladder; he merely elevated it to a comfortable climbing angle. He would extend it as Sam and Mark became more comfortable. Fully extended, they would be climbing over eight stories.

Michaels explained the workings of the truck as Mark stared nervously up at the ladder. When the ladder was in position, Daniels completed a final walk-around and then joined them.

"Who wants to go first?" Michaels asked, glancing from Sam to Mark.

"I'll go," Sam volunteered, throwing her helmet on her head, and working her hands into her gloves.

The truck crouched beside the tower like a glistening beast, the ladder like an enormous horn protruding from its back. Daniels and Mark stood off to the side, watching as Sam followed Michaels to the side of the truck. Michaels showed her where to position her feet and Sam followed the footholds mounted on its side that led up to the rounded platform housing the base of the ladder. Once she made it onto the platform, she glanced skyward. The ladder was composed of two thirty-five-foot ladders mounted together. The fly section was propelled via large hydraulic lifts on either side. When not extended, its tip reached about forty-five feet with the added height of the truck beneath it.

Sam checked her chin strap, yanked at her gloves, and began the climb using the hand-over-hand technique they had been taught. She climbed cautiously yet smoothly, her arms and legs working in unison, and when she finally reached the top of the ladder, she locked her leg through the rungs. She paused to rest, taking a few deep breaths, and looking out over the back side of the training field, taking in the fading fire of the sinking sun. She then unlocked her leg and carefully climbed back down.

When she reached the bottom, Michaels gave her a nod. "No problem," he said as he turned to Mark.

Mark approached the truck, tightening down his chin strap and glancing nervously up at the ladder. Michaels directed him to the footholds and Mark slowly made his way to the top of the truck. Once on the platform, he checked and rechecked his gloves and chin strap. He glanced up the ladder again, took a few deep breaths, put a foot on the bottom rung, and then froze. Daniels and Sam watched from the ground. The conversation between Michaels and Mark was swallowed by the noise from the truck's idle. Michaels leaned in, one hand on Mark's back, the other working in an upward motion as he gently coaxed him to mount.

Mark took the first few rungs, glanced up, and then scrambled nervously back down to the platform. Michaels continued talking to him and slowly Mark made upward progress. Michaels followed him onto the ladder, pausing each time Mark froze, tossing him words of encouragement with each step. When Mark was halfway up, he froze again, this time putting his arms through the rungs and locking his wrists. Michaels continued his monologue and finally got him moving again, staying right beneath him on the ladder. Sam held her breath as the men approached the top. Ever so slowly, they made it. When Mark reached the tip, he looked out over the training field, then down to where Daniels and Sam were standing and gave a quick wave. Michaels stayed with him, always just a few rungs beneath, as Mark slowly worked his way down. Sam breathed a sigh of relief as the men stepped onto the tarmac.

Daniels returned to the panel, this time extending the ladder to its full height. The ladder pierced the darkening sky, its tip miniscule from their spot on the ground. The lights had come on around the tower and they were bathed in their brightness. The metal on the truck was reflected in soft glints as the first stars appeared overhead.

When the ladder was fully extended, Michaels led Sam back to the truck. She climbed onto the platform, checked her gear, and started climbing. The higher she went, the cooler the air grew around her. She glanced to her right and could see the tops of the pines moving ever so slightly in the light wind. The sky was ocean blue with a razor slice of red on the western horizon. She kept climbing, the ladder gently rocking with each step, lulling her with its rhythm. She reached the top and rested for a few minutes, taking in the view. A pale arc of light hovered above the city and Sam watched as the last bit of daylight was swallowed by the darkness. She looked down to where the men stood, their helmets angled upward as they watched from below. They stood with their hands on their hips, like miniature soldiers.

After a few deep breaths, Sam started her descent, concentrating on hand and foot placement. The monotonous rhythm of her boots on the rungs seemed to stretch on as the truck slowly grew beneath her. She finally stepped safely onto the platform, then turned and made her way down the side of the truck.

Michaels followed Mark back onto the platform, and they worked through the same routine: Michaels gently coaxing as Mark slowly climbed. He paused once before reaching the top of the first section but continued after a few words of encouragement. As he made his way onto the second section of the ladder, where foot placement was confounded by the overlapping edges, he started to panic. The sway of the ladder under their combined weight only fueled his anxiety. The muscles in Sam's neck had formed a knot from staring upward against the weight of her helmet. She rubbed unconsciously at her shoulder; her eyes glued to the men.

One cautious rung at a time, Mark continued his ascent until he finally reached the tip of the ladder. After a moment's rest, they began their slow descent. Sam watched Michaels with admiration. She could see the effect his words were having on Mark. Mark occasionally nodded his head as Michaels kept up his encouragement. Finally, they both stepped safely onto the platform. Mark bent forward taking deep breaths, shaking his hands out to release the tension in his arms.

Daniels suddenly turned to Sam. "Why are you here?" he asked, a quizzical knot in his brow.

Sam stared at him. "Why am I where?"

"On the training field. You obviously didn't need the practice." His piercing eyes were softened by the hint of a smile playing across his face.

"It never hurts to practice," Sam shrugged, smiling, and swinging her eyes back to the ladder. Daniels looked at her in profile before following her gaze to the truck.

Michaels and Mark took a breather and then prepared to run through the exercise again. It was obvious Sam was comfortable, so Michaels concentrated his efforts on Mark. While Daniels checked the gauges on the panel, Sam strolled over to the side of the tower and plunked herself down on the tarmac, stripping off her helmet and gloves and leaning back against the side of the building. With the sun down, the temperature was dropping and the first whiff of fall hung in the air. The deep scent of pine skirted the tarmac and the truck idled in a steady hum. Sam put her head against the wall and closed her eyes, relaxing her arms and legs.

When Sam opened her eyes, Daniels was standing beside her. He had taken up a position against the wall just to her right. He had one leg bent with his foot against the wall, arms crossed over his chest. It was the exact stance he had taken in the search room, standing there in the darkness, surrounded by swirling smoke. Fine cords of muscle lay in strands along his forearms. He watched Mark's skyward progress and from her position on the ground, Sam could read the sharp angle of his jawline. The bright lights above the tower threw a soft halo around the perimeter of his helmet. His face was relaxed but his eyes retained their laser sharpness.

They watched the men make their way up the ladder. Mark was moving better, his arms less rigid, his climbing more graceful. Michaels continued to encourage him, only less frequently. When they finally reached the top, Mark positioned himself to try to lock in, but struggled to get his leg up and over the top of the ladder. Michaels directed him to try locking in sideways, but Mark would have none of it. He shook his head, refusing to budge. They rested for a moment and then Michaels motioned for him to descend.

Sam and Daniels watched from the sidelines; Sam hyperaware of Daniels' body next to her. He did not bother with conversation; he seemed content in the silence and Sam didn't push it. She remembered her ramblings from the night in the library and didn't want to repeat the blunder. They leaned against the cool of the building, watching the men descend.

When Mark finally made it onto the platform, he and Michaels stripped off their helmets and reviewed the climb. Daniels pushed from the wall and reached a hand down to Sam. Sam hesitated, her hand in midair, as she shot a glance over at Michaels and Mark. Daniels remained poised above her, his grey eyes burning into her, his arm outstretched. The men were still locked in conversation, so Sam reached up, took his hand, and he guided her to her feet.

~

When Sam passed on dinner, Ty had showered, changed into clean clothes, and headed out with Johnny and Tate. The others would meet them at the restaurant. They lugged their gym bags across the parking lot and were waiting for Johnny to pop his trunk when Ty happened to look out over the training field. Heading across the field to the tower was Sam. *She said she was going to the library.* Even more perplexing was the fact that she wasn't alone. Daniels walked closely beside her. Ty watched them disappear around the back of the tower.

"You coming, buddy?" Johnny called as he slid in behind the wheel.

"Yeah," Ty muttered before slamming the trunk. He glanced once more at the tower before climbing into the passenger's seat.

The next morning, Ty picked Sam up for class. She bounded out to the car, threw her gear in the back seat, and climbed in. Ty watched her, searching her face.

"How were the burgers?" Sam asked as she pulled her book from her backpack. "Did you drown in grease?" She laughed and placed her hand on his shoulder as Ty put the car in gear.

"Practically," Ty replied dully, his eyes on the road. Ty's mind churned. *What the hell was she doing at the tower and why, of all people, was Daniels with her?* Daniels was always surrounded by his cadre of instructors. It baffled Ty to see the commander alone with a student, especially when that student was Sam.

Sam flipped open her text and began grilling him in preparation for the afternoon's exam. Ty lost himself in his worries.

"Ty, you're not listening!" Sam griped. "Do you want me to repeat the question?"

"I think I'm good," he replied absently before falling silent again. Sam watched him for a moment before turning her attention back to the book. They arrived at campus and were pulling their gear from the car when Ty slammed his door, catching the ID tag that hung from his bag.

"Fuck!" he exclaimed, yanking on the bag. Sam strolled around to his side of the car. "Hey, what's going on with you this morning?" she asked as Ty threw open the door and yanked his bag free.

"Nothing," he grumbled under his breath before turning for the building. Sam followed in silence.

The day passed uneventfully, although two more students were ejected following the exam. Ty kept an eye on Sam throughout the day, noting her temper, her mood, seeing if he could catch any indication she was holding something back. But Sam seemed her normal self. She talked animatedly at lunch and seemed unconcerned with anything beyond the usual stressors of the course.

Ty also watched Daniels. The commander had slid soundlessly into the classroom that morning, making his usual rounds among their desks. He then braced at the back of the room, seeming lost in the lecture as Tanner extolled the virtues of fire suppression systems. Ty sat along the right side of the classroom; Sam sat to his left. By glancing over his shoulder, Ty could watch Daniels leaning against the back wall. The commander stood like a statue; arms locked across his chest. *God, the man is intense.* He never seemed to let up; always razor sharp and searching.

What Ty didn't realize was that he was witnessing Daniels' singular weakness, the one chink in his armor. Daniels was staring intently at Sam.

Ty shifted a startled glance to Sam and then back to Daniels. As he did, Daniels' eyes darted over, locking Ty in his penetrating gaze before slowly sliding his attention back to Tanner.

~

The day Mark had been dreading finally arrived. He and Sam had spent the lunch periods leading up to the test going over Michaels' instructions: approaching the jump calmly, taking a deep breath, and facing the fear. He just had to stay focused.

The cadets were lined up on deck. Daniels stood off to the side, surveying the activity as the adjuncts completed the final preparations for the exercise. Four instructors were on hand for the test. Sam was relieved Lee was not among them; one less thing for her to worry about.

The instructors readied the airbag as PT began. As the students ran laps around the field, the bag slowly inflated, blooming beneath the tower like a Macy's balloon. When the bag was fully inflated, it sat like a giant pillow. It was constructed of thick burlap, with vents on each side that allowed air to escape under pressure, reducing the impact on landing.

The instructors would take them up in groups of four. Those waiting their turn would be forced to stand at attention on deck and watch. The entire setup was designed to intimidate. It was having its desired effect. Some of the men could not bring themselves to look up at the window where, in a matter of minutes, they would be jumping. One student never even made it through PT. As they ran their first lap, he took one look at the airbag, reported to Tanner, and quit.

The first four were taken from the deck and escorted up to the third floor. They wore bunker pants, boots, and gloves. Their helmets would not be needed; they would only get in the way when they struck the bag. Each student would step up into the window, be given a count by one of the instructors, and then jump. No one would be pushed; that was not the purpose of the exercise. If a student refused to jump, he simply packed his shit and went home. It was that simple.

Mark would be in the second group. He braced nervously on deck, his eyes never leaving the window. Sam could see him talking to himself, focusing on the task at hand. It was frustrating standing in formation; Sam would have liked to throw him a few words of encouragement.

Sam braced next to Ty, who wore a stony expression. He had been quiet the last few days, but Sam chalked it up to the confidence test. Perhaps he was dreading it like the others, although he hadn't mentioned it. Sam gave him a light poke with her elbow. Ty glanced at her and Sam grinned. Ty met her eyes, but his expression remained frozen. He slid his eyes to where Daniels stood off to the side. Sam followed his gaze, then turned back to him, questioning. Ty shifted his eyes back to the window.

The first group went smoothly. Bo was the first to jump and what he lacked in the classroom he more than made up for on the training field. He approached the window, placed his arms across his chest, and stepped off without missing a beat. When his body hit, the air escaping from the side vents sounded like someone popping an enormous balloon. He rolled off to the side and swung his legs over the edge, dropping onto the tarmac. The next cadet braced in the window as the pump refilled the bag.

The first group finished, and it was time for the next four to ascend. Sam watched Mark as he marched past. Mark caught her eye and gave her an anxious smile. He was sweating heavily. His position in line meant he would be the last in his group to go. Sam knew the minutes would be agonizing but hoped he would use the time to go over Michaels' directions.

One by one, his group jumped, each of them landing with a loud "POP!" and then rolling off. Mark climbed slowly up onto the sill.

Sam watched Michaels talking to him as Mark positioned himself in the window. Michaels kept his hands braced behind his back, the intensity in his face matching that of Mark's. Mark cautiously stood up, his large frame filling the window. Sam could see him falter; at one point turning away from the window and shaking his head. But with a few words from Michaels, Mark stood up again, his hands clutching the frame on either side. He slowly released his hands and brought his arms together across his chest. With a final reaffirming glance at Michaels, Mark stepped off.

He seemed to fall in slow motion. As he left the ledge, his feet came together in front as he positioned his body in space so that he would land flat on his back, just as they had been coached. Sam watched him fall, his body striking the airbag with a resounding slap.

The students stood in silence, holding their breath, waiting for movement from the top of the bag. Finally, Mark let out an ear-splitting, *"Fuckin' A!"* as he rolled his giant frame off the bag.

Michaels looked down from the window and gave an assertive thumbs-up, which Mark returned once he got to the tarmac. As he jogged by, he grabbed Sam's shoulder and gave it a painful squeeze.

The next group to go included Tate and Peterson, although Tate was nowhere to be seen. He had been holed up in the locker room most of the morning, unable to control his nervous bowels. As his group assembled, he came trotting across the field.

"You finally over the nervous squirts, Tater?" Peterson yelled loudly as Tate approached.

"Put a lid on it, Peterson," Tanner grumbled.

Tate fell in line and his group headed upstairs. The first two in the group went without trouble and then it was Tate's turn. He climbed into the window on shaky legs, clutching the window frame as if the building would fall out from under him. Michaels stood beside the window, using the same words of encouragement he had used with Mark.

Tate finally let go of the frame, crossed his arms, and jumped. He emitted a high-pitched scream as he fell, causing a ripple of laughter among the cadets. He smacked the airbag and rolled off so quickly that he nearly landed face-first on the concrete.

The instructors heckled him good naturedly from the side lines. Sam glanced over at Daniels and could just make out a smile peeking from beneath his mustache. The last they saw of Tate he was running back across the field.

"I believe we got a Code Brown in progress!" Tanner exclaimed, grinning and pointing with his toothpick.

Finally, it was Sam's turn. Johnny headed for the stairwell and Sam followed, with Ty and Jeff bringing up the tail end of the alphabet. They arrived on the third floor and positioned themselves around the window. Johnny climbed right up, set his jaw, crossed his arms, and before Sam knew it, he was gone. She leaned out the window to see him calmly climbing off the bag.

Sam turned and faced Ty. She gripped his arms, forcing him to look her in the face. "Are you all right?" she whispered so the men around couldn't hear.

"Fine," he replied, his eyes on the window.

"Your turn, Smith," Michaels barked. Sam slowly turned from Ty.

Sam approached the window with confidence. Living fifteen stories up had made her used to excessive heights. The third floor of the tower seemed nothing in comparison. She followed Michaels' directions, positioning herself in the window and crossing her arms. She glanced down and could see Daniels watching her. His shoulders were straight, his stance rigid. Sam could just make out his eyes from that height, could feel their penetration even from that distance. Daniels gave a slight nod of his helmet and Sam stepped off.

The sensation was pure exhilaration, total freedom. Having nothing beneath her was like floating. Until she hit the bag. The impact jolted her back to earth, to the painful reality of gravity. Her teeth rattled in her head. Sam slowly rolled off the bag and dropped to the ground. She gave her head a shake as she stripped off her helmet.

"Good job, Sam!" Mark exclaimed, his face relaxed and beaming. Sam shot him a wink as she got back in line. Ty approached the window in much the same manner as Johnny. He simply stood up, got into position, and jumped. Sam didn't even have a chance to catch his eye. Before she knew it, he was falling.

Jeff was the final student to jump. He climbed into the window, slowly straightened his body, and then froze. Michaels coaxed him, trying the same tactics that had worked so successfully with Mark, but to no avail. The cadet refused to budge. Michaels finally ordered him down from the window and their class was reduced once again.

Once the cadets had leapt from the third floor, they now had to face the fourth-floor jump. But the second jump went much smoother than the first. Whoever was going to fail had already thrown in the towel. Those who had made the lower jump knew they could stand another ten feet. Even Mark seemed confident as he stepped into the sill.

One by one, they stood, braced, and jumped. By the time class broke, another major hurdle was behind them. Not only had they made it through their first confidence test, but they were also almost halfway through the course. From where they stood, they could almost envision the end point: graduation.

To mark the occasion, the group decided to meet at Johnny's for dinner, despite a turn in the weather. By the time Ty picked Sam up, a light rain was falling and the skies to the south were roiling black. Johnny and Mark wheeled the grill close to the back door and took turns darting in and out of the house, shuttling burgers and bratwursts. The rest stood in the kitchen, talking over the week's events. Their sense of relief was palpable. Not only had they passed the first test, but their confidence in completing the course was growing. The reality of becoming full-fledged firefighters was crystallizing.

Sam watched Ty throughout the evening. Something had shifted between them. A void had opened over the last few days and Sam could not put her finger on it. Ty had reverted to his old habit of avoiding eye contact, and not just with her. Sam noticed it even when he spoke to the others. He had withdrawn into himself, not overtly, but in subtle ways only she could note, having spent so much time with him.

At one point in the evening, as Lance was spinning one of his Michigan tales, Ty looked up and locked eyes with her. Sam held his gaze. Ty dropped his eyes, only to look up again before giving her a weak smile. Sam returned the smile, but it was clear they needed to talk.

By the time dinner broke up, the rain was coming down heavily under blackened skies. They were loath to break from the comfort of Johnny's house. The men were sprawled out, dirty dishes and empty beer bottles strewn throughout the room. Bill finally took the lead, gathering up bottles, kicking their feet to get them moving. They picked up the dinner debris, cleaned up the kitchen, and then slowly filed out of the house. The rain was coming down sideways as they darted for their cars. Ty and Sam were soaked by the time they climbed inside. Ty pulled away from the house, driving slowly through the wind and rain.

They arrived at Sam's condo and Ty pulled up close to the building. He turned off the engine and sat staring straight ahead. "Let's talk," Sam began, twisting in her seat to face him. She could see the hesitation in Ty's face. His eyes never left the windshield. Sam waited for him to break the silence.

"The night we went for burgers, you said you were going to the library. Did you?"

"No, I didn't," Sam replied. "I met up with Mark so we could work on the ladder. He was worried about the jump and didn't think he was going to be able to do it. Michaels worked with us on the ladder truck that night."

Ty's face relaxed a bit. The strain fell away from his eyes. He glanced from the windshield to Sam as he turned her words over in his mind.

"Why didn't you tell me about it beforehand?"

"Mark was embarrassed," Sam replied, shrugging. "I thought the fewer people who knew, the better. I'm sorry I didn't tell you. I didn't think it was a big deal, I didn't mean to hurt you." She paused before asking, "Is that what's been bothering you all week?"

"Yeah, I just couldn't figure out why you had kept it from me. Sorry for being such a limp rag." He put his head back and closed his eyes. "I'm ready for the class to be over. I'm sick of being stuck with assholes like Peterson and being screamed at by instructors all day. It'll be great when it's done."

Sam looked at him in profile. The rain on the windshield was painting his skin in shadowed rivulets. They trickled down his face and neck, disappearing against his collar. She could see his pulse in his throat and was reminded of the night he had been sick from drink.

Sam reached over, placing her hand alongside his face, stroking his eyebrow with her thumb. Ty turned and looked at her before closing his eyes again, taking in the feel of her hand. Sam reached over and drew Ty to her. She held him tightly before releasing him. She then threw her hood over her head, gave him a quick smile, and ran for her building.

When Sam arrived upstairs, she stood in the dark hallway, replaying their conversation. She didn't know why she had excluded Daniels' presence at the ladder training. She hadn't intended to deceive Ty; it was simply easier to leave Daniels out of it.

Sam thought about Daniels often. She found she watched for him, hoping to see his long stride crossing the field. Sam felt safer when he was around. He instilled in her a sense of security, a feeling of protection she associated only with her father. Although Sam admired him as an instructor, Daniels had taken on an added dimension in her mind. Sam felt connected to him. His presence was something she sought, even as it made her nervous and self-conscious.

Daniels and Ty contrasted sharply in Sam's mind. They occupied separate realms of her sub-conscience; she could not imagine discussing one with the other. Their age alone set them apart. Ty was three years her junior; Daniels had to be at least twenty years older. Sam drew from both men, yet they touched different aspects of her emotions.

But Sam could share none of this with Ty, despite the closeness they nurtured. Where Daniels was rigid and stifled, Ty was open, like an exposed wound. His sensitivity left her in awe. His vulnerability seemed innate despite his physical and emotional strength. It felt only natural to protect him.

When Sam disappeared inside, Ty continued to sit, watching the rain stream down the windows, listening to its steady drumming on the roof. Why hadn't she mentioned Daniels? Why had she excluded him from the training?

But Daniels' exclusion wasn't the main thing bothering Ty. When he thought back to that evening, seeing Sam and Daniels crossing the training field, it hadn't been the fact that they were alone that had bothered Ty as much as the way they had walked.

Whenever students moved on the training field, it was standard for instructors to lead, students to follow. It was a form of reverence on the field; a protocol all of them followed. But when Sam and Daniels crossed the field, they didn't move as two people separated by rank, a subordinate following a superior. They moved as one, side by side, their bodies close enough to touch. It was the intimacy of their movements that had caught in Ty's chest. Sam's explanation hadn't touched any of that.

Ty cranked the engine and drove off into the rain.

X

It began as a simple prank, the result of a long morning filled with Peterson's incessant complaining. Part of the problem was the training itself. They were working through another day of hose evolutions and the monotony had become excruciating. Tanner had berated Aaron repeatedly with no success. Aaron had performed over a hundred pushups, but still would not shut his mouth. Each time they went to load the hose, he launched into one of his tirades.

"Why the fuck do we have to go over this shit again and again?" he exclaimed as he thrust the folds of hose onto the hose bed.

"Peterson, shut the fuck up or you'll be giving me twenty more!" Tanner yelled. The threat had little effect.

They were gathering the remainder of the hose when Sam noticed a dead black snake in the ditch near the tower. It had been beautiful in life, its color a deep blackish purple. She jumped down into the ditch and picked it up by its tail, holding it up to examine it more closely. Aaron happened to spot her, and his blathering increased tenfold.

"You better put that fuckin' snake back where you found it, Sam!" he yelled from a safe distance.

"What's the matter, Aaron? Don't tell me a big guy like you is afraid of a harmless black snake."

The students clustered nearby, waiting to see how the altercation devolved.

"You bring it any closer and I'll kick your cute little ass from here to the tower!" he bellowed. "And you know I can do it!" He turned with bravado and hawked a giant loogie onto the tarmac.

It wasn't the remark about the ass-kicking that got to Sam, it was the fact that the threat was laced with Aaron's usual sexism.

"Asshole," Sam muttered as she wandered off, dangling the snake.

That should have been the end of it, but as Sam finished her lunch, Aaron's remark kept eating at her. She eyed the group, then rose from the grass.

The cadets had congregated on the south side of the tower. Since the weather had cooled, they would spend the last few minutes of lunch tossing a football. Sam retrieved the snake and carried it over to where their gear was neatly lined up along the tower. She removed Peterson's helmet from the line, coiled the snake into a tight circle, and then tucked the helmet back in place. She then slipped back to her spot on the grass.

Following lunch, the cadets lined up on deck as Tanner and Michaels handed out the afternoon assignments. The adjuncts lounged beside the tower, waiting for the class to break into groups. Once the assignments were given, Tanner released them, and the students gathered their gear. Sam stood back and waited.

Aaron approached his gear, laughing loudly following some lame attempt at humor that aroused only a half-hearted response from his friends. He reached down for his helmet and as he hoisted it from the ground, he recognized the shiny black coil of the snake.

With a high-pitched shriek, he launched his helmet into the air and stumbled backwards, his arms pin wheeling as he lost his footing. He landed on his ass with a loud "*grumph!*" as the class erupted around him. Gear flew as the students pelted Aaron with gloves and water bottles. Tanner barked orders to bring the class under control, but as he went to scream, he choked on his laughter and his toothpick went flying.

Aaron scrambled to his feet, fuming. He lunged toward the cadets, his big head swiveling as he searched out Sam among the crowd. Reading his intention, Tanner and the adjuncts sprang into action. The officers grabbed hold of Aaron just as he dove for Sam.

"*You fucking bitch!*" Aaron yelled as Sam unconsciously backed away. Ty slid in beside her as they watched Aaron struggle.

"*Let go of my fucking arms!*" Aaron screamed as he thrashed against the instructors.

The laughter had died, and the cadets watched anxiously. Tanner grabbed a fistful of Aaron's tee shirt. "*You move and you'll be doing pushups for the rest of the fuckin' afternoon!*" Tanner yelled into his face. Aaron had flushed a deep crimson. He glared past Tanner as he raged at Sam.

"*You wait, Sam! I'll kick your ass!*" he yelled, pointing a meaty finger. Tanner grabbed hold of Aaron's arm and twisted it behind his back.

"*You can shut the fuck up or you can pack your shit right now! Which is it going to be?*" Tanner yelled, wrenching the cadet's arm for emphasis.

Aaron yanked himself free and stormed off in the opposite direction. The students gathered their gear as the adjuncts rounded up their groups. Ty took hold of Sam's arm as they headed for the tower.

The instructors worked them hard. The students ended the day by running laps in their bunker gear, the ultimate penalty for bad conduct. As the exhausted group headed for their lockers, Mark sidled up next to Sam.

"Nice job," he nudged her, grinning.

"Bad idea," Sam mumbled, shaking her head. Sam knew she had crossed the line with Aaron, but she could not have realized the effect the joke would have. Had she known, she would have thought twice about screwing with Aaron. Sam couldn't have imagined what his anger would compel him to do or that Ty would pay the price for her recklessness.

~

Sam lay low following the incident. She did not know how Aaron would retaliate but felt sure it would come. She stuck close to the group; she didn't want to give him the opportunity to catch her alone. Aaron knew the penalty for fighting. Sam didn't think he would risk his position in class, especially considering they were almost halfway through. But still she was cautious.

Over the next few days, the class was subdued. Aaron kept to himself, avoiding even his usual cronies. Without his incessant yammering, a strange silence fell over the group. Sam would have enjoyed it, had it not been so menacing. She kept to herself and avoided eye contact.

Things slowly returned to normal. After two days of silence, Aaron's booming voice could be heard once again, berating his cohorts, dousing everyone within earshot with his opinion.

They spent the next day on the training field as they prepared for their first interior live burn, which would take place the following week. They drilled continuously, discussing tactics and various ways to approach the fire, working with forcible entry tools, and throwing ladders to advance hoselines into the tower. By the end of the day, they could barely move, their legs whipped from scaling the tower, hauling equipment, and loading hose. But with an exam scheduled the next day, the group decided to hit the books before heading home.

They dragged themselves across the field to their locker rooms. Sam could barely pull her bag from her locker, her arms spent from working with the heavy tools. Her shoulders were in knots. She collapsed onto the bench, stretching her arms behind her back to loosen her joints. She didn't hear the door open. She looked up with a start to see Aaron looming above her. Sam watched in panic as the door swung closed behind him.

~

"Tater, you gotta get some new underwear," Mark griped, shaking his head in disgust as he stripped out of his towel. He reached into his locker and withdrew a pair of black mid-length briefs. "How about trying some of these?" He held the briefs up for display before stepping in and pulling them up. "They show off your package *and* your quads." He cupped a hefty fist of genitals while flexing a thick, muscled leg.

Tate stood awkwardly in front of his locker, sporting a worn-out pair of dingy jockey shorts. He eyed Mark's chiseled physique before glancing down at his own less-than-substantial package. "Thanks, but I don't think I can pull that off," he replied morosely, shaking his head.

The men had just emerged from the showers and were in varying stages of undress. Shorts, tee shirts, and underwear, soaked through from the long day on the field, lay scattered in wet clumps about the floor as the cadets toweled off and donned clean clothes.

"Well, check out Ty, then," Mark countered, flicking his towel in Ty's direction. Ty grinned and plucked at the legs of his boxer shorts. "Boxers are never a bad option," Mark added as he slipped on a pair of sweats. "The ladies seem to like them and anything's better than lookin' like a fuckin' Boy Scout. You'll never drum up any business in those shitty shorts." He eyed Tate's tattered briefs with disdain.

"What about Lance," Tate retorted, nodding in Lance's direction. He too sported the loathsome jockeys.

"Lance doesn't know any better," Mark replied nonchalantly as he pulled on his boots. "What do you expect from a fuckin' Yankee?"

"Hey, I happen to like the support," Lance exclaimed, running a comb through his damp hair, and then jabbing it in Ty's direction. "I don't know how Ty stands floppin' around all day in boxers."

"I enjoy the freedom," Ty replied, grinning and stuffing his dirty clothes into his bag.

"Hell, when you're that pretty, you can get away with anything," Mark interjected, chuckling and eyeing Ty. "Ty could pull on a fuckin' trash bag and still get the chicks."

"Here," Mark continued, reaching into his locker, and tossing a pair of briefs to Tate. "Try a pair on and see how you like 'em." The briefs sailed past Lance in Tate's direction. Tate darted sideways, dodging the underwear as if they were a bullet.

"Please, Mark!" Tate exclaimed. "I prefer my own shorts to sharing with others. Besides," he continued dejectedly, kicking the shorts back across the tiled floor, "I'd look ridiculous in those things. You gotta have a bod like yours to pull those off." He hung his towel up neatly in his locker and stepped gingerly into a pair of uniform pants.

"Don't sell yourself short, Tater," Mark replied, running a towel vigorously over his head. "You're shaping up nicely." He flashed Tate a reassuring smile before popping him with his towel. Tate grinned as he slipped his arms into his tee shirt.

The men finished dressing and gathered their dirty clothes. Mark scanned the length of the lockers, noting the unusual quiet that had settled over the room and the absence of a certain loud-mouthed cadet.

~

"Did you think I'd just let it go?" Aaron muttered as he approached Sam in the locker room.

Sam had seen Aaron angry on many occasions; toward Ty, toward his friends, even toward the instructors, but the hatred in his face went beyond anything he had displayed in class.

Sam jumped to her feet, hoping the bench would afford her an extra second to break and run. But Aaron stood between Sam and the door. There was no other way out. She knew she would have to get past him. Perhaps if she yelled, someone might hear her, although the men's locker room was at least twenty feet down the hall. Sam doubted they would hear her over their usual din and besides, she would rather fight than resort to screaming.

Aaron darted to his left, not intending to come after her, just jerking to make her cringe. Sam flinched in response. He crouched into a wrestler's stance, knees flexed, thick arms raised, his fists opening and closing like an angry crab. As Aaron turned to lunge for her, the door behind him suddenly swung open, slamming into the wall with a resounding crack.

Mark's beefy frame filled the doorway. Aaron froze, torn between the easy grab at Sam and Mark's threatening proximity. But even someone as big as Aaron was no match for Mark's size and strength.

"You better get your ass out of this locker room or I'll rip your fuckin' head off," Mark said in an even voice.

Aaron slowly stood up. He glared at Sam, pointing a thick finger. "You are so fuckin' lucky." He slowly turned toward the door. Mark took a step inside to let Aaron pass. Aaron shot Sam one last menacing glance before Mark pushed the door closed behind him.

Sam collapsed onto the bench, her legs weak. She buried her head in her hands. Her temples throbbed. *What if Mark hadn't come? What if he hadn't been watching?* Sam didn't know what Aaron might have done. Perhaps nothing. Perhaps he only intended to scare her. But with a guy like Aaron, one never knew. It was impossible to predict whether he would risk his standing in class over a stupid joke.

"Everything OK, Sam?" Mark stood in the doorway, glancing anxiously around the locker room. Sam rose from the bench and approached him.

"I'm fine, but god, do I owe you for that." She reached up and embraced his large frame.

"Hey, you helped me out," he replied, giving her a jarring pat on the back. "The least I can do is keep that asshole away. You let me know if he so much as looks at you, all right."

"Thanks," Sam replied. "Now let me make sure the coast is clear." Mark moved away from the door and Sam stuck her head out, glancing in both directions down the hall. There was no one in sight, so with a quick jerk of her head, she opened the door enough for him to squeeze by, quickly shutting it behind him.

Sam returned to the bench and sat for a few more minutes before forcing herself into the shower. She didn't think Aaron would return, but knew she would be unable to watch the door, so she laid out fresh clothes just outside the stall, showered in record time, grabbed her things, and headed for the library.

~

Aaron sat hunched behind the wheel, trying to control his rage. If only that fuck-face hadn't shown up, he could have set that bitch straight. She would have *never* fucked with him again.

Aaron had no intention of hurting her. He wasn't going to get kicked out of the academy on account of some smart-ass bitch. But he wanted her scared. The way she had backed away from him, the fear in her eyes – God, he loved that! *There's nothing better than to stand over someone who's scared shitless.*

It was the same feeling he got at his uncle's place, when he would hide out in the tree stand near the feeder they kept stuffed with corn. He'd crouch in the darkness as the sun slowly crept through the trees and those first tentative deer made their way across the open field. Aaron would raise his rifle slowly, relishing the weight of it in his hands, knowing he was about to inflict a devastating injury. And as the deer began to eat, he always did the same thing: he would give a sharp whistle, just enough to startle the animal. The deer would freeze, head locked in the direction of the noise, and for a split second, Aaron could enjoy the look of panic on its face just before he blew it away.

It was the same thing with women. They always felt better to him when there was fear involved. Something about knowing *he* was the one making them cower, that was what really got him off. And he had seen that look in Sam's eyes. He had her cornered, he just needed a few more seconds and she would have tried to bolt.

Aaron imagined grabbing her as she tried to get away, throwing her against the lockers and forcing her to be still. Thinking about the fear in Sam's face made him aware of the tightness in his crotch. Aaron shifted in his seat and unzipped his pants, reaching into the glove box and pulling some napkins from a wad he kept for just such occasions. He leaned his head back, enjoying the hardness of his cock, remembering Sam's fear.

When Aaron was done, head back, eyes closed, enjoying the warmth that had settled in his belly, the idea hit him. If Mark was going to butt in and ruin his plans, Aaron would just have to take the long way around. He wouldn't hurt Sam directly; he'd hurt her by other means. He'd not only get revenge against her, he'd revenge that little cocksucker who hung him on the hook. Kill two birds with one stone, so to speak.

~

It was Friday morning and Ty was sick. He had woken in the night with a sore throat and now his head was splitting, his joints ached. He made it through PT but the run left him wasted. Fortunately, they were in the classroom, but the "halfway point" party was that night and Ty didn't want to miss out.

It was a class tradition for everyone to get together at the local pub to celebrate making it halfway through the course. Even the instructors attended. The cadets buzzed with anticipation throughout the week, which seemed to alleviate some of the tension following Sam's prank.

But now all Ty wanted to do was sleep. Class ended and he and Sam drove home.

"Are you going to make it tonight?" Sam glanced at him from the corner of her eye. "I'll be glad to stay home with you." Ty was sweating and flushed and seemed shriveled in the passenger seat.

"I think if I go home and crash for a bit, I'll be OK by the time we leave," he replied, sounding more confident than he felt. Ty didn't want to miss the get together nor disappoint Sam. He was also still leery about Aaron, not sure if he had completely gotten over being humiliated by Sam's joke. Ty didn't trust the guy and felt better about accompanying Sam to the party.

Sam dropped him off and Ty dragged his bag inside, stripped out of his uniform, and climbed into bed. He set his alarm for 7; Sam would come by at 7:30. Ty figured with some rest and a hot shower he would be much improved.

Ty slept hard, but when the alarm went off, its ringing cut through his brain in a painful arc. He forced himself up but couldn't seem to get his body in gear. He finally threw off the covers and made his way to the bathroom. As he waited for the shower to warm up, he unlocked the front door so that Sam could let herself in.

Her punctuality was a joke between them. Sam ran her daily schedule like a drill sergeant: never late, always exactly on time. Ty climbed under the steaming stream and tried to work through some of the soreness in his limbs by flexing his arms and legs. When he finished with the shower, he toweled off and headed back to the bedroom. He had pulled on a pair of jeans and was wrestling a shirt over his head when he heard the front door click open. He glanced at the clock. Right on time, as usual, he thought to himself, smiling.

"I knew you'd be on time . . ." he said as he walked into the living room. He looked up to see Aaron standing in the center of the room.

~

It rarely happened, but tonight Sam was late. After dropping Ty off, she had decided a hard swim was in order. It had been a rough week of training and Sam knew the smooth resistance of the water would be just the thing for her sore muscles.

But she had lost track of time amidst the monotony of the laps and was now scrambling to get to Ty's, berating herself for her tardiness.

She showered with academy quickness, threw on a pair of jeans and a blouse, and grabbed the rest of her things as she headed for the door. She drove the short distance to Ty's and whipped her car into the driveway, noticing the dark interior of the house. *Perhaps he's fallen asleep.* Sam jogged up to the front door, surprised to find it standing open a few inches.

She eased it open and peered inside. If Ty was sleeping, she would simply leave him a note and let him sleep. Rest would probably do him more good than going to the pub. She made her way through the dark living room, switching on a small lamp beside the couch. The bathroom light was on, but the house was otherwise dark, silent.

"Ty?" she called softly, not wanting to wake him, yet not wanting to startle him if he was getting dressed. No answer. Sam approached the bathroom and glanced inside. Ty was sitting on the floor, his back against the wall. He held his face in his hands, and the first thing Sam noticed was the blood covering the towel.

Sam dropped to the floor beside him. "What happened?" she cried. "Who did this?" Sam felt panic rise in her throat as Ty lifted his face from the towel. The right side of his face was swollen and already turning a deep purple. His lower lip was split and the blood from his nose was drying in dark smears down his face and chest.

"What happened?" Sam repeated. If Ty didn't say something, Sam felt she would scream.

"I got jumped when I went to the store for medicine," Ty mumbled through the mess of his face. He hadn't planned to lie; it just came out as he tried to focus. Though dizzy and nauseous, a deeper part of him knew that if he admitted it had been Aaron, Sam would have blamed herself, knowing this was part of Aaron's retaliation for the snake.

"How did you get home in this condition?" Sam exclaimed as she braced her hands against his shoulders, examining his wounds.

"I managed," Ty muttered, struggling to smile but finding it impossible with his cut lip. He tried to focus. Ty's vision was covered in a haze; he wasn't sure if it was from the dried blood or the impact of Aaron's fists. He fought to replay the events as they had unfolded.

Ty remembered walking into the living room to find Aaron standing there, like an odd piece of furniture, his oversized frame too large for the room. But before Ty could react, Aaron had struck him hard. After the first blow, they seemed to just keep coming. Ty was hit twice more in the face, the second blow splitting his lip, bloodying his nose. The force of the blow knocked his legs out from under him. He crumpled to the floor as long red globs dripped onto his shirt, painting his chest in bloody splatters.

Ty tucked into a defensive ball, one he had used successfully on countless occasions against his father. Aaron swung another massive fist, striking Ty with a crushing blow to the left side of his chest. The wind escaped him with an audible wheeze and Ty gasped for breath, his chest ablaze in pain with each ragged inhalation. Ty thought he would pass out. The room was spinning, and Aaron was standing over him, yelling in that familiar coarse voice from the academy. Aaron's rant conjured Sam's image, but Ty could not make sense of the words. The rest of Aaron's outburst was lost in a haze.

The room fell silent after Aaron stormed out, and Ty had somehow crawled into the bathroom. That was the last he remembered before Sam arrived.

Sam bolted from the floor, throwing open drawers, the medicine cabinet, searching for something more than the towel to use on Ty's face. There wasn't much: razors, deodorant, toothbrush and toothpaste. Nothing to treat his injuries. Sam grabbed another towel, wet it under the cold water, and dropped to her knees beside him.

She began wiping the blood using gentle strokes, flashing back to the evening in the tower when Daniels had done the same for her. Sam remembered the lightness of his hands, the concentration in his face as he held her jaw. Sam shoved the memory aside and concentrated on Ty.

"Let me take you to the ER." As Sam wiped the blood from his face, her mind ticked off potential injuries: concussion, facial fracture, eye trauma.

"No, I don't need the ER," Ty mumbled through swollen lips. "I just want to rest." He closed his eyes and put his head against the wall.

"I can't care for you here." Sam stared at the bloodied towel with exasperation. Ty remained silent. Sam continued to wipe his face.

Once Sam had removed most of the blood, she carefully peeled off Ty's shirt and tossed the bloodied ball into the tub. She hurried to his bedroom and flicked on the lamp, grabbed another tee shirt from the closet, and rushed back to the bathroom. She worked the shirt over Ty's head, careful to avoid the wounds on his face. Sam then took hold of his arms and guided him up.

Ty rose on weak legs. It seemed he would crumble if Sam let go. She walked him out to the living room and eased him down onto the couch. Sam leaned him back and handed him the towel. Ty's nose still bled, but it had slowed to a trickle. Sam returned to the bedroom, sidestepping the bloody trail that led to the bathroom, and grabbed Ty's gym bag. She stuffed some clothes inside and turned out the light. The bathroom illuminated the living room and Ty sat in the faint light, barely moving. Sam threw the bag over her shoulder and then eased him up, guiding him to the front door.

"I've got medicine at my house. I'm taking you there." Ty followed blindly.

Sam eased Ty into the car and threw his bag onto the back seat. She drove to her building, guiding him in through the lobby and up to her apartment. Sam led him into the kitchen and ran his hands under warm water, working them over with soap to remove the blood that caked his palms. Ty didn't speak. His face was a wreck and he merely stared straight ahead in a blank stare.

Once Ty's hands were clean, Sam guided him into her bedroom and sat him down on the edge of the bed. She rushed to the bathroom, reaching under the sink for the small bag of medical supplies. She wet a washcloth and carried it and the bag to the bed. She sat down on the bed, facing him.

She slowly turned him toward her and started working on the wounds on his face. His nose had stopped bleeding, but there was dried blood beneath it. Sam cleaned the blood from that area first, gently rubbing to lift it from his face. The blood from his lip had congealed into a mass; she dabbed at it until it broke up, then wiped the remainder off with the cloth.

After applying a disinfectant to his cut, Sam broke open a cold pack, wrapped it in a thin bandage, and placed it against the side of Ty's face. Whoever had attacked him had been a lefty, she noted, since the wounds were confined to the right side of Ty's face. Ty began to cough, grimacing and clutching at his left side. Sam put the cold pack down and gently lifted his shirt over his head. Ty flinched as he raised his arms. A large red welt extended from his sixth to his tenth rib, the wound apparently caused by a large fist.

Sam pushed the rest of the materials off the bed and yanked the covers down. She then guided Ty's shoulders onto the bed. She pulled off his shoes and socks and then lifted his legs onto the bed. Sam wanted to remove his jeans but was not sure how to do it without embarrassing them both.

"Take these off, Ty," she whispered, placing a light hand on his hip. Ty tried reaching with his left hand, but the pain in his side stalled his movement. Sam tentatively unbuttoned his jeans, slid his zipper down, and slipped them off before pulling the covers up over his legs. She took a moment to examine his ribs, gently palpating the area, checking for signs of fractures. The ribcage was stable but painful; Ty cringed each time her fingers neared the wound. She put her hand on his forehead and noted its heat. It was then she remembered Ty had been sick all day. *And now this.*

Sam returned to the bathroom and cracked opened a bottle of ibuprofen. She went into the kitchen and filled a glass of water, picking up the pills on her way back to the bed. She eased him up so that he could swallow the tablets and then laid him back down. She walked around to the other side of the bed and gently sat down, trying not to jar him.

Sam touched Ty's shoulder to soothe him. She wanted him to sleep. She wanted to keep him still, so that his body could mend. She thought about the academy, how they would be performing their first live burn the following week and wondered how Ty would ever be well enough to participate.

He soon fell asleep, breathing heavily through his mouth. Sam spent the night in the living room, a dim light burning as she read. She checked on Ty constantly. As he slept, the right side of his face morphed into a bruised, swollen mass. She replaced the cold pack near his eye as each one warmed.

Sam had texted Johnny to let him know they wouldn't make it to dinner. She simply told him Ty was sick and that she was going to hang out with him instead. Johnny said he would let the others know, and to call if she needed anything.

~

Daniels hated this. The class get-togethers were something he had to force himself to attend. He enjoyed spending time with his instructors. In fact, he got together with them regularly over dinner and drinks. But being among the students always made him uncomfortable.

His discomfort was two-fold. On the one hand, he believed in a rigid social division between students and instructors. It was the only means of maintaining a level of deference among the cadets. The training field demanded such deference. If students did not follow orders, the chance that something would go wrong, or someone would get hurt rose exponentially. Daniels felt if the instructors socialized with the students, the officers would lose their edge when commanding the cadets.

The other source of Daniels' discomfort stemmed from his own interaction with the students. It was never easy, and he knew much of it was his fault. He ran a rigid academy and was known for his strict adherence to rules. His role as commanding officer caused the students to shrink from him; they avoided his gaze, stiffened when he approached. It didn't bother him at the academy, where such reactions were expected, but in social situations, it relegated him to outcast.

To make matters worse, Daniels was uncomfortable with the idea of seeing Samantha in public. The thought of her at ease, talking and drinking among the other students caused a tightening in his chest. Daniels was not one to get nervous, but the idea of seeing her and talking to her beyond the safety of the academy was the closest he had come in some time.

He sat with his officers, trying to join in the conversations, trying his best not to watch the door. He had done a quick headcount upon arrival, noting that most of the students had already arrived, but still no sign of Samantha. He also noted Williams' absence, which renewed the tightness in his chest.

Daniels had seen them together; in fact, it was rare to see them apart. He had wondered whether there was more to their relationship but had not allowed himself to dwell on it. It was none of his business and as commanding officer, he had more vital concerns than the personal relationships of his students. Yet he found himself watching them.

Daniels noticed the way Samantha and Ty interacted, the calm surety of their friendship. They even resembled each other in many ways. They were close in height; in fact, Samantha's height put her equal to many in the class. Samantha's short hair, Ty's striking features, and the similarity in their coloring gave them the appearance of siblings, as if sprung from the same seed.

But it was the way their bodies moved together that struck Daniels most of all. They moved with familiarity, but a familiarity born not of sexual intimacy. They communicated on a deeper level, their actions, and reactions perfectly in sync. It was unusual. Daniels had never seen anything like it among his cadets. Sure, he had seen the men react to the female students, usually with leers and sideways glances. But there was a simplicity to the way Samantha and Ty interacted, a natural connectedness that Daniels admired, even envied.

The only incident that threw him was when Ty had caught him staring at Samantha in class. Daniels was trying to focus on the lecture, trying to keep his eyes on the front of the room. But despite his efforts, they naturally sailed to where she was sitting.

Daniels couldn't see her face from where he stood at the rear of the room, but he could read her perfect posture, the cut of her shoulders, and the way she bent her head down and to the left while writing. When he locked eyes with Ty, Daniels had not only felt caught, but he'd also felt as if Ty were challenging him. Ty's stare was not merely a declaration of protection, there was an element of possession to it, as well.

Daniels glanced at his watch again. Samantha wasn't coming. He tried not to dwell on the issue; he assumed she had a good reason for skipping the dinner. He said his goodnights and headed for home.

~

Ty's dreams were dark and painful. When they came, he tried to pull himself from sleep, but the pain in his face and chest anchored him to a realm just beyond waking. He couldn't shake himself free. Aaron would be standing over him, fists clenched even though they had already done their damage. It was like waiting for the crash of a tremendous wave; suffocating and unstoppable.

But it was Aaron's words that truly cut. Ty scratched through the fog in his brain, trying to feel his way over the surface of those words, to read the letters with his fingertips, yet they continued to elude him. What remained was the sense of pain upon hearing them. Not like the pain in his face or the searing burn each time he breathed; it was a pain that tore deeper, one that struck at Ty's essence.

Ty could feel Sam's presence off and on throughout the night. He could feel her moving beside him, touching his face, replacing the cool bandage at his eye. He tried to open his eyes but could not find the strength. He wanted to talk to her, to hear her voice. He wished she would say something, to reassure him it was really her, not just some wish for her beside him.

The dreams returned whenever she left, her presence drove them off. Ty wished she would stay; just lie down beside him and keep the demons at bay, keep Aaron's voice from entering his brain. There was something evil in the dreams, something Ty's mind was fighting. His subconscious hammered away at them, driving them down into the depths. When he slept, they returned.

When Sam entered the bedroom the next morning, Ty's eyes were open, but he retained the dazed look of a prizefighter. It took him a moment to focus when she sat down beside him. Sam placed her palm against his forehead, relieved by its coolness. She retrieved more ibuprofen, which Ty gratefully accepted. The welt on his chest had turned to a dark stain overnight. The area around his eye was blackened, but the cold packs had reduced the swelling. His lip was painfully torn, still congealed with old blood. Sam wet another cloth and held it against the wound, loosening up the clot. Ty stared at her while she worked.

He sat up slowly, the pain tearing at his side. Sam braced his arms, trying to provide support. "A stupid question, but how do you feel?"

"Like I was hit by a truck," Ty replied, trying to match her weak smile.

"Would you like me to run a shower for you?"

"Yeah, that might work." He slowly threw off the covers and forced his legs over the side of the bed. He grimaced as he moved, each motion causing small cascades of pain through his face and chest.

Sam went into the bathroom and turned on the hot water. She laid out a fresh towel and carried his gym bag in so he could change into fresh clothes. She returned to the bed and helped him up by guiding his arms. Ty stood up, trying to straighten his back through the pain in his side. He looked terrible. His wounds stood in stark contrast to the beauty of his face. The hair around his forehead stood on end, encrusted with dried blood from the night before.

Sam helped him into the bathroom and laid out his things. "Call if you need anything," she said as she pulled the door closed behind her. While Ty showered, Sam stripped the bed and put down fresh sheets. She then went into the kitchen and put on a pot of coffee. The morning was cool and the glass door to the balcony was open, letting in bright morning sun.

Ty emerged in clean clothes, his wet hair sticking up in all directions. He moved slowly to the couch and Sam poured him some coffee. "Should we call the police and file a report?" Sam asked as she sat down, handing him a cup. Ty froze for a second, his cup half-way to his lips. He then took a sip, wincing as the hot cup contacted his cut.

"I don't think it'll make a difference," he replied casually through stiff lips. "I didn't get a good look at the guy. I doubt I could give an adequate description. It was probably just some punk looking for cash." He glanced at the balcony. "Can we move outside?"

"How about if I meet you out there? I'm going to jump in the shower," Sam replied, placing her cup on the coffee table, and rising from the couch. Sam noted Ty's discomfort when she mentioned the beating. She didn't push it. Instead, she walked him slowly out to the balcony.

Her eyes burned with fatigue as Sam stood under the hot stream. She would try to catch some sleep later while Ty rested. Sam flashed back to the way he had looked last night, his wounded body tucked between her sheets. Her thoughts suddenly shifted to Ty standing beneath the shower, the water running over his battered skin. She gazed at the puddle at her feet, imagining him standing in the exact spot, naked and bruised. She remembered the feel of his torn lip beneath her fingertip. Sam pushed the thoughts from her mind and reached for the shampoo. Her feelings for Ty were as confusing as her thoughts of Daniels.

The warmth she felt for Ty ran deep, but not in a sexual or intimate way. In fact, her thoughts of men, in general, tended toward the platonic, the safe. Sam had always attributed it to her military upbringing and the fact that she had been raised by her father. She had missed out on the typical stages a girl passes through as she reaches sexual maturity. Sam had never experienced the "boy-crazy" phase of most young girls. She regarded men reservedly, as things to be studied from afar. She had been exposed to a male-dominated world at an early age and was perfectly comfortable navigating within its waters. That's what made the fire service such a perfect fit. Within its confines, she could move among men, yet remain detached, separated by her sex.

Sam had always preferred the company of males. Even when she was young, her best friends were usually boys. Girls seemed frivolous to her. They fretted over silly things, were concerned with issues that, to her, seemed meaningless. Sam gravitated toward the masculine, although she preferred to remain separate and detached. At one point her level of detachment towards men made her question her sexuality. But as she got older, she settled into a comfortable relationship with the opposite sex. She craved the company of men, loved being a part of their world, but would always treat relationships with the off-handed carelessness of someone welded to her independence. Sam nurtured her detachment.

Ty slept much of the day. Sam pulled pillows and a blanket from the closet and got him settled on the couch. That evening, they sat on the balcony watching the last bit of light fade from the sky.

"I should probably go home," Ty muttered with little conviction as he sipped his hot cocoa, swiping the whipped cream from his lip with a flick of his tongue.

"Why don't you stay another night in case you need something? Besides, we have your nest all made up," Sam replied, grinning. Ty's bedding on the couch had grown steadily throughout the course of the day. He had pulled together more pillows and another blanket, creating an elaborate construction perfectly conformed to his body. He had spent the day nestled within, sleeping off and on, relishing its cozy comfort.

Ty spent the weekend at Sam's. She drove him home Sunday night so that he could do laundry and prepare for class. She helped him clean up the mess in the bathroom and was reminded of the brutality of the assault when she collected his bloodied shirt.

Ty walked her to the door, and they stood outside under the faint light of the porch. The light struck his face sideways, so his wounds were hidden in shadow. Ty hugged her fiercely and Sam felt her eyes well. She pulled away from him quickly, smiling over her shoulder as she waved goodbye. She then returned to the emptiness of her apartment.

~

As Michaels ran alongside the cadets, he thought about how to approach the situation. When the students had assembled for the run, he'd noted Williams' battered face, the obvious result of a fight. The kid looked like hell but seemed to be keeping up with the group well enough. Still, something like this could not go unaddressed.

As they wrapped up their run and were cooling down, Michaels eyed Tanner, motioning him over with a quick nod. Tanner jogged to his side. "Tell Daniels we're heading to lineup," Michaels grumbled as he stripped his whistle from around his neck.

Lineups only occurred when there were issues with the class or when the cadets were due for an inspection. Since no inspection was scheduled for the day, Tanner assumed it was to address the issue of Ty's face. He headed for Daniels' office.

"You can go on in," Miss Davis announced when Tanner arrived.

Tanner found Daniels at his desk, rifling through paperwork, his head cocked to the side cradling the phone as he listened intently. Daniels motioned for Tanner to take a seat.

He hung up the phone and turned his attention to Tanner. "What's up, Bill?"

"Scott's lining up the cadets." Daniels threw him a knowing glance. "Lineup" was code for trouble when it did not involve an inspection.

"Let's go," Daniels replied, rising from his desk, and grabbing his coffee cup on the way out.

Daniels and Tanner marched into the gymnasium as the students shuffled into formation. Michaels approached Daniels and the officers exchanged knowing glances. Tanner was always amazed by their silent communication. As hard as he tried, Tanner could never master the skill. It seemed he would always be relegated to the periphery of their conversations.

Daniels slowly approached the line of cadets. He worked his way down the line until he came to Ty. He stopped briefly, ran his cold grey eyes over Ty's face, and then proceeded on. He reached the end of the line, did an about-face, and slowly made his way back, his eyes scanning in a downward direction as he completed the inspection. When he was finished, he walked briskly over to Michaels and with a jerk of his head, indicated Ty was to be pulled from lineup and brought to his office.

"Williams, come with me," Michaels announced.

Ty froze for a split second before falling out of line and following Michaels into the hallway. Tanner took over.

"You waitin' for breakfast or what?" he barked as the cadets broke from formation and began their pushups.

Ty followed Michaels down the hall towards Daniels' office. He wasn't sure what was happening, but assumed it had something to do with his appearance. He knew fighting was against the rules and anyone caught would be dismissed immediately, but surely, they wouldn't hold him responsible for being the one getting hit. Besides, they did not know it was Aaron who had done the hitting and Ty was not about to step in another pile of shit by ratting him out, as much as he craved Aaron's dismissal.

The hallway seemed to stretch for miles. Ty was still sweating freely from the run yet was too nervous to wipe his brow. When they arrived at Daniels' office, Miss Davis took one look at Ty's face and quickly motioned them inside.

Michaels held the door open as Ty took a few tentative steps inside. Daniels stood up behind his desk and motioned for him to take a seat. Ty eased himself down, working hard to fight the grimace that bubbled beneath the surface of his bruised face. Michaels stood at attention next to Daniels' desk, his eyes trained on Ty. Daniels took his seat.

"Is there something you'd like to share with us, Williams?" Daniels asked in a measured tone.

"No, sir," Ty replied, fighting to maintain eye contact with the commander. He laced his fingers to keep from fidgeting.

"I assume your injuries are the result of a fight."

"No, sir, I was jumped Friday night. A guy outside a grocery store. There was little fighting involved," Ty replied, trying for a smile, hoping to break the tension in the room.

Daniels continued in a softer tone. "Are you all right? Did you get checked out?"

"I'm fine, commander. Just a few bruises."

Daniels looked to Michaels to see if he had anything to add. When Michaels remained silent, Daniels ended the meeting. "You can return to PT," Daniels said with a nod. Michaels marched over and opened the door as Ty rose from the chair. Daniels could see the pain in his face as he moved.

"I'll see you back at the gym," Michaels muttered to Ty as he left the commander's office. Grateful to be released without a reprimand, Ty made a hasty exit. Michaels took a seat on the edge of the chair in front of Daniels' desk.

"He was able to keep up during the run. I'll keep an eye on him today, make sure he doesn't have any problems." Michaels noticed Daniels' face had grown cold.

"That asshole Peterson's left hand is cut; it's broken open at the knuckles," Daniels growled. He had noted the right-sided injuries on Ty's face and quickly deduced they were the result of a left-handed assailant. When he took a second pass down the line of cadets, he had scanned their hands, looking for injuries. Peterson's left hand was swollen and cut. *That stupid fucker.*

"If Peterson so much as blinks, I want his ass ripped from class," Daniels added. Daniels had been keeping tabs on Aaron. He knew all about his bullying, his aggression toward Ty following the hook incident, and his reaction to Sam's prank with the snake. He felt confident this was Peterson's way of not only getting back at Ty, but striking Sam as well, and Daniels would not tolerate it.

"You got it," Michaels responded with a quick salute. Michaels shared Daniels' low opinion of Peterson and would like nothing more than to toss him out on his ass. The guy was a misfit and a mean one at that. He would keep an eye on him and if he so much as looked in Ty's direction, he would kick his ass to the curb. Michaels stood up, gave Daniels a nod, and marched from the office.

XI

It started as small grey wisps, gentle puffs that found their way around the cracks and seams of the boarded windows. It was the color of dirty cotton and swirled against the brick of the building as it gained density and bulk. In a matter of minutes, it had morphed into a black acrid cloud that seethed from around the windows as the heat inside intensified.

The cadets stood nervously at attention, lined up along the deck. They had been standing for almost an hour, watching the instructors work. The officers moved methodically, the tasks familiar, routine. Three worked the interior, stacking bundles of hay and wooden pallets into every corner of the burn building, stuffing it like you would a holiday turkey. They would accompany the students into the fire once it was lit. Two more on the outside set up the engine that would supply the water for their attacks. Another would work the periphery as the safety officer, monitoring the progress of the burn, surveying for hazards. A separate team in full gear was standing by. They would serve as the RIT: the Rapid Intervention Team, whose sole purpose was saving the cadets' asses, should something go wrong.

Overseeing the entire effort was Daniels, standing off to the side, slowly sipping his coffee. He wore bunker pants and boots. His helmet shaded his eyes, and his gloves were shoved into the low pocket on his right thigh. His arms were crossed, as usual, and he raised and lowered his mug with slow, steady precision while he scanned the scenario, looking ahead, seeing in his mind's eye how the evolutions would unfold, who would go where and in what sequence. The students would enter in teams of three: one to work the nozzle, one to back up the nozzle man, and one to feed the hose to the two up front. The cadets would rotate throughout the day, so each would have a chance to work the various positions.

While some teams attacked the fire, others would be performing search and rescue, locating victims hidden throughout the structure. They would work in concert, synchronizing their efforts. The fires were controlled from a small operations room in the rear of the building. The instructors would communicate via radio, monitoring the progress of the interior teams, coordinating the attacks. The man in the control room would stand at the panel, his hand on the "dead man's switch," adjusting the flow of gas throughout the structure so that conditions remained extreme. "E-Stop" switches strategically mounted on the walls could be mashed in the event of an emergency, cutting off the flow of gas. The hay and pallets would provide the dense smoke lacking in natural gas fires. They would also intensify heat conditions, and it was going to be hot.

The cadets stood on deck, nerves rattling, eyes never leaving the burn building, watching the instructors as they worked. It was like watching henchmen construct the gallows from which they would swing. Every action was intended to make things as realistic as possible. The fires would be allowed to build. Only then would they be permitted to enter.

They broke the students into groups and handed out assignments. Everything started moving quickly. Timing was crucial. The instructors wanted to maximize their exposure to the heat and flames. They wanted them moving. The training ground erupted in shouts and screams as each instructor took hold of his team, hustling them into position as the students frantically donned their masks, helmets, and gloves.

They would attack the building in sequence. The first entry team dropped into position at the door, the backup team right on their heels. The search team crouched nearby, poised to make entry alongside the attack teams. The instructors stood over them, screaming to be heard through their masks, their voices muffled, as if yelling through pillows. They used their hands to get the students' attention when their voices failed, landing a hearty *whack!* on the cadets' helmets to emphasize their commands.

Johnny, Ty, and Sam made their first entry on the backup line. They watched as Mark, Bill, and Shane crawled forward. The fire was consuming the far corner of the room, the heat and smoke just starting to bank down. As they moved forward, the fire rolled overhead until they were crouched under a canopy of flames as the heat drove them to the floor like a crushing fist. They awaited the signal from the instructor crouched next to them; they were to attack only on his command. The officers wanted to be sure the cadets experienced the full intensity of the fire before opening their lines. Just when the students thought they would have to lie flat to escape the heat, the instructor gave the signal: a forward chop with his arm through the air.

"HIT IT!"

The cadets opened their hoses in unison, the first team attacking the left side of the room, the backup hose dousing the right. They hit it in small bursts, "penciling" the flames so the water had a chance to cool the fire without bathing them in steam. The search team was making its way through the room, frantically shoving furniture aside as they tried to locate the victims.

The teams continued their attack and the fire kept coming. They would knock it down and it would spring back to life, dancing above their heads, driving them to the floor. Sam could picture the instructor at the panel: a radio clutched in one hand, his fingers massaging the switch, a wicked grin creasing his face as he cranked up the gas.

The fire was a beauty to behold, being in the room as it licked over their heads, mesmerizing. Sam stole a quick glance at the crews and could just make out the outline of their upturned helmets as they stared in awe at its power and magnificence. The evolution seemed to end quickly. Too quickly. Their adrenaline was surging, and Sam could not help wondering how many of the men were sporting hard-ons.

As the smoke cleared, they backed out of the building, dragging their hoselines and assisting the search crews with the victims, who would be dragged right back in for the next round. They stumbled out onto the tarmac, ripping off their masks, slapping each other on the back in acknowledgment of their concerted efforts. They were ushered over to the shade where a team of medics stripped them down, monitoring their blood pressure and pulse as the cadets filled their lungs. They were given water and ordered to drink. They then made their way back to the tarmac and prepared for another entry.

The morning progressed in a steady succession of evolutions. By lunchtime, they were exhausted, famished. The fires were allowed to die down as the cadets broke for lunch, collapsing on the field, attacking their food.

The afternoon was capped with an academy tradition. The fires were relit for the final time and allowed to build. The entire class was then hustled inside the burn building on hands and knees where they huddled on the floor, tucked against the wall. And there they sat – no hoselines, no search. They were there for one reason: to appreciate the punishing heat of an interior fire.

Ty was to Sam's left, his body tucked neatly against her. There was no sound, aside from the fire eating away at the interior of the building, the flames frustrated by the burn-resistant coating. As the fire intensified, Sam scanned down the line of helmets to her right. Near the doorway, she could make out the figure of Daniels reclined against the wall, one leg out straight, the other bent, an arm thrown over his knee as if he was kicked back on the beach watching the surf. His face was hidden behind his mask, but the angle of his helmet informed Sam he was looking directly at her.

As the flames grew, the heat drove the cadets down. It had a physical dimension to it, as if the ceiling were being lowered on top of them, crushing them beneath its weight. Michaels stayed in communication with the controller, and when the temperature at the ceiling approached six hundred, they were ordered out of the building and were done for the day.

Sam was standing beside the tower, assembling her gear, when Daniels approached.

"How did it go today, Samantha?" He held his gloves in his right hand and was pulling them through his left, enjoying the feel of the coarse material against his palm.

"Very well. An amazing experience." Sam smiled self-consciously at the impotency of her words.

"Everyone did well. A smooth day."

Sam noticed how relaxed Daniels' face appeared, even as he scanned the tarmac. He then swung his eyes and looked directly at her, noting the faint line above her mouth from the rope, a reminder of their night at the tower. Sam dropped her eyes, wondering if the others were looking on. She wanted to look at him and, at the same time, disappear into the concrete, to melt away quickly like a drop of rain on a hot day.

"Good work, Samantha." Daniels turned slowly and walked away. Sam continued to stare at the ground before glancing up to watch him leave. She then returned to her gear, stowing her gloves in her coat, securing her pockets. She looked up to see Ty standing near the wall, staring in her direction, not saying a word.

~

It had been a remarkable day and Ty was ecstatic. They had made it through their first burn, the class was more than halfway through, and his injuries were healing quickly. The cut on his lip would leave a scar, a perpetual reminder of that asshole, Peterson, but the pain in his chest was minimal and the bruising around his eye had faded to a sickly yellow.

Ty was busy working on the air bottles, shuttling the empties to the back of the tower where they would be filled, carrying the filled bottles into the first floor. He was coming back around the building when he stopped, noticing Sam standing in front of Daniels. He couldn't hear their conversation, not that they were speaking much. They simply stood there, mostly just looking at each other, few words being exchanged.

Ty froze. Something flashed in his mind, some echo in his brain that played against the back of his skull, jarring him. Suddenly, he was back at his apartment, Aaron standing over him, the pain in his chest severe, his mind unable to focus. He was trying to shake his head clear when Aaron bent down and spoke. The words came flooding back, those same words that had danced through his nightmares following the assault. They rushed in with total clarity as Ty stood there, staring at the outline of Daniels and Sam.

"By the way, asshole, your little girlfriend is fucking Daniels!" Aaron had yelled through gritted teeth. *"I saw them come out of the tower the day Lee tried to break her, that just-fucked look on their faces. I guess he got to her first!"* Aaron had then spit on the floor and stormed out.

Aaron had been saving that little tidbit for just the right occasion. He had watched Daniels and Sam leave the tower the evening she had cut herself with the rope and he knew just when to dole it out to crush Ty. *That will fix their little "friendship."*

Ty stood there, unable to move, even as Sam returned to her gear and swung her gaze in his direction. Suddenly, Ty didn't know her. It was like seeing a stranger; a stranger who resembled someone he once knew. Sam looked over at him, smiled, but could see that something was happening; that Ty was being whisked away by a thought process that seemed as if it would drown him. He stared at her, a burning pain searing the outline of his features.

Sam stood up slowly and Ty couldn't tell if the look in her eyes was one of concern or guilt. Either way, he fled. He dropped the bottles – they clattered to the pavement with hollow thuds and he quickly grabbed his gear and headed across the field.

Sam watched him go, unable to call to him. Something had caught in her throat. She couldn't tell if it was guilt at having been seen standing so close to Daniels or the fact that a deeper part of her feared that whatever had just transpired between her and Ty meant the end of their friendship, dissolution of their bond. She knelt on the tarmac and fumbled blindly with her gear.

~

Ty sat silently as the darkness settled around him. He didn't bother with the lights. He didn't need to see. The thoughts consuming him played before his eyes in vivid detail. Sam showing up late that night at the library, distracted and silent. Daniels and Sam walking across the training field, their bodies almost touching. Her omission of Daniels' presence at the training session with Mark. And the way Daniels had been staring straight into her during class. Ty felt foolish for not seeing things for what they were. Sam had kept it all hidden from him, a whole side of herself locked away.

Ty had tried working through his feelings for Sam. They shared something he had never experienced, a closeness beyond friendship, yet without the complications of intimacy. Not that Ty had much experience. In fact, aside from a few sexual encounters, he had never shared true intimacy with a woman. His responsibilities on the farm had kept his social life to a minimum. There had been a few brief romances in high school, but nothing real, nothing lasting. He didn't think about it much. Ty spent most of his time avoiding the wrath of his father, focusing on his responsibilities, flying under his father's radar.

Since the start of class, Ty had come to trust Sam completely. He felt different around her, unencumbered by the need to act a certain way, behave in accordance with the other men at the academy. They had spent so much time together that their closeness had become the backdrop to their friendship. Neither tried to explain or define it, they simply nurtured and enjoyed it.

But now Ty realized that a part of Sam had been parceled off, that Daniels had taken something that even he had never come close to. How else to explain her behavior?

The day Lee had humiliated her with the rope was the same night she showed up late in the library, distracted and silent; the same night Ty had noticed the cut above her mouth and had tried to get her to talk about it. That had been the night she had gone to the tower with Daniels. Perhaps she had still been fuming from the run-in with Lee. Perhaps Daniels had merely followed her out to discuss the issue. Perhaps it hadn't been planned, it had just happened when they found themselves alone. Perhaps, perhaps, perhaps. Ty could run through a million scenarios and still not come up with an adequate explanation for why Sam had betrayed him with secrecy.

~

As the students made their way across the training field, Johnny jogged up beside Sam, grinning and bumping shoulders to get her to smile.

"Can you give me a ride home?" Sam asked distractedly as she hurried across the field.

"No problem," Johnny replied, staring at her.

They met up outside the locker rooms after showering and drove home in silence. Johnny made small talk but as hard as she tried, Sam couldn't hold a conversation. She sat silently, going over Ty's reaction in her mind, wondering what could be happening between them. As an afterthought, she added, "Just drop me at Ty's." Johnny nodded and kept driving.

Sam stood on Ty's porch, her gear bag slung over her shoulder, and waited for Johnny to pull away. She gave him a quick wave and watched him disappear in the darkness. There were no lights on in the house, but Ty's car was in the driveway. Sam knocked and waited. She heard nothing from inside, so she knocked again, louder in case Ty was in the back. Still, nothing. She reached for the knob, turning it slowly.

Sam stood in the doorway, waiting for her vision to adjust, which didn't take long in the darkness of the living room. She could just make out the outline of Ty's body on the couch. He sat with his head in his hands, not moving. He didn't even look up when she stepped inside and turned on the lamp.

Sam dropped her bag and tentatively approached the couch. Ty finally looked up, confusion marring his face. Sam knelt in front of him, her hands on his knees. Ty leaned back, examining her as if trying to dissect her features. Sam placed her hands on his wrists cautiously, feeling at any minute he might jerk away. There was a tense, formidable look to him Sam had never seen before.

"What has happened?" Sam asked, her voice small in the heavy silence of the room. Ty's gaze had shifted from her face to somewhere beyond her, his vision going straight through, no longer seeing.

"When you were standing there," he stammered, "standing there with Daniels, I remembered something Aaron said."

Sam's face hardened at the mention of Peterson.

"He saw you," Ty continued, his voice soft, paper-thin. "He saw you and Daniels the night you were with him in the tower. He said you were . . ." At this point, Ty's voice cracked. He paused for a moment, swallowing hard. "What happened that night at the tower?" he began again, this time looking directly at her.

"Nothing happened," Sam replied, bewildered. As far as Sam knew, no one had even known she'd been in the tower with Daniels that night. They hadn't seen anyone, but Aaron must have been watching. From where, Sam couldn't imagine.

"I was there practicing my knots. The commander showed up. He helped me and then we left," Sam added, her words picking up speed as she spoke.

"What did Aaron say to you?" she pleaded, shaking Ty's arms when he didn't respond. "Tell me!"

"He said the two of you had been together," Ty replied, but with the first hint of doubt creeping in as Aaron's story began to unravel.

"Ty, nothing happened. If you wanted the truth, you should have asked me. I will never lie to you."

"But something is going on. I've seen you together, I've seen him looking at you," Ty continued, wanting everything out in the open.

Sam wanted it out in the open, as well. But she could barely understand Daniels herself, much less explain him to Ty.

"I can't speak for Daniels," Sam replied, settling back on her haunches. "I barely know the man. But he has been nothing but professional throughout our training. Nothing has happened, there is nothing to explain." She gripped his hands.

Ty sat for a moment, relief easing the lines on his face. Then he abruptly stood up, almost knocking Sam over in the process. He began pacing the room, his hand moving quickly through his hair as he grappled for words.

"I don't want you to think you have to clear anything with me. Wait, that's not what I mean," Ty began, pausing midstride, trying to articulate the thoughts racing through his head. "I don't want you to feel you can't tell me anything, even if it concerns someone else." He glanced at her then dropped his eyes to the floor.

Sam stood up and smiled. "I appreciate that. I feel the same about you." She approached him and took up his hands again. "I'm sorry I kept those things from you – the incidents with Daniels at the training tower. But there was nothing to tell. He found me out there working on my knots, he helped out with Mark's training on the ladder. That was it."

"But how do you feel about him?" Ty asked, unconvinced it was that simple.

Sam took a small step back. "I don't know how to feel about him," Sam replied, staring at him in earnest. "You've been around him; he's not an easy person to know. We've spoken some and he's been helpful concerning the class. I admire what he's done, his achievements, and I find myself thinking about him, but I feel I hardly know him."

A vicious headache was creeping up Sam's neck, radiating to her temples. She sat down on the couch, rubbing the sides of her head. Ty settled in next to her and Sam gave him a weak smile. Suddenly, the exhaustion of the day settled over them. All the energy seemed to drain from their bodies and Ty was out of questions.

"I'm going to head home." Sam smiled and patted his knee, then stood up and hoisted her bag from the floor. She braced her hand against her sore back, stretching, before turning for the front door. She had her hand on the knob when she remembered she had no ride home. When she turned, Ty was dangling his keys, grinning.

"Let's go," he said, taking her bag in his hand and throwing an arm over her shoulder.

Sam paused at the doorway and stopped him with a hand to his chest. "Ty, when did Aaron say these things to you?"

Ty bit his tongue, remembering his lie about the beating. "This afternoon, after the burn," he replied as he quickly ushered her out the door.

After he dropped Sam off, Ty drove home slowly, replaying their conversation in his head as he navigated the darkened streets. His physical exhaustion was countered by the relief he felt following their conversation. But as he thought back over the pain Aaron had caused, both physically and emotionally, Ty's anger rose. Aaron had tried to destroy their friendship. Ty would not forget. He filed it away with the other infractions Aaron had committed and it only stiffened Ty's resolve for revenge. As he pulled into his driveway, he realized just what he would do.

~

The next day on the training field felt anticlimactic compared to the excitement of the burns. Stations were set up throughout the tower and they were back to running drills. The forcible-entry station was set up at the front of the tower; ladder drills would be conducted on the north side; ropes and knots would be held on the first floor; and hose evolutions would run out of the third. Sam saw with disappointment that Lee had returned.

Ty had picked Sam up that morning and they seemed to be back on track. The ride in was normal, although Ty still seemed contemplative. But when Sam asked about it, Ty had simply smiled and changed the subject.

The morning went smoothly. Sam worked through the stations and even performed well under Lee's scrutiny, thanks to Michaels' hawk-eye. He had kept careful watch over Lee's station as Sam moved through, much to her relief and Officer Lee's annoyance.

At lunch, the cadets spread their coats in the shade as Tate launched into a recap of a documentary he had watched the night before. He rambled on about the origins of radio communication until Lance lobbed his banana peel at Tater's head, pleading, "Come on, man! Give us a break."

"But you don't understand the significance of Hertz's experiments on Marconi's eventual success in sending and receiving the first transmissions!" Tate whined. "Now, that occurred in . . ." but before he could finish, Lance buried his head beneath his turnout coat and rolled onto his belly. Tate relented and continued munching quietly on his sandwich.

Sam was laying back, enjoying the cool of the late October sky, when she looked around and could not locate Ty. *He must be in the tower.* Ty appeared a few minutes later, smiling and plopping down next to her in the grass.

Lunch ended and they were ordered back to formation. They stood on deck as Michaels made the rounds, clutching his trusty clipboard, outlining the afternoon's activities. Sam glanced over at Ty. "What's going on with you?"

"Not a thing," Ty replied, rolling back on his heels. As the students broke from formation, Ty waited and watched.

Aaron lumbered over to his gear and snatched it from the tarmac, folding his coat over his arm and plunking his helmet onto his head. He was making his way to the tower when he froze in his tracks. He ripped his helmet off, only to discover the top of his head covered in motor oil.

"What the FUCK?!" he screamed, as everyone on deck turned. The top of his head was covered in a thick mat of oil, his arms were frozen out at his sides. He dropped his gear to the tarmac, turned his helmet in his hand, and noticed the large swath of aluminum foil lining the inside, which had been coated with oil, a traditional prank among firefighters. He threw the helmet to the concrete, fuming.

"Who the fuck did this?" he screamed as he scanned the group. The students on deck slowly backed away. Mark and Bill stood off to the side, unfazed. The instructors, who had been heading for their stations, were slowly turning toward the deck. Michaels and Tanner were making a beeline. But before they could reach the deck, Ty stepped forward.

He stood in bunker pants and helmet; his gloved hands clasped behind his back. "I greased your helmet, you fat motherfucker. Now what are you going to do about it?" Ty stated in a calm, even voice.

The cadets froze. Sam's heart leaped into her throat as she watched Aaron move forward, fists clenched.

At first, Aaron didn't respond, he simply moved toward Ty, a look of fury on his face, the oil slowly seeping down his forehead. By this time, Michaels and Tanner were running toward the tarmac, the rest of the instructors hot on their heels.

Ty stood his ground, his hands locked behind his back. Aaron moved in, clenching a massive left fist and in that moment, Sam realized it had been Aaron who had beaten Ty, not some stranger in a parking lot. That's when Aaron must have said those things about her and Daniels. Sam felt a flare of hatred as she watched Aaron closing in.

Sam wanted to scream, to push Ty to the ground so that Aaron's fist wouldn't find him, but it was too late. Aaron's arm had already entered its devastating arc, speeding toward Ty's face like a missile. Just as Aaron was about to land the punch, something in his thick head registered the strangeness of Ty's actions. *Why was he just standing there? Why wasn't he ducking or raising his arms?*

But while Aaron's strength may have been great, his reasoning skills were less than stellar. As his fist came in for a landing, the last thing he saw was the smile on Ty's face, causing him to rein in the punch just enough so that when it landed, it lacked the full force of Aaron's rage. And the moment he made contact Aaron realized exactly what Ty had done. By drawing Aaron into a fight and refusing to fight back, Ty had just sealed Aaron's dismissal from class.

As Ty reeled backwards, Aaron stumbled forward, trying to regain his footing. Michaels and Tanner landed on him like a couple of linebackers, throwing him to the ground, yanking his arms behind his back. Ty managed to stumble to his feet, clutching the side of his face as he regained his balance. When he stood up, he was still smiling.

Aaron was yanked to his feet and escorted from the tarmac, but not before Mark had a chance to sidle up. "If you ever come near Ty or Sam again, Bill and I will hunt you down. You hear me?" Mark sneered in a low voice. Aaron didn't respond, but the communication was clear. He hung his head as the officers escorted him across the field.

Ty was taken to the clinic where he was checked out, given a cold pack, and sent straight to Daniels' office. He wasn't sure which made him more nervous: his involvement in Aaron's dismissal or having to face Daniels after everything he and Sam had discussed. There was no time to decide. Daniels was waiting for him when he entered the office.

Michaels occupied one of the chairs in front of Daniels' desk, Ty settled into the other.

"Are you all right?" Daniels began. "Officer Michaels says you took quite a hit."

"I'm fine, sir," Ty replied, glancing from Daniels to Michaels.

"We're scheduled to be out at the tower tomorrow, but you'll take a day of light duty," Michaels announced. Light duty was doled out when cadets were injured and could not perform on the field. They were typically given office detail to avoid racking up absences.

"You'll spend tomorrow inside," Michaels continued. He knew Ty would fight it, but he didn't want to take any chances, especially considering

Ty's previous injuries. Michaels was furious with Peterson but thrilled that he was gone. He would have liked to give Ty a ferocious bear hug for his performance.

"I really feel OK. I'd rather not miss a field day," Ty replied, hoping for a reprieve. The last thing he wanted was to spend a day doing office work while the rest of the cadets were on the training field.

Daniels put an end to the discussion with a raised palm. "One day won't kill you," he responded, almost smiling. "I'm sure we'll have you back out on Monday."

Michaels stood up and headed for the door. Ty rose, but Daniels motioned for him to keep his seat. Michaels walked out, closing the door quietly behind him. Daniels folded his fingers into a teepee, his elbows on the arms of his chair as he hit Ty with those icy eyes. "The assault last week, it was Peterson, wasn't it?" he asked in a quiet voice.

Ty remained silent. With Aaron gone, it didn't really matter at this point, yet he still felt uncomfortable confessing. Daniels didn't wait for a response.

"It's OK, he's gone and it's done," he added, leaning forward. "He wasn't cut out for the job and it's better he find out sooner than later."

"How did you know it was him?"

"I saw his hand: cuts and swelling on his left hand, which matched the injuries on the right side of your face," Daniels replied.

Ty stared in silence. *The man misses nothing.*

"So, tomorrow . . ." Daniels continued, leaning back in his chair. "Skip PT and report to my office. I'll have Miss Davis rustle up some exciting paperwork for you." That near-smile played across his face again.

"Yes, sir," Ty responded reluctantly.

As Daniels ushered him out of the office, his hand floated naturally to Ty's shoulder, taking them both by surprise. Ty smiled and Daniels quickly dropped his hand. They stopped in the lobby on their way out.

"Miss Davis, this is Cadet Williams. He'll be reporting for light duty tomorrow; will you see that he has work?"

"I'm sure we can find something for him to do," she replied, smiling from behind her computer. "It's nice to meet you," she added, shaking Ty's hand.

"You, too," Ty replied. Daniels gave him a nod and returned to his office.

What would it be like, working in such proximity to Daniels? Ty wondered as he pulled the door closed behind him. He forced it from his mind. He would worry about that tomorrow. Right now, all he wanted was to escape the office and return to the group. As he left, he took a moment to savor the fact that Peterson was truly gone. He practically floated down the hallway.

Ty arrived at the tower as the cadets were packing up for the day. When Sam saw him crossing the field, she finished securing her gear and stacked it on top of his, which she had already bundled. As Ty approached, the students dropped their gear and gathered on the tarmac, applauding, and slapping him on the back. Even those close to Petersen were relieved he was gone. Aaron was a thug, even to his friends.

Mark grabbed Ty in his massive arms, lifting him off the ground and swinging him in a wide circle. Ty looked miniscule next to Mark's giant frame.

"Way to go, pretty-boy!" Mark cried, plunking him down on the concrete. Ty laughed, despite the exploding pain in his head. His group encircled him, checking out the new wound on his face, which had transformed the yellowed area into a deep reddish-purple. The swelling was not as bad, but the area was raised and painful. The men filtered off to gather their gear.

"We're having a 'Goodbye, Asshole' dinner at Johnny's tonight!" Bill announced to the group as they collected their gear. "Let's get the fuck out of here and go get some beer!" As far as Bill was concerned, no party was complete without a few cases.

Ty approached Sam with a sheepish grin. Sam placed a gentle hand to his face, gauging the damage from Aaron's fist. Ty closed his eyes. Sam's touch had become something he craved, a means of reaffirming their bond.

"That was a very brave and stupid thing you did," Sam said, her hand still on his face. Ty's eyes flickered open and he glanced at the men around them. Sam quickly dropped her hand and squatted to rearrange her gear. Ty crouched next to her, placing a light hand on her arm.

"I'm OK. I just wanted the guy gone and that was the only way I could make it happen."

Sam looked at him, at the earnestness of his face. She knew part of the reason Ty had taken the hit was because of the things Aaron had said following the assault; the accusations about her and Daniels. Sam forced her eyes from him and gathered her gear. She stood up and handed Ty his coat. As they walked across the field, she found his hand.

XII

The next morning, Ty reported to Miss Davis for light duty. She popped up from behind her desk and greeted him with a warm handshake. She then clutched her hands in front as if about to lead him in prayer before ushering him into the room with a gracious sweep of her arm.

"Welcome!" she chirped as she led him to a small desk in the corner. Paperwork and file folders formed staggering piles atop the worktable. Ty glanced nervously at Daniels' door as Miss Davis offered him a small chair.

"So glad to have you here," she announced as Ty took a seat at the desk. Even with Ty's limited height, the chair was a tight fit for his muscled frame.

Maggie enjoyed working around the cadets. She was looking forward to having an extra set of hands to assist her with the mass of paperwork that flowed from the commander's office. Her motivations were also selfish. The first time Ty entered the office, Maggie had taken one look at him and deemed him the best-looking cadet to have ever graced their training field.

"Now, Cadet Williams," she began before Ty interrupted.

"You can call me Ty."

"Now, Ty," she began again, speaking in a light staccato, her ample frame hovering above him like a giant balloon. "Commander Daniels generates paperwork like a beaver does woodchips. I'll need your help sifting through his latest venture, which is separating the past three years' special training courses into subcategories. We need to run stats on how many units from different departments have participated in the various types of training. The commander wants to add to the current program, so we need to determine which courses lead in attendance so that we can plot out the schedule for next year. All set?" she said, standing back and smiling.

Ty's head hurt. He had forgotten to take aspirin before leaving his house and the pain was working its way across his face.

"All set, Miss Davis," Ty replied half-heartedly. She hurried over to her desk and pulled a small laptop from one of the drawers. She then plopped it onto his desk, turned it on, and stood back, hands spread on her wide hips, waiting for it to power up.

"Are you familiar with Excel?" she inquired, eyeing him.

"Yes, ma'am." Ty flashed back to the bookkeeping he had assisted his mother with on the farm. She had taught him at an early age the necessity of good recordkeeping. Ty had often helped her with managing the farm's finances and had become proficient with numbers and spreadsheets.

Once the computer was up and running, Ty began by sifting through the piles on his desk. Satisfied he was settled in, Miss Davis returned to her desk where she tapped away on her computer, glancing his way every few minutes.

An hour passed before the commander emerged from his office. Seeing Ty mired in stacks of paperwork brought a smile to his face. He could tell Miss Davis had been busy; the kid had enough work to last him all month.

"How are you doing this morning, Williams?" Daniels asked, pausing near Ty's desk.

"Fine, sir," Ty replied, peering from between the stacks. Daniels noted the intensity in the boy's face and could see the workings of a long spreadsheet on the computer.

"How's the work coming?" Daniels bent forward to peer at the computer screen.

"Pretty well. I'm just dividing the training into subcategories and inputting the attendance numbers. I've broken down the attendance columns by department so we can track it regionally as well as numerically."

"Nice work." Daniels smiled and straightened.

Daniels was impressed. Ty was obviously well-organized and understood how to analyze data. He wished Michaels and Tanner were so inclined. They were excellent on the field but a mess when it came to office work. Michaels' skills were a hair above Tanner's. When placed in front of a computer, Tanner became frustrated in a matter of minutes, banging on the keyboard and ranting about the needless waste of time that is office detail.

"How about a cup of coffee?" Daniels flicked his head in the direction of the pot.

"That would be great!" Ty jumped up from his seat, happy to take a break from the screen. He followed the commander over to the coffee pot, which Miss Davis kept perpetually fresh. Maggie peeked from behind her computer as Ty walked by.

Daniels filled two cups. "Cream or sugar?"

"No thank you, sir. Black is fine."

"Good choice," Daniels replied, smiling.

Black coffee was a rule Sam had imposed. The first time they went to the café, Ty had asked for a bit of cream, since he found some blends too strong to take straight. Sam had harassed him for drinking candy-ass coffee, insisting that good coffee was ruined by cream and sugar; a house rule her father had enforced when she was very young. Sam had berated him to such an extent, Ty quickly surmised black coffee was preferable to her verbal abuse. He drank it straight from that point on.

But Daniels' coffee was not the rotgut version inflicted upon students in the cafeteria. It was a rich, mild blend, although Ty's first eager sip left a scald on his tongue. He blew over the top of his cup as Daniels motioned him into his office. Ty followed him to the leather chairs, and they took their seats, both relishing the savory warmth of the coffee.

"How did you become interested in the fire service, Williams?" Daniels asked as he leaned back in his seat and studied Ty. "Do you come from a family of firefighters?"

"No, sir, my family owns a large farm in Ocala." Ty leaned forward in his chair; elbows braced on its arms. "My father breeds horses. I grew up there. As far as I know, no one in my family has ever served." He took another guarded sip, enjoying the coffee even more as it cooled.

"And how is the training going?" Daniels was always curious to know how his cadets were faring.

"I love it. Tactics are my favorite. The pump calculations leave me a bit baffled, but overall, it's been a great experience. I'm looking forward to being done, though." Ty glanced nervously at the commander, self-conscious of his ramblings.

Daniels was struck by Ty's honesty. When asked, most cadets

layered on the bullshit to score points with the instructors. Ty seemed completely at ease with the truth. Daniels couldn't help but envy Ty for sharing that level of openness with Samantha.

"What else do you do when you're not at the academy?" Daniels asked, and then caught himself. He had not meant to get personal. He remembered the look Ty had shot him when he caught him staring at Samantha and didn't want to come across as prying. He tried to cover the blunder. "Do you play any sports?"

"I ran track in school. I still love to run," Ty replied, oblivious to Daniels discomfort. He found he was enjoying talking to the commander. He'd had a fixed opinion of the man as strict and unyielding, but Ty was finding that, although a serious-minded professional, Daniels was down to earth, comfortable in his own skin.

"Distance or speed?" Daniels asked, his curiosity piqued. Daniels' love of running matched his love of training. Both were a source of solace in his life that kept him balanced and fulfilled.

"Distance. I'm not much for speed. I'm too short," Ty replied, grinning. Again, Daniels was struck by his honesty.

"Do you ever go over to the greenway?" Daniels asked, warming to the conversation.

"I don't even know where that is," Ty replied with a shake of his head.

"It's a great spot. The path stretches through ten miles of green space. It's on the north side of downtown, just off the Expressway. I go there on weekends for my long runs."

"How far do you usually go?"

"Typically, ten. I run it like a track; one time around is a pretty good workout. Michaels joins me on occasion, but now that he's married, he can't get away from home as often on Sundays." Ty noted the twinge of disappointment in Daniels face.

"I'll have to check it out. I'd be glad to run with you, if you want," Ty added without thinking, immediately regretting the offer. Not that he wouldn't like to run with the commander. Ty just didn't want to be perceived as speaking out of line. He tried to cover his misstep. "But I'm sure you have other instructors to run with," he muttered with a flip of his hand. He sipped his coffee.

Daniels noted the awkwardness but again, appreciated Ty's honesty. "I'd like that," he replied, and now it was Daniels' turn to feel awkward. He had just broken his cardinal rule about socializing with cadets.

But Ty didn't appear to be a typical cadet. He was more thoughtful than most, more self-possessed. He was open; he didn't try to put on airs like so many of the men who came through, always trying to outdo each other or show off in front of the instructors. Ty's manner was simple. What you saw was what you got.

"I'll be there Sunday morning around six. I park at the main lot. You're welcome to join me."

"That'd be great," Ty replied. "I'll be there." They returned to their coffee and Daniels glanced at his watch. Ty caught the signal and stood up.

"Thank you for the coffee, sir. I'll see you Sunday morning."

Daniels stood up, smiled, and headed for his desk.

~

"You're going where with whom?" Sam exclaimed as they stood in the middle of her kitchen. Ty had skillfully handed her a beer before dropping the news that he was meeting Daniels for a run on Sunday. The bottle was poised halfway to her mouth.

"I'm meeting him for a run," Ty repeated, ducking behind her to stir the big pot of spaghetti that bubbled on the stove. It was the one meal Ty felt confident enough to cook, so he had taken over Sam's kitchen to prepare dinner: a payback for Sam's tending to him after Aaron's visit. He busied himself at the stove, smiling.

"How in the world did this happen?" Sam threw her head back and chugged her beer. She couldn't escape the irony, considering all that she and Ty had just worked through concerning Daniels.

"It just came up," Ty replied, holding a sauce-stained spoon in one hand. "We were talking over coffee," he continued when Sam interrupted.

"You had coffee with the man?" she shot back, almost laughing. Sam flashed back over the day she had had at the tower: mindless evolutions, back-breaking hose work, topped by three laps in full gear because of the class' lack of enthusiasm on the training ground.

"You are such a bum!" Sam exclaimed. "I've had a shit day on the field, and you got to sit around having tea and crumpets with Daniels." She laughed as she took another pull from her beer. It tasted wonderful against her parched throat and the smell of the spaghetti was making her stomach rumble.

They settled in over heaping plates of pasta as Ty recapped his day in the office. It was obvious Ty had enjoyed his time with Daniels, that he felt a connection with the commander. Sam wondered if it stemmed from the lack of connection with his own father. For the first time in his life, Ty had an older man to talk to on equal terms, absent his father's bullying.

Sam sat back as Ty chattered on, smiling in between bites of spaghetti and sips of beer, enjoying seeing him relaxed and happy. Each time Ty grinned, the bruise on his face would crinkle, the area around his eye resembling a withered plum. But the wound did nothing to detract from his perfect lines. Later, they watched a movie as Ty burrowed into his nest on the couch. He was soon fast asleep. Sam turned out the lights and left him where he lay.

~

When Daniels arrived at the greenway, Ty was already there, stretching his legs on the grass adjacent to the parking lot. Ty had not wanted to chance being late, so had risen before dawn and driven through the dark streets following the directions Sam had written down.

Daniels stepped from his SUV and gave a wave as he strolled across the parking lot. Without a word, he began stretching next to Ty, working the kinks out of his legs.

"We'll start just over there and head west on the trail." Daniels pointed to an area on the path to their left. Ty gave a silent nod, already settling into the soothing mindset of a long run.

They started out at an easy pace. Ty followed Daniels' lead, matching his stride as their bodies slowly warmed up. The air around them was cool and a half moon was sinking in the western sky, turning a faint orange in anticipation of sunrise. Neither of them spoke, which Daniels appreciated. He hated running with men who felt the need to chatter. The silence was what Daniels loved best about running, hearing only the faint sounds of his feet striking the path, the constant rhythm of his breathing.

Ty shared his appreciation for silence. When he and Sam ran, they had a no-talking policy. The first time they had ventured out, Ty felt compelled to make small talk. But Sam had quickly shushed him, laughing as she did so. "It's bad enough trying to keep up with you!" she had exclaimed in between breaths. "Don't make me entertain you with small talk!" That had put an end to chatting during their runs and they enjoyed them that much more in silence.

As Daniels and Ty progressed along the path, the light slowly crept through the surrounding trees. It settled onto the glassy lake, bouncing its faint color skyward. The Canadian geese had found their way south and were skidding to a stop on the water, their landings slicing through its still surface. They honked wildly to each other as the group swelled.

The run took them just over an hour. They sprinted the last half mile, arriving winded and sweaty. They walked in small circles as their bodies cooled.

"Good run," Daniels said through deep breaths.

"Excellent," Ty added, smiling. Although Ty enjoyed the runs with Sam through the dark streets of downtown, running along the greenway had reminded him of home, of long runs through the countryside during the early morning hours. Ty loved listening for the sounds of animals waking, in the woods and among the neighboring farms. It was his favorite part of the day.

Daniels strolled over to his vehicle and pulled a towel and two bottles of water from a cooler on the back seat. He tossed a bottle to Ty and they drank in silence, unconsciously continuing their small circular wanderings. When their breathing had slowed, they walked over to a nearby picnic table, each straddling one end of the bench. Their eyes combed the green space before Ty finally broke the silence.

"Thanks for letting me join you. This is a great place to run. I can see why you like coming here."

"I'm glad you came. I think it's the best area around," Daniels replied, taking another sip of water. "Is your dad a runner?"

"No, my father only knows the farm. Nothing else really exists for him. I was lucky he let me participate in track. He kept a pretty tight rein." Ty stared off toward the lake. Daniels noted the tightening in Ty's face. He dropped the subject and waited for Ty to choose a new one.

"Sam tells me you're from San Diego," Ty continued, immediately realizing his mistake. The minute he mentioned Sam's name, Ty flashed back to the classroom. He remembered Daniels' eyes on Sam and he silently cursed himself for bringing her up.

But Daniels let it slide. He took another sip before responding.

"Yes, I spent seventeen years with San Diego Fire," Daniels replied, his eyes focused on the distant tree line. "It was a great place to work, very training-centric. I got to develop a lot of new programs there. It was a wonderful place to learn and develop as an officer." He glanced over and smiled to put Ty at ease. Daniels had also flashed back to the incident in the classroom, but he didn't want it to spoil their run.

Ty relaxed and their conversation naturally flagged. They watched the morning settle in and by the time they stood to leave, the fields were bathed in full light.

"Michaels and I run before class each morning. Join us any time you like," Daniels said, realizing he had broken his rule a second time. He held out his hand and Ty gave it a hearty shake. Daniels smiled as he turned to get into his vehicle.

"See you tomorrow," Daniels called as he climbed in. He gave a quick wave before driving away.

Ty stood for a few minutes in the parking lot, watching Daniels' vehicle disappear through the trees. Ty felt relaxed, which surprised him. It had been hard to imagine what it would be like spending time with Daniels outside of class and Ty had tossed and turned the night before, unable to sink into a deep sleep. But now Ty felt he had gotten a slight handle on the commander. He was slowly recognizing the boundaries within which he could navigate. He finished off his water, jumped into his car, and headed for Sam's.

When Ty arrived, Sam was nowhere to be found. He texted her to find she had headed to the beach, taking advantage of having the morning to herself. As much as Sam enjoyed being with Ty, the stress of the academy and the lack of time alone were wearing on her. Her favorite escape was a solitary day at the ocean.

Sam followed a regular routine. She would rise before dawn, grab her beach bag, which was kept perpetually packed, and head out early with a mug of scalding coffee, driving east onto vast grasslands that flanked the St. Johns River, crossing relic dunes that unfolded toward the Atlantic as the rising sun turned the landscapes myriad shades of green. Once there, she would stroll out onto the white sand, spread a sheet near the dunes, and watch the sun slowly climb the sky. Her earliest memories were of the ocean. Sam could remember her parents' voices, even though she could no longer picture what they had looked like back then. She remembered the blinding light reflecting off the sand and the pounding of the surf sounding like the footfalls of giants.

The beach was where she felt most peaceful, where she could spend the day alone, reading or sleeping on the sand. She glanced at her watch. It was just after seven as she settled in. The sun was cutting through a thin bank of clouds, throwing pale columns of light skyward. The breeze coming ashore was laced with the chill of fall and carried with it the briny smell of the surf.

She imagined Ty and Daniels running side by side along the greenway, could picture their bodies moving in a steady rhythm in the early light. Sam felt a connection to each of them, yet in different ways. Ty had become a form of security to her, and she to him. It was hard to imagine moving through the process of the academy without Ty beside her; impossible to conceive what it would have been like had Ty not been in her class.

It was the same for Daniels, only from a different angle. Daniels was ingrained in Sam's thoughts of the academy, as if he formed the backbone of what the academy stood for, its strength and intensity. When Sam thought about the experiences of the last seven weeks, it was impossible to tease out his presence, so intertwined had he become in the process.

To think of the men together made for confusion in Sam's mind.

Sam shook the thoughts from her head, instead focusing on the warmth of the sun and thoughts of her father. He always returned to her when she neared the ocean, the smell of salt and sand always brought him back. But thoughts of her father typically ushered in a melancholy that settled in her chest when she thought of all they had missed since his death. Sam often wondered what he would have thought of her joining the fire service. It was the life lessons he instilled that had led her to the academy.

Despite the beauty of the day, whenever she left the shore, Sam always carried home that familiar sense of loss. Today was no different.

On those occasions, Sam would usually head home and settle in on her balcony with a stiff glass of gin to numb her thoughts and ease her mind.

She had just sat down when Ty showed up at her door. Sam ushered him in with a smile but could not bring herself to ask about his time with Daniels, her need for silence overwhelming. Ty could sense her mood and instead, settled in next to her. They sat in silence as the sun dipped below the horizon.

Ty warmed the leftover spaghetti, put on soft music, and then led Sam inside. They ate quietly, exchanging small talk but avoiding anything of substance. When they were finished, he cleared the table as Sam drifted into the living room and curled up on the couch.

Ty turned out the lights in the kitchen, leaving only the fading light from outside spilling across the living room floor. He lifted her head and slid onto the couch. Sam settled back down on his lap as Ty laid his head back, eyes closed, his hand blindly stroking her hair. Ty stayed until the dark closed in, until he knew she was asleep.

Daniels also spent the day in introspection, but instead of his mind flashing to Samantha on a regular basis as it did on most days, he found himself thinking about Ty and the brief time they had shared. The boy had made an impression on him. It went beyond what Daniels had seen of him as a cadet – the serious student, the hard worker – to who Ty was as a person.

Over the years, Daniels had seen scores of young men move through the training process. He had developed the ability to gauge their merit with a few simple questions, a few brief observations. He could discern those who had integrity and drive from those who were willing to play the system as long as they succeeded, as long as they graduated. The second type were not there to learn and grow as individuals, but merely to brandish the title of firefighter.

Ty was unique. Daniels admired his honesty, his directness, his work ethic, and even his vulnerability. When Ty mentioned his father, Daniels had noted the constriction of his features, the subtle tightening in his face. He recognized it because he suffered from the same affliction, ever since the events that forced him to flee San Diego. All it took were the right words to activate the reflex.

Perhaps that explained the connection he felt with the boy. When Daniels looked at Ty, he saw so much of himself.

~

Ty and Sam arrived at school an hour early so that he could meet up with Daniels and Michaels for their morning run. Sam was pleased Ty was forming a bond with Daniels. It seemed to affect something deep inside him, something even beyond her touch. As they were walking into the building, the officers emerged, both dressed in shorts and tee shirts. Sam met Daniels' glance, both uncomfortable in the presence of the other men.

"Glad you'll be joining us," Michaels said, breaking the silence.

"Thanks," Ty responded. "I just need to drop my bag. I can meet you on the field."

Daniels nodded, glanced once more at Samantha, and he and Michaels headed for the field. Sam followed Ty inside, smiling and calling after him, "Good luck!" as he broke into a run toward the locker room. Sam headed for the library and settled into their new routine.

~

Michaels was pleasantly surprised when Daniels broke the news that Ty would be joining them. Michaels enjoyed his time with the commander, but the price of spending time with Daniels typically meant sacrificing any chance of outside participation. Their time was usually restricted to just the two of them.

Michaels' decision to marry had been hard on Daniels. Daniels had come to depend on him, both professionally and personally. It seemed he was the only person Daniels felt comfortable around; the only one he could open up to, and even that was done in small, metered doses. Their morning runs were now the only time they had together that was guaranteed. It was part of their daily schedule, non-negotiable. Michaels was encouraged by the fact that Daniels had invited Ty to join them, especially considering the policy Daniels adhered to concerning fraternizing with students. Maybe Daniels was finally permitting himself some latitude. Perhaps he saw something in Ty that allowed him to drop his defenses and mentor on a more personal level.

Michaels had liked Ty from the start. Ty was serious without being uptight. He was likable and seemed to care for the students around him. And the kid was a worker. He was never idle, always looking for ways to help out. If something needed to be done, Ty could usually foresee the task at hand. He'd be on it before the instructors could issue the order. But what had really won Michaels over was the way Ty had handled Peterson. Michaels couldn't have scripted a better way to get rid of that piece of shit. When he saw Peterson going for Ty, he initially thought Ty was a goner. But Ty seemed to know exactly what he was doing. He made Michaels' day when he got that ass-wipe to swing.

The only thing that gave Michaels pause was Ty's relationship with Smith. He couldn't figure out what the hell was going on there. They were always together, yet they didn't act like a couple. Michaels could usually tell when students were banging each other. It was usually pretty obvious. That was another reason he preferred the all-male classes: no hassles with female cadets. He hoped Ty wouldn't get bogged down in a relationship. The kid had a lot going for him. He didn't need to be saddled with a commitment.

Michaels should know. Ever since he got married, his life seemed to be on a collision course with suburbia. His wife was already talking kids, even though they had only been married a year. The whole thing gave Michaels a sinking feeling in his gut.

Michaels admired Daniels, even envied his freedom. Sure, the guy seemed isolated, but he seemed to thrive on the isolation, something Michaels found hard to understand. Michaels may have gripes about being married and on a leash, but at least he had companionship, even if it was imposed. He took Ty's presence as a good sign, something he felt was long overdue in Daniels' life.

XIII

It was going to be a long week. For starters, the students were condemned to the classroom for five days straight. To make matters worse, they would be studying hazardous materials; hardly their most stimulating subject.

They would spend the first three days on hazmat. On Thursday, they would move on to basic first aid. Lance, Trey, Johnny, and Sam were already certified as paramedics. Most of the other students were emergency medical technicians, so much of the medical training would be redundant. Ty was one of the few who lacked either certification.

Lunch was the only time they got a break from the tedium of the classroom and they harassed each other to no end in an effort to alleviate the monotony. Lance even went as far as shooting a spoonful of peas at Tate, who was foolish enough to launch into one of his scientific elucidations concerning the migratory patterns of insects. It was a tough week. By Thursday, they were fit to be tied.

The only bright spot was Ty's new running routine. Each morning, he and Sam arrived early so that he could join Daniels and Michaels on the track. After only a week, Sam noticed a change in Ty's demeanor. Ty had always seemed content, but his time spent with the officers seemed to instill in him a greater sense of self, more focused and intensive. It was as if he was coming into his own as a man, as if his inclusion elevated his self-worth. The change was immediate and profound.

The cadets spent Thursday going over cardiopulmonary resuscitation. They reviewed the protocols for managing cardiac arrest and the techniques for treating choking victims. After the tedium of hazmat, it was a relief to be up from their desks, simulating rescue procedures on each other, even if it entailed receiving numerous back blows to dislodge imaginary objects. By Friday, they were out of control. They couldn't take another day locked up inside, so Michaels relented and allowed them to drag their medical equipment out to the tower. The cadets piled out of the classroom and sprinted to the locker rooms. They stripped off their uniforms, donned their shorts, gathered their bunker pants, boots, helmets, and gloves, and bolted across the field.

They spent the morning practicing bandaging and splinting. They took turns playing the victim, so that everyone could experience applying and receiving treatment. During the afternoon, they practiced spinal immobilization. One of them would simulate the patient, usually mimicking someone who had fallen from the top of the tower to make it a bit more interesting. One rescuer would position himself at the head of the patient and take control of the head, keeping the patient's neck perfectly in line. The team would then logroll the patient onto a backboard. A second rescuer then would perform a head-to-toe examination, working his way down the body, looking, and feeling for injuries.

They would palpate the skull, searching for depressed cranial fractures or lacerations. Pupils were checked for reactivity and equality, followed by the ears, which were checked for blood and cerebrospinal fluid.

They checked the neck by palpating along the spine. The stability of the chest was assessed by pushing on the sternum and compressing the sides of the ribs. They palpated the abdomen, checking for rigidity that accompanies a belly bleed, and then moved down to the pelvis. They compressed each hip and then "rocked" it as they leaned over the patient, a hand on each hip, moving carefully side to side. The rescuer then worked his way down each extremity, checking for fractures by palpating the limbs. And finally, grip strength was checked by having the patient squeeze the rescuer's fingers.

When the full assessment was completed, a cervical collar was put in place and the patient was strapped down for transport. Once the patient was completely packaged, the scenario was over.

They worked in groups of four. One person would play the patient, the other three would be the rescuers. One of the rescuers would take the lead and conduct the patient assessment. Ty, Johnny, Tate, and Sam worked together. The men had rotated through as the patient; now it was Sam's turn. She sprawled face down on the concrete, so that they'd have to perform a logroll. Ty called the lead, much to Sam's relief. Tate got so nervous when it came to placing his hands on her that Sam figured she'd end up with an actual injury if he were to take the helm.

Johnny coached them through the logroll, making sure they kept Sam's spine in alignment as they rolled her onto the board. Once they had her on her back, Tate knelt at her head to maintain control of her cervical spine. The simple act of handling Sam's head caused his face to break out in a sweaty sheen. He gripped her temples between sweaty palms, his face hovering above her as she lay flat on the pavement. Sam issued a stiff warning.

"Tater, if you so much as shed a drop, you'll be taking my place on this board," Sam griped, forcing a frown as Tate took a swipe at his brow with his sleeve.

Ty positioned himself alongside Sam to begin the assessment, one leg tucked beneath him, the other bent aside so he could reach over her to perform the exam. Sam was eyeing him, trying to keep a straight face, when she noticed a shadow glide into view: Daniels. Sam panicked. She already felt ridiculous, lying on the ground with Tater gripping her head and sweating like a cardiac patient, and now Ty was going to be working his way down every inch of her body. The last thing Sam needed was Daniels' laser-like stare. But Ty was oblivious to the commander's presence. He grinned, stifling a laugh, enjoying finally having Sam at his mercy. Sam could feel a line of sweat break out across her lip, which didn't escape Ty's notice.

"Don't be nervous, miss" he chided, leaning over her. "This won't hurt a bit." Daniels cracked a rare smile.

Sam wanted to warn Ty, to let him know the commander was standing behind him, if for no other reason than that he take the scenario seriously. But Ty was oblivious, and Daniels seemed content to sit back and watch.

Ty started with Sam's head, ruffling her short hair, and giving her skull a good squeeze, as if he were choosing a melon. He then checked her pupils by bending way too close to her face, their noses almost touching. All Sam could make out was a flash of white teeth as his head blotted out the sun. He then ran his hands over her face in an exaggerated manner, like a blind man deciphering her features. With each move, he verbalized his actions so that Johnny would know what he was checking for. Johnny sat opposite Ty, throwing conspiratorial smiles to Daniels. Sam could just make out Johnny's grin from her vantage point on the tarmac.

Ty then checked her neck, pushing down on her trachea and causing her to gasp. *I'll get him for that one*, Sam scowled. Ty checked her shoulders by giving them a tight squeeze and then shifted his position so that he could examine her chest. Suddenly, his smirk evaporated when he realized he would be palpating her torso, as if it hadn't occurred to him until that exact moment. Sam grinned, thinking she would finally have her revenge. Ty's hands hovered anxiously above her chest before coming in for a gentle landing on her sternum. Sam was about to toss out a sarcastic reply when she happened to glance up at Daniels.

Like Ty, the smile had faded from his face, but with Daniels it had been replaced by an anxious intensity, as if Ty were venturing into uncharted waters only Daniels was experienced enough to navigate. Suddenly, Sam felt vulnerable, ridiculous. It was bad enough having Ty run his hands over her body; Daniels' presence only intensified her anxiety. Between Ty's hands and Daniels' eyes, Sam felt totally exposed; she might as well have been lying there naked. She glanced up at Tater, who by now was sweating buckets, swiping his brow every few seconds while trying to maintain control of her head.

As Ty began, everything seemed to slow down. His movements became cautious, systematic. Using the base of his palm, Ty pushed gently on her sternum, then repositioned his hands to her ribcage. He felt his face flush as he placed his hands alongside her breasts. He squeezed the sides of her chest and felt his fingers slip into the indentations between her ribs. He then slid his hands down to her belly, carefully palpating all four quadrants of her abdomen, noting the tautness of the underlying muscles. Daniels' eyes remained locked on Ty's hands.

Ty moved down to Sam's pelvis. He positioned himself on his knees next to her hip and leaned over her, his hands on the outside of her pelvis. Sam noticed the concentration in his face, how his eyes tracked the methodical movement of his hands. He squeezed inward and then repositioned his hands on top of her hips, his fingers conforming perfectly to their arches as he rocked slowly side to side, his body braced above her.

Ty drew himself up beside Sam's chest and worked his way down each arm, squeezing gently as he made his way toward each hand. He slipped his fingers into her palms and had her squeeze simultaneously to check her grip strength. Sam noted the warmth of his fingers. He returned to her hips, working his way down the length of each leg, running his hands over her thighs, knees, and calves. By the time he was done, Sam realized she had been holding her breath. She exhaled slowly as Johnny handed Ty the straps.

Tate slipped a C-collar around Sam's neck as Johnny positioned the straps. Ty took over, securing the first strap over her left shoulder and clipping it onto the board near her right hip. He then secured the second strap over her right shoulder, clipping the other end next to her left hip so that the straps formed an 'X' across her chest. He gave each strap a slow tug to cinch it down. The third strap was placed over her hips, the fourth over her thighs. Ty sat back on his haunches, wiping his forehead with the back of his hand, scanning up and down Sam's body to check his work. Sam noticed Daniels doing the same thing.

Johnny slapped Ty's shoulder and brought the scenario to a close with, "Nice job!" Daniels ran a rough hand over his jaw and disappeared. Ty never even knew he was there.

~

It was just after four when Ty checked his watch in the darkness. He had fallen asleep on Sam's couch again; the second time this week. It was becoming a habit, as was the urge he indulged as he pulled himself up and treaded lightly to her room.

Sam was curled beneath the covers, her face hidden in shadows. Soft light spilled through the large window above her bed, bathing the smooth contours of her body in the predawn glow. Ty settled soundlessly in the corner. He leaned forward, elbows braced on knees, hands clasped as if he had come to worship.

He searched the shadows for the outline of her face, craving a glimpse of the features that had become engrained in his brain. Added to them now was the feel of Sam's body beneath his hands: soft skin, solid bone, firm muscle, and those beautiful curves.

Ty sat back and watched her until the dawn chased him from her room.

XIV

The cadets spent Monday morning reviewing their knots before moving on to attaching the ropes to equipment. Even though they had covered the material a few weeks ago, they were rusty, their brains overloaded by the curriculum.

Sam lucked out the first day. When the instructors broke them into groups, hers was placed with Tanner instead of Lee. Tanner took them through securing ladders, hoselines, and hand tools before moving on to raising and lowering equipment through the tower windows.

Sam enjoyed working with Tanner. Like Michaels, he was serious about the training, but he maintained a good-natured playfulness, even while berating them for their mistakes. As he supervised their work, he kept up a constant monologue, as if he were incapable of keeping his thoughts to himself. He would wander through the room, slow walking with one hand on his hip, the other fondling his toothpick, his sharp eyes catching even the simplest mistake. When he eyed a slip-up, he'd pounce. Lance and Trey were about to get an earful.

They were struggling to secure a pike pole, but their knots kept slipping each time they went to tighten both ends. Just as they'd get one end secured, the other would slip off and the tool would clatter to the concrete. Trey was exercising patience, but Lance, with his short fuse, was growing increasingly frustrated. His griping increased exponentially as his frustration mounted.

"Just try reworking the hitch," Trey hissed under his breath as he eyed Tanner closing in. As Trey struggled with the tool, Lance's arms wound into their usual gyrations.

"Well, obviously I don't know what the fuck I'm doing here!" he exclaimed loudly. "I keep trying to secure the bastard, but something's not working! I've tried tying both ends, and it just keeps sliding off!"

The rest of the students were struggling to maintain straight faces and stay focused on their knots. Trey rubbed at his forehead with a gloved hand as Tanner moved in.

"Boys, what the fuck are you doin' over here?" he bellowed in his thick twang. "This is about the most pathetic display yet. You got a goddamned monkey fist on this tool." He picked up the tool and examined the clove hitch, which had bunched up on itself, losing all semblance of a knot. "Strip it down and do it again." He handed the tool back to Trey and continued through the room, mumbling under his breath.

"I tell you what," he grumbled. "We go through these fuckin' knots over and over and still you guys can't seem to find your butts with both hands. Jeeeee-zus. I've never seen such a bunch a retards."

Sam was hoping they would be with Tanner for the entire three-day session. Her luck ran out after just one day.

When they arrived at the tower the next morning, Sam realized her gloves were missing again. She found them on the top shelf of her locker, but by the time she made it back out onto the field, the cadets had dispersed. After berating her for her carelessness, Tanner ordered her to run a quick lap before joining her group. As she returned from the run, Johnny waved her over. Sam noted the grave expression on his face. He stood alongside their regulars: Ty, Tate, Lance, and Trey. She glanced over at Ty and noticed he too was scowling.

"Why the grim faces, boys?" Sam said as she tried to catch her breath. The men stood silently as Lee strode up behind her.

"All right girls, grab your shit and meet me on the third floor," he barked as he headed for the stairs. Sam's heart sank. She glanced around for Michaels, hoping for a reprieve, but Michaels was nowhere to be seen. He had already taken his group into the tower.

~

Michaels had thought about the day's schedule on his way in to work. He continued to mull as they completed their morning run. He knew Lee would be heading up the three-day session, since ropes and knots were his area of specialization. Daniels allowed the instructors with the most training and experience to coordinate their respective sessions. It was not meant as a slight to Michaels; Daniels knew Michaels was more than capable of running the entire course, but it was an act of deference. Lee was a wizard with ropes. He had been coordinator of the county's high-angle team before retiring and teaching full-time. Michaels had never had a problem with Lee leading ropes and knots. The man knew his shit.

What concerned Michaels were the group assignments and the fact that Lee had assigned himself to Smith's group. Michaels knew that if he changed up the procedure and dictated the groups, Lee would take it as a slight. Since Lee provided three of the specially trained adjuncts from his former team, Michaels wanted to avoid a power struggle.

He took comfort in the fact that Lee had behaved himself the last time Sam moved through his station. Of course, Michaels was there watching, but he noticed that Lee hadn't put her in his section for the first or third day of training, so perhaps he was through riding her. Michaels would do what he could to keep an eye out, but with students working on various floors of the tower, he knew it would be difficult. His main focus was getting Mark through the emergency escape drill. He hoped the extra work on the ladder, combined with his successful airbag jumps, had improved the cadet's confidence. Hopefully, things would go smoothly.

Daniels was leery about the lineup, as well, but he had made it pretty clear in the tower the day he confronted Lee that any inappropriate behavior would mean his ejection from the academy. He noticed Lee had assigned Samantha with Tanner on the first day; to Adjunct Wilson's group on the third. Although she was assigned to Lee on the second day, Daniels felt confident Lee wouldn't cross him. Even Lee wasn't that reckless.

Lee had planned carefully. He knew Michaels was keeping an eye on him. No doubt he and Daniels had conspired. The two communicated as if by radar and Lee resented being monitored. He had scheduled Smith with other instructors for the first and third days, just to keep things low profile. But he would have her for the second day, and he could always make changes on the fly. Lee figured if he were going to be teaching three days in a row, he might as well have something nice to look at and working on the floors of the tower would provide a bit of cover.

Let's see how far I can push her.

~

Johnny led the group as they filed into the tower. He glanced over at Sam as they mounted the stairs. The last run-in with Lee had been humiliating; Johnny wondered what was in store for the day. The tension enveloped them as they climbed to the third floor.

When they arrived on the floor, Lee was standing near the window, slapping a piece of webbing against the palm of his hand. It made a hearty "*thwap*" each time it landed.

"Take out your webbing, girls," he grumbled, eyeing Sam as he used the derogatory term. They took out their piece of webbing, which had been distributed the previous afternoon.

"First, we'll practice making the quick-seat." He scanned their faces to ensure they were listening. "I'll take you through it first. Smith, come on over." His face cracked into a sneer.

Sam approached reluctantly, stopping a few feet from where Lee stood. The thought of the officer's hands on her made Sam cringe. She hoped he would simply have her lead the construction of the seat by showing the others how to do it as he talked her through. The fact that he had used her real name instead of "Pet" gave her a brief glimmer of hope. It was short-lived.

Lee spread out his piece of webbing, which was knotted to form a large loop. He gathered it in one hand and approached her. Sam tensed, and Lee took note.

"Don't you worry, Pet. I don't bite." His grin spread across his face and Sam was hit with a strong whiff of aftershave as he positioned himself in front of her.

"First, you take your webbing and loop it behind you." He addressed the group, stepping up against Sam so that he could pass one end of the loop to his other hand, which had encircled her waist. His face was only inches from hers, the brim of his hat almost touching her forehead. Sam fought the urge to knee him in the balls. Lee spread the loop behind her, his arms sliding around her torso like a snake winding a tree. The top of the loop crossed over Sam's lower back, the bottom of it lay across the backs of her thighs. Lee turned to address the men. Sam glanced past Lee at Ty and Johnny. They stood close together, their faces set. Ty clutched his webbing in his right hand and Sam could see his veins standing out even from where she stood. Tate was growing nervous at the display and shifted in his boots, trying to relieve tension.

"Then you pull the loop tight," Lee continued, drawing the webbing tight across Sam's backside. Despite the coolness of the tower, she could feel sweat spring up along her back as she tried to remain still. Lee gave the webbing a subtle yank to get her attention.

"Next, you move your hands between the front loops and reach between your legs to bring the back of the loop forward." He brought the front of the loop together, crossed it, slid his hands between the ends and reached down between Sam's legs, grabbing the lower back half of the loop and drawing it up and forward. He worked the webbing with speed and precision. Sam felt the backs of his hands brush the insides of her thighs. She could see Ty tensing as Lee worked. She couldn't bring herself to make eye contact.

The webbing conformed perfectly to Sam's pelvis. Lee pulled it tight to emphasize its snug fit. He then stood back, holding onto the front of the webbing with one hand in front of her crotch.

"Any questions?" he asked, grinning. No one said a word. "Good." He then released one side of the webbing as the seat fell away. But before Sam could step away, Lee pivoted up against her as he grabbed the back of the webbing with his free hand and slowly drew the material between her legs. Sam could feel it slide across her crotch, his hand applying tension on one end as he pulled it between her legs with the other.

Johnny dropped his eyes, embarrassed on Sam's behalf and not wanting to make it worse by watching. Ty's gaze never wavered. The look of hatred emanating from his face had transformed his appearance, making him look years older. He was wringing his webbing between his hands, twisting it into a tight braid as he imagined wrapping it around the officer's throat.

Lee stepped away from her and tossed her the webbing. "OK, girls. Now you practice." He sidled over to a chair in the corner. He sat down, spreading his legs in front, and crossing his arms over his chest. He glanced over at Sam, raised a finger to push the brim of his hat back off his forehead, and grinned.

Sam returned to the group and they practiced constructing their seats. She positioned herself as far from Lee as she could, her back to the wall, swiping at the sweat that had accumulated on her lip. Ty stood in front of her, swinging his head to glare at Lee as the cadets worked in silence.

Lunch was a solemn affair. Ty stared off into space, refusing to even crack a smile when Sam gave his boot a kick as they lounged in the grass. Sam had already worked through much of her anger. As she practiced her quick-seat, she screamed at Lee in her head: *Asshole-motherfucker-shitforbrains-cocksucker-pieceofshit-sonofabitch-dick!* By the time they broke for lunch, she had gotten most of it out of her system.

It took Mark and Bill joining them for the silence to be broken. They plopped down in the grass and scanned the morose group. "What the hell's going on over here?" Mark griped.

"Just another wonderful day with Lee," Johnny replied, rolling his eyes. Mark had heard about Sam's previous incident with Lee. He didn't push the issue.

Sam turned to Mark and held out a section of her orange. "How are you feeling about the rappel?" She dropped the slice into his large, outstretched hand.

"Like hell. I just hope I don't get up there and shit my pants." He popped the orange into his mouth, grimacing at its tartness.

"Just follow Michaels' lead." Sam knew having Michaels with him at the window would be an asset. Watching them work on the ladder truck was the perfect example of what a student-instructor relationship should be: one mentoring, the other lapping it up.

Sam tried once more with Ty, tossing a piece of orange peel at him and hitting him in the nose. He managed to crack a smile and then laid back in the grass, losing himself in his thoughts.

After lunch, they assembled on their respective floors to resume the webbing drills. The afternoon would be spent rappelling out of the tower windows using their quick-seats. The drills would be performed in bunker pants, boots, helmets, and gloves. Tomorrow, they would add full gear and tools to the mix to simulate a true emergency escape.

Ropes were anchored within the room and one of the adjuncts took up position as safety outside on the tarmac. He would control the belay rope, which would be secured to the backs of their harnesses and rigged from above the window through a pulley system, providing a controlled descent, should the students have problems with the rappel.

Once Lee had talked them through the maneuver, it was time for them to perform. Lance decided to go first, if only to get it over with. Tate stood back, nervously checking his watch, hoping the day would end before he would be forced to go.

Despite his gangly size, Lance's rappel went smoothly. It seemed to bolster Tater, who perked up once he saw Lance survive his first attempt. Sam watched carefully as Lee assisted the others, hoping she could perform flawlessly without his help. When it was Ty's turn, Lee hung back and let him manage on his own, as if daring him to attempt the rappel without his guidance. But like Sam, Ty had been paying close attention and was ready. He exited the window without a hitch.

Finally, Sam could put it off no longer. Lee flicked his head toward the window. "You're up, blondie." Sam constructed her seat and clipped onto the rope. She threw her right leg into the window and straddled the sill, gripping the rope with her right hand and checking with the safety on the ground. Lee took the opportunity to lean into her, sticking his head out the window and getting a confirmation from the belay that he was set.

As Lee leaned out, he slid his hand high up on Sam's thigh. Sam could feel his fingers digging into her flesh as she calculated the distance between her fist and his narrow face. She jerked her leg to shake him off and Lee jumped back, feigning surprise. By this time, Ty had made it back up to the floor. He entered the room just as Lee spoke.

"Take it easy, blondie. I'm just here to help," Lee cooed, patting Sam's leg as if to reassure her. The pat turned into a stroke and suddenly, a piece of webbing came hurtling toward Lee's face. They jumped when it hit, their heads pivoting toward the source. Ty braced in the center of the room, his fists knotted at his sides, anger morphing his features.

"You just better stand the fuck over there, Williams!" Lee shouted with an angry flick of his head. He snatched the webbing off the floor and threw it at Ty, who caught it in one hand as he crossed the room, his eyes never leaving Lee.

That was just the break Sam needed. She glanced down at the safety, gave him an affirming nod, and she was gone. She slid out of the window into a kneeling position against the wall and then stood up. She gripped the rope firmly, keeping her hand pressed against her hip to ensure her arm did not waver. As soon as she felt stable, she started her descent and never looked back.

~

The mornings had grown cooler and both men were dressed in sweatshirts. Their rhythm, by now familiar, was perfectly in sync. They made their way around the training field in silence under the lingering darkness of dawn.

Michaels had taken the morning off to catch up on paperwork. He didn't worry so much about missing the morning runs, now that Ty accompanied them. If fact, he sometimes got the feeling Daniels preferred to be alone with Ty. Michaels had watched as the commander had grown increasingly comfortable around the cadet. It gave Michaels a sense of peace, knowing there was someone else who could bring Daniels a bit of solace.

When they met up that morning, Daniels had noted Ty's dark mood. He was quieter than normal and seemed to be brooding. At first, Daniels attributed it to Michaels' absence. Perhaps Ty felt more comfortable with Michaels around. But Michaels didn't participate in their weekend runs and yet Ty always seemed at ease. Daniels didn't pry, he simply waited and watched.

When they were finished, they began their customary cooldown: two or three laps walking the course, depending on how much time they had. Today they were early, so they took their time. Normally, Ty would break the silence, not wanting to waste an opportunity to discuss tactics with the commander. When Ty didn't launch into his normal chatter, Daniels' concern grew. As they approached the backside of the course, Daniels put a hand to Ty's arm. The physical contact broke him from his reverie.

"What's going on this morning, Ty?" Both men stood with hands on hips as they slowed their breathing. Ty's eyes shifted to the pavement.

Ty was anxious to discuss the incident in the tower with Daniels, but felt constrained by his loyalty to Sam. When they had arrived home from training, Ty was still fuming. Sam tried to brush off the incident with Lee, but her dismissive attitude had further infuriated Ty and they had come close to their first argument.

What Ty could not understand was Sam's need to stay above the fray. Sam knew the last thing she needed was a complaint against an instructor. That was the surest way to be branded a "problem female" and Sam would have none of it. She could put up with Lee's bullshit and was not about to cause waves. She had left Ty's last night, refusing to discuss the matter further, both still angry. Now she sat in the library, poring over her notes, her demeanor still tinged with the chill from their discussion.

"I want to talk to you about something, but I don't want to betray a trust." Ty was unable to look at Daniels as he spoke. Daniels assumed he was referring to Samantha. He remained silent and waited for Ty to continue.

"We were with Lee yesterday," Ty began, eyeing Daniels before continuing. "The guy was out of line." Ty dropped his eyes again, hoping Daniels could interpret his silence.

Had Ty been looking at Daniels, he would have noted the tightening around the commander's mouth. Daniels felt a sinking feeling in his gut, knowing he shouldn't have allowed Lee free rein with the schedule. He flashed back to their confrontation in the tower, furious that his threats had been ignored.

"What happened?" Daniels asked stiffly. "I have to know in order to handle the situation." This was only partially true. Daniels knew he could depend on Ty's word without going into detail, but he was concerned about Samantha. Daniels remembered the look on her face when he saw Lee berating her about the knots; the subtle shake of her head, urging Daniels not to approach, to let her get through the incident on her own. Daniels felt confident that unless it was a truly egregious infraction, Sam would simply take it from Lee and never come forward.

"He kept putting his hands on her; during the quick-seat, even during the rappel. The guy's a piece of shit." Ty paused before muttering, "Sorry," hoping Daniels would excuse the insubordination.

"I'll take care of it," Daniels replied quietly, putting a hand on Ty's shoulder.

They finished their cooldown and headed inside.

~

Sam rubbed at her neck to relieve the tension, then shut her books and headed for the cafeteria. She was settling at a table, her coffee balanced precariously on her stack of books, when a team from Miami marched in. There were five of them and they were massive. They stood in line, gripping their small trays, laughing, and shoving as they pushed their way through the line. One of the men sported a dark sleeve of tattoos. He caught Sam's eye, elbowing the firefighter next to him, and throwing her a wink. Sam glued her eyes to her book as their laughter floated across the cafeteria. She shifted in her chair and tried to concentrate.

The men worked their way through checkout and settled noisily at a nearby table. They attacked their breakfasts and continued to banter. "That's one sweet little cadet!" Tattoo announced loudly as the men swung their heads in Sam's direction. Sam threw them a dirty look and returned to her studies.

"Whatcha' reading, sweetie?" he called over as the team continued shoveling, forks flying, the men grinning. Sam shot him a stink-eye as she held the book up for display. Tattoo jumped to his feet and sauntered over to her table, yanking out a chair and plunking himself down across from her. His teammates snickered as they gulped their food.

"Let's see." He snatched the book from Sam's hands, then slammed it shut and glanced at the cover.

Sam took a deep breath and leveled her tone. "Give me back my book, please."

He leaned toward her and grinned. "What's the matter? Can't I interest you in one of Miami's finest?" He puffed out his chest as the men encouraged him with grunts and nods.

Sam glared at him. "Only two things come out of Miami," she responded evenly. "Assholes and coconuts."

The men burst out laughing as Tattoo shoved her book across the table. He bolted to his feet, knocking over his chair in the process. He leaned over the table, bracing himself on powerful arms. "You've got a pretty smart mouth," he muttered through clenched teeth.

He didn't see Tanner sidle up to the table. Neither did Sam, until suddenly, he appeared, looming over Tattoo. Tanner came at him with a hard shove. The firefighter staggered sideways, trying to regain his balance as the chair went flying. "Get the fuck back to your group," Tanner growled.

Tattoo straightened, hitched up his belt, and kicked the chair aside with his boot before making his way back to his table.

"Good one, Sam," Tanner said with a wink before calmly strolling away.

~

The students gathered at the base of the tower for their final day of rappelling. Today, they would practice emergency escapes in full gear so they could become accustomed to the added weight of their packs. Although his first attempt had been clumsy, Mark had been buoyed by his second rappel. Michaels had worked through the rest of the group and then stayed late to allow Mark extra time on the rope. Mark was able to perform the rappel with few hiccups the second time around and was even confident enough to go a third time without assistance.

Sam was relieved to have their session with Lee behind them. As she and Ty headed out to the tower, Ty briefly touched her arm, trying to bridge the void that had opened during their argument. Sam gave him a quick smile.

The entire group seemed to have started the day in better spirits. They were feeling more confident about the session and tomorrow they would move on to extrication, where they would have the opportunity to destroy cars; something everyone was looking forward to.

The cadets stood loosely in formation, awaiting their instructions. They spoke in low tones through the sides of their mouths to avoid detection by the officers.

"Nice haircut, Tater," Lance whispered down the line. "They shave poodles where you got that done?" Snickers rippled through the cadets.

"Better than that fuckin' fright wig of yours," Mark replied with a smirk.

"Hey, I look damn good," Lance muttered through tight lips.

"Sam, what do you think?" Mark stole a glance in her direction. "We need a girl's opinion."

"First off, I'm not a girl, I'm a *wo-man!*" Sam chided quietly, grinning. "Second, I think Tater looks like a badass and makes all of you look like a bunch of pansies." Tate gave an appreciative snort.

"Put a lid on it, guys," Jimmy hissed. "I'm not in the mood for an ass-chewing."

"What the heck's goin' on over there?" Ty murmured, squinting into the morning sun to peer at the officers.

The instructors were locked in a huddle, poring over their clipboards, sorting through some issue that had arisen prior to class. Michaels looked especially perturbed. He was having heated words with Lee and didn't seem to be making any progress. Tanner finally broke from the cluster and stomped over to the students.

"Hit the deck!" he barked as the students snapped to attention.

Lee sauntered over and began detailing the day. The groups would head into the tower to perform their emergency escapes. The instructors were lining up in front of the cadets, waiting for them to break from formation. Just as Lee was about to release them, he turned to Johnny. "Simms, your group's with me again."

The cadets stood in anxious silence. Ty fumed. Not only were they stuck with Lee again, but Daniels had let it happen. Ty would never have confided in the commander, had he not believed Daniels would look out for them.

"You girls got a problem?" Lee grumbled when the group failed to move.

"No, sir," Johnny replied, as he bent to gather his gear. The cadets slowly filed into the tower. Ty glanced across the field, searching for Daniels, but the field was empty.

~

Michaels was livid. He realized what Lee was up to the minute he saw the change in the schedule. There was only one reason to switch up the groups and he knew it had to do with Smith. Why Lee wanted to push the issue was beyond Michaels. Surely Lee knew they were keeping an eye on him.

The change in schedule had launched an all-out turf war. Tanner resented the change, since he had hoped to work with his same group. Lee had even reassigned Mark to an adjunct, which Michaels refused to go along with. He had worked long and hard to prepare Mark for the rappel and he'd be damned if he was going to let Lee fuck it up.

Lee finally relented on Mark's group but refused to give up Smith's. Michaels knew it would be impossible to monitor Lee's behavior, since the groups would be working on different floors. The guy would have free rein and there was no time to get word to Daniels. Michaels gathered Mark's group and headed to the second floor.

Sam knew the change in assignment was her fault, which meant the group would have to suffer just so Lee could give her a hard time throughout the day. They trudged up the stairs to the third floor. The only sounds were voices floating in from the other floors and the instructors' shouts as they directed their groups. Ty's face was like stone and Sam feared he would lash out again and threaten his standing in class. The last thing Ty needed was to get embroiled with an instructor. Lee's reputation at the academy was secure and Sam felt sure he would prevail if it came down to a battle of wills.

When they arrived on the third floor, they donned their turnout gear. They threw their airpacks on and stood in a semicircle around the window as Lee reviewed the exit. Sam felt more protected in full gear. It gave her an added layer of defense against Lee's hands.

"Here's how it's going to go down," Lee announced, leaning against the wall adjacent to the window, his gloves gripped in a tight fist against his hip. "You'll perform your exit and then stage below on deck. When all of you are through, we'll break and go through it again."

Immediately reading Lee's intent, Sam quickly stepped forward. "I'll go first!" She yanked her gloves from her pocket and slapped them against her thigh to loosen them up. Sam didn't want to take a chance on Lee saving her for last and having her alone on the floor. Lee glared at her.

"Not so fast, blondie. I say who goes when." Lee scanned the group. "Williams, get in the window." When Ty didn't move, Lee's voice rose a decibel. "I said get your ass in the window, pretty-boy, or you'll be kissin' my fuckin' boots!"

Ty glanced at Sam, furious that he would be stuck on deck while Sam awaited her turn, certain that Lee would save her for last. Lee eyed him and grinned. "Don't worry about Pet. I'll see that she's safe." He casually slipped on his gloves, cracked his knuckles, and then folded his arms across his chest.

Ty marched to the window and grabbed hold of the rope. He clipped in, straddled the sill, threw one more glance at Sam, and then made a hasty exit. When he landed on the tarmac, he threw off the rope and slammed his helmet to the concrete.

"You're next, Draper," Lee said with a flick of his chin.

Trey prepped his gear and clipped on to the rope. His slender frame was well-suited for the rappel. He was able to slip into the window, even with the added bulk of his airpack, and swing out onto the exterior of the building with little trouble.

Lance went next and one by one each member of their group performed the exit. Tate was the last man called. He touched Sam's arm lightly as he passed and then anxiously maneuvered himself into the window. Twice his tank clanked against the window frame, sending a jarring reverberation through his teeth, but he hung in there patiently and was able to adjust. He smiled nervously as he disappeared below the sill.

"So here we are, blondie," Lee sneered as he stood before the window. The light was cutting harsh lines over his shoulders, carving his face in cynical angles. He strolled the few steps to where she stood, then eyed her up and down. "Let's just do an equipment check before you head out." The words slid from his tongue. Sam could feel the blood rise in her face, and she took a few quick breaths to alleviate the tension. Her hands felt numb and she thought she might hyperventilate before she ever had a chance to exit.

Lee started by examining her gear. Sam knew she was prepared, and he would find nothing wrong, yet he kept up the charade of the inspection. "Everything here looks good," he said, stepping back and looking her up and down again. "Just be sure those straps are down tight." He stepped up close and shoved his hands beneath the shoulder straps of her pack, just below her collarbones. Sam remembered how Daniels had released her chinstrap during inspection, how carefully he had handled her gear. Lee forced his hands under and gave her straps a quick jerk, which resonated through her body. He then pulled her close. Sam held her breath as his face came within inches. She shifted her eyes to the window, which seemed to break his intent. He gave an angry jerk of her straps, but instead of releasing them, he left his hands in place and slid them down and over her chest. It happened so fast Sam didn't even have time to knock them away. She stood frozen, too stunned to respond. Suddenly, a booming voice broke from the back of the room.

"*Officer Lee!*"

Their heads shot in unison toward the voice. Daniels stood in the doorway, his feet set, hands shoved stiffly in his pockets. Lee ripped his gaze from Daniels long enough to shoot a daggered glance at Sam, but she couldn't tear her eyes from the commander. His presence had immobilized them both. Lee stood dumbly, still gripping Sam's straps before dropping them like hot coals and backing away. Lee glanced from Daniels to Sam before giving a disgusted huff as he marched from the tower.

XV

The first day of extrication training was spent in the classroom, going over tools, technique, and safety procedures. In the morning, the students would be shuffled onto a bus, driven to a junkyard, and let loose. They couldn't wait. It would be good to get off the training grounds; they craved a change of scenery.

On Friday morning they loaded their gear onto the bus. Tanner and two of the adjuncts accompanied them; Michaels followed in a separate truck with the tools. Tanner lounged among the students, laughing, and jawing and blending in as if he were one of them. Everyone liked Tanner. The guy was so amiable they could even forgive his constant barking.

Sam had noticed a subtle change in the instructors. Although they still kept up a constant barrage of orders and never missed the opportunity to dole out an ass-chewing, they had mellowed in temperament. They spoke to the students like normal human beings more often. They didn't seem to hold them in such low esteem as they had the first weeks of class and Sam wondered if it was all part of the process: degradation slowly morphing into respect.

"Who's got the fuckin' water?" Tanner yelled over the heads of the cadets as they bounced along in the bus.

"Here you go, sir," Tate called from the rear, cocking his arm, and launching the bottle. The bottle sailed, careening past Tanner's head in a near miss. With lightning-fast reactions contradicting his bulk, Tanner ducked, and the bottle went skittering along the dusty floorboard.

"What the fuck, Tater?" Tanner exclaimed, clambering from his seat to retrieve the bottle.

"Sorry, sir. My fault," Tate replied sheepishly, shriveling in his seat.

"How many times a day do you think Tanner says 'fuck'?" Trey asked thoughtfully, eyeing the burly officer as the group looked on.

"I have no fucking idea," Ty replied, grinning, and craning his neck. "Mark?"

"Fuck if I know," Mark replied with a shrug, swinging his head. "Sam?"

"It's a fucking mystery," Sam declared, cocking her brow.

"Assholes," Trey muttered, as the group around him chortled.

They pulled into the junkyard and drove to an area in the back where four dilapidated cars were spread out on an open field. These would be their guinea pigs. They would practice using a variety of tools to familiarize themselves with how the tools worked, to get a feel for the heft of them in their hands. The instructors broke the students into groups and assigned each group to a vehicle.

They started small. They were each allowed to take out a window using the center punch. Johnny went first. He clutched the small, screwdriver-sized tool in his hand and pressed the sharp tip of the punch against the window, waiting for its lethal response. As the spring-loaded punch inside was activated, its tip jetted out, shattering the window in tiny fragments. It was pure magic.

Then they moved on to the larger tools. Each group would work on their respective vehicle while the tools circulated between them, so that each student would be given the opportunity to test his skills. Sam's team was composed of the regulars. The smaller number of groups was a vivid reminder of how much their class had shrunk.

They started with the reciprocating saw, cutting through the hood of the car to get a feel for its bite and kick. Its blade cut cleanly, reminding Sam of those T.V. commercials that show the angry chef slicing tomatoes and tin cans.

Next, they used the hydraulic rams to lift the steering column. They positioned the rams beneath the column and slowly extended them, forcing the column up with little trouble. Then they moved on to the cutters. Also run by hydraulics, the cutters were shaped like a parrot's beak and cut through the posts of the car as if slicing cheese. The power of the tools was astounding. The students quickly transformed the car into a convertible by cutting through each of its posts and tossing the roof aside amidst cheers.

Finally, they moved on to the true workhorse of the extrication toolkit: the jaws. Sam fought against the weight of the tool as Mark and Bill made a purchase in the door jamb. She shoved the tip of the tool into the purchase and twisted its handle, causing the jaws to slowly spread, easily tearing the door away from the Nader pin. As the door pulled away from the pin it issued a resounding "pop." Tanner looked on with a grin. "Now that's how you pop a door!"

The morning wore on and they were so caught up in the destruction, they worked straight through lunch. They finally broke midafternoon, collapsing in the grass, exhausted. They had scarfed their lunch, chasing it with gallons of water to ward off dehydration, when Tate wandered back to the car. Originally, it had been a Chrysler four-door, its interior at one time a deep brown to match the mud-brown exterior. Now it was the color of a dried-out turd, the interior sweat-stained, torn, and smelling strongly of mold.

Tate was soon joined by Bo, who had grown up around his uncle's shop. Bo continued to struggle with his grades, barely holding onto a C. His position in the class remained tenuous and the stress forced him into long bouts of silence. He rarely spoke.

They managed to pry the torn-up hood from its hitch, using the pry bar to brace it open. Then they started to tinker. Their tinkering soon drew other students as one by one, they abandoned their lunches and made for the car. Sam watched them gather like flies to fly-paper; once they landed, they were stuck. Within minutes, Tanner was drawn into the group.

"What are you boys doin'? Tryin' to resuscitate her?" he asked as he diligently worked his toothpick to dislodge a stubborn shred of salami from between his teeth.

"I think we can get her going, Sir," Tate replied enthusiastically. "We've inventoried her guts and she seems to have all her main components in place. You mind if we give her a shot?"

"Tater, if you can get her goin', you boys can take her for a spin, for all I care," he answered, chuckling. Tanner knew by looking at the vehicle its days of running were long past. Their destruction had been total. The car no longer had a roof, the doors and windows were gone, they had used an ax to chop through the windshield, and all four tires were flat. This would take a miracle, but let them go at it, if they wanted. He lumbered over and spread out on the grass near Sam.

Over the course of their training, Sam had noticed that Tanner never seemed to get too close. He always maintained a safety zone of at least three feet whenever they spoke. Sam did not take offense; the distance seemed to put the officer at ease. They sat back and watched the men work.

After twenty minutes of tinkering, the cadets gave it a try. Tate twisted wires beneath the dash while Bo worked on the engine, tweaking its rusty components. After several failed attempts, the engine choked twice and died. They made a few adjustments and tried again. This time they were rewarded with a mild sputter from the engine. Buoyed by the sputter, they continued to tinker until finally the engine gasped and wheezed. It backfired a thick blot of smoke from its tailpipe and idled with a loud metallic rattle. Tate sprang from the car and grabbed Bo, joining him in a giant bear hug to celebrate their success. It was the first time Bo had smiled in weeks.

They glanced over at Tanner, who was lying back, his thick arms folded behind his head, grinning as he chewed on his pick. He gave them a nod and they were off. Tate jumped behind the wheel; Bo climbed into the passenger's seat. They threw the car in gear and eased it onto the open grass, bare wheels grinding against its twisted frame. The engine sputtered and threatened to die, but they managed to keep it going as they whooped and hollered, spinning it in wide donuts across the field, waving as if they were grand marshals in some dilapidated parade. The rest of the group stood by, cheering them on.

When the class arrived back at the academy, they quickly unloaded the equipment and headed for the showers. They changed into whatever clothes they had with them – shorts, sweatpants, sweatshirts – and Sam's group drove in a small caravan to Johnny's, stopping on the way for groceries and alcohol. They arrived at Johnny's, unloaded the supplies, and filtered throughout the house. Johnny and Bill worked the grill; Tate, Sam, and Trey prepped the food. Shane and Bo assisted with the grilling while Ty and Lance lounged on the couch, ribbing each other and sorting through Johnny's CDs in search of music they could agree on.

They gorged on burgers and baked potatoes, ravenous from the day's training. They sat back afterwards, full and content, clustered in small pockets of conversation. Sam and Mark were sitting at the table, their heads together, discussing aspects of the military; their favorite topic. Ty watched them from the couch, noting how the bottle of gin they had been nursing was quickly evaporating. Mark and Sam were laughing. Mark was shoving her shoulder as she made fun of him for some arcane comment. Ty couldn't help but notice how small Sam looked next to Mark's giant frame. Their arms, side by side, were incomparable: Mark's massive bicep next to Sam's slender limb. She looked almost delicate, as if Mark could snap her in two with one quick jerk.

The evening progressed and the group soon tired. They headed for their vehicles and Ty steadied Sam as she climbed into the car. They arrived at her condo and made their way through the lobby and into the elevator. Sam entertained herself by making fun of Ty's sobriety, yanking on the hood of his sweatshirt as he stepped from the elevator. Ty held her arm to steady her as they made their way to her door. He used the key she had given him, since Sam seemed incapable of locating hers, and she stumbled into the hallway with a giggle. She then swung her head around, inspecting her palms.

"I forgot my stuff in your car!" she exclaimed, doubling over with laughter.

"I'll go get it." Ty placed a steadying hand to her shoulder. "You get yourself together," he griped in his best parental tone. He then headed back down to the car.

Damn Mark and his bottle of gin, Sam thought as she struggled to brush her teeth without staggering. All she wanted to do was sleep. Her back and shoulders were aching from the tools and the stiffness of fatigued muscles was closing in fast. She tossed her toothbrush onto the counter and headed for bed. She didn't bother undressing. She wore her academy shorts and sweatshirt, so she simply curled up on top of the bed and was asleep instantly.

When Ty came back up to the apartment, he looked in the living room, but Sam wasn't there. He glanced at the balcony, thinking she had stepped out for some air, but it was empty as well. He moved softly down the hallway to her bedroom and could see her curled up on her side, her breathing deep and steady against the silence of the room. The picture window ushered in moonlight, recreating the familiar scene of his early morning wanderings.

Sam loved an open window in winter; the smell of the cold and the noise of traffic lulled her to sleep. Tonight, the window stood open a few inches and the cool night air lifted the curtains in gentle puffs. Ty walked to the other side of the bed and eased himself down beside her. He smiled to himself when he thought how he would tease her in the morning.

He rose to go, but then faltered. He lowered himself back onto the bed and stretched out on his side, his head resting in his palm above a bent elbow. Sam lay with her back to him. Ty studied the outline of her body and thought back to how she had looked next to Mark, how delicate she had seemed at that moment, and suddenly he realized the word that had been playing against the back of his mind, one he normally didn't associate with Sam. Sitting next to Mark, Sam had looked feminine.

It wasn't that Ty never thought of Sam as feminine. His memories of her on the tarmac were proof positive. Ty was all too aware of her fine features: her shapely legs, her warm smile, and the fluid movements of her body. It's just that he usually tried to think of her asexually, as a brother thinks of a sister; aware of her sexuality but feeling a twinge of guilt for noticing.

Occasionally, he had been moved by her: the closeness of their bodies as they worked in the tower or searched a darkened room. But Ty refused to entangle his thoughts of Sam with thoughts of sex. His few sexual encounters in high school had been awkward affairs that had left him feeling embarrassed and obligated. He didn't want to muddy their relationship with the confusion of sexual intimacy. Things were too good between them. Sam resided in a place in his mind free from the discomfiture of sex.

Yet he couldn't stop looking at the smooth S-curve she made on the bed, how the mattress conformed to the lines of her body. He reached out and touched the back of her head, gently stroking her hair. His hand moved to her neck and he noticed how soft the skin was just below her hairline. He could just make out the fine hairs that graced the back of her neck. They were mesmerizing.

His hand found its way down her back. Without thinking, he reached underneath her sweatshirt to touch the base of her spine, feeling the small knots of vertebrae, the tautness of the overlying skin. His hand worked its way up her back, his fingers following the dual line of muscle along her spine. Sam's breathing deepened and Ty felt himself grow hard. The guilt came in a rush, yet he couldn't stop. The beer and the lateness of the hour anchored him in place; his limbs refused to move.

Ty rolled onto his back and unzipped his pants. He turned his head to look at her as he reached inside, taking hold of himself. He closed his eyes as his mind struggled to separate the feel of his cock from the sight of Sam next to him, but the juxtaposition was confounding. Suddenly, it wasn't Ty's hand but Sam's. Ty imagined her leaning over and slowly stroking him as he gazed into her eyes. The imaginary Sam then moved down on him, taking him into the warmth of her mouth. For a split second, Ty could feel the faint ridge of Sam's teeth before her lips encased him.

Ty gave an audible moan and was jolted back to reality. He rolled off the bed and hurried to the bathroom, shutting the door behind him, and flicking on the light. He leaned against the wall, head back, eyes slammed shut, as he fought to control his breathing. He quickly arranged himself and zipped his pants. He sat down, his head in his hands, trying to erase the image of Sam from his mind.

He splashed cold water on his face, buried it in the sweet smell of her towel, then snapped off the light and stole back to her darkened room. Sam still slept, her breathing steady and deep. Ty grabbed his keys from the dresser and fled.

~

As Sam slept, she dreamt of the tower. She was standing on one of the upper floors, yet when she peered out the window, the skies were dark and painted with stars. A cold wind streamed in from the darkness, bringing with it the smell of pines and the aroma of burnt wood, reminding her of the mountains outside of Asheville where she and her father would hike, their long walks along rocky paths that cut through thick, fragrant forests. She remembered the icy winter air, its painful sting in her lungs.

And suddenly Daniels appeared before her. They stood together in the center of the tower floor, a dim light burning in the back of the room, his eyes lowered to his hands in which he held a section of rope. He worked the rope into a knot, but his hands kept faltering. He manipulated the smooth material into intricate folds, doubling it back on itself to complete the knot, but his efforts were in vain; the rope seemed to stretch forever.

Sam watched his face as he worked, noting the sharp curve of his jaw, how the muscles along his face tightened and relaxed with the movement of his hands. She noticed his brown lashes, how they contrasted with the grey of his eyes. They flickered as he monitored the progress of the knot.

As Sam watched, Daniels' eyes darted up to meet hers. They stared with that steely intensity, burning into her until she slammed hers shut to escape the assault. And then his hand was on her. He stroked the back of her hair, his fingers gently following the contours of her skull. His hand rose and fell, gliding against her hair until it made its way to the back of her neck. Sam kept her eyes closed, but she knew intuitively that he still clutched the rope. She could smell his skin, just inches from her face; feel the warmth radiating from it.

His fingers traced the back of her neck, barely touching her skin. They continued down her back and her flesh rose to meet them. When they got to the base of her spine, they found their way under her shirt and she could feel the smoothness of their surfaces as they made their way back up. And then his mouth was on her. Sam felt unsteady on her feet, as if swaying against the cold air flowing in through the open window. The next thing she knew she was falling, falling through that cold window and out into the night.

XVI

With ten weeks behind them and an equal number of students dropped, they were feeling the effects of the intensive training. Because they had only three weeks left, their exposure to live fire would increase, with another burn scheduled for Tuesday, and special burns slated for Wednesday, including a simulated car fire. It was going to be a working week. The only saving grace was having the long weekend off for Thanksgiving.

The cadets had just finished PT and were heading out to the tower to practice firefighter survival tactics. The morning ride in had been quiet. In fact, the entire weekend had been subdued. Sam spent Saturday morning recovering from her hangover, swimming endless laps trying to rid herself of the headache and nausea. Ty had come over that evening but had been quiet and standoffish. Sunday hadn't been much different. He had met Daniels for a run, which had become their weekly ritual, but had spent the rest of the day on his own. Sam didn't push the issue. She never minded a quiet day alone, especially considering their week ahead.

But when Ty remained withdrawn on the ride in, Sam became concerned. "Everything OK over there?" she asked as they drove in silence. Ty kept his eyes on the road.

"Yeah, I'm fine," he replied, distractedly. "Sorry," he muttered with a weak smile.

"Let me know if there's anything I can do." Sam flipped open her book as Ty gave a nervous glance in her direction.

Sam let him brood. Being surrounded by the men for so long had left her insensible to their dispositions. She felt numbed to their presence, as if she could no longer distinguish where one left off and the other began. They had become one giant blur of testosterone. Even when her hormones peaked, it had passed with barely a notice. Being exposed to so many belches and farts simply destroyed a woman's sense of mystery.

The morning would be spent practicing survival tactics. The afternoon would culminate with a sequence of drills where the students would combine their skills to make an emergency exit from the structure. First, they would simulate assisting a partner who had run out of air. They would begin with a two-man search, during which one of the students would play the role of a firefighter whose tank had run dry. The victim would be chosen by a slap to the helmet from one of the instructors. The student with air would then have the victim lock into his system through a quick-connect hose located on each airpack. Once the victim was hooked in and breathing off his partner's tank, the pair would reverse their search and exit the room.

The entire drill would be performed blindfolded to simulate the blackout conditions of a real fire. First, they would partner up and practice the quick-connect drill sitting face to face on the floor. Once they had the technique down, they would integrate it with the search.

Michaels was in charge of their group. Sam looked forward to being under his direction; she had developed such a deep respect for the officer after seeing his efforts with Mark. His demeanor had a calming effect on everyone around him.

They sat on the floor in pairs, facing each other. Michaels handed out the blackouts and they slipped them over their masks. The rest of the drill would be done via touch. Ty and Sam sat close together, one leg bent in front, the other spread to the side so they could keep their bodies close enough to connect their hoses. Sam would play the firefighter who had run out of air and hook in with Ty. They would then reverse roles and Sam would assist Ty. Once everyone was blacked out, they started the drill.

They sat in full gear, breathing off their tanks. Sam reached out blindly and tapped Ty on the chest. "I'm out of air, buddy!" she called, her voice muffled by her mask.

Ty reached back and located his quick-connect hose by tracing it from the base of his tank to the point where it attached at his shoulder. He unclipped it and reached forward. In the meantime, Sam unclipped hers and their hands grasped open space until they came in contact. Sam guided his hand to her hose and after a moment's fumbling, he was securely clipped in. They then reversed roles and worked through the drill as if Ty were the one in distress.

Once everyone had the hang of it, they congregated in the hallway so they could take turns incorporating the emergency assist into their search. Lance and Trey went first. They were instructed to search the room until Michaels slapped one of them on the helmet. At that point, the tagged individual would advise his partner he was out of air, and the two would work through the quick-connect drill. Once connected, they would reverse their search and make their way out of the room.

The drill began. Trey moved with ease, but Lance's gangling frame was all arms and legs. The blackouts didn't help matters. Lance had trouble maintaining contact with Trey, so he kept up a running monologue as they crawled.

"How we doin', Trey? I'm right here, buddy! We're makin' good progress," Lance shouted, his muffled yells becoming more chopped as his breathing increased from the effort.

"Shut the hell up, won't you!" Trey shot at him as he crawled along the edge of the room. When they were deep in, Michaels slapped Lance's helmet to start the quick-connect drill.

"*Trey, I'm out of air! Trey, hook in! Hook in!*" Lance yelled as he waved an arm through the air, trying to locate his partner.

"I'm right here, asshole!" Trey replied, winded. They stopped the search, groped until they located each other, and then got into position. Trey tried to take hold of Lance's hose while at the same time, Lance waved his arm about, trying to locate Trey's hand. They blindly slapped at air, making no progress.

"Lance, what the hell are you doing?" Michaels yelled from across the room.

"Sir, I'm trying to save my own life, here!" Lance replied as the rest of the students stifled their laughter. They finally got their hoses connected, but then had to find their way out of the room. Trey tried crawling forward, only to run headlong into Lance, who had gotten on all fours and frozen.

"Get the fuck out of my way!" Trey yelled, swinging a glove, hoping to locate Lance's head. Lance finally got moving, only to get tangled in the hose, binding them in a knot. Each time they moved, the hose was pulled tight, their crawling brought to a halt.

Michaels finally stomped over and ripped off their blackouts. "You guys are a complete clusterfuck! Get the hell up and let someone else go! You can try again later." He turned back for the group to choose the next victims.

Sam and Ty looked at each other as their hands rose simultaneously. They donned their masks, blacked them out, and dropped into position in the doorway. Sam would lead the search. Ty would maintain contact by keeping his right hand in contact with her boot. Michaels gave them the go-ahead and they were off.

They worked methodically through the room, Sam following along the wall using her right hand, Ty sweeping the floor with his left. When they were about twenty feet in, Michaels slapped Ty's helmet. Ty grabbed Sam's leg. "I'm out of air, Sam!"

They slid into position: face to face with their right legs bent, left legs extended. Ty located his hose, Sam found hers, and their hands touched in midair, perfectly aligned. Sam clipped into Ty's hose and they got back on their hands and knees, this time with the wall on Sam's left as they reversed their search. She could feel Ty beside her, his body close. She noted their breathing was practically in sync, both consciously controlling their respirations. After several minutes, they found their way out and the drill was done. They ripped off their blackouts, smiling and panting.

"Now *that's* how you do it!" Ty announced to the group. Michaels smiled dryly, slapping Ty's helmet as he passed through the doorway.

The rest of the pairs went, and they broke for lunch, heading to their usual spot under the trees. They lounged around on the grass after devouring their sandwiches, catching up on their weekends. Sam glanced over at Tate, who was lying back in the shade, his arms flung out at his sides as if he had just fallen from the sky.

"You're looking pretty slim, Tater. Nice job," she said as Tate sat up and brushed the grass from his shoulders.

"Thanks. I've been trying," he replied, smoothing his tee shirt to show off his contours. "It's really just a matter of regulating how many calories I consume and trying to offset it by the amount I'm burning each day on the field. It seems to be working." He beamed with pride.

Lance could not resist. He slowly sat up, rolled onto his hands and knees, and started crawling toward Tate like a stripper onstage. "Oh, Tater, I just can't keep my hands off you," he said in a girlish tenor, licking his pouty lips. "You are such a fuckin' studmuffin! Come here and let me have a bite!" His arms and legs pumped as he reached Tate and pounced. Tate tried to evade him but wasn't fast enough. Before he knew it, Lance was on top of him, planting smacking kisses on his cheeks, which by now were flushed a deep pink. Lance's long legs kicked at the air, trying to gain traction.

"Get off me, you big moron!" Tate cried, trying to force Lance's gangling frame aside.

They rolled around in the grass, Tate grunting, Lance making loud smacking sounds beside his face. The wrestling eventually worked Lance's bunker pants low on his hips, revealing white cheeks and a hairy crack of ass. Trey howled at him.

"For Christ's sake, Lance! Crack kills! Pull up your fucking pants!"

The group laughed raucously, throwing remnants of their lunch at Lance to try to move him off. He finally tired and rolled away, sprawling in the grass next to Tate. By then, Tanner was standing over them, shaking his head.

"Don't make me turn the hose on you two," he said as he strolled away, chuckling.

"Take it easy, Lance," Sam teased, throwing Trey a quick wink. "You wouldn't want to make your husband jealous." Trey eyed her but played along.

"What are you talking about?" Lance replied earnestly, staring at Sam as he clambered to his feet. He hitched his suspenders over his shoulders and planted his spindly hands on his hips.

"You know," Sam cajoled. "Trey," she said with a flick of her head in Trey's direction. "It's OK, we all know you guys are a couple." She bagged up her trash, working hard to keep a straight face. "Besides, it's not like you're the only couple in the group." She gave another flick of her head, darting her eyes to Mark and Bill. Mark's jaw fell open and Bill instinctively puffed out his chest.

"What the fuck, Sam?" Mark exclaimed, big-eyed.

"Look boys, there are plenty of gay firefighters out there. You guys have nothing to be ashamed of." Her eyes twinkled as she glanced at Ty. Ty ducked his grin behind a water bottle.

"That's it!" Mark exclaimed, bolting for her, Bill automatically following his lead.

Mark grabbed hold of Sam's legs as she tried to scurry away. Bill snatched her arms and they carried her, kicking, and screaming, to a large grassy puddle near the hydrant.

"Don't be ashamed, Mark! It's OK that you're queer!" Sam hollered, laughing maniacally, and kicking her boots. Mark was now laughing along, as he and Bill swung her up and over the puddle.

"Here's what you get, Sammy!" he yelled, as they let go of her limbs. Sam landed with a fantastic SeaWorld splash, her bunker pants and tee shirt, drenched. She gripped her belly, laughing, as she wallowed in the water. The men around her howled as Mark and Bill plunked down in the grass.

"You guys know I'm not gay, right?" Lance whined, igniting another round of hysterics.

The afternoon session would be like the morning, only they would first have to locate a victim before simulating the out-of-air scenario. They would then have to get themselves and the victim out of the room. The challenge would be dragging the victim while being clipped into each other's packs.

The groups headed to their respective floors. As they assembled their gear, Michaels emerged from the stairwell with Daniels close in tow. The students' chatter came to a halt when they noticed the commander standing in the doorway. He crossed his arms, leaned against the frame, and scanned the group. Sam quickly dropped her eyes. Daniels' sudden appearance brought forth the remnants of a dream.

She was in the tower and Daniels stood before her. He held a piece of rope and Sam was watching him work. The dream turned hazy after that, but as she stole a glance at him in the doorway, pieces of it emerged from the fog.

She remembered his hand on her head, his touch at the base of her spine. Sam felt her face flush as she focused on the floor. The smell of the tower intensified the memory, and she could suddenly remember the feel of his mouth. She nervously checked her pack and readjusted her helmet.

"Smith and Williams!" Michaels barked, startling her gloves from her hand. She snatched them from the floor and then turned to Ty. They quickly donned their masks and helmets, then dropped into position at the doorway as they slipped on their gloves. Sam noted the determination in Ty's face. He gave a quick nod before slapping on his blackout. Sam returned the nod and pulled the blackout over her mask.

They worked the same way as before, quickly yet methodically. Ty took the lead, Sam following on his left, sweeping the floor with her tool to locate the victim. They had moved deep into the room and Sam had the same feeling she'd had when Daniels had watched her search. She could feel him moving through the room, monitoring their progress. But this time, she felt he was there to see Ty work. Sam had noticed how Daniels watched Ty. Not with the same intensity with which he looked at her, but with a look of admiration, as if he enjoyed seeing Ty work and progress. He looked on Ty with pride.

They located the victim, each grabbing hold of an arm, and reversed their search. That's when Michaels slapped Sam's helmet, indicating she was out of air. Sam called to Ty and they quickly slid into position, bodies close, legs overlapping. They located their hoses, found each other's hands, and were clipped in in no time. They then resumed crawling, dragging the victim between them. Ty hugged the wall as they shared the burden of the dummy. Sam crawled beside him, their shoulders touching.

They worked by sense of touch, the floor smooth beneath Sam's hands, Ty's arm constantly sweeping the wall to lead them out. When they finally made it out the door, they pulled off their masks and inhaled deeply, trying to catch their breath. As they stood up, Daniels strode past them, slapping Ty on the back and smiling.

~

Ty felt better. The incident on the bed with Sam had bothered him for days. He felt guilty; immoral, even. His feelings for Sam ran deep and he felt he had betrayed her with his actions. Ty tried to write the incident off as too many beers, too little sleep. But seeing her again ushered in the confusion he had felt lying next to her. Ty wanted things to remain simple, he wanted their friendship free of confusion. He was determined to keep his head.

Being back on the training field helped. It brought them back to familiar turf. They performed so well together, like two parts of a single mechanism. They had spent so much time as partners that they could read each other's movements, anticipate each other's actions. Ty was glad Daniels had seen them work. He seemed pleased with their performance.

His time with Daniels had become another important aspect of Ty's life. The more time they spent together, the more comfortable Ty felt around him. Daniels didn't intimidate him as before. Ty was still in awe of the man: his accomplishments, his demeanor on the field, and the way he ran the academy. But he'd noticed a subtle change in the commander. Not only was

Ty more relaxed around Daniels, but Daniels also seemed more relaxed around Ty. Daniels smiled more, even laughed on occasion. It was hard to believe he was the same stern individual from the first weeks of class.

Ty wondered if Daniels was ever lonely. He never spoke of other people in his life. Ty didn't even know if the commander had children, if he had ever been married. Although Daniels seemed more at ease, he still resided behind a wall; a wall Ty had yet to breach.

~

Daniels was pleased. He got so much pleasure from watching Ty on the field. The boy followed instructions well, his performance was exceptional, and he was making good grades on his exams. Daniels had come to appreciate their time together. He looked forward to their morning runs at the academy, and when the weekend rolled around, he always anticipated their runs along the greenway. After the run, they would make their way to the picnic table set off from the path, take their water and towels, spread out along the benches, and catch up on the week's events. Ty would discuss his lessons, drilling Daniels relentlessly on procedures and tactics, admitting when he was having difficulty with a certain subject. Daniels was always surprised by Ty's candor. Ty kept nothing hidden. Everything about him was out in the open, tangible.

In a way, Daniels was Ty's polar opposite. He envied the boy's ingenuousness. Talking to Ty made Daniels long to open up; his candidness worked like a salve, drawing the emotions Daniels had buried for so long slowly to the surface. Sometimes, when they were cooling down, Daniels found himself wanting to discuss the events of his past, as if wanting to unburden himself, to shed the weight of grief he had carried for so long. He grappled with these feelings. As Ty's superior, he felt he should maintain some semblance of authority, a degree of distance. But Ty was so unassuming, so completely without guile, that Daniels felt his barriers crumble. He truly cared for the boy.

~

Michaels had noticed a change. Daniels seemed different, as if the man had morphed into a warmer version of his former self. Not that he had shed his cool demeanor on the field; Daniels was still relentless when it came to running the academy. His rigid standards remained in place and Daniels guarded them like a sentry. But on their morning runs, as they made their way around the field in the early light of morning, he noticed a new cheerfulness about Daniels, a lightness of heart. The change was most apparent whenever Ty approached: the softening of Daniels' features, the way they laughed together, the perfect ease the two men shared.

Michaels envied them. His relationship with Daniels had always been foremost in his life, yet despite their friendship, Michaels had made little progress in developing a deeper closeness with the commander. He knew how Daniels battled his past, his hesitancy to engage with others. Seeing him with Ty gave Michaels a renewed hope that the commander might one day open up. Michaels found it amazing that a boy as young as Ty had been able to penetrate Daniels' tough exterior; that Ty had been the one person Daniels chose to let in. It was something beautiful to watch.

~

The Tuesday burns went well. Since their training was drawing to a close, they started combining their skills. They no longer simply entered the burn room with a hoseline. Now they practiced arriving on scene, advancing a hoseline, positioning for entry, and working in unison to achieve their goals. After numerous practice evolutions, they were now working in well-coordinated teams. The instructors were pleased, their hard work coming to fruition.

The evolutions also gave the students an opportunity to lead; Johnny was a natural. His calm reserve was perfectly suited for directing crews and he was able to coordinate the teams without letting the activities overwhelm him. His years as a medic, overseeing the care of critical patients and directing complex treatment strategies, translated easily on the fire ground. Michaels and Tanner were impressed.

The afternoon would be spent combatting car fires. The simulator was a burned-out hull in the shape of a generic automobile, positioned just south of the tower in the middle of the adjacent field. It was plumbed with natural gas lines that were controlled by a panel on the other side of the field. The instructor could adjust the flames, depending on the actions of the crews.

They broke for lunch as the skies darkened and a steady rain began to fall. As long as there was no lightning, they could proceed with the training. Michaels stood by, ear cocked to the horizon, listening intently for the first crack of thunder, searching the skies for random bolts. As the instructors set up the drill, the cadets stood in small clusters, their helmets forming rivulets of water down their backs. The November days had grown chilly and they shivered despite their heavy gear.

Johnny, Tate, Ty, and Sam were standing in a huddle, discussing their approach as they watched the first group advance. Mark and Bill wandered over, bored with awaiting their turn. Bill was stomping his oversized boot in a nearby puddle, trying to get a rise out of Mark. Mark ignored him until finally turning and tackling him to the ground. They rolled around in the mud until Bill finally surrendered. The group was caught up in their antics, oblivious to the silent approach of Michaels and Daniels.

Johnny was the first to notice the officers and quickly braced, clearing his throat and barking, "Guys!" The students snapped to attention, surprised by the officers' sudden appearance, the sternness of their faces. The last they had seen of Michaels he had been coaching one of the groups.

"Ty, can you come with us?" Daniels said quietly as the rain poured over the brim of his hat. His jacket was soaked through, but he appeared not to notice. Michaels' expression was just as serious; his face chiseled in stone.

Ty glanced at Sam as the officers turned abruptly and marched toward the tower. Ty followed them inside as the group stood by in silence. A moment later, Michaels stepped from the tower and called to Sam. She threw a worried glance at Johnny before jogging over.

Sam followed Michaels into the tower and stood for a moment as her eyes adjusted to the darkness. She could just make out Daniels standing off to the side, his hands braced on Ty's shoulders as if he were confiding some dark secret. Sam stood still, unsure if she should approach, not wanting to disrupt the intimacy of their conversation. Daniels looked up, glanced back at Ty, and then walked towards her. Ty didn't move; he stood frozen, staring straight ahead.

As Daniels approached, Sam realized she was shaking. She didn't understand what was happening, but instinctively knew that this moment would change the trajectory of their training; that whatever was happening was impacting Ty in such a way that he was unaware of his surroundings.

Sam fought the urge to run to him.

Daniels stood before her, the rain still running down his face. He cleared his throat before muttering in that same quiet tone, "Ty's father has died."

XVII

They left Orlando and headed north on I-75, Sam behind the wheel so that Ty could focus on the days ahead. His father had been planning to purchase an adjacent three hundred acres, expanding the farm to one of the largest in the county. He was walking his property line with an appraiser when he collapsed. Responders were called, but because of his location off the roadway, their response had been delayed. By the time they got to him, he was in full arrest. His pulse never returned, and he was pronounced dead an hour later at the local ER. Ty put his head back and closed his eyes.

They cut east on Highway 40 and the nondescript topography gave way to rolling, open farmland. Oak hammocks sprouted like small, gnarled cities and the sun dropped behind them as the darkness from the east crept ahead. At one point, Ty dozed, only to awaken with a start, as if shaken by an unseen hand.

It was full dark by the time they turned onto Williams Road. Named after Ty's great grandfather, the road ended where their property began, at a large wrought iron gate that continued east and west along low stone walls. Fields stretched away into the darkness and the large outbuildings that housed the stallions loomed like giant stones against the horizon. They drove through the gate and up an oak-lined drive before pulling in front of a massive Colonial structure of brilliant white. The front porch extended the width of the house; an upper balcony was accessed via French doors lining the second story. Cars were parked along the length of the drive and lights blazed in every room. It was a magnificent home and Sam tried to imagine the violence that had existed within its refined walls.

Ty stared up at the house through bleary eyes. He put his hand on the door handle, yet seemed unable to open it, overcome by flashbacks of his father's rage, the heft of his fists, and the familiar tension he associated with home. Sam turned off the engine and placed a light hand on his arm.

Ty swung his head, his face blank, and then slowly climbed from the car.

The evening became a blur of nameless faces, crowded rooms. It seemed everyone in the county had come to pay their respects. Ty's mother, a lovely woman with the same exquisite coloring as Ty, moved through the house like a ghost, greeting guests with formal handshakes, responding to words of condolence with Ty's same blank stare, as if they were both shell-shocked victims of some long-running conflict. Sam was captivated by the resemblance between mother and son. She could understand why Ty's looks had so enraged his father. Ty was her spitting image. Photographs of Ty's father lined the walls of the study. His dark, grave features were nowhere to be found among Ty's fine bones.

The night wore on and the crowd slowly abated. Sam slipped upstairs and changed into sweats. She found Ty in the den, staring blankly at a photo of his father receiving a key to the city. He placed the frame carefully among the others on the mantle, then sank into the soft depths of the couch. He put his head back and smiled as Sam settled in beside him.

"Thanks for coming with me, Sam. It's great to have you here." He stared at her before dropping his eyes to his hands. Sam reached over and squeezed his arm, then laid her head back and closed her eyes.

The house had grown quiet, the staff having called it a day. Ty took Sam's hand and drew her up from the couch. He led her out onto the front porch where they took up one of the swings suspended from the high ceiling. They drifted back and forth as the night sounds intensified, broken occasionally by a lonesome whinny from the stables. Eventually, Ty's head sank onto his chest. Sam rose carefully, woke him with a gentle hand, and led him back into the house and up the vast staircase. They exchanged goodnights and Sam watched him drift off to his room.

Ty kept busy with funeral preparations and spent much of his time with his mother. Sam set up camp on the porch, her academy books littering the wicker table beside her as she swung contentedly and studied. Ty would check on her from time to time, escaping from the flurry of activity to spend a few quiet moments beside her.

"You OK out here?" he would ask, gripping her hand for confirmation.

"I'm fine," Sam would reassure him. "See to your mother."

Ty would duck back into the house, only to reappear an hour later and go through the same routine.

Friday night they attended the wake, which was held in the large cathedral in the heart of downtown. People filtered quietly through the aisles, paying their respects, speaking in the low tones reserved for somber occasions. Afterwards, they returned to the house and Ty's mother quickly disappeared upstairs.

Sam showered and headed down to the den. Ty drifted in a while later, his hair wet, eyes red. Sam settled onto the couch and Ty collapsed beside her. She pulled one of the small pillows and placed it on her lap, then guided his head down as Ty curled up beside her like a fetus.

Sam reached up and clicked off the small lamp next to the couch. The high lights from the porch streamed through the windows in acute angles, but the depth of the room kept the couch in shadows. Sam ran her fingers through Ty's damp hair, feather soft beneath her touch. He closed his eyes and was transported to a glassy lake where he drifted beneath a warm autumn sun as giant oaks bristled in the breeze.

Sam began to doze. Ty was lost in sleep, so she eased out from under him and pulled a blanket from the back of the couch. Her absence registered deep within his slumbering brain and he let out a gentle moan in protest. Sam tucked the covers over his shoulder and crept from the room. Once upstairs, she climbed into the broad bed and fell instantly asleep.

In the morning, Sam woke with a start to find Ty sleeping beside her. He lay tucked on his side, his body turned toward her. She took in his features as he breathed softly against the pillow. His hands were curled; they twitched as he dreamed. Sam rolled toward him and with a gentle finger, touched the hair along his forehead. Ty slowly opened his eyes, heavy lids batting against the bright morning light. He rolled onto his back, rubbing at his eyes with the base of his palms.

"Sorry, Sam," he muttered. "I woke up and you were gone." He turned his head and searched her features. Sam threw him a hesitant smile.

"Let's go find some coffee. I'm famished." She gave his shoulder a quick squeeze, then got up quickly and headed for the bathroom. Ty stood up slowly and straightened the covers.

"I'll see you downstairs?" he called, as Sam poked her head out from the bathroom, toothbrush in hand.

"Sounds good," she replied, smiling as she squeezed toothpaste onto the brush. "I'll be down in a minute." She disappeared into the bathroom. Ty closed the door quietly behind him.

They arrived early for the service. Sam lingered in the lobby as Ty and his mother made last-minute checks on the arrangements. The crowds soon gathered, streaming into the church as Ty's aunt and uncle greeted the guests.

Sam appraised her outfit by running her hands down the front of her dress, smoothing the dark fabric. After months spent in heavy turnout gear it felt strange to be in a dress. She had come to love the feel of her gear. It gave her a feeling of toughness and invincibility. The dress and heels left her feeling exposed and vulnerable; as if someone could simply walk by and knock her over.

As she contemplated her appearance, she glanced up at the arched doorway. In walked Johnny, dressed in a dark suit, looking like a formal version of the medic she knew so well. She grinned and headed for the door. In that moment, Michaels and Daniels materialized behind him, marching in like beautiful soldiers. Their appearance stole Sam's breath. They were dazzling in dress uniforms, their dark coats and white shirts laced in the insignia of their rank, their chests adorned with a multitude of ribbons, proof of their heroism on the fire ground.

"I can't believe you all made it!" Her eyes darted from face to face. Johnny smiled warmly and gave her a sturdy hug. Michaels shook her hand formally and flashed a quick smile. Sam turned to Daniels, who cautiously took up her hand. Sam held on, placing her other hand atop his. He gave her hand a brief squeeze before letting go.

"How's Ty?" Daniels interjected, anxiously squaring his shoulders and adjusting his tie.

"He's doing well," Sam replied, holding his gaze. "It's been a hectic couple of days, but he seems to be handling it well. Let me go get him." She turned and walked briskly across the lobby, disappearing into the alcove where Ty was conferring with the church staff. Daniels watched her go, taking in the fine curves of her legs. Michaels and Jimmy exchanged grins before Daniels checked himself, acknowledging them with a guilty smile.

Sam stood inside the doorway as Ty spoke in earnest with the minister. Ty glanced her way and Sam gave a quick jerk of her head. He wrapped up his conversation and hurried over.

"God, I'm ready for this to be over," he whispered, his eyes patrolling the crowded alcove. Sam noticed how polished he looked in his suit, the sharp outline of his shoulders, the exquisite tailoring. His hands were buried in his pockets and he suddenly swung his head in her direction and peered into her face. He drew up on his toes to bring their eyes in alignment, grinning as he compared their heights.

"You're too tall in those things!" he exclaimed in a low voice, turning his back to the crowd to hide his smile.

Sam grinned and gave him a nudge. "There are some people asking for you in the lobby. Can you come?"

"Sure. It'll give me an excuse to get out of here." He took her arm and steered her toward the door.

As they entered the lobby, Ty saw the men. He rushed to Johnny and enveloped him in a bear hug as they slapped each other on the back. He did the same with Michaels, who reciprocated Ty's warmth while maintaining his rigid posture. He then turned to Daniels. The commander offered his hand, which Ty cradled in both of his, just as Sam had done minutes before. Daniels then pulled Ty toward him, embracing him warmly and holding him for those few extra seconds that define tenderness. He released Ty and stood with his hands braced on his shoulders, just as he had done in the tower when breaking the news. They smiled at each other as the others looked on.

As the service progressed, Daniels tried to focus. Seeing Ty and Samantha had moved him deeply and his mind drifted as he tried to sort through his feelings. Embracing Ty had left a lump in his throat. He wanted to tell him how sorry he was, that if there was anything he needed, he hoped Ty would turn to him. But seeing Ty's face and the welling of emotion his presence summoned had caused the words to catch in Daniels' throat. He tried but couldn't get anything out.

The sight of Samantha had stolen his breath. Whenever Daniels thought of her, it was as she appeared on the training field: her legs cloaked in bunker pants and boots, the suspenders reaching over her square shoulders or hanging loosely at her hips, her tee shirt clinging to her frame, the academy emblem spread across her back. That image had become etched in his memory. Seeing her in a dress, her high heels emphasizing the length of her legs, had stunned him. The feel of her warm hands had only added to his confusion, his inability to speak.

Daniels looked to the front of the church where Sam and Ty sat, their bodies close, shoulders touching. He imagined their hands locked and it left him with a sense of longing. He remembered watching them in the tower as they performed their quick-connect drill, the way their bodies appeared as mirror images, their movements perfectly coordinated. He had watched the way their hands worked, how they found each other despite their blacked-out masks, the way their legs intertwined as they sat on the floor. It was as if they had morphed into twins through the course of their training. It was hard to think of one without picturing the other.

Ty stood up as the minister approached and gave a slight nod of his head as they shook hands. As he turned to sit down, he caught Daniels' eye and they exchanged a moment of silent communication. Daniels felt the familiar welling of pride in his chest, as if he had somehow laid claim to the boy. When Daniels watched Ty perform on the training field, it was as if Ty represented a part of him. Daniels couldn't explain the sensation, yet it gave him such keen satisfaction that he indulged himself.

As for Samantha, a pattern had developed. Just when Daniels thought he had a handle on his feelings, he would see her on the field or hear her voice among the men and that part of him reserved for her would be yanked to the forefront. Seeing her today, dressed as she was and miles from the academy, intensified his longing and exposed his wound afresh.

~

Sam kept an eye on Ty during the ceremony, curious how he would handle a service celebrating his father's life. As the succession of people spoke of his father's community service, his philanthropy, and his contributions to the church, she wondered if Ty was taking an inventory of the times they had fought, of all the times he had been subjected to his father's fists. Ty gripped her hand, sometimes painfully, and Sam touched his arm from time to time to remind him she was there, thinking of him.

The graveside service was brief, the family monument flanked by generations of Williams markers. After the casket was lowered, the crowd drifted away. Ty left with his family and Sam drove with the men back to the house. From her position behind Michaels she could see Daniels' face in profile. He squinted into the sun, the sharp lines of his face reminding her of a hawk searching for prey. He was truly beautiful.

They parked in front of the house and headed inside. People were already arriving, and the house was soon full. Ty joined them as they grabbed drinks from the bar and staked out a large corner of the porch. They talked about the academy, their upcoming finals, and the state exam to follow. The cadets used the time to pump the officers for information, but the men simply smiled and held their cards close. Ty ushered Michaels and Johnny out to show them the horses. Sam had gone inside to change. Her heels were aggravating her, and the afternoon was turning cool. She slipped on jeans and a light sweater and headed back downstairs. When she returned to the porch, Daniels was reclined in a chair, his eyes on the horizon. They swung her way as she spoke.

"Would you like to take a walk?" Sam asked, once again struck by his penetrating gaze.

Daniels smiled and stood up. He had stripped out of his jacket and tie and his sleeves were rolled to the elbows. Sam's eyes fell naturally to his forearms.

They turned off the porch, following a stone path that led away from the house under massive oaks that had stood for over a century. The land stretched in all directions and the afternoon sun cut ribbons of shadows on the grass.

They walked in silence until they came to a low bench set beneath a cluster of oaks. Sam tried to gauge his mood, but as usual, he left her confounded. They settled on the bench and Daniels slid his hands into his pockets, stretching his legs out before him, as Sam had seen him do so many times at the tower.

"I'm glad you came," Sam began, quickly adding, "I know it meant a lot to Ty." She fingered one of the small pearl buttons on her sweater.

Daniels smiled, his eyes returning to the horizon. Sam puzzled over their conversation, but after a brief pause, he spoke. "Where are your parents, Samantha? Are they local?" Daniels looked at her in profile.

"Both of my parents are dead," Sam replied, her eyes still on her button. "My mother died when I was very young. I don't remember much about her. My father died several years ago." She glanced up at him. "What about yours?"

"My family's in California; both parents and three brothers."

"Three brothers? Your poor mother," Sam grinned. "Are there other firefighters?"

"Two of us; the other two are police officers. My youngest brother works for San Diego. Do you have brothers and sisters?"

"No, it's just me. I bet it was nice, growing up in such a big family. Do you see them often?" She forced her fingers from her button and folded her hands in her lap.

"I go out a few times a year. Two of my brothers are married with kids so it's quite an ordeal when the whole family gets together." Daniels smiled, crossing his ankle over his knee, and folding his hands in his lap. Sam noticed the curve of his leg, remembering how he looked on the morning runs: the fine, muscled legs of a runner. Sam shifted her eyes to the field.

"Is it hard for you, Samantha, not having a family?" Daniels asked after a moment.

Sam paused, surprised by the personal nature of the question, the hollowness of the statement. Sam had never thought of herself as without a family, at least not since the early days following her father's death. Her isolation was simply the norm. Even when her father was alive, he travelled extensively. By the time Sam could stay alone, she had grown accustomed to the seclusion. It was all she had ever known.

"I miss my father," she replied wistfully, her eyes fixed on some distant spot. The funeral had brought back the memory of his death. Sam remembered standing beside his grave as rifles were fired in salute, their deafening crack reverberating in her ears, the somber look on the officer's face as he placed the long casings in her hand, the metal still warm from firing. Suddenly, the force of the memory enveloped her, and she swallowed hard to fight back tears.

Sam stared at her hands, not trusting herself to look up. When she finally did, Daniels was examining her face, searching her features. She watched him, noting that up close, the grey of his eyes was edged in pale blue. She had the distinct urge to touch his face. Her hand moved before her brain could stop it.

Sam placed her palm alongside his face. She thought he might pull away, but instead, his eyes slowly closed, his lashes featherlike upon his cheek. She took in the firm line of his jaw against her palm. Her thumb grazed his mustache, coarse against her finger as she stroked it softly. He opened his eyes, looking directly into hers.

Sam knew she was treading on dangerous territory. Daniels placed his hand over hers, pressing it before lowering it to his lap where he stared at it as if seeing one for the first time. He traced an imaginary line over her palm with his finger. Suddenly, her thoughts flashed to the academy and how this would play out when they returned to training. Here, under the trees and far from the academy, it was easy to push the boundaries. But in two days they would be forced back into their roles: he as commander, she as cadet. Sam didn't think she would be able to look at him on the field if she didn't stop herself now.

Sam slowly pulled her hand away and stood up. She gazed out over the lawn and could see the men heading back to the house. "The others are back," she murmured. Daniels stood up and placed his hand on her arm, just below her shoulder, and then turned to walk away. He glanced back, waited for her to catch up, and they made their way back to the house.

The men were returning from the barn when Ty glanced up to see Sam and Daniels winding their way back up the path. Ty's familiar bolt of tension was reignited; the same sensation he experienced when he saw them crossing the training field together. A whistle shrieked somewhere in his brain, blocking out Johnny's conversation, as an anxious rigor mortis settled in his limbs. He marched mechanically up to the house, his eyes never leaving the commander.

After refilling their drinks, they congregated on the porch. Ty was exhausted, anxious to leave, yet he surprised himself when Johnny asked when he and Sam would be returning to Orlando. Ty had planned to leave that afternoon. He had already spoken to his mother, who assured him she had plenty of support on hand at the farm, and his bag was packed in anticipation of a quick escape. But seeing Sam and Daniels together had triggered a sense of possession Ty wasn't ready to relinquish.

"We're going to stay one more night."

~

The house was finally empty. They had seen the men off and Ty and Daniels had planned to meet at the greenway the following evening for a late run once he and Sam returned to Orlando. Ty's mother and the staff had turned in early, drained from the day's emotional events, and the noise in the house had faded to a blissful silence.

Ty and Sam remained on the porch, watching the sun tuck itself into the folds of the western fields as the early stars blinked on in the darkening sky. They talked for hours; about the future, the past, and Ty's feelings concerning the death of the person who had caused him so much anguish. As Ty spoke, Sam concentrated on his face. Although his words flowed freely, there was something disconnected behind his eyes, as if he were directing the discussion through some mechanical force. Sam assumed it was the exhaustive process of grieving.

As Ty rambled on, a part of him stood back, monitoring their conversation. That *other* whispered in his ear, recalling the scene of Sam and Daniels crossing the lawn, their bodies close, as they had been on the training field. Ty pushed the *other* aside and tried to focus, but the *other* wasn't so easily assuaged.

It must have been the *other* that caused him to wade into the chilled stash of champagne his parents always kept on hand. Ty had gone inside for a glass of water, but had instinctively reached for one of the heavy, iced bottles instead. Surely, it wasn't the memory that flashed before his sub conscience: Sam's form tucked on the bed, the smooth outline of her body as she slept off the effects of the gin. Surely, Ty wasn't that conniving. But the *other* was driving him and his exhausted brain simply followed.

Sam was battling her *other* as well; the voice that whispered she had had enough to drink, reminding her of the hangover she had suffered after the gin. She berated herself as they cracked the second bottle. But Ty was laughing now and the sound of it was like music. The more they drank, the more he let go of his grief. He was relaxed and happy and Sam simply enjoyed it.

They finished off the second bottle and made their way into the house, laughing as they helped each other up the winding staircase. Sam was having trouble focusing and craved a hot shower; the need for sleep was overwhelming. She said goodnight to Ty outside her door, but before he turned to go, he placed unsteady hands on her shoulders, looking intently into her face before grinning and dropping his eyes. Their bodies swayed as Sam hugged him tightly.

Sam showered and collapsed into bed. The dream came quickly, whisking her back to the darkened tower. But this time the surrounding air was warm, the smell of earth intense. She stood with her eyes closed, but could feel Daniels approach, the soft swish of his body moving towards her. The familiar touch of his hand reappeared, this time on her shoulder as he drew a finger down her arm to the curled hand at its end. Her mind flashed to sitting under the oaks as he traced her palm.

Sam kept her eyes closed, refusing to meet the intensity of his gaze. His hand made its way onto her belly, sliding against the smoothness of her skin. He lifted her shirt, placing the side of his face against her for warmth as he knelt before her. Sam stroked his head, then placed her hand lightly against his face. Daniels moved up against her and she realized they were no longer standing. She could feel the press of his body, his weight upon her.

As she grappled with the change in position his mouth moved onto her. It grazed her face, barely touching her skin, tentative. His body was warm, and her hands instinctively floated to his sides, feeling the muscles along his torso flex as he positioned himself above her. Sam relished his firmness against her pelvis. His mouth covered hers, still tentative, so different from the previous dream. This time, his mouth was soft and seeking, his tongue gentle against her lip. The realness of the dream left her spinning.

In that moment, the first hint of danger crept in. Her mind fired a warning shot, startling her from the depths of dreams. As Daniels explored her mouth, her hand returned to his face. He was moving on her now and Sam was being slowly drawn into his rhythm. She slid her hand to where his mouth met hers. Suddenly, she realized it wasn't Daniels against her, the clean-shaven face a dead giveaway. Sam's mind raced as her hands reached for his shoulders. She grabbed hold of them, realizing the familiarity of their shape, the body she had come to know so well in the tower. Ty.

Sam ripped through the haze, pulling her face from his while bracing her hands against his shoulders. "No, Ty," was all her disoriented brain could come up with.

Ty froze on top of her, his body unable to downshift. Sam repeated the words, only quieter, as if not to startle him. Ty quickly moved off her and was gone.

~

Ty knew it was over. In one fell swoop, he had destroyed everything he and Sam had built. He had gambled their friendship in exchange for a sense of ownership and now he would pay the ultimate price: losing everything they had.

A part of Ty knew his intentions as soon as he opened the first bottle. Not that he had planned to go as far as he did. He simply wanted to be beside her again, to touch her smooth skin. Ty knew it was wrong, but he told himself as long as he maintained control, he wasn't crossing the line. He would never do anything to endanger their friendship, yet after each glass, the urge to touch her had grown; with each thought of Daniels, Ty's need for Sam intensified.

When he slipped into her room, he told himself he wouldn't stay. But his mind flashed again to Daniels, and the conflict that surfaced whenever he thought of them together. Ty could deal with them as individuals; he had come to care so much for them both. But when he thought of them together, something within him took over. Ty wanted them to be part of his life, yet not be a part of each other's. He knew it was selfish, yet where Sam was concerned, Ty's need for possession overrode his sense of reason.

When Ty saw her sleeping, his desire to touch her had been replaced by the urge to own her. He started with her arm and saw the subtle reaction it produced: the twitching of her hand as his fingers glided toward it. When he lifted her shirt, the smoothness of her flesh had drawn him in, and when her hand floated to his face, he took it as encouragement and kept going. Once he had moved onto her, there was no turning back. His body took over, blank with drink, overwhelmed by the feel of her.

When Sam awoke and held him off, Ty took it not only as a rejection of his feelings, but as a severing of all that held them together. He had fled to his room. When Sam failed to appear, every minute that passed was further confirmation of his fears.

~

Sam crept down the dark hall and stood before Ty's door, berating herself for her complacency. She knew Ty was vulnerable, yet she had dismissed her worries in exchange for too much drink, a loss of control. Had she encouraged him during the evening? Had she misread his signals? Sam knew Ty would never take advantage of a situation; that he was above the manipulations employed by some men. And yet he had come to her room again, not simply to sleep next to her, but with the intention of having her. How could their friendship have taken such a leap without either of them declaring it?

She had to talk to him. She hoped the appropriate words would come when she saw his face. She knocked lightly and waited.

When Ty didn't answer, Sam slowly opened the door. The room was dark, but she could make out the pale outline of his body, perched on the edge of the bed, his head buried in his palms. Sam knelt before him. Ty's face was contorted in grief. Throughout the weekend Sam had waited for him to express himself, yet he had remained unmoved until this moment. Perhaps he was simply overwhelmed. It had been an exhausting few days; Ty had to be feeling the strain.

Sam slid in between his knees. Ty's hands dropped to his sides. He was like a rag doll, limp and dejected. Sam placed her hands on his shoulders, forcing him to look at her.

"Ty, please talk to me."

Ty remained silent, his face wet and flushed. He turned his head away from her, his tears illuminated in the faint light. He swiped at his eyes, humiliated and ashamed. How could Sam ever forgive him?

Sam moved up against him, wrapping her arms around him and drawing him near. She held him, waiting for a response from his deadened limbs, and for a moment, Sam thought he would remain frozen. But Ty's arms slowly encircled her, clinging to her tightly.

"I'm so sorry." His words were broken, his head buried against her neck.

Sam didn't speak. She didn't need to. She held onto him, communicating through the strength of her arms, the warmth of her body. She stood up and they climbed into his bed. Sam curled up behind him, drawing Ty against her. Ty lost himself in his newfound safety: his father gone, Sam at his side. They slept until morning.

XVIII

The drive home was quiet. They put the night behind them and spoke of the days ahead. In two weeks, they would graduate, followed a week later by their state exam. They focused on the academy, the safety of the subject a balm against the drama of the previous weekend.

Ty walked Sam up to her apartment, carrying her bag inside and placing it in her room. Ty's familiarity with her home comforted her; it reinforced the fact that Ty was engrained in her life. They hugged without speaking, smiled, and parted.

When Ty arrived at the greenway, Daniels was already warming up in the grass. He had arrived early, anxious to see how Ty was holding up after the long weekend. Leaving the farm had been difficult. Although he had gone in support of Ty, Daniels' allegiances were split. He knew Samantha would be there and, for the first time, he would have the opportunity to see her away from the academy. He wondered if the connection he felt when he watched her on the field – her intensity, focus, and determination – would be evident outside the boundaries of the academy. Daniels couldn't help but recognize aspects of himself in Sam; yet with Sam, the lines were softer, the edges smooth to the touch.

But seeing Sam at the farm had only strengthened his connection; their moment under the trees had intensified Daniels' deep feelings for her. At times, he felt foolish. He was almost twice her age, had a full career behind him, and a second which kept him stretched to the limits. And yet scenes of her played like a reel in his mind. Samantha doing pushups in front of Lee, that steely determination with which she refused Daniels' intervention. Samantha in the tower, her face bloodied, and the way she had looked at him as he tended her wound, that intensity boring straight through him, cutting an inner part of him that hadn't bled for years.

Initially, Sam had reminded him of Madeline. His eyes had been drawn to her because of some hint of recognition in her appearance – hair color, eyes, the focus in her face – yet he had quickly deduced they were two very different women. Madeline had been assertive, yet in a calm, reserved manner. What he saw in Samantha was a razor-sharp intensity, a lucidity rare in women her age. He watched the way she handled herself on the field, the way she interacted with the men without being distracted by them. Daniels had watched how other female cadets behaved, how they played up their sex to be the focus of attention. Or the opposite extreme: the women who lacked any semblance of femininity and prided themselves on being as butch as possible.

Samantha had struck a rare balance. She was tough and determined yet retained an element of femininity that held her apart from the men. She worked well with others without needing to be the center of attention. She blended with the men, and yet held fast to an aloofness that enabled her to rise above the pack and distinguish herself on her own terms.

The way she handled Lee was proof of her ability to cordon herself off from becoming emotionally involved in the events around her, almost to a fault. For some strange reason, it was one of the things Daniels admired most about her: her ability to withstand an assault, see it for what it was, process it, shut it out, and move on. He would never want her to tolerate an abusive situation, and hated to think that Lee had gotten away with mistreating her, and yet it was the way Samantha had contained it that truly impressed him; as if she were gifted with an indifference that held her against the outside world.

Daniels knew it must be tied to her upbringing: the loss of her parents, the lack of family support. He tried to imagine what her life had been like, imagining himself going through the loss of Madeline without his family to turn to, their care and attention.

Daniels longed to know more about her, what made her tick, and how she had attained the emotional resilience that was so evident on the training field. That's what had made the time at the farm so special. To have the chance to talk to her, to ask questions and learn more about her, was something he had longed for. His mind flashed repeatedly to their brief conversation beneath the oaks: the far-off look in her eyes when she talked about her father, the smoothness of her hand on his face, and the intricate lines of her palm, which he could still feel when he closed his eyes and remembered. Daniels carried all of it with him, filling the void that had taken up residence in his chest so long ago.

As Ty approached, Daniels was moved by other emotions: the feelings he had for Ty, the closeness they had achieved over the past weeks. Watching him progress through class had given Daniels a sense of Ty's intelligence and drive. Watching him handle the death of his father had revealed Ty's emotional strength and resilience. Daniels admired how the boy handled himself. He watched him throughout the ceremony, how Ty attended to details instead of moving through with the passivity of the grief-stricken. Daniels was anxious to talk to him, to spend time with him without the intrusion of others. He watched his bounding approach and smiled.

"Am I late?" Ty exclaimed as he jogged up.

"I'm early." It was good to be back in their routine. Daniels had come to associate Ty with the freedom and ease he felt during those long runs along the greenway. They shook hands warmly.

"How are you?" Daniels asked, examining Ty's face.

"I'm OK. Glad the weekend's over. It's good to be home," Ty replied as his smile waned. Daniels was struck by Ty's use of the word "home," especially considering he had spent his entire life in Ocala.

"I'm glad you're back, and again, I'm sorry about your father. I'm sure it's difficult." Daniels was shaken by Ty's response.

"I'm glad he's gone," Ty said with hardness in his face Daniels had never seen before. "I've spent the last few years wishing he were gone, wishing he had never been in my life, blaming myself for his cruelty." Ty swung his gaze to the distant trees and swallowed hard.

Suddenly, he dropped his head and broke down. It was so unexpected Daniels was caught completely off guard. Ty put a hand to his face, embarrassed by his outburst, yet unable to control the pain that had been roiling beneath the surface. Having to move through the formalities of the funeral had forced the feelings deep into his psyche. They now came rushing out with an intensity he couldn't control and the fact that it was happening in front of the commander humiliated him.

Daniels approached him tentatively, cautiously putting his arms around him, drawing him close. He didn't know what to say so he said nothing. Ty kept his hand over his face but tucked his head on the commander's shoulder. Daniels could feel Ty's body shake as his emotions poured forth. Daniels felt his own emotions well, so moved was he by Ty's display. He forced them back, focusing his eyes on the ground. His hand moved to the back of Ty's head and he held onto him until he calmed, and the tears subsided. Ty slowly withdrew.

"God, I'm sorry," Ty muttered, shaking his head, and staring at the ground as Daniels stood with his hands braced on Ty's shoulders.

"Don't apologize." Daniels dropped his hands and they separated. Ty wiped his face using his sleeve and they both began stretching. Daniels gave Ty a reassuring pat and they were off.

They ran for over an hour before heading to their picnic table to cool down. They straddled the benches on opposite sides of the table, staring off in the same direction toward the lake. Finally, Ty broke the silence.

"Thanks for earlier," Ty said, still embarrassed by his outburst.

"Don't worry about it." Daniels smiled and took a sip of water. "It happens to us all," he added offhandedly. Ty looked at him.

"You've been through this? The loss of a parent?"

"No," Daniels responded, pausing. "But I've been through loss."

Ty waited, hoping Daniels would continue. When he didn't, Ty spoke.

"What kind of a loss?" he asked and again, Daniels was moved by his frankness. Daniels took another slow sip, then looked Ty in the eye.

"My wife. We weren't married long; only three months. In some ways, it feels like I barely knew her. There just wasn't time." Daniels shook his head at the memory and returned his gaze to the lake.

"What happened to her?" Ty stared intently at the commander; eyes wide.

Daniels looked at him, unsure whether he should wade in to such a personal discussion yet feeling a return of the desire to open up, get it out.

"She was killed in a car accident. Entrapment," Daniels added, as if it explained the seriousness of the wreck without having to go into details.

"When?" Ty continued, aware that he was seeing a side of the commander he never knew existed.

"A long time ago. Almost ten years," Daniels replied, counting back the years in his head. A faraway look came over his face as he recalled the accident in all its vivid detail.

An emergency room physician, Madeline's shift in the ER had stretched late into the night due to a bus accident that sent fifteen patients to her hospital. As she drove home, weary from the long night, she lost control in the dense fog. Her body had been trapped in the wreckage for more than two hours before crews could reach her. Daniels had been summoned to the scene by his coworkers. He stood by, rigid with shock and grief, the enveloping fog splashed in the red and white of emergency lights, the smell of exhaust and blood heavy in the air. The only noise was the sound of tearing metal, the constant hum of generators, and the idling of the nearby trucks. No one spoke. They led him away after she was removed.

"You never remarried?"

"No. I doubt I'll ever remarry. It doesn't seem to be in the cards." Daniels flashed a wan smile.

"You don't have any kids?"

"I'm not exactly the kids type," Daniels replied, his smile warming.

Ty responded with a "Humph," before continuing. "Do you get lonely?" he asked with the openness of someone oblivious to the protocol of formal communication.

Daniels chuckled. "You ask a lot of questions, you know that?" He stood up and popped Ty on the head with the end of his towel. He waited for Ty to rise and they headed for their vehicles. Daniels placed a light hand on Ty's shoulder.

"I'll see you tomorrow," Ty called as he climbed into his car, smiling.

"See you tomorrow." Daniels watched Ty drive away. He leaned against the car as his mind drifted backwards, the familiar ache of loss etching its way into his chest.

The accident was almost ten years in the past, yet Daniels still marked each anniversary of her death. The date stood out in his mind, more so than the date they met, or the date they married. Her death had torn a hole in his soul, left an indelible gulf in his psyche that could only be filled with constant work, constant study; anything but the silence that rang in his ears.

The grief was a living thing. It had stalked him, day and night, like some unseen giant. He tried to shake it, his daily runs lengthening into long stretches where he lost track of time and distance until he would rein in, miles from home, unable to remember how he got there.

He tried a change of scenery. He left the Training Division, which stunned his coworkers, and returned to combat as a Battalion Chief. But with that first extrication call – a van that had been broadsided by a BMW, whose driver had turned away for a split second to check the market's closing – the beast of grief had reappeared, bloodied and hungry.

The damage to the van was devastating. The mother was trapped in the passenger seat, two children hidden somewhere in the folds of wreckage. The father, who had escaped injury, was being restrained on the sidelines by two beefy police officers. They held onto his arms as he struggled, moving with him as he thrashed, the three of them locked in a strange, hysteric dance. The officers did their best to be tolerant (*What if that was my wife and kids?*) but were no match for the husband's frantic rage.

Daniels had sat in his command vehicle, locked in a paralysis so intense it took great effort just to reach for the radio handset and respond to dispatch's repeated requests, "Battalion One, acknowledge!"

Before Madeline's accident, Daniels had been singled out by administration as a future leader of the department. Following her death, he withdrew into himself. He had always been a loner. Daniels never craved the company of other men, unusual in a field dependent on group cohesion. When Madeline was gone, there seemed to be nothing left. She had filled something in Daniels he'd not realized was empty until her death ripped it from him.

He fled the west coast to start again in the east. His position at the academy had proven a balm for his soul and the last ten years had seen the slow closing of his wound. And now the inclusion of Ty in Daniels' daily routine had become a source of joy and fulfillment; one he had never experienced or expected. Daniels never envisioned himself in a paternal role, but Ty stoked feelings Daniels never knew he possessed.

As for Samantha, she stirred something in him he thought had died with Madeline: a warm sense of desire that had lain dormant for almost a decade.

~

It was good to be home. Sam took in the quiet of her apartment, the hum of the building, the soft rush of traffic far below. She unpacked, showered, filled a tall glass with gin, and headed for the balcony. The days were getting shorter and the low sun was slipping from the sky. She settled in and took an icy sip, enjoying the burn as it slid down her throat.

The drive home from Ocala had been quiet, but it had given Sam a chance to sort through the conflicts of the weekend. They were numerous. The incident with Ty had unnerved her. It was difficult to hold a conversation with him without flashing back to the feel of his body pressed against her, the slip of his tongue on her lip. For the first time, Sam was relieved when he left. The strain of acting normal had given her a splitting headache.

And then there was Daniels. Sam relished the memory of sitting quietly alongside him, surrounded by the open beauty of the farm, the vastness of the distant fields. It had been a few moments of blissful escape. For once, they were free from the students, officers, and the constant activity of the training field. To be close to him out in the open was liberating, his body next to hers reassuring, soothing. Sam wondered what it would be like to have Daniels alone in a room, with no one else around, no eyes watching; nothing but stillness and silence.

Sam found herself returning to the feel of his hand, the way his finger carefully traced the lines of her palm. His touch was featherlight, reminding her of the way he had cleared the blood from her face, corrected her gear. It seemed a contradiction for a man of his intensity to communicate in such a gentle manner. But Sam was learning there was nothing straightforward about the commander. Sam was slowly chipping away at the aloofness he presented on the training field and the excavation was revealing a different man underneath, one she felt increasingly drawn to.

~

Ty picked her up in the morning and they returned to the comfort of their routine. Quizzing each other kept them focused on school, away from the emotional confusion of the weekend. This week they would prepare for finals: classroom sessions would be spent reviewing the curriculum, field drills would focus on polishing their skills. At the end of the week, they would take their final physical assessment.

As the cadets were heading in from PT, Miami-Dade's Technical Rescue Team emerged from the locker room. The team had returned to the academy for another week of confined space training. They moved like a herd of wildebeest, shuffling down the hallway, parting the crowd of students with elbows and leers, dwarfing the cadets with their size and strength. As Mark tried to pass, he banged shoulders with one of the team members, a firefighter equaling Mark in mass, and sporting a dark sleeve of tattoos. Sam recognized him from her encounter in the cafeteria. A shouting match quickly erupted.

"Watch it, motherfucker!" Tattoo growled as his team closed in around Mark. The cadets watched nervously from outside the huddle.

"Sorry," Mark replied sarcastically. "Next time I'll be sure to halt for pussies." He turned to break through their line.

The team refused to be dissed, especially by a sorry-ass cadet. Another hulking member shoved Mark as he tried to pass, and the hallway erupted in a skirmish. Bill jumped into the middle of it, Johnny and Lance right behind him. Sam stood further down the hall, her hand braced on the door to her locker room, as all hell broke loose.

Within seconds, Michaels and Tanner appeared, wading through the crowd, shoving men aside. They managed to quell the fight before it devolved into a rumble.

"*Cadets, get your asses into the locker room!*" Michaels yelled. "*Miami, get the fuck onto the training field! NOW!*"

Sam slipped through her door and pulled it closed.

The students spent the morning reviewing for the final exam. The end of the week would also mark their second confidence test: the church raise. Mark was nervous. He had made it through the airbag jump and had even managed to rappel out of the fourth-floor window, but climbing a three-story ladder suspended by four slender ropes was beyond his worst imagining. For the jump, he had had the calming presence of Michaels beside him; on the ladder, he would be on his own.

He confided in Sam over lunch. She had just loaded her plate at the salad bar and was making a beeline for a table when he caught her.

"Hey, Sammy, do you think Michaels would mind going through the ladder drill with us one more time?"

Sam smiled to herself with his use of "us," as if she shared in his trepidation. "I'm sure it wouldn't be a problem," she replied, balancing her tray on one arm, and popping a cherry tomato into her mouth. "Want me to set it up?" she mumbled.

"You don't mind?"

"Not a bit," she replied, smiling and swallowing. "I'll talk to Michaels after class."

Over lunch, the group quizzed each other as they gulped their food. They were just wrapping up when the team from Miami swaggered in. They were decked out in bunker pants and tee shirts. They marched in with their helmets under their arms, breezing past the students' table as the cadets tried not to stare. Mark glanced down at his own barren uniform, devoid of a badge and any form of rank, and he was whisked back to his brief stint in football: the humiliation of being cut, the heavy weight of his failure.

He looked up as Tattoo grinned at him from across the room and raised a meaty middle finger in Mark's direction. Mark's feelings of inadequacy morphed into anger.

The team jostled their way through the line and were heading for a table when Tattoo veered toward the cadets and tossed an apple onto Mark's tray. It landed with a wet slap in the center of his mashed potatoes, causing a shower of gravy to spring from his plate, splashing the front of Mark's shirt in dark, clumpy streaks. Mark slammed his fists onto the table and leaped to his feet and it was only through sheer force that Bill and Trey were able to yank him back to his seat. Mark fumed and shoved his tray aside.

That afternoon, the team was making their way into the academy as the cadets were heading out to the field. This time, the guys from Miami were ready. As Mark and the others walked by, Tattoo went straight for Mark, ramming him in the chest and knocking him to the pavement. Mark's gear was flung onto the sidewalk, his helmet skittered into the parking lot. Tattoo chuckled as Mark clambered to his feet.

"Better watch your step, cadet," Tattoo smirked as his group marched past. Mark seethed as he shook out his coat.

"Fuck 'em," Bill said quietly as he handed Mark his helmet.

~

Sam headed to Michaels' office on her way to the library. The office lobby was empty, Miss Davis' desk stood vacant. Sam poked her head through Michaels' door, but he was nowhere in sight. She was turning to leave when Adams, one of the special ops instructors, emerged from Daniels' office. Daniels followed him out, brightening when he noticed Sam. Adams threw her a cursory nod and strolled from the lobby.

"What are you doing here, Samantha?" Daniels smiled and leaned against the doorframe; arms crossed in front.

"I was looking for Michaels. Mark and I were going to see if it would be possible to hold one more training session on the ladder to prepare for the church raise."

Sam stood awkwardly in the middle of the lobby; her gear bag draped over her shoulder. The bag's weight was wearing her down, but she didn't know whether to drop it or turn to leave. As if reading her mind, Daniels approached her, slipped the bag from her shoulder, and carefully placed it on the floor.

"Michaels ran next door to the police academy. He'll be back in a minute. I'm grabbing some coffee. Would you like some?" He turned for the pot. Sam wasn't sure how it would look sipping coffee with the commander, but as she formed the words, *"No, thank you,"* the reckless side of her brain intervened.

"That would be nice," it replied, before Sam had a chance to squelch it.

Daniels poured Sam a cup and pointed to the cream and sugar.

"Black, please," she replied, which brought another smile to his face. Daniels filled his mug and flicked his head toward his door.

"Come on in," he said as he strolled into his office. Sam glanced at her bag, unsure whether to leave it or pick it up. She didn't want to wrestle it with a hot cup of coffee in her hand, but habit compelled her to grab it. The fact that she was debating over a goddamn bag reminded her of her nerves. *The man is just so confident.*

She left the bag and walked into Daniels' office, expecting to find him sitting behind his desk, but Daniels had taken up one of the soft leather chairs. Sam settled into the opposite chair, crossing, and uncrossing her legs before focusing on her cup.

"I'm sure you're looking forward to your training being done." Daniels gripped his mug in one hand, the other elbow cocked on the arm of the chair, his fingers bracing his chin.

"I am," was all Sam could come up with. *Fucking dunce.* She glanced up, flashing back to the feel of her hand on his face, his grey eyes slowly closing. She took a quick sip, wincing against the heat.

"What are your plans after the academy?" Daniels continued, snapping her back to the present. He eyed her over the rim of his mug.

"I'll be testing for Orlando next month."

"Good. They're one of the best," Daniels replied, smiling. "Will you be applying anywhere else?" Daniels was familiar with the stiff competition of OFD's entrance tests; it sometimes took candidates several attempts to get hired. Not that he thought Samantha would have a problem, especially being a female, which gave her minority status. But OFD's tests were notoriously rough, especially for women. He knew if she could make it through the test, she would be a prime candidate.

"No. I don't intend to work anywhere else," Sam replied, sipping her coffee, enjoying its warmth.

Daniels watched her mouth on the cup. He was about to ask another question when Michaels blew in. Sam quickly stood up; the commander reluctantly followed.

"Smith is here to see you," Daniels said as he headed for his desk.

Michaels nodded. "Follow me," he muttered as he led Sam out of the office. Sam glanced at Daniels and held up her cup, silently thanking him for the coffee. He smiled and turned to his paperwork.

Later that evening, after their study session had broken up, the group filtered out to the parking lot. Sam caught Mark, whispering, "All set for tomorrow evening."

"Fuck," he grumbled, digging for his keys.

~

The instructors worked the cadets hard on Wednesday. The state test would consist of several timed drills. To get them ready, Michaels set up stations throughout the tower. An instructor was assigned to each, armed with their usual paraphernalia – stopwatch and clipboard – and as the students moved through each station, they were graded on time and accuracy. They worked through airpack drills, ladders, hose evolutions, and search and rescue. The instructors kept them moving at a steady pace and by the end of the day, the students were exhausted.

"You up for studying?" Ty asked.

"You go ahead," Sam grumbled crossly as they dragged themselves down the hallway, stopping in front of the men's locker room. "I'm going to the field with Mark to train on ladders." She shifted her gear to her other arm, wincing at the stiffness in her back.

"Can I come?" Ty stood in helmet and boots; his coat draped over one shoulder.

"I don't know how Mark would feel about it. How about I just meet you in the library when we're done? I don't think we'll be long. My back is killing me and I'm too tired to climb, so we should be back in about an hour." She shifted her gear again. "I'll come find you."

Ty gave a resigned shrug. "OK, I'll see you later." He pulled his helmet from his head and watched as she walked away.

Sam clumped across the field, cursing the weight of her gear. The ladder truck was already set up and she dumped her boots and helmet in a pile at the base of the tower. She had been curious to see if Daniels would be joining them. Part of her hoped he wouldn't. She was exhausted and didn't think she could face the pressure of his presence. Michaels and Mark were standing beside the truck, discussing the climb. Sam scanned the tarmac, but Daniels was nowhere in sight, which gave her a brief rush of relief followed immediately by disappointment.

The ladder was set vertically, and its tip reached high toward the darkening sky. Sam was exhausted just looking at it, her limbs drained from the day's training. Mark grinned as she approached, the nerves playing across his face.

"Sam, you want to go first?" Michaels said, turning to her.

The last thing Sam wanted to do was climb the goddamn ladder, but Mark was shooting her desperate puppy eyes, so she relented. "Sure," she replied with forced enthusiasm.

Sam plodded over to her gear, kicked off her boots, and stepped into her bunker pants. She gave an aggravated sigh as she donned her helmet and gloves. By the time she clambered up the side of the truck and onto the platform, her breath was coming in ragged gasps. *This is going to be a bitch!*

She had hoped to sit back against the tower and watch, perhaps even doze a bit while Mark practiced. Sam took a few deep breaths before beginning the climb. She started her ascent and had made it about a third of the way up when she glanced down and noticed the addition of a third helmet on the ground: Daniels.

By the time Sam made it to the top, she was breathing heavily and sweat was trickling down her spine, despite the night's chill. She took a few more breaths before locking in.

On the church raise, they would lock their leg in over the top rung. They would then have to let go, lean straight back with arms spread, as if performing a backwards swan dive off the top, one leg locked, the other braced on a lower rung. After reaching full extension, they would return their hands to the ladder and unlock, then climb over the top of the ladder – no easy feat four stories off the ground with the ladder swaying side to side. Once they made it over the top, they would climb down the other side and the exercise would be over.

Once Sam was locked in, she released her hands and spread them wide. She slowly lowered her body until she was parallel to the ground, holding the pose for a few seconds and then pulling herself back to the ladder using her abs. She took another few deep breaths before climbing cautiously over the top, and then carefully descended the other side. She finally arrived on the platform and climbed down from the truck, bending forward to catch her breath.

"Nice job, Sam," Michaels said with a guarded smile. Sam had noticed Michaels using her first name more often, usually when there were few students around. It was a nice change from his usual bark, "Smith!"

Daniels had taken up the bench against the tower, arms locked across his chest, long legs extended in front and crossed at the ankles. He watched as Sam approached.

"Good job up there, Samantha," he said with a relaxed smile.

Sam eyed his mug on the ground beside him. She settled in next to him, removing her helmet and placing it next to her on the tarmac. She stripped off her gloves and attempted to tame her short hair back in place, to no avail. She leaned back and breathed slowly. Her damp shirt and the cool air quickly brought on a chill.

Daniels picked up on it but was without a jacket himself. He wore a long-sleeved academy tee shirt, the sleeves pushed up to his elbows. He leaned down and picked up his mug. "Here," he said, offering her the cup. "Take some. It will warm you up."

Sam hesitated before lifting a tired arm and accepting the mug, caught off guard by the intimacy of the gesture. She nestled the vessel between her hands, pausing before taking a sip.

"Is it black?" she asked, slyly.

Daniels gave a nod and for a moment that seemed to stretch into a blissful hour, they stared at each other before finally turning away.

The coffee was hot and rich, and Sam could feel it snake its way down through her chest. She glanced at the cup, smiling to herself as she drew parallels between the mug and its owner: the smooth, metallic exterior disguising a dense layer of insulation, and contained deep within, an intense heat at its core. She put her head back against the wall, relishing its warmth.

"Thank you. That's wonderful." She passed the mug back. Daniels took a deep sip as Sam watched him out of the corner of her eye, remembering the smooth bristle of his mustache beneath her thumb. She forced her eyes to the truck.

They watched as Mark mounted the platform. The climbing angle made it difficult for two people to be on the ladder, so he tried it on his own first, but only managed to make it halfway before freezing. Michaels was soon in tow and the two made slow progress until Mark finally reached the top. Michaels perched several rungs below as he talked Mark through the leg lock. Mark struggled, but finally managed to get his leg over the top rung and locked in place. Getting him to let go would be another struggle.

His massive arms clung to the rungs. They could see Michaels talking to him, giving him direction with one hand while holding on to the ladder with the other. Even from that distance, Sam could make out the powerful muscles that kept Michaels affixed to the ladder. After several minutes of coaxing, Mark finally let go, holding himself upright with his locked leg. His arms slowly came away from his body and he achieved a half-hearted spread before anxiously grabbing back on. Michaels talked him into letting go again and finally, Mark was able to lean back, arms spread wide. Although he did not achieve the full angle, he came close; close enough to satisfy Michaels, who then talked him over the top and back down the other side.

Daniels and Sam continued passing the mug between them. Sam sipped from the cup, keeping her eyes glued to the men. When they arrived safely on the ground, Mark whooped and hollered as Michaels gave him a bear hug, backslapping each other like long-lost friends. They took a quick break, chugging water and reviewing their tactics. Sam and Daniels settled in as the men remounted.

~

Ty had intended to head to the library, shouting to Johnny he'd meet him there, and had books in hand when he found himself skirting the training field, scrambling along the backside of the hedgerow like an assassin. He pushed the guilt aside, compelled by the need to see Sam and

Daniels together.

He crouched at the edge of the field, hidden beneath the dense foliage, and had a clear view of the tarmac and truck. He watched Sam approach Michaels and Mark, but Daniels was nowhere to be seen. Perhaps it was just the three of them this time. Perhaps Ty had been anxious for no reason. Just as he was getting up to leave, Daniels emerged from the tower. Ty tucked himself back in among the leaves.

Sam made her ascent as Ty watched from the sidelines. But he wasn't watching Sam, his eyes were drawn to Daniels. He watched the way the commander's eyes never left her, the intensity in his face, the rigidity of his body. Daniels barely moved the entire time Sam performed, as if he would spring from his position, should Sam stumble in the slightest. When Sam was finished, Ty watched Daniels glide over to the bench and Ty's heart rate took a leap when Sam settled in beside him. When Daniels handed her his mug, the familiar pain returned, ripping Ty's security into bloody halves.

As he hid in the shadows, Ty wrestled his anxiety. Sam had become part of him, someone he relied on completely, while Daniels filled a void Ty had carried since childhood. It was impossible to imagine his life without either one, yet he couldn't help but feel they were stealing from him to give to each other.

But as Ty watched, something else drew his attention. From his position on the field, Ty was able to see their faces, and for the first time, could watch the expressions passing between them.

Ty was struck by the serenity in the commander's face, and the warmth highlighting Sam's delicate features. And for the moment they stared into each other's eyes, the emotion passing between them was palpable. Despite the closeness Sam and Ty shared, she had never looked at him with the depth in her eyes reserved for Daniels. And even the blissful calm following their runs along the greenway was nothing compared to the peace that now etched the commander's face.

Even when they weren't speaking, their expressions reflected the affection that lived between them. And for the first time, Ty's feelings of jealousy and possession faded as he shared in their happiness. Sam's contentment was well established, most of which she achieved on her own. But seeing Daniels' joy moved Ty profoundly.

Ty thought back to Daniels' appearance at the funeral, the way the commander had held him, the power of his gesture. He thought about the incident at the greenway, when Ty had broken down; the caring Daniels had shown him as Ty grappled with his grief, and the pain in Daniels' eyes when he spoke of his own loss. Most of all, Ty thought about the pride Daniels seemed to take in watching Ty perform on the field. In his subtle way, Daniels gave Ty the recognition and acceptance he had craved from his own father, the acknowledgment that had always been denied. Ty's hard work on the farm had never elicited a single ounce of praise. Even on the rare occasions when his father attended his track meets, a winning ribbon would barely earn him a handshake.

The bond Ty shared with Daniels had become as important as the one he shared with Sam, Daniels' happiness just as important as Sam's or his own. Surely there was enough of each of them to go around. Certainly, the emotion Sam and Daniels shared between them would not be deducted from their feelings for him.

As the clarity settled over him, the pain in his chest was given final release. Ty stood up, brushed himself off, and made his way back to the academy.

XIX

Thursday passed uneventfully and before they knew it, Friday was upon them. It was going to be a long day. They would spend the morning in the gymnasium, completing their final physical assessment. After lunch, they would be back out on the training field running evolutions to prepare for their final live burn, which would take place the following week. The day would end with the church raise.

Ty had the added burden of driving home to Ocala after class. The family would meet in the morning for the reading of his father's will and his mother wanted him to be present, despite his protests. Sam offered to come along, but Ty wanted to make it brief: in and out. Besides, he knew everyone was getting together at the pub later and didn't want Sam to miss the party.

The final physical assessment was the same as their entrance test. They finished the run and then were shuffled into the gym. They knocked out their pushups and sit-ups, with Tate scoring the most improved, going from a measly fifteen pushups at the start of class to pumping out the max of fifty. He spent the rest of the morning strutting around the gymnasium like a peacock. They tested their grip strength and body fat, both of which had improved for almost every student. Sam scanned the group and was amazed at the metamorphosis that had taken place. They were all leaner, stronger, and more confident. The cadets had evolved both physically and emotionally over the course of their training and it was apparent in the way they held themselves.

After lunch, they performed evolutions before breaking to prepare for the confidence test. They then congregated on the field with their gear lined up on deck and braced at attention as the instructors went over the procedure for the church raise.

Everyone would rotate through both positions: climbing the ladder and then serving as anchor on one of the ropes. Two of the adjuncts retrieved the ladder from the tower and walked it over to the center of the field as the students looked on anxiously. Sam glanced over at Mark and noted the trepidation in his face.

Michaels and Tanner joined the adjuncts and together they secured four long ropes to the top of the ladder. They laid the ropes out so they would not interfere with the raise, which the adjuncts accomplished with smooth efficiency. The ladder appeared to weigh nothing in their hands and Sam flashed back to when Lee had made her raise it on her own, the backbreaking humiliation of the incident.

Once the ladder was upright, Tanner and Michaels took over. Tanner pressed his hip against its base while Michaels exerted pressure from the opposite side. Tanner then grabbed the halyard and raised the fly with steady pulls. The top half of the ladder rose smoothly skyward, its dogs clicking as it extended toward the sun. When it was fully raised, each instructor grabbed hold of one of the ropes and slowly backed away from the base of the ladder, maintaining constant pressure on their lines to keep the ladder from toppling. With the men on anchor, the ladder appeared to stand magically on its own.

The anchors had to work together. If one pulled too hard, it could throw the whole thing off and the ladder would come down. It would be even trickier once the climbs began. The climber's movements had to be counteracted by the men at the ends of the ropes. The exercise not only instilled confidence in the climber, but was also meant to reinforce teamwork, since the climber's life literally rested in the hands of those holding the ropes. One lapse in concentration meant the climber plunged almost four stories to the ground.

Bill volunteered to go first. His nerves were apparent, but he seemed to be doing it for Mark's sake, as if to say, *If I can do it, so can you.* He worked his way up the ladder slowly and methodically. His weight caused the men on anchor to constantly adjust their footing, as if flying a massive kite. He reached the top and hefted his leg over the top rung, struggling to maneuver his boot in between the rungs, but eventually locking in and slowly letting go. He grabbed on twice before finally extending his arms out to his sides and leaning back. The shift in weight caused the anchors on one side to be pulled forward. They manhandled the rope, bracing themselves by digging in their heels. Sam panicked, wondering if she would be heavy enough to anchor the rope when her turn came.

Bill unlocked and carefully worked his way over the top. As he descended, his face slowly relaxed. By the time he made it to the ground, he was grinning. He swiped at the layer of sweat that had worked its way over his face as he approached Mark.

"Piece of cake, Buddy!"

Mark looked on nervously.

Ty jumped forward just as Daniels appeared on the field. Bill took Michaels' place on the rope, starting the rotations. Michaels then positioned himself near the base of the ladder so he could coach the students as they ascended.

Ty approached the ladder with confidence. Michaels gave a few quiet words of encouragement and Ty began his climb. He moved as he always did, smoothly and efficiently. His arms gripped the ladder easily, his body seemed to float up the rungs. Sam glanced over at Daniels, who stood with his hand braced above his eyes to block the sun, a warm smile playing over his face. His eyes traced Ty's progress, much to Sam's disappointment. She felt a keen urge to see that flash of grey.

Ty made it to the top, slid his foot over the top rung, and was quickly locked in place. He released the ladder and spread his arms wide, leaning back as if plunging backwards into a pool. The cut of his body was beautiful against the pale sky, his narrow waist broadening to perfect shoulders. The muscles of his arms stood out, flexing as he drew himself back to the ladder. He climbed over the top and before Sam knew it, he was safely on the ground. He grinned broadly and glanced over at Daniels, who held up his hand, finger to thumb. Ty dropped his eyes to conceal his pride. When he collected himself, he flashed Sam that beautiful smile as he took over one of the ropes.

As the students progressed through the drill, those awaiting their turn were able to fall out of formation. Sam sidled over to Mark.

"You all set?"

"God, I hope so," he muttered, chewing on a fingernail and turning his head to spit.

"You're up, Sam," Michaels called from the base of the ladder.

She gave Mark a quick pat and headed for the ladder. As she approached the base, she cut her eyes to Daniels and almost laughed out loud. Ty and Daniels stood next to each other, their feet the same distance apart, arms crossed in front of their chests; mirror images. Ty had adopted Daniels' stance without even realizing it. As she took hold of the rungs, she thought how much they resembled father and son.

Sam made her way up the ladder with little trouble. Her training on the truck had prepared her for the climb and she barely paused when the ladder began to sway. She focused on the tree line, noting the sun dropping in the west. From her vantage point, she could make out the police cadets running their obstacle course and the team from Miami working down in the trench. The men appeared miniscule from her vantage point.

She threw her leg over the top rung and locked in with ease. She then let go, enjoying the feel of open air, spreading her arms wide as if sacrificing herself to the sky. She lay back, parallel to the earth, relishing the pull of gravity that drew her earthbound. She held the pose and then pulled herself back to the ladder, climbed over the top and down its backside. Daniels and Ty were smiling as Ty shot her a quick thumbs-up. She took her position on the rope as Mark anxiously approached the ladder.

Michaels stood alongside him, talking quietly. Mark was taking deep breaths, trying to remain calm. He started his ascent, taking each rung methodically, slowly. He looked enormous on the ladder, as if it were too small to accommodate his bulk. His arms and legs worked in unison and he was making smooth progress. He faltered about halfway up but gathered himself and kept moving. He got to the top of the ladder and took a quick break. Everyone watched as he positioned himself for the leg-lock.

Like Bill, he had trouble getting his massive leg over the rung. His thigh resembled a giant ham beneath his bunker pants. He got it over the top and worked to manipulate his foot in between the rungs. His large boot made it difficult, but he persevered and was finally locked in. Now he just had to let go. He braced himself, at one point glancing down at Michaels, who encouraged him with a firm nod of his helmet. Michaels was gripping the base of the ladder, as if communicating his support through its beams.

Mark stared off at the horizon before releasing the ladder. Sam held on to her rope, bracing herself for its inevitable sway. The anchors had wrapped the ropes around their backsides and were digging in. As Mark leaned back, Sam felt the ladder pull in his direction.

The anchors jockeyed their feet and after several seconds of frantic positioning, were able to hold it steady. When Sam looked up, Mark's massive frame was outlined against the sky, his arms extended like a crucifix. He held the pose and then quickly pulled himself back to the ladder, whooping and hollering once his hands were safely attached. Sam looked over at Michaels, who was smiling skyward. His hands still gripped the beams, the veins in his arms standing in high relief. Mark descended as the cheering cadets welcomed him back to earth.

~

They were to meet at the pub at seven. Johnny would come by to pick Sam up since Ty was heading straight for Ocala. As class broke, Sam walked him out to the parking lot. Everyone was in great spirits now that the final confidence test was behind them, especially Mark, who was walking on air. Ty threw his bag in the back and slowly approached her.

"Are you sure you don't want me to go?" Sam asked, dropping her gear bag to the ground. "I hate to think of you driving up by yourself." She was even more uncomfortable with the idea of his driving back. There was no telling what was outlined in the will, especially considering Ty's abandoning the farm. Sam wondered if his father would use the document to take a final swipe at his son.

"Go, have fun and enjoy the drinks. You earned them," Ty replied, placing his hands gently on her shoulders. He then pulled her close, pressing his forehead to hers.

"Are you OK?" Sam whispered. She could feel the heat of Ty's hands on her shoulders.

"Yeah," he whispered back. "I better go." He turned to climb into his car when Sam pulled him back, held onto him tightly, and then graced his cheek with a light kiss. Ty grinned and was gone.

Johnny showed up late at Sam's with Mark and Bill in tow. They had arrived at Johnny's house already well along into the night's drinking. They continued their roughhousing as Sam grabbed her keys and herded them toward the elevator. Bill brandished a bottle of whisky, his arm draped around Mark's massive neck as their laughter reverberated through the vestibule.

"It's going to be a long night," Johnny muttered as the elevator doors slowly closed.

As the men spilled out of the elevator, Sam flashed an apologetic smile to the elderly couple waiting in the lobby. Johnny grabbed Bill's thick arm and pulled him toward the door. As they reached the car, the men continued their banter as Johnny fumbled for his keys.

"Thanks, Sammy!" Mark said loudly as he planted a wet kiss on her cheek.

Sam rolled her eyes as she held the car door open. Mark and Bill piled into the back seat. "Fuck, it's tight back here!" Bill griped as he passed the bottle to Mark. But the cramped quarters did little to dampen their mood. They laughed and sang the entire way to the pub as Johnny and Sam tried to hold a conversation up front.

"How's Ty doing?" Johnny shouted over the noise in the car.

"He still seems a bit distracted, but I think he's handling it well," Sam replied loudly. "They meet with the attorney in the morning and then he'll be heading back, so I'm sure I'll see him tomorrow night."

The noise in the back overwhelmed their conversation. Sam twisted in her seat.

"What the hell's gotten into you boys?" The relief on Mark's face was apparent. Sam hadn't seen him that happy since the academy began.

"One more week, baby!" Mark yelled as Bill joined in with an accompanying holler. "Can you believe this whole fucking experience will be over?" He took a deep drag from the bottle before thrusting it at Sam. "Take some, sweetie!"

"No, thanks," Sam grinned. "But how about I hold onto this until we get to the pub." She tucked the bottle beneath her seat.

"Anything you say, Mom!" Mark cried, laughing as he and Bill wrestled like toddlers.

It was hard for them to believe they were almost done with their training; that in two weeks, they would be fully certified firefighters. Their graduation would enable them to sit for the state exam, which would consist of a written and practical test. The practical would take place on the training field, with the instructors from the academy assisting the officers from the State Fire College. Everything they had worked for was about to come to fruition.

The first person Sam saw as she entered the pub was Daniels, sitting at a large corner table, flanked by his instructors. He spotted her the second she strolled in. Her quick smile was answered with a slight nod, as the men around him talked animatedly. He looked like a king holding court. Michaels and Tanner sat to his immediate right, Taylor and Adams to his left. The adjuncts filled the remaining seats, their proximity to Daniels reflecting their status within the group.

Sam grabbed Johnny's arm as he wove his way through the crowd. Mark and Bill stumbled after them, slapping the backs of other students as they rambled toward the bar. The rest of the class was already there. The lights in the pub were low, the atmosphere warm and comfortable. The noise level was deafening as the men tried to talk over each other. It seemed the entire pub was occupied by either firefighters or cops. Sam recognized some of the police academy instructors, who were throwing back drinks as they conversed with their students. The place was packed, and the air reeked of testosterone.

Their class congregated at the end of the bar. Michaels and Tanner broke from the instructor's table and shoved their way into the group. Tanner yelled to be heard, bringing the noise level down amongst their huddle.

"Boys! Boys! And Sam," he added quickly with a sheepish grin. "We are here to celebrate your final week of class!" he yelled, as the group broke into cheers, clinking glasses. Sam glanced over at the instructors, who had been following along with the celebration, their glasses raised, their cheers blending with those of the students. She caught Daniels' eye and he gave his glass a subtle hoist and smiled. Sam smiled and was soon swallowed by the crowd.

The group settled in for a rowdy meal and as soon as the last fork dropped, they resumed their place near the bar. The air in the room had shifted while they ate. The Miami team had arrived and was crowded around a corner table. One of the members had grabbed a bottle from the bar and they were taking turns knocking back shots.

Mark, by now thoroughly trashed, directed his attention toward Tattoo. Tattoo stood next to his table, brandishing the bottle in one hand as he raised his glass in Mark's direction. Bill was jockeying for position between Mark and the team as Mark shoved his way toward the corner. Sam made a beeline for the opposite end of the bar.

It didn't take long for Tattoo to fire the first shot. He started throwing words Mark's way, none of which Sam could hear, but she could see the effect they were having. Mark was growing increasingly angry, his arm raised, fist clenched.

Michaels and Tanner had rejoined Daniels, unaware of the drama brewing in the corner. Sam threw a pleading glance in their direction, hoping to catch Michaels' eye, but the instructors were engrossed in their discussion, their heads crowded in a huddle. She watched Daniels, distracted by the intensity in his face, the fine lines of his features. Sam was so distracted that she missed the first punch being thrown. In a flash, Mark and Tattoo were on the ground, tearing at each other with fists as the crowd backed away to make room.

As the noise in the corner erupted, Michaels and Tanner bounded from their seats. Daniels didn't move. He took a slow sip from his glass, his eyes on Sam.

The men were finally separated, but not until they had both sustained injuries. Tattoo had a large welt developing on the left side of his face. His left eye was practically swollen shut and his mouth was bleeding freely. Obviously, Mark had gotten the upper hand. Mark had sustained a large cut to his lip which would require stitches, but other than that, he appeared unfazed. He laughed and taunted the team as they gathered Tattoo in a protective huddle, ushering their fallen comrade to the door.

"That's right, Miami! Get the FUCK out of our pub!" Mark yelled in between laughter as the team made their way out into the night. Bill grabbed him, forcing him into a chair so that Johnny could examine his face. The cut was deep, and a thick ooze of blood was making its way down his chin. Johnny used a clump of napkins to staunch the flow. Mark jerked his head from side to side, yelling to the men around him, making Johnny's job that much harder. Each bout of laughter opened the wound afresh. Johnny finally gave up, holding the blood-soaked clump of napkins dejectedly at his side.

"I'm going to have to take him to the ER," Johnny yelled at Sam. "Can you get a ride home?"

Michaels stood close by, monitoring the situation.

"Don't worry about me," Sam yelled back. "I'll be fine. Let's get him out of here."

Michaels spoke up over the noise. "I can give Sam a lift home," he offered, to Sam's relief. Tate, Lance, and Trey had arrived together, but were beyond hope. Lance was standing behind Tate, his arm around his neck, manhandling him and laughing hysterically. Trey was standing next to them, flicking Lance with wet fingers he repeatedly dunked in his glass. They were a mess.

"Let me say my goodbyes," Michaels said loudly.

"I'll meet you outside," Sam yelled back. "I want to give Johnny a hand!"

They got Mark to his feet and Bill stumbled along behind them. They folded Mark into the front seat of Johnny's car as Bill collapsed in the back and commenced snoring. Johnny rolled his eyes, gave Sam a quick hug, and headed out of the parking lot.

Sam scanned the parking lot for Michaels' red pickup just as the door to the pub flew open. Michaels emerged with Daniels on his heels, a deep scowl marring the commander's face.

"You ready, Sam?" Michaels asked, flashing a rare smile.

"I'm ready to be out of there," she replied with a jab of her thumb. Sam glanced at Daniels, but he kept his eyes forward.

They made their way out into the parking lot and the source of Daniels' tension was soon revealed. Michaels had offered Sam a ride home, yet he had no ride to offer. He had come with Daniels.

~

I'm going to catch hell for this one, Michaels thought to himself as Daniels wove through traffic, his eyes firmly affixed to the roadway. Yet he couldn't help reveling in Daniels' discomfort. Michaels had spent the last three months watching Daniels watch Sam. The commander's feelings were apparent, even if he wouldn't admit it. Michaels concurred with Daniels' rule about mixing with students. He would never consider being involved with one himself, even if he weren't saddled with a wife. But his concern for Daniels overrode his sense of decorum. He had never seen Daniels respond to anyone the way he responded to Sam and one thing was certain: the man needed to get laid.

Michaels was willing to take a hit for the setup. The academy was almost done and in less than two weeks, Daniels would no longer be Sam's commander. They would be free to do as they liked. He was confident Daniels wouldn't put himself in a compromising position while Sam was his cadet. The man had the patience of Job and prided himself on his adherence to rules. Michaels simply wanted to give them some time away from the academy. He had watched them on the farm, glad they had a few moments to themselves, and was hopeful a foundation had been laid. Maybe Daniels would actually open up a bit, allow himself to enjoy a woman's company after so many years of living like a fucking monk.

Daniels' isolation bothered Michaels. No one should waste their life mourning. You had to move on at some point and that point had finally come. Michaels wasn't going to sit by and watch Daniels blow an opportunity. Michaels had come to respect Sam. She was smart, a hard worker, and a serious student. He knew she had a bright future and, above all, she was tough. She didn't take shit off the guys yet handled herself with propriety. In many ways, she and Daniels were a lot alike. They both tended to be stern perfectionists and seemed to enjoy pushing themselves. Perhaps their similarities would work in their favor, perhaps not. Michaels wasn't trying to plan a wedding, but if someone could break through Daniels' rigid exterior, more power to them.

Michaels had initially worried about Sam and Ty, at one point suspecting they were a couple. But the past months had shown that they simply enjoyed a strange form of friendship. Michaels had never seen anything like it and couldn't imagine having a female as a friend. It was bad enough he had a wife at home who insisted on wasting dinnertime discussing current events instead of catching up on ESPN. He felt confident Ty would accept Daniels, should something develop between him and Sam. After all, the two men had grown close and obviously cared about each other. Michaels would leave it to them to work out their bizarre triangle.

Come Monday, Michaels would take his lumps. But then again, perhaps Daniels would thank him. Michaels stepped from the vehicle, grinned, and waved goodnight.

As Daniels drove, he contemplated the many ways he would ream Michaels come Monday. The guy had set him up and there was no way out of it. Not that Daniels had a problem spending time with Samantha, it was just he worried so much about appearances that it quelled much of the joy he felt at getting her alone.

Once they dropped Michaels off, they drove in silence and Daniels became aware of the long stretch of quiet. Sam was content to remain mute. The last thing she wanted was to push him into a conversation. It seemed each time she did, her reckless side took over and before she knew it, she was delving into dangerous territory. She kept her mouth clamped shut, refusing to give her brain an opportunity to sabotage the conversation.

"Where do you live, Samantha?" Daniels finally asked, relieved to have a topic of conversation.

"Downtown. Where do you live?" she asked, then bit her lip.

"Just north of downtown, in Winter Park." Their conversation stalled as the streetlights flashed by.

As they entered downtown, Sam directed him to her building. Daniels parked his SUV, then came around to open her door. It had been some time since a man had opened a door for her. Ty sometimes did it as a joke, but other than Ty's attentions, there had been such a lack of chivalry in Sam's life she had forgotten how pleasant it could be.

Sam thanked him as she climbed out and the silence accompanied them to her building. Her mind was racing, wondering what she should do once they reached the door. She couldn't ask him up. If he said no, she would feel like an idiot. If he said yes, Sam worried he would regret the transgression. Sam was all too familiar with his propensity for rules; she assumed mixing with students was at the top of the list. It was a no-win situation. As they approached the lobby, Sam gave up and simply let it play out.

Once they reached the door, Sam turned to him. "Thank you for bringing me home. I appreciate the ride." She could feel herself stalling. Daniels extended his hand and Sam took it, but he didn't shake it, he simply held on, staring at it as if it were a foreign object before covering it with his other hand. He finally looked up at her.

"Good night, Samantha." He released her hand and turned to go.

Sam watched him walk away just as her saboteur spoke up. "Would you like to come up for coffee?"

Daniels turned toward her and smiled. "I'd love some."

Sam wasn't the only one battling an inner voice. Daniels' sane side was telling him to leave immediately; to get away from there as fast as he could. He didn't trust himself to be alone with her, not after having spent the last three months watching her, replaying their brief conversations over and over again in his head. The thought of being alone with Samantha caused such a nervous tug that he could feel his pulse bound in his chest.

And still he followed. Like Sam, a reckless force was compelling Daniels forward. Both mutely went along with the tide.

They were silent in the elevator. They arrived on her floor and Sam ushered him into the dark apartment. The lights from outside streamed in and she clicked on a small lamp in the hallway. Daniels followed her into the kitchen and Sam set up the coffee pot as he stood in the doorway, leaning against the frame. Sam could picture him in the tower, in the classroom, anywhere at the academy in that same stance. He watched her intently as she worked. She scooped out the coffee with an unsteady hand, spilling a bit on the counter as Daniels stood behind her, smiling at her discomfort. Finally, Sam dropped the scoop and spread her hands on the counter before turning to face him.

"Look, you're making me nervous standing there watching." She stood with her feet defiantly spread, hands planted on her hips. "I feel as if any moment, you're going to demand twenty pushups for the mess."

"I tell you what," Daniels replied casually, pushing from the wall. "I'll wait outside. Is that a safe enough distance?"

"It's a start," Sam murmured, turning back to the coffee. Daniels grinned and headed for the balcony.

As the coffee brewed, Sam stole into the bathroom to freshen up. She washed her face and brushed her teeth, hoping the cold water would clear her head. She had only had two drinks, thanks to Mark's misbehavior at the pub, but her nerves were taut knowing the commander was right outside.

She returned to the living room and could see him standing outside, hands spread on the railing, his shoulders outlined by his jacket. His head swung slowly as he took in the view. He wore a pair of jeans that hung loosely on his body and a buttoned-down shirt, the sleeves rolled up. A faded leather jacket held him against the cold. Sam shook her head at the sight of him and headed for the kitchen.

For the past three months, Sam had grown accustomed to seeing Daniels in a position of authority: the operations he oversaw, the breadth of his charges. That the commander, with all his responsibilities, should be here in her house, relaxing and waiting for coffee, was a strange juxtaposition Sam could not get her head around.

She poured two cups and carried them to the balcony. Sam settled in and Daniels took Ty's chair, stretching his long legs up onto the railing. From the side, his body formed a beautiful check mark.

"How long have you lived here?" Daniels asked, taking a deep sip from his mug, and putting his head back. He stared at her as she spoke.

"For three years. I bought it after my father died." Sam wrapped her hands around her mug, savoring its heat.

"How did your father die?" Daniels wished he could simply shake all the information from her. He lacked the patience to wade through their lives one question at a time. He wanted to know everything at once.

"Cardiac," Sam replied, her eyes on the dark horizon.

Slowly, their conversation loosened and flowed freely. Daniels spoke of San Diego and the programs he had implemented for the department. They laughed about the academy and the antics of her fellow cadets. Eventually, their talk turned personal again.

"You've never been married?" Sam asked, unaware of his history. Ty had not spoken of Daniels' past.

"I was married once," Daniels replied, tentatively. It was such a heavy topic; he didn't want to quash their conversation with its weight.

"When did you divorce?" Sam was growing uncomfortable with the thought of a past wife, a past life. Perhaps she didn't want to know after all.

Daniels paused. "We didn't divorce. She was killed shortly after we married." Daniels could see Sam stiffen as he spoke. He was used to the response. Everyone reacted in the same way. There was no easy way to tell it. Only Ty had pushed on with more questions, unaware of and unconcerned with decorum.

Sam remained silent. She was familiar with people's response when hearing about loss. She had heard it enough whenever anyone asked about her parents. She hated it and was not about to go that route. Instead, she simply gave him a thoughtful look and then stared out into the night, her hands on her mug.

Daniels stared at her in profile, appreciative of her silence. The death of her parents had branded Samantha with a degree of loss greater than even he had experienced, and her perspective was apparent in the way his words flowed over her. They sat for a while without speaking.

Eventually, Daniels noticed her shivering. The air had grown cold and she wore only a light sweater. "You're cold. We should go in," he said, standing up and picking up their mugs.

Sam rose and led him inside. The warmth of the apartment was bliss, she rubbed her arms to warm her blood. Daniels strode into the kitchen and placed the mugs on the counter. He then returned to the living room as Sam stood at the glass door, staring out into the night. Her reflection showed her deep in thought. Daniels came up behind her and placed his hands on her shoulders.

Sam turned to face him and without thinking, without trying to plan her next move, she slipped her arms beneath his jacket, encircling his waist. She placed her face against his chest and Daniels buried his face in her hair, breathing in her scent. Sam could feel the muscles in his back respond as he slid a hand up to the back of her head.

After a few minutes, Sam pulled from him. She looked up into his face and smiled. "As much as I don't want you to leave, you probably should."

Daniels quietly took her hand and led her to the front door. He held her once more, opened the door, and left.

~

Ty arrived from Ocala the next day as a bronze sun was disappearing through the trees. Sam was scrambling out of the pool when he strolled up. She darted for her towel in the brisk air, snatching it and throwing it over her shoulders. She was anxious to hear about the family meeting. Ty approached her, grinning, and grabbed her around the waist, swinging her in a wide circle.

"I'm soaked! Put me down!" Sam exclaimed, slapping his shoulder. Ty laughed as he held her off the ground.

Ty was happy. He had made it through the final stage of his father's passing and was finally free. "Down you go," he said, placing her gently on the ground.

Sam wrapped the towel around her waist, threw on a sweatshirt, and grabbed his hand. "Come upstairs. I've made dinner and I want to hear all about it," she said, pulling him along as she headed for the lobby.

When they got inside the apartment, Sam ordered him to the balcony as she headed for the shower. Ty stopped in the kitchen and fixed them both a drink before settling into his usual spot. The low sun was turning the cypress around the lake a rusty orange and the smell of a distant fire hung lazily in the air.

Sam joined him on the balcony bundled in sweats, her hair damp. She settled into the chair next to him and accepted the tall glass of gin. Ty raised his glass. "To my new life," he announced as they clinked glasses. Sam smiled as she took a sip.

"Well?" she interjected when Ty remained silent.

Ty simply put his head back and stared off into the distance. Sam watched him, waiting. "Tell me what happened!" she exclaimed.

Ty swung his eyes to her, smiling. "Nothing much to tell," he replied, shrugging, and taking a sip. "He wasn't quite as heartless as I thought." He put his head back and closed his eyes, his face relaxed.

As curious as Sam was, she did not want to pry, so she launched into her tale about their night at the pub. She described Mark's run-in with the men from Miami and his trip to the ER, where it had taken six stitches to close his wound. Johnny had described in vivid detail the embarrassing display Mark had made in front of the ER staff, while Bill had slept through the whole thing on the backseat of Johnny's car. Johnny had finally made it home after three, dumping Mark and Bill on the living room floor to sleep it off.

"Sounds like a fascinating evening," Ty said, laughing. Then his mind clicked.

"If Johnny took Mark to the hospital, how did you get home?"

"Michaels offered me a ride. Daniels took us both home," Sam replied. She took a sip of her drink.

"Who did he drop off first?" Ty probed, grinning.

Sam glanced over at him. "We dropped Michaels off first. Daniels brought me home. He came up for coffee," she added, not wanting to keep anything hidden.

"Did you guys have a nice time?" Ty inquired quietly, watching her.

Sam blushed before dropping her eyes to her glass. "Yes, it was nice."

Ty could see it in her face, the same thing he had seen on the training field as she sat next to Daniels: a pleasant calm. He didn't push the issue. He figured Sam would open up eventually and if he pushed too hard, she might shut him out. Ty wanted her happy. He wanted Daniels happy. The situation still made him anxious, but he didn't want to be excluded from their lives. Ty knew if the issue were to form a wedge between them, everything they had so carefully constructed would come apart.

Ty put his head back, relieved to be home. What he hadn't told Sam was that his father, on a whim of generosity, had seen to Ty's future beyond anything he ever expected. His mother would be taken care of; her monies were vast, and his uncle would take over the farm, freeing her from responsibility. She would start a new life as soon as she signed over her holdings.

As for Ty, his father had left him over a quarter of a million, tucked away in an investment fund. But Ty was too overwhelmed to discuss figures with Sam. Instead, he simply relished the fact that he would be able to take care of her, should she ever need anything.

~

Daniels was looking forward to seeing Ty. As he drove to the greenway, he wondered about his weekend. Ty had filled him in on his planned trip home; Daniels could tell he was anxious for the whole affair to be over. Daniels was curious if Ty would discuss any of it with him.

He was also thinking about Sam and whether he should broach the subject with Ty. Daniels felt he had a pretty good handle on Ty and Sam's relationship, but perhaps it was more complicated than he assumed. Sometimes Daniels wondered if Sam's hesitation with him was due in part to her feelings for Ty. They didn't act like two people in love, although their closeness was undeniable, but how could he discuss the matter without overstepping his bounds with either of them? He was forced to simply wait things out, which he hated. Daniels was never good at standing by and seeing how things played out. He preferred to direct the course of events, to have a hand in their outcome. The role of passive observer stuck in his craw.

When Daniels arrived, Ty was already waiting. As he climbed out, Ty jogged over, grinning. "I beat you this time!" he exclaimed; his face bright with excitement. The two men embraced briefly, then made their way onto the path. "So how did things go?" Daniels asked. "Everything settled?"

"Yes, we met with the attorney and had the reading. My mother will turn over her holdings in the farm to my uncle. She intends to move to Savannah to be closer to her sister."

Daniels waited to see if Ty would continue. Ty could sense his anticipation. "My father took good care of me," he said, glancing up at Daniels. "I was shocked. I didn't expect anything from the man, but apparently he felt enough to look out for my future."

"I'm glad, Ty," Daniels replied, placing a hand on his shoulder. "Perhaps it was his way of apologizing."

"Maybe so." Ty shrugged. "Anyway, it's done and I'm ready to run!" He slapped Daniels on the belly and bolted.

When they finished, they headed for the table and settled in for their cooldown. The air was brisk, the sky a clear fall blue. They glanced at each other, both waiting for the other to speak. As their breathing slowed, Ty plunged forward.

"Sam filled me in on the other night. I guess Mark won't be paying Miami Fire a visit anytime soon," he said grinning, hoping to ease into the subject of Sam.

"Well, it had been a rough week. I think Mark was looking for a way to vent." Daniels also wanted to discuss Samantha yet was unsure how to broach the subject.

"Sam said you gave her a ride home," Ty continued, tentatively.

"Yes, I did. Johnny seemed to have his hands full with Mark and Bill. Michaels was with us," Daniels added.

Ty smiled. "I'm glad you were there."

Daniels didn't respond at first. Finally, he said, "You and Sam are close." He didn't pose it as a question, simply a statement of fact.

Ty glanced over at him. "Yes, we are. She's the best friend I've ever had." He kept his eyes on Daniels, who stared straight ahead. A pause hung in the air before Daniels proceeded. "Do you love her?" He was unable to look Ty in the face when he said it. He spun his water bottle in circles within his palm, watching it as it turned.

"Yes, I love her, as a friend," Ty replied before adding, "We aren't romantic." He continued watching Daniels, noting the discomfort in his face. Ty would have liked to reach over, to give him a reassuring nudge that it was OK, that he understood there was something developing between him and Sam and that Ty would adjust, that they would work through it. Instead, he choked on his words and the silence grew.

Instead of speaking, Daniels straightened on the bench and looked meaningfully at Ty. At once, Daniels could read his face, could see the understanding in the way Ty looked at him. As Ty's face broke into a grin, it reassured Daniels that all was well. Daniels smiled a hesitant smile and then cut his eyes to the tree line. Nothing more was said, but a truce over Sam had been sealed.

XX

Monday morning arrived and Daniels was pacing the field when Michaels pulled into the academy. As he jogged out onto the field, he tried to read the commander's face, anticipating the degree of ass-chewing he was about to receive. Daniels watched him approach, his expression blank.

"Good morning, Scott," Daniels said with little emotion, but the fact that he was using first names eased Michaels' anxiety.

"Morning, Matt," Michaels replied, happy to go along with the familiar tone. Neither man spoke for a moment.

"I suppose you're pretty pleased with yourself," Daniels muttered, staring out across the field, hands on his hips.

"Not sure what you mean," Michaels replied quizzically as he stretched his legs.

Daniels finally swung his eyes to him. "I think you do." He fought the smile working its way into his features.

"How'd things go?" Michaels asked tentatively, moving in close.

Daniels exhaled and shuffled his feet. "It was a nice evening. Very pleasant," he replied sheepishly, unable to convey how much he had enjoyed being alone with Samantha. His thoughts had returned to her throughout the weekend. He found he missed her. He yearned to talk to her, learn more about her. That Michaels had understood his feelings moved him; it reassured him of the bond the two men shared. Michaels had been the one person who knew his history, who understood his grief but never pushed. That is, until now. But perhaps it was just the nudge Daniels needed.

"So glad," Michaels replied, giving him a quick pat on the back. The officers glanced up as Ty and Sam pulled into the parking lot. Ty came bounding over as Sam headed inside, throwing the officers a quick wave.

"Speak of the devil," Michaels added, grinning.

~

As their final week kicked off, the cadets were ordered into the classroom following PT. The instructors had something special in store; so special, Daniels was in attendance. He slipped into the back of the room as the students settled noisily at their desks. Ty grinned and Daniels returned the smile with a quick nod. Michaels and Tanner braced up front.

"Congratulations on your final week," Michaels began. "Our goal is to get everyone through the final phase so listen up as we lay out the schedule. Today, we'll continue practice drills in preparation for your practical final and the state exam. Tomorrow, we'll have one more class review to prepare for the written tests." He then skipped forward in the week.

"Thursday, you'll have your final practical exam. Friday, the final written in the morning, graduation that evening, at least for those of you who pass," he added with a smirk. It was met with nervous laughter.

"But Wednesday, we have something special planned. We've arranged to participate in an off-site burn. It will be a joint training exercise between Orlando Fire and Orange County. The building is a condemned hotel just outside of Zellwood." He slid his glance to Tanner, who stepped forward, flipped open a file folder, and began handing out the paperwork. "You've each been given a copy of the floor plan," Michaels continued as the cadets stared anxiously at the layout. "It's a three-storied, wood-frame. It's been abandoned for a while, so it's in pretty shitty shape, but it will give you guys a taste of the real thing. As you can see, there are three wings that jut off its main front." All eyes were glued on their sheets. Michaels began pacing the front of the room.

"OFD will train in the middle wing, Orange County on the south, and you all will have the north wing. The building will be lit off in stages. You'll get to practice forcible entry, search and rescue, and perform a series of hose evolutions. We'll have you work through attack scenarios and you'll finally have the opportunity to fight real fire." The class buzzed with nervous anticipation.

Daniels leaned against the back wall, the concern simmering in his chest. He relished the joint operations and enjoyed training alongside area departments, and the exposure to live fire and the chance to witness experienced teams making entries was a rare opportunity for the students. But off-site burns carried certain risks. The buildings were typically dilapidated structures that frequently contained hidden dangers. Many of them were balloon construction, with spaces in the walls that ran continuously into the attic above. This allowed hidden fires to race upward, funneling straight into the attic where they could spread undetected. In no time, the fire could run the length of the building, surrounding unsuspecting crews.

Live burns were always a trade-off between safety and experience. In the burn building, an instructor could monitor the amount of heat, controlling safety, to a degree. The experience afforded the students exposure to simulated fire conditions and prepared them for the real thing. But off-site burns were a different beast. They provided a much more realistic scenario and better prepared the students for actual fire, but they posed increased risks for inexperienced rookies. Close monitoring by the instructors was critical. Daniels would send the best of his team.

As the students filed out of the classroom and headed to their lockers, they chattered amongst themselves in hushed tones. The week was going to be intense. They had their finals to prepare for, the state test to dread, and now the joint training exercise to anticipate. Stress levels within the group were sky-high.

During lunch, Daniels came out to the field to meet with his instructors. They would have several formal meetings in preparation for the burn, but Daniels was feeling hyper-cautious and wanted reassurance that everyone was on board. They stood in a huddle, seven in all. The special ops instructors, Taylor and Adams, would also participate in the burn. The class size had shrunk considerably, so the safety ratio could be met by a smaller corps, but Daniels wanted all his lead instructors in on the action.

The students watched the officers from their positions on the grass. The late afternoon sun was striking the huddle at an angle, casting elongated shadows, their presence magnified by the effect.

Tate was nervous about the burn. Although his confidence around live fire had improved, his bowels still kicked into overdrive whenever he was fully packed out. Johnny sat next to him, stripping apart blades of grass, running through tactics in his head in anticipation of the scenarios. Bill and Mark were hungry for the experience. Mark was particularly hyped. Knowing he had mastered his fear of heights gave him a feeling of invincibility; the pounding he gave that dick from Miami only intensified the feeling. He fingered his stitches, smiling to himself.

Trey looked forward to the opportunity to see Orange County Fire in action. He had his heart set on working for the department, having a cousin who had been with the county for six years. He also held serious doubts about his ability to compete for a position on OFD, although he would never admit it out loud. Lying next to him, Lance wasn't thinking much of anything. He was sprawled out on the grass, barely noticing the instructors nearby, wondering what the hell he had eaten to produce such horrific farts. Trey was none too pleased with the effects and scooted farther afield.

Ty and Sam sat together, sharing the last of her water. They watched the men in the huddle, but for different reasons. Ty watched as Daniels led the discussion, noting the way Daniels stood, the subtle movements of his hands as they emphasized his speech. Ty noticed the way the men listened to him; their attention rapt. It always amazed him, the way Daniels' mere presence commanded respect and authority. How did one achieve that? Did it come naturally or was it something Daniels had developed during his years as an officer? Ty tried to imagine himself in that position: making command decisions, supervising subordinates, leading men. He had come to idolize Daniels and was no longer content to simply be close to him. Ty wanted to be just like him.

Sam's attention was also consumed by Daniels. Like Ty, she spent much of her time admiring Daniels' easy command, his natural ability as a leader. Daniels reminded her of her father: his authoritative interaction with the men under his command and the heady air of rank that surrounded him like a vapor. Daniels' authority, which at times intimidated her, also provided a blissful comfort she had grown used to as the daughter of a naval captain. Proximity to his power was like coming home.

But Sam's admiration was not restricted to Daniels' authority. It also included the radical swing in his character she was privy to whenever they were alone, a softness that seemed so at odds with the man on the field before her. Sam's ability to elicit that side of him created her own sense of authority, a fine sensation of command over someone always in command of others. The experience was intoxicating.

As the huddle broke, Daniels glanced over at Sam and Ty. *Two peas in a pod*, he thought to himself. They sat in identical positions on the grass: knees bent, elbows atop, feet spread, their bodies, as usual, touching. Their heads were turned in his direction, but their eyes were hidden beneath the shade of their helmets. They passed a water bottle back and forth and he couldn't help but envy Ty's mouth sharing with hers. They appeared to be watching him, but he couldn't quite tell. The question was answered as Ty raised a hand and waved. Daniels smiled, waved, and headed across the field. When he glanced back, they were still watching.

~

The two officers grabbed their beers and headed to a quiet corner away from the bar. They settled in and pulled out their copies of the building plans. Their files contained the safety checklists that had been completed by the Inspectors tasked with ensuring the building was up to code for the burn. This included removal of all asbestos, electric wiring, insulation, appliances, and carpet. Ventilation cuts had already been made in the roof directly over where the burns would take place and the windows had been cleared and replaced with removable plywood panels. All the outlets in the structure had been removed or knocked into the walls, the holes filled with expanding, fire-resistant foam to prevent the spread of fire.

Daniels scanned the safety measures again but still fought a nagging apprehension in his belly. "You're sure everything's kosher?" he grumbled, flipping through the paperwork. "You know these big fuckers make me nervous." It was one thing to light off an old house or small apartment complex; it was another to try to control the spread of fire in a multistoried hotel that had never been retrofitted.

"Everything looks good. You sure you're not just nervous because you have a vested interest in this class?" Michaels eyed the commander, grinning.

"Hilarious," Daniels replied sarcastically, glancing up from the file to flash his icy greys. He glanced over the paperwork one last time before pushing it aside and turning to his beer. Michaels quickly changed the subject.

"I finally got Tanner to agree to hold the party at his house." The end-of-semester party would take place on Saturday night. The instructors usually rotated the responsibility, but for the past year, Tanner had dodged his rotation. He had finally relented, even agreeing to supply the keg.

"You really want the students exposed to that man's squalor?" Daniels replied with a grin. "It's not exactly a pleasure palace. The bathroom alone's enough to send you screaming for the bleach." Daniels had experienced it first-hand when he had the misfortune of having to piss after giving Tanner a ride home when his dilapidated Chevy took a dump on I-4.

"Why don't I host the party," Daniels offered, taking a swig of his beer and waiting for Michaels' shock.

"*You* would host the party?" Michaels exclaimed; his beer paused in midair. "Since when do you open your home to . . ." and the sentence died on his lips as his face broke into a grin. "I get it. Now that you have the twins, suddenly you're not so opposed to company," Michaels added slyly, nodding his head and slipping over the term his brain used to refer to Ty and Sam. Daniels caught the slip and looked at him questioningly.

"What the hell do you mean by twins?" Daniels asked gruffly, although he couldn't deny the resemblance between Ty and Sam.

Michaels stammered, fingering his bottle. "It's just that Sam and Ty are so much alike. They work and act like twins. Haven't you noticed, or is it too Freudian for you to delve into?" He chuckled and took another sip.

Daniels struggled to keep a straight face, flashing back to Sam and Ty on the grass, the strong similarity in their appearance. Michaels had a point. Sam and Ty were so much alike, and Daniels sometimes wondered if their similarities were part of what drew him to the cadets. He shook his head, unable to articulate his thoughts, and took another pull from his beer.

Michaels took note and followed suit. They gathered their paperwork, drained their beers, and headed out.

~

The exam was only three days away, so the students spent Tuesday locked in the classroom. Late in the afternoon, they were released to their locker rooms. They were instructed to assemble their gear and meet at the tower where Tanner would issue their airpacks for tomorrow's live burn. Once at the tower, they arranged their bunker gear next to their assigned packs to expedite their departure in the morning.

As they assembled their gear, Michaels and Tanner performed safety inspections. They checked the students' gear for wear and tear and any holes that would allow the heat to work its way in. They checked their Nomex hoods, gloves, and boots, and then had the students don their entire assemblage and breathe off their tanks.

The students stood in line, their faces hidden behind their masks, the hiss of their regulators falling in a constant, steady rhythm. They no longer shouldered their gear awkwardly like rookies. There was no more shuffling of feet, no more nervous adjustments to their straps, no more tugging of their face masks to insure they were snug. The cadets had spent enough time dressed out that they now wore their gear like a second skin. They had come to depend on it: the weight of their helmets, the snug fit of their boots, and the secure encapsulation the entire assemblage afforded. The gear would see them through the fires that would be set the next day. Tomorrow, they would be released from the confines of the academy and let loose amidst conditions that would only be controlled through their concerted efforts. The instructors would be watching, but the students would be on their own, ready to take on that force they had spent the last three months learning to fight: fire.

XXI

The bus bumped along for over an hour before arriving with a squeal of rusty brakes in the desolate municipality of Zellwood. The back of the bus was piled high with gear and helmets; the students were spread out toward the front. The instructors followed in two academy SUVs. Tanner, in the engine, brought up the rear. Daniels would join them later in the morning.

The hotel was located just west of the city's boundary, on an expanse of land surrounded by vast fields of corn. How the hotel had managed to stay in business for over eighty years was anyone's guess, being so far removed from the small clump of buildings that served as downtown.

The hotel had fallen into disrepair in the '70s and been abandoned in foreclosure soon after. The structure had stood vacant since then, serving as a refuge for transients and a source of wood for poverty-stricken locals. Its walls were crumbling whitewash, the decorative shutters that had once hung aside its many windows either missing or dangling by remnant screws.

When the convoy pulled up, the hotel grounds were already flanked with fire apparatus. OFD had three engines, two rescues, and a ladder truck staged near the end of their wing. Their District Chief was parked off to the side. Orange County's units were staged to the south, and because of the distance spanning the wings, they would have little interaction with the cadets.

The students unloaded their gear and airpacks, placing them in neat piles in the grass. The instructors made their way over to where the officers were gathering in a huddle. The students watched the men from OFD as they prepared their equipment. Their rigs were the best money could buy; expensive, sophisticated units that provided the latest technology in fire suppression. The students looked on with envy.

The crews filtered over to where the students were gathered, flashing back to their own first nerve-wracking experience with live fire, graciously shaking hands with each cadet. They joked and backslapped to put the students at ease. Johnny knew many of the men, having worked alongside them during his years on the ambulance.

The drivers began setting up their rigs. Tanner positioned the engine alongside the north wing, setting the parking brake and engaging the pump before hooking into the nearby hydrant. Mark and Bill assisted him, stretching the supply line. Tanker trucks would also be utilized in case the need for water overwhelmed area hydrants.

When the instructors and officers were through with their meeting, Michaels gave a shriek of his whistle and motioned for the students to assemble in a group. He waited as the cadets gathered in a nervous cluster.

"The hotel will be lit off in stages, starting with the first floor," he began, his brow knotted above his sunglasses. "Hay and pallets will be used, just like in the burn building, and your group will make entry via the end of the wing." He twisted and pointed to the wooden doors. "Groups on floors two and three will use the exterior stairwells," he continued, and the students squinted into the sun, peering at the metal stairway that scaled the end of the wing. "An instructor will be monitoring the interior end of the wing to make sure the fire doesn't get away from you. We want all activity confined to the wing of the building."

"You'll attack in teams of eight: two on the first hoseline, two on the backup, two to perform search and rescue, and two to ventilate," he continued, ticking off the teams on his fingers. "Dummies are hidden inside and it's up to the search crews to locate them and drag them out. Ventilation crews, report to Adams. He'll give you the signal when to ladder and ventilate. The groups will take turns and those not fighting fire will move through forcible entry drills on the other floors."

The students were broken into groups and would remain in those groups throughout the day. Sam, Ty, Johnny, Tate, Mark, Bill, Lance and Trey made up group three. Group one would be first in and attack the fires on the first floor while the others practiced forcible entry. Group two would be assigned to the second floor; group three, the third.

The instructors and students donned their gear. "Give your partner a thorough safety check," Michaels yelled over the noise of the fireground as the cadets nervously jumped into action. When Sam and Ty had completed their checks, Ty gave her helmet a tweak, smiling to break the tension.

Silence settled over the cadets. This was not going to be like the drills in the burn building. There was no instructor with his hand braced on the kill switch, should something go wrong. They would have to be alert and on their toes, once they were inside. It would be up to each of them to ensure the safety of everyone involved and the weight of responsibility settled over them like a pall.

Michaels and Taylor, their faces set, performed a final check of the perimeter. Michaels seemed naked without his clipboard, despite being fully dressed out. Taylor would serve as the safety officer, patrolling the exterior of the structure, watching for changes in fire conditions, deterioration in the building's integrity, and for any safety violations on the fireground. Adams would assist exterior crews in ventilation, guiding the crews through ladder operations. An adjunct would be poised inside the structure where the wing joined the main building, monitoring the students' progress on the fire floors. Once everything was set, the evolutions began.

~

Daniels was on edge and this asshole from the Health and Safety Board was wasting his time. Daniels, along with Commander Phillips from the police academy, were stuck playing tour guide to a small battalion of public officials who insisted on a walk-through of the Institute's training facilities. These public displays occurred several times a year and were simply formalities requiring patience and the ability to dole out heaping piles of bullshit.

Daniels and Phillips were partners in loathing. They hated the PR side of their jobs. They were busy men with too much responsibility to be escorting bloated public officials around their grounds.

Daniels was especially perturbed. He would have liked to have gone out to the burn with the others instead of having to wade through this nonsense. As one of the officials droned on about budgets, Daniels recalled Michaels' ribbing from the other night. He knew his keen interest in the class was grounded in his feelings for Samantha and Ty. Although Daniels felt tremendous responsibility for all his students, seeing the two of them safely through was foremost in his mind.

When Michaels first brought up the opportunity for the burn, Daniels had initially refused. Live burns were always problematic and a bitch to regulate. But with OFD and Orange County handling all safety preparations, the academy would be granted inclusion free from the lengthy procedures required to bring the building in line with NFPA training regulations. It would be a great opportunity for the students, Michaels argued.

Daniels knew Michaels was right. It was a rare opportunity for students to get to fight live fire outside the safety of the burn building. But the freedom from safety preps also meant Daniels was not the one overseeing those preparations. His lack of involvement did not sit well with him. He would have preferred to be the one in charge. He had worked extensively with OFD and Orange County. They had good people on the job, and he trusted their judgment. Perhaps Michaels was right; perhaps he was just being overcautious because of his concern over Samantha and Ty.

Daniels' foul mood was made worse by lack of sleep, which he had tried to combat by chugging several cups of strong coffee. He now found himself strung tight from too much caffeine, which only added to his irritation. He had tossed and turned the night before, unable to clear his head. He had finally dozed off, only to be woken by a haunting dream.

He was climbing the stairs of the tower and the smell of smoke hung heavy in the air, yet each floor was clear, and silence reverberated against the barren walls. He climbed several flights yet seemed unable to reach his destination. He finally made it onto one of the floors and found Michaels and Tanner braced along the perimeter of the room. They were decked out in full gear, their gloved hands locked onto their waist straps, their masks hanging loosely around their necks. They were staring at something beyond Daniels' view. They swung their heads silently as he approached, then slid their gazes back across the room.

Daniels took a few tentative steps inside the room. Sam and Ty sat tucked against each other on the floor, their backs against the far wall. They wore bunker pants, boots, and tee shirts. They sat as they had in the grass: knees bent, hands resting on top, their bodies so close they appeared as one. They watched him intently from across the room.

Daniels glanced back at Michaels and Tanner, who continued to stare at the cadets. When he returned his gaze to Sam and Ty, they had moved from their position against the wall. Sam now lay on her back in the middle of the room, arms and legs spread eagle on the concrete, her suspenders lying loosely at her hips. Ty knelt between her legs, as if just completing a patient assessment. As Daniels watched, Ty lowered himself onto Sam, blocking Daniels' view of her face. Daniels froze, his voice mute, his muscles locked in place. He glanced urgently at Michaels, but Michaels continued to stare at the cadets, as if evaluating their performance.

Daniels' eyes flew back to Ty, who was now moving slowly against Sam. His arms and shoulders flexed each time his body made its upward thrust, his suspenders cutting a sharp X across his back. Daniels was straining to get a glimpse of Sam's face, yet seemed trapped behind an invisible wall of glass. Sam slid her hands to Ty's hips, gripping the cinches below his waist, her leg bent to fold him against her. Her hands followed his movements as their bodies worked in a slow rhythm.

Ty gasped and extended his arms, raising his chest high above her, arching his back in release. Daniels tore his eyes from Ty to stare at Sam, who was now visible beneath him. Her eyes were closed, lips barely parted, her face serene and turned toward the men who watched. Ty slowly lowered himself onto her, his arms encircling her head. He buried his face against her neck as Sam's arms closed around him. Daniels slammed his eyes shut and when he finally summoned the courage to open them, Ty was gone, and Sam was staring intently at him. The dream disintegrated and Daniels was wrenched from sleep. He awoke bathed in sweat, his heartbeat a ragged thunder in his chest.

Sleep never returned. Daniels worked to decipher the dream, straining to put the pieces together. He knew it was grounded in the bond between Sam and Ty, and his own perplexity when it came to their relationship. Perhaps he had yet to accept the nature of their friendship, the intensity of their commitment to each other. Perhaps it stemmed from the envy he felt when he watched them together; the closeness of their bodies, the familiarity with which they moved. To have that freedom with Samantha was something Daniels craved. Just as Ty longed for Daniels' natural abilities, Daniels longed for the one thing only Ty possessed: access to Sam.

Daniels pushed the dream from his mind and tried to focus on the meeting. His urgency to attend the burn intensified with each passing minute and when the meeting finally wrapped, he fled.

~

The first fire was lit off as group one huddled near the doorway at the end of the wing. They readied themselves, checking and rechecking their gear. The radios were alive with chatter and when the fire was licking the ceiling, the call to enter was given. The door was thrown open, black smoke belched forth, and the group was swallowed by the darkened hallway.

On the third floor, Sam's group was busy forcing doors and tearing through walls using tools they had lugged up the dilapidated stairway. Group two practiced on the second floor and the halls reverberated with the sounds of crashing plaster, splintering wood.

The first evolution went smoothly. Shane and Bo had manned the attack line and were so jacked with adrenaline they could barely stand still. They talked animatedly about conditions inside: the dense smoke, the intense heat. They prattled on as group two prepared for their attack.

As Daniels neared Zellwood, he switched his portable radio to the "talk-around" channel being used on the fireground. He listened as group one made their attack, pleased at the smoothness of the operation, the swiftness with which the fire was brought under control.

Group two braced on the stairwell as the fires on the second floor were lit. Dense smoke seethed from the second story windows as the exterior crew assembled their ladder in preparation to ventilate. The group's entry was confounded by the narrow stairwell, which led to small platforms outside the second and third floor doorways. The crews were forced to approach single file, slowing their entry time. Sam's group sat in the grass, watching the action on the second floor. They talked quietly amongst themselves as they planned their attack.

Ty jumped at the chance to man the attack line; Sam would back him up. Mark and Bill would perform search and rescue, while Johnny and Tate manned the backup line. Lance and Trey would ladder the building to perform ventilation. As they schemed, Michaels approached the group.

"Listen up, guys," he said as the group gathered 'round. "We may only get one shot at the third floor. The fires are burning hot and we're seeing signs of hotspots in the attic, so we'll have to move quickly if you guys want real action. As soon as group two is done, prepare for entry." With this, the group sprang into action, readying their gear.

Daniels arrived just as group two was exiting the second floor. The first thing he noticed was the condition of the stairwell. With radio in hand, he approached Taylor, who as safety was pacing the outside of the building.

"What's the condition of that stairwell?" Daniels barked over the noise from the trucks.

"It's pretty shitty, but we double-checked the joins, and the hardware is in fair shape. It should be fine," Taylor yelled. Daniels watched as group two made their way down, noting the small cascades of rust filtering from beneath their boots as they backed their equipment down to ground level.

He looked over and saw Ty's group donning their gear. He watched Sam throw her pack onto her back, catching her eye as she adjusted her straps. She gave a quick smile and returned to her work. He could see the anxiety in her face. He could see it in all their faces: that look of intensity, determination, and the faintest hint of fear.

"Light it off!" Michaels barked into his radio.

Group three was now breathing off their tanks and assembling their hoses and tools. They mounted the stairwell, Ty and Sam in the lead, followed closely by Mark and Bill. Johnny and Tate were maneuvering the backup line into place as the first four ascended, while Lance and Trey repositioned to the side of the structure, awaiting the signal to ventilate.

Ty and Sam advanced their hoseline up the stairwell as Mark and Bill followed hot on their heels. Mark's excitement was apparent, even from ground level. He was practically chomping at the bit as he followed Sam up.

Once they reached the third-story platform, Ty and Sam huddled at the doorway, awaiting the call for entry. Acrid smoke seethed through the crack above the door, floating high above their heads in a thick, grey column. Dense puffs emerged from the vast row of windows as the pallets inside were quickly consumed. The call was given, the door thrown open, and one by one, the crews disappeared into the smoke. Daniels held his breath.

He pressed his radio to his ear, monitoring the chatter from the interior instructor, who watched from the far end of the wing. Ty and Sam groped their way down the hallway as Mark and Bill tore through the rooms, searching out the victim. Deep in, they stumbled upon the dummy. They gave the signal to the instructor, who relayed the information via his radio to Michaels on the ground. Mark and Bill grabbed hold of the dummy and hustled toward the exit.

Johnny and Tate materialized in the thick smoke, squatting closely behind Ty and Sam. The teams continued their attack, but the fire kept coming, building in intensity the harder they fought. They would open their nozzles, give a quick burst, but instead of damping down, the fire seemed to expand, quickly spreading above their heads. The smoke was growing thicker, banking to the floor. Ty peered beneath it and could just make out the instructor crouched at the opposite end of the hall, his radio held close to his mask. The instructor gave a jab of his radio and Ty opened his line, but the result was the same, their stream impotent against the mounting wall of flames.

Mark and Bill dragged the dummy out onto the platform and were jockeying into position to get it down the stairs. The tight confines of the platform, combined with the bulk of their bodies, made for difficult work. Daniels noticed another shower of rust as they began their descent. Inside, the fire intensified as Ty and Sam continued to struggle. The heat was driving them back toward the stairway, and Johnny and Tate were forced to retreat. Ty peered through the smoke and flames but could no longer see the instructor at the end of the hallway. The fire had cut him off, forcing him to withdraw via the interior stairwell. The students were on their own.

As the heat forced them to the floor, Sam slapped Ty's helmet, jabbing her thumb in the direction of the door. They needed to back out. They were practically on their bellies, the heat above their heads, intense. The smoke was banked down along the floor. Johnny and Tate had already made it to the stairwell and were maneuvering their hose for the descent. Sam ducked her head and could just make out the reflectors on Ty's helmet as he continued to battle the flames.

Sam smacked him again and he finally got moving. They worked to back the line toward the door, swinging the nozzle in quick circles to ward off the intense heat, but as they struggled toward the exit, Ty ended up behind her. Sam glanced beyond him and could just make out the base of the doorway. They were almost there. Ty slammed the nozzle shut and backed out onto the platform just as Sam turned to crawl out. She took one last look down the hallway.

Fire was racing across the ceiling toward them in thick, rippling waves. The dense smoke beneath it was coal black and pulsed with each wave. The heat was like nothing they had experienced in the burn building. Sam could feel her ears burning despite her Nomex hood. She took one last look before turning toward the doorway. But as she turned for the exit, the smoke parted just enough for her to glimpse the dim light of the gaping doorway. Ty had vanished. The platform was empty.

Sam's heart leaped in her chest. Ty had been there mere seconds ago, but now the platform outside the doorway was a pale void of light. Confused, Sam swung her head toward the fire, thinking perhaps Ty had made it back inside. But the tight confines of the hallway would have prevented his passage. She crawled forward and when she reached the doorway, her mind went blank as the sight before her registered: Ty and the stairwell were gone.

Sam felt the panic rise in her throat. She didn't care about the stairwell; she didn't care that she had no hoseline. She didn't even care how the fuck she was going to get down from the third floor. At that moment, all she cared about was Ty.

Where was he? What happened to him? Had he fallen three stories? Her mind raced, but the heat was forcing her out, the smoke quickly engulfing her.

Sam crawled out onto the small platform. The fire followed her out the door, blowing over her shoulders like a wave. She tried to make herself as small as possible, keeping her back to the doorway and tucking into a tight ball. The heat penetrated the back of her gear. She could feel it searing her shoulders, working its way around her neck. She lifted her hands for cover and could feel the fire scorch her wrists. She glanced at the ground and could just make out the men racing forward. Michaels was screaming into his radio as a crew from OFD sprinted over with a ladder.

Her mind returned to Ty. Suddenly, Sam felt their separation like a mortal wound to her chest. To have him ripped away was like having a knife plunged into her breast, her heart felt torn from its moorings. Her throat clamped shut with emotion and for an instant, she couldn't draw breath.

The fire was on her now. Thick fingers of flame gripped her shoulders, the mounting heat was unbearable. She tucked her head against her chest, drawing her knees up, trying to control her breathing. The pain at her wrists intensified as the flesh sprang into blisters. Her shoulders were burning, her neck felt on fire, and her hands were immobilized in agony. Sam closed her eyes, wondering at the slowness of it all. The fire was turning her inside out and she exhaled slowly, waiting for it to end.

Daniels watched it all from the ground. It unfolded before him like some horrific nightmare. He stood, fixated, as the platform holding Ty came down. But the collapse was initiated before Ty even made it out.

As Mark and Bill manipulated the dummy, their weight had snapped the last of the rusted joins holding the stairwell in place. The bulk of their bodies, the weight of their gear, and the extra burden of the dummy were too much for the ancient hardware. The wood beneath had long since been devoured by termites. What had appeared stable on the outside was an illusion. The stairwell could never have held.

Mark and Bill had just made it to the ground when Johnny and Tate emerged onto the platform. They were halfway down when Daniels saw the first of the joins spring. The second-floor platform tore away, leaving the entire stairwell hanging from the third floor. Michaels was screaming into his radio, trying to communicate with the instructor on the third floor, trying to warn him to evacuate the crew via the laddered window. But by that time, the instructor had been cut off and forced to retreat through the building's interior stairwell. He raced around the rear of the building just as the stairwell fell away, taking Ty down with it.

But the worst was yet to come.

As the stairwell crumbled to the ground, Samantha emerged onto the platform, the fire chasing her out the door, striking glancing blows against her back. She had nowhere to go. She tucked into a ball, trying to protect herself from the flames. Daniels watched as the reflectors on her coat melted and was seized with a paralysis so intense, he could do nothing but watch her be consumed.

Michaels reached her just in time. Two members of OFD had watched the scene unfold and grabbed a thirty-five-footer off their rig, throwing it against the building. Michaels scaled the rungs before the men even had a chance to tie it off, grabbing Sam by her rescue strap and yanking her from the platform. Freed from the direct heat, he straddled her across his lap and carefully made his way down the ladder. They reached the ground, and she was whisked away by the medics. They laid her in the grass and stripped the smoldering gear from her body.

Daniels rushed over, trying to maintain his composure as a scream rose in his throat for the crews to hurry. They removed her helmet and mask, and he could finally see her face. She was stunned, unable to speak. The skin on the left side of her jaw was bright red and she stared blankly ahead as they removed her tank. Johnny had jumped in and was unzipping her coat. Pain marred her face as the sleeves tore at the blistered flesh on her wrists. Once her tank and coat were off, Johnny laid her back in the grass and the medics took over.

Where's Ty? What happened to him? Is he all right? Why isn't he here? The men moved around her in a blur. Before Sam knew it, she was staring up into a clear sky and could smell the grass near her face through the stench of singed flesh. Her mind tried to focus, tried to piece together the events, but all she could think of was, *Where's Ty?*

As the medics worked, Daniels stood over her. Sam could see his eyes, always those eyes. He stood with arms folded taut, a radio in one hand, the other bracing his jaw as he watched the medics administer oxygen. She couldn't understand why he wouldn't tell her where Ty was. Couldn't he read her face? Didn't he know that was all she cared about? Why wouldn't someone tell her something? She pleaded with her eyes, but he only stared back, his intensity unwavering. Sam forced the obvious from her mind. If Ty were all right, he would be there with her. Nothing would keep him from her. His absence confirmed her worst fear.

Within moments, she was placed on a stretcher, loaded into the Rescue, and on her way to the hospital beneath lights and sirens. Johnny had jumped in the back and he and the OFD medic worked to get her comfortable. The medic radioed the ER as Johnny gave her a shot of morphine. Sam stared at the ceiling as she slipped into a numb haze.

The next thing she knew, she was in the ER, lying on a bed as a nurse cleaned her wrists. Johnny stood by with his hand on her boot. Johnny: always there, always helpful. A smile touched her lips at the thought of him. The scar on his face formed a deep furrow along his cheek, his eyes held deep sorrow. Then she remembered: where was Ty? Sam closed her eyes and sank back into the morphine.

Sam awoke sometime later. She didn't know how much time had passed, but she was alone in the room and could hear the bustle of the ER on the other side of the door. She looked around, trying to shake the haze. The side of her face burned, as if it had been touched with a hot skillet. Her wrists were bandaged, it hurt to flex her fingers. The skin on her shoulders was painful, as if she had fallen asleep in the sun. She flexed her arms and legs, returning the blood to her numb limbs, assuring herself she was intact.

The door to her room opened and Daniels and Michaels marched in. She dropped her eyes to her hands, unable to look at their faces. Sam knew why they were there. They had come to tell her about Ty. She bit the inside of her lip to keep her emotions in check, drawing blood across her tongue. She thought back to her father's funeral and the efforts at self-control she had employed to get through his service. She had refused to cry. She would take the news of Ty as she had taken her father's death: with stoicism and courage. She stared at her hands and waited for them to speak.

Out of the corner of her eye, she watched as their boots were positioned next to her bed. They stood close together on her left. A silent pall fell over the room. As she waited for one of them to speak, she felt a hand on her right ankle, someone standing at the foot of the bed. Her mind whirled and she assumed it was the morphine playing tricks. She slowly lifted her eyes, first to Daniels and Michaels to confirm their position in the room, then she slowly swung her gaze to the foot of the bed, as if trying to see through a fog. She saw the hand on her leg and her eyes followed it upward until she could make out Ty's form standing before her.

The haze engulfed her in another wave, heavy black curtains closing over her eyes. She forced them to focus. It was him. He was real. Ty stood before her, filthy in tee shirt and bunker pants, the exhaustion painting his beautiful features. He dropped his face into his hands and Michaels and Daniels quickly exited the room.

The next thing Sam knew Ty was holding onto her. She blinked repeatedly, trying to get her mind around the fact that he was there; that he was in one piece, he was safe. Sam closed her eyes and drifted in the warmth of the morphine, holding onto Ty with all she had.

After a while, Sam dozed, and Ty stole out of the room. Daniels came in on silent feet, approaching the bed cautiously, placing a gentle hand on her arm. Sam's eyes fluttered open. Too weary to speak, she managed to place her hand over his and smile. He left without a word and she drifted off again.

Sam awoke hours later, her head clearing as she struggled to sit up. Ty was curled in the corner, fast asleep in a chair. Sam watched him as she worked her legs over the side of the bed. She stretched her back, wincing at the tightness of her shoulders, but the pain had subsided to a dull ache and all she could think of was getting home. She stood up cautiously, not trusting her legs. Her wrists stung, but the pain was tolerable. She slowly approached him, carefully lowering herself before him, kneeling between his knees. She laid her bandaged wrists on his thighs. Ty opened his eyes and smiled. He went to sit up and flinched, his hand automatically going to his side.

"What happened?" Sam placed her hand over his.

"Just got banged up on the way down." He winced again.

Sam lifted his shirt and could see the bruised area over his ribs where his chest had struck the railing. As the stairwell came down, Johnny and Tate had managed to jump clear. Ty had landed in a heap among the twisted metal. He was fortunate the stairwell collapsed beneath him, absorbing most of the impact. He was able to roll away from it and escape serious injury. Once on the ground, he had been pulled off to the side as a medic examined his ribs. He struggled to catch his breath, which had been knocked from him when he impacted the ground. He tried to scream at the medic to hurry; that he had to get back to Sam.

Ty had watched with horror from below as she tried to fend off the flames. It seemed like an eternity, Sam huddling on the platform. Finally, Michaels had raced up the ladder and snatched her, bringing her down as if she weighed nothing. Ty could only watch, impotent, unable to help.

Sam placed her hand over the wound, the curve of her palm conforming to the side of his chest. Ty stroked her hair as Sam laid her head in his lap. They held on to each other, relishing their safety. Daniels entered the room quietly and stood watching before they turned their gaze to him, smiling in unison. Michaels was right, Daniels thought. They were so much like twins.

"Are you ready to get out of here?" Daniels asked, returning their smiles. Ty helped Sam up as she shook off the residual effects of the morphine. The nurse entered with a clipboard and Sam took a seat on the side of the bed as they completed her release. Michaels entered tentatively and Sam watched from the bedside as he approached and stood before her.

"You scared the shit out of us," he said, smiling but disconcerted by the closeness of the room.

"Thank you so much," Sam said, taking his hands. She had replayed the scene in the midst of her haze: Michaels flying up the ladder, his large hand pulling her from the platform, the ease with which he brought her down. The man's abilities had always impressed her, and her appreciation swelled each time she flashed back to the rescue.

Embarrassed, Michaels gave her fingers a gentle squeeze and backed away. Ty was standing next to Daniels and Sam smiled, noting again the similarities in their stance.

"Samantha, the practical exam is tomorrow but we're going to reschedule you and Ty for next week," Daniels announced as she stood up from the bed.

"That's not necessary," Sam replied, flexing her legs, glancing from Daniels to Michaels.

"You can't perform injured. Ty's injured as well. It won't be a problem," he assured her. But Sam would have none of it. The thought of having to reschedule ignited her fury. She didn't want to come back for the exam; she wanted to take it alongside her classmates. Arranging a special exam smacked of preferential treatment and she refused to have that stamp placed on her after all the hard work she had put in.

"Commander," Sam replied sternly, "I'm taking that exam tomorrow if it kills me." She stood before him, shoulders set, her bandaged wrists at her side, reminding Daniels of her spilling the coffee in her kitchen. Daniels smiled despite himself, shaking his head.

"I think that's a really bad idea, Samantha."

Ty jumped in. "Commander, I don't want to reschedule either. We both want to go through with the others; graduate with our class." The earnestness in Ty's face prevailed.

"All right, you two hardheads can have it your way. But if you screw up, there's not much we can do for you."

Michaels ruffled Ty's hair as they headed for the door. Sam leaned over and whispered to Daniels, "You're only supposed to call me Samantha when we're alone." She touched his hand lightly as she passed.

XXII

The test was going to be harder than she thought. Daniels was right; it was going to be torture putting on an airpack and manipulating gear and equipment with her injuries. *Damn that man for always being right!*

Ty had spent the night again, this time shunning the couch in exchange for curling up next to Sam. They couldn't imagine separating after what they had been through. Sam refused to let him out of her sight. They had left the hospital and returned to the academy to collect their gear. Sam moved cautiously, guarding her injuries. Ty grasped at his side from time to time, but eventually, they stowed their gear and ambled out to the parking lot.

"We move like a couple of senior citizens," Ty said, grinning as they slowly climbed into the car.

They grabbed a pizza on their way home, devouring it on the balcony, their hunger kicking in once they finally sat down and relaxed. Ty carefully covered Sam's bandaged wrists with plastic wrap and she headed for the shower. Afterwards, once Ty was bathed, Sam treated his chest with an antibacterial as he sat on the edge of the bed, staring out the window, lost in thought. Sam gave his knee a light squeeze. His eyes sailed back to the room and he smiled his golden smile.

They climbed into bed and Sam curled up behind him. She flashed back to the platform, the intense fear that had nearly strangled her. She stroked Ty's head, not wanting to waste a moment sleeping, so close had they come to being separated forever. Ty slept soundly, his breathing a soft rhythm that eventually lulled Sam to sleep. They woke as the first light crept stealthily into the room.

Once Sam was up, she realized how painful the test was going to be. The side of her jaw was still red but had faded to a pale blush overnight. Ty had coated her shoulders with lotion before bed, which eased the tightness, but her wrists still ached. She flexed her fingers with difficulty and fretted at the thought of grasping tools. She had been given a prescription for pain, but fearing it would impact her performance, she downed three ibuprofens instead, hoping they would knock the edge off. She laid three tablets out on the counter for Ty.

They donned their academy clothes and then headed to class, reviewing tactics as they drove, going over techniques; reminding each other of the pitfalls. They arrived as the officers were heading in from their run. Daniels examined them critically.

"How are you two holding up this morning?" he asked with skepticism. Michaels stood next to him, eyeballing the cadets. Like Daniels, he doubted they would be able to successfully navigate the exam.

"We're just great," Ty exclaimed with mock enthusiasm, drawing doubtful smiles from both men.

"Well, we'll just see how great you are once you have to throw a ladder," Michaels grumbled, despite his grin.

They headed inside to their respective locker rooms. There would be no PT this morning since the cadets would be on the field all day for the final. It was a welcome break from their normal routine. Sam was relieved they wouldn't have to run.

Sam's group welcomed her back. The class assembled their gear and headed across the field to the tower. Their final was designed to mimic the state exam. If they passed, they were shoo-ins for the state test, unless something went wrong, which was always a possibility when working around equipment. But the academy prided itself on its pass ratio; the students who made it through their course typically sailed through their state certification.

As they headed across the field, Mark jogged up beside Sam, glancing anxiously at her bandaged wrists. He stopped her with a hand to her arm as the others went ahead. Sam dropped her gear to the ground, wincing. Mark placed his alongside. He swiped at his mouth with the back of his hand.

"Are you all right?" he asked hesitantly, shifting his stance and eyeing her.

"I'm hanging in there. I feel like shit, my face hurts like hell, and my wrists ache, but I think I'll make it," she replied, forcing a smile. Mark dropped his eyes.

"I feel terrible," he said, staring at the ground, fumbling with the clasp on his suspenders. "I feel like the whole damn stairwell deal was my fault." He glanced up at her before dropping his eyes again. "Bill and I jerked around with that fuckin' dummy for so long, I think maybe we caused the stairwell to come off."

Sam laid a hand on his arm. Mark slowly lifted his eyes.

"The stairwell failed because it was old. I'm sure your big ass didn't help matters, but it was bound to come down, sooner or later," Sam said, grinning. "We're all OK, Mark. Don't beat yourself up."

Mark gave a sigh, smiled, and straightened his stance. As they bent to pick up their gear, Sam bumped him with her hip, knocking him off balance, making him drop his helmet. Mark laughed, snatched his helmet from the ground, and tapped her on the backside with it as they headed for the tower.

The stations were already set up, the instructors standing by, clipboards poised and ready. The test was divided into two sections; the cadets would move through each station sequentially. The active section would begin with an airpack drill, during which they would have ninety seconds to don the entire ensemble and be breathing off their tanks, ready to make entry. From there they would continue to ladders. They would throw a twenty-four-foot ladder and advance tools or a hoseline, depending on the whim of the instructor. Both were laid out nearby on the tarmac.

Using proper technique, they would climb into the window, straddle the sill, and verbalize checking the floor by rapping on it with their tool or nozzle. After a cue from the instructor, they would descend, reverse the throw, stow the ladder, and proceed to the smoke maze.

They would have three minutes to complete the maze. Upon exiting the maze, they would perform a search during which they would locate and evacuate a dummy. Their final station would involve advancing a charged hoseline and striking three targets. This would conclude the active stations. The second section of the test would be made up of skills stations where they would perform a patient assessment, tie a series of knots, answer tactical questions, and identify a variety of tools. It was going to be a long day and they still had their written test to prepare for, which was scheduled for ten the next morning.

The bottom half of the alphabet started with the second section of the exam. Sam performed her patient assessment and then moved on to ropes and knots, focusing her concentration, blocking out the pain. When it came time to tie a figure eight, she flashed back to Daniels' hands guiding her that night in the tower. She made the last turn of the rope, pulled it tight, and had a perfectly formed figure eight in her hand.

By lunchtime, the top half of the class had completed the active stations, the bottom half, the skills. After lunch, the groups would switch. Bo and Shane sailed through the active section and the relief showed in their faces. The students would not receive their grades until tomorrow, but they knew they had made it through without any major blunders. Mark, Trey, and Bill had also made it through successfully. Sam and the rest would go after lunch. They nervously chewed on their sandwiches.

Ty and Sam sat side by side. Ty polished off his lunch and then leaned into her. "How are you feeling?" he whispered, eyeing her wrists.

"Pretty good," Sam replied, flexing her hands as proof. "I'm not exactly looking forward to throwing my pack on, but I think I'll make it. How about you?"

"My chest hurts but my straps should clear it. Are we studying tonight?" The group had planned a final study session to review for the written exam.

"I'm up for it. Tate said he met with Bo last night and seems pretty confident he'll do OK, but an extra session can't hurt any of us."

"Sounds good." They finished their water, noting the instructors assembling at their stations. "Here we go," Sam muttered, rolling her eyes as Ty jumped to his feet. He pulled her up from the grass and they made their way to the tower.

When Sam threw her pack on the pain was intense. The straps rubbed along her shoulders where the heat had penetrated her coat, smarting each time she flexed. Her mask rode painfully along her jaw, rubbing the scorched area, bringing stinging tears to her eyes with each turn of her head. But her wrists beat all. Sam had smuggled two wristbands in her pocket, hoping they would protect her blistered skin. But they slipped from position as soon as the work began. By the time she arrived at the maze, the pain was so intense she could barely feel her fingers. She managed to make good time, but her legs felt weak and her stomach was beginning to churn.

When Sam arrived at the search room, she was dizzy from the pain. She tried to focus, giving her head a swift shake, trying to clear the cobwebs. But the jarring caused her to lose her balance; she lurched forward and stumbled. Michaels was watching from the sidelines. He marched over and yanked her aside. The sudden movement caused her mask to slip, sending a bolt of pain along her jaw. A muffled cry escaped her lips as his hand gripped her arm. He released it immediately, but the damage was done.

Michaels had her near the wall. Sam fumed as she stared at the floor, her eyes brimming with hot tears.

"What are you doing?" he whispered fiercely. "Do you want to fail?"

Sam concentrated on the floor as she clenched her fists in frustration.

"Sam," he continued, quieter, "you don't have to finish. You can come back." Sam turned and marched to the door of the search room. She dropped into position, fighting to see through her tears as she prepped her gear. Exasperated, Michaels followed her to the door, laid out the instructions, and covered her mask with a blackout.

Sam wouldn't remember much about the search. His command, *"Go!"* reverberated in her head as she blindly pushed forward. She scrambled along the wall before finally locating the dummy. It was reclined atop the battered couch, so she paused to take a few ragged breaths before jerking it to the floor. She turned and reached out for the wall, but her hands found only air.

Sam became confused, her sense of direction, scrambled. She frantically felt the surrounding floor, imagining the clock ticking, her score falling with each passing second. She kicked her boot out, finally striking the wall. She grabbed hold of the dummy and started crawling, tracing the wall with her left hand while dragging the massive weight behind her.

Suddenly, it was as if the room had doubled in size. Certain she had missed the door, she paused to catch her breath, torn between backtracking and pressing forward. She decided to push on and after several minutes of desperate crawling, her hand finally located the door. She scrambled on her knees, pulling the dummy clear of the doorway, then snatched her search tag from her pocket. She fumbled blindly for the doorknob, rapping her knuckles against it and sending painful ripples through her wrist, before slapping the tag on the handle and signaling the room was clear.

"Time!" Michaels called as he scribbled on his clipboard. Sam bent forward, her face to the floor, and tried to control her breathing. Her head pounded as she stripped the blackout from her mask.

Suddenly, Michaels' large hand took hold of her arm and he gently lifted her to her feet. Once Sam was standing, she reached up to remove her helmet and mask, but her arms were sapped. They hung limply at her sides as she fought to catch her breath. Michaels dropped his clipboard, which had to be a first in academy history, and carefully unclipped her strap and removed her helmet, placing it beside her on the concrete. He gently slid her hood off, gathering it around her neck. He loosened the spider of her mask and carefully removed it, trying not to drag it along the side of her face. Once her mask was off, he bent down, retrieved her helmet, and handed it to her. Sam gave him a grateful nod and headed out of the tower for the final station.

Sam stood in position for the hose pull, spreading her feet wide to build momentum. She clutched the nozzle and brought it forward over her shoulder, gripping it in front of her chest so she could use her weight to provide leverage.

The instructor yelled, "*Go!*" and she took off.

The weight of the charged hose was immense. Filled with water, it felt as if she were dragging an automobile. Her shoulder burned with such ferocity that she forgot about her wrists; at least until she found her first mark and went to open the nozzle. She braced the nozzle's handle against her forearm, reawakening the pain in her wrists. The blinding tears returned, and she blinked to clear her vision as she struck the first target.

She slammed the nozzle closed, threw the hose back over her shoulder, and hauled it forward to the second mark. Ignoring the pain, she rammed the nozzle open, striking the second target, almost dropping the hose in the process. Only one more to go.

Once again, Sam slung the hose over her shoulder, which by this time had grown numb from the pain. She leaned into it, heading for the final mark, working on reflex as she struggled across the tarmac. She made it to the final mark, but when she went to open the nozzle, her hands refused to cooperate, her fingers felt paralyzed. She beat the lever with the base of her palm as lightning pain surged through her wrist. As the stream sputtered and stabilized, she took aim. After a few shaky seconds, the stream finally found its mark. She hammered the nozzle closed and the test was done.

As the adjuncts threw her a thumbs-up, she dropped the nozzle to the pavement and headed for the backside of the tower, stripping off her gear as she stumbled forward. She had to get away from the men. She needed to compose herself and clear her face. She was humiliated by her tears. She rounded the backside of the building, relieved to find it vacant.

She dropped to her knees, dumping her pack, and stripping off her coat. As she pulled her wrists free from her sleeves, one of her bandages snagged and was ripped free, exposing the burns on her wrist. Sam cried out in pain and before she knew it, her stomach heaved, and she vomited a small clear puddle onto the concrete.

She tried to control her breathing. Her eyes filled with another round of tears as she struggled to clear her throat when suddenly, Ty's hands were on her. He slid a soothing hand to her back, gently rubbing. Sam swiped at her eyes with the back of a numb hand. When she finally turned around, it wasn't Ty but Daniels kneeling beside her, his hand lightly stroking her back as her breathing quieted. She was done.

~

The drive home was quiet. Sam had her head back, eyes closed, and Ty lost himself in thought. He was relieved their practical was done. Everyone had done well, their confidence bolstered for tomorrow's written exam. Ty had performed flawlessly, and Daniels had even been there to see him finish. But with the written final in the morning and graduation tomorrow night, Ty contemplated the future looming before them.

Sam was determined to work for OFD and had already begun planning the physical training she would undertake to prepare for the grueling entry tests. Ty knew she would do well. She was already a paramedic, had two degrees, and would be one of the few females able to pass OFD's notoriously difficult skills test. Johnny, Mark, and Bill were also applying, so she would be among familiar faces. As for Ty, he was enrolled in EMT school and would work toward his paramedic degree. His lack of EMS certification put him behind many of his classmates and he would be unable to work for a department until he had completed his coursework.

But Ty's concerns over his career paled in comparison to his anxiety over the status of his relationships. What would happen between him and Sam now that they would no longer be together every day? How much would he see of her and would their closeness remain intact? Ty couldn't imagine daily life without Sam in it. The thought of not having her near him caused the same familiar pain in his chest as when he thought of Sam's future with Daniels; the uncertainty of what would happen between them now that they would be free from the boundaries of the academy. Would Ty be replaced by Daniels?

Ty worried about his own relationship with Daniels. Would they still run together on Sundays and if so, would that be the only time he would have with the commander? He had come to cherish his time with Daniels. It fulfilled him in ways even Sam could not. He felt he drew strength from Daniels' presence, as if some essence of the commander infiltrated Ty via osmosis – simply by being close to the man. Ty felt certain Daniels enjoyed their time together, as well. He noticed how pleased the commander seemed when Ty performed well on the field and the way their conversations flowed easily now that they had spent so much time together.

But Daniels had not given any indication they would see each other after graduation. Ty was not even sure if they would be meeting on Sunday to run, since no words had been exchanged on the subject. These thoughts plagued Ty as he drove Sam home. He felt part of his life slipping from him, the very best part. The last three months had shown him what it was to have special bonds and the thought of those bonds slipping away caused a tearing sensation in his gut.

They arrived at Sam's apartment and Ty helped her out. Once upstairs, Ty carried her bag to her room and turned on a hot shower. The bandages around her wrists had been destroyed during the exam. Her left wrist was bare, the right barely wrapped; the remnants of the bandage twisted and dirty from crawling through the tower. Ty carefully cut it away and Sam stumbled toward the shower, too tired to speak, too exhausted even to thank him for his efforts.

When Sam was clean and bundled in pajamas, Ty bandaged her wrists and gave her more ibuprofen. Too tired to eat, she curled up on the couch as Ty went home to change. When he returned, Sam was still on the couch, the cool evening air streaming in through the open glass door.

Sam watched as Ty settled at the other end of the couch. He grabbed one of the small pillows, patting its surface playfully, beckoning her down to his end. Sam gratefully complied, placing her head in his lap, and curling up on her side, her face turned toward him.

As Ty stroked Sam's head, his fears returned. A part of him longed for a continuation of their training. As long as they were students, nothing changed. He and Sam could continue to nurture their closeness, and he and Daniels could still enjoy their time together. Graduation meant the end to all they had come to know and the thought of it filled Ty with trepidation.

Staring down at Sam, he thought about Daniels and the feelings developing between them. Daniels would no longer be her commander. The restraints that had held them in check would dissolve upon graduation. Ty felt as if he were playing against a clock when it came to Sam. Ty would no longer have her friendship exclusively and he wondered what it would be like, sharing her with Daniels.

Sam rested peacefully in his lap. Her face was relaxed, and she appeared to be free of pain. Occasionally, she would glance up, as if reassuring herself he was still there.

Ty slid down so that his body was almost flat. His feet were crossed on the coffee table and he continued to stroke her head. Sam reached up and carefully lifted his shirt, revealing a ragged purple bruise on the left side of his chest, reminding her of Aaron's assault. Ty's skin had been torn by the railing and she examined the fine abrasions as if sifting for gold. Her face lay only inches from the wound. She touched the area gently, tracing the outline of the bruise with a light finger.

Ty's skin was smooth, his scant body hair blond, feather soft. Sam continued tracing her hand across his belly. She didn't know what compelled her, other than the feelings she unknowingly shared with Ty: worries about the end of their training and an unknown future for them both. Touching him reassured her.

Ty was now a part of her. Sam was even becoming used to having him in bed beside her, which she knew was reckless, but she didn't care. Sleeping beside him was like returning to the womb, the thrumming of his heartbeat, a hypnotizing metronome.

When Sam was young, she had wondered what it would be like to have a sibling, someone whose blood ran through her veins, whose genetic code was inherently linked to hers. Sam looked on siblings with a sense of wonder and mystery, a concept foreign to her and her isolated childhood. Ty was the closest she had ever come. Her connection to him had been instantaneous, unexplainable. Sam had no intention of letting go.

As Sam drank in the comfort of his lap, she reflected on the fact that she and Ty were only children, and although they had both grown up without brothers and sisters, their family lives otherwise had been polar opposites. Sam had grown up with a loving father, yet most of her life had been spent on her own, a groundless existence where she moved from place to place. Ty had a home and the familiarity of family and friends, yet a father who kept him ostracized and afraid.

Perhaps what Sam and Ty lacked in their childhoods they found within each other. Sam found a constancy her father was unable to provide, Ty, loving security free from fear. It was as if their voids had been filled the moment they came together.

Sam slid her arm behind him, drawing him closer. She placed her head on his belly, relishing his warmth against her face. Ty continued to stroke her hair and Sam began to doze. He woke her gently, drew her up from the couch, took her hand, and led her to her room. He tucked her in carefully, walked around to the other side of the bed and climbed in silently, curling his body behind her. Ty knew he should go home. He was becoming too accustomed to sleeping beside her. It was unnatural, something he could not explain, but having Sam beside him was like sinking into a warm bath; the soothing silence found beneath its surface.

Ty coveted his nights with Sam and knew that as their lives changed, his time sleeping beside her would grow scarce. But for now, he had her exclusively to himself.

XXIII

Their final morning broke as a clear December day, a cold rush of northern air providing a crispness to the sunrise. The cadets assembled in the cafeteria, nervously poring over their books, gulping steaming cups of coffee as they quizzed each other over untouched breakfasts. Their exam was in less than an hour. Their final grades would be announced as soon as Michaels could scan the answer sheets and calculate their overall scores. Final grades would include fieldwork, exams, and the practical and written finals. Those who passed would attend graduation that evening; those who didn't could petition the State Fire College to retake the test, repeat the entire three-month training, or decide on an alternative career.

The successful cadets would also be given an invitation to the graduation party the following evening and for the first time in his tenure at the academy, Daniels would play host. The students closed their books with the finality of an execution and filed out of the cafeteria, their fate about to be decided.

They settled quietly at their desks as Michaels and Tanner braced up front. A pall fell over the room as they waited for the officers to speak. "You have two hours to complete the exam," Michaels announced solemnly as Tanner distributed the exams. "When you're done, you can wait in the cafeteria. Return to the classroom at one o'clock sharp for your results. You may begin."

The students tore open their packets as Tanner scribbled the time on the board in childlike, jagged numerals. The cadets wrote frantically, the two hours slipping by as they plowed through the questions. As the last few minutes wound down, the stragglers scrambled desperately for answers. Tate had finished first. He had sailed through the course and was expected to receive top honors. The rest of the class slowly filtered into the cafeteria, chattering excitedly, comparing notes. They picked at their lunches and watched the clock.

At two minutes to one, they bolted from the cafeteria, raced down the long hallway, and filed into the classroom. They settled stiffly at their desks, nervously fiddling with pens and pencils. Finally, the door swung open and Michaels and Tanner marched in, their faces blank. Michaels braced at the front of the room, emerald eyes scanning the rows of cadets. He placed his clipboard on the podium, cleared his throat, and began.

"We have calculated your scores and totaled your final grades. They include all coursework you've turned in, your exam scores, and your final exams. We've also graded you on your performance, both in the classroom and on the training field. Your performance scores were based on your attendance, assertiveness on the field, and your overall attitude throughout the course of your training." He raked his eyes over the room one final time.

"We are pleased to announce that all of you have successfully passed your Minimum Standards Training and will be attending graduation this evening!" he exclaimed, his face cracking into a smile.

The class erupted in cheers as handshakes and high fives were exchanged between desks. Mark grabbed Sam's arms and shook her like a ragdoll, yelling, "Holy fuck!" as the cadets celebrated. As Sam straightened her uniform, she glanced over at Bo, who was focusing all his will to keep his emotions in check. He swallowed hard and looked up, catching Sam's eye, shaking his head in disbelief.

Tanner raised a hand to get the class' attention. "Guys!" he shouted. "Listen up! We have your graduation notices and your invitations for the party tomorrow night. The invites include a map, so be there at seven sharp!" He handed out the envelopes. "Graduation's in about five hours, so go home and make yourselves presentable. Be at the auditorium pronto. I'll shit-can your badge if you're late!" he yelled, grinning.

Once the invitations were handed out, Michaels and Tanner headed for the door. Michaels turned and cleared his throat loudly as the noise in the room was squelched.

"Williams," he said sternly, eyeing Ty and silencing the room, "report to the Commander's office ASAP!" He then marched out of the room with Tanner on his heels.

The cadets froze. Sam's head flew toward Ty, who looked as if he had been slapped. He stared at Sam a moment before jerking from his desk.

As Ty made his way down the hall, he wracked his brain. They had all passed, so failure wasn't the issue. He flashed back to Daniels' summons on the training field when he informed him of his father's death. His stomach churned.

Ty entered the lobby and Miss Davis glanced up. "They're waiting," she said in a brittle tone before swiveling toward her computer. Ty approached the door and knocked lightly. "Enter," Michaels called, his voice muffled through the door. Ty opened it slowly and forced his legs into action. Daniels was seated behind his desk, Michaels and Tanner stood alongside. The men made an imposing trio, their faces locked.

"Have a seat, Williams," Daniels said, and the meeting began.

~

Sam was going crazy. She glanced at her watch again as she paced outside the classroom, her head swinging every few seconds in the direction of Daniels' office. The others had left, their faces, which moments ago had been joyous, now marred with concern. It couldn't be anything good. No one was summoned to the office unless it was serious. Perhaps Ty had committed a rules violation without their knowledge. But how could he have passed?

"I'll call you as soon as I know something," she had told Johnny as the rest of the group reluctantly headed out.

Sam glanced up from her watch just as Ty materialized in the hallway. Her stomach gave a nervous flip as she ran up the hall to meet him. She too had flashed back to the rainy day on the field when he had been informed of his father's death. But surely this had nothing to do with his family. The situation was further confounded by Ty's relationship with Daniels: surely Daniels would have given him a heads-up if Ty had done something wrong.

As Sam slowed to a walk, she tried to read his face. He wore a quizzical expression, which morphed into a smile as he drew near. "What the hell?" Sam exclaimed, breathless from the sprint.

"I've been offered a job," Ty said, grinning. "Daniels has offered me a job, here at the academy while I'm in school. I'm going to assist with program scheduling. Apparently, Miss Davis raved about my mastery of the computer spread sheet. Daniels asked me himself. Can you believe this?" A look of wonder had settled in his face as he stared at Sam.

"That's wonderful, Ty!" Sam cried, throwing her arms around him. Ty clung to her as he rocked her back and forth.

Sam was thrilled. For weeks, Ty had been excluded from the excited chatter over job prospects. But now, his new position would enable him to be part of the fire service while he completed his EMS certification. Ty grabbed her hand, and they made their way out of the academy.

~

Ty picked Sam up for the ceremony and they emerged from her building looking sharp and polished in their uniforms. They talked excitedly as they drove, Ty still overwhelmed by the idea of working with Daniels.

"So, when will you start?" Sam sat stiffly in the passenger seat, trying to keep her uniform from wrinkling. She ran an unconscious hand down the front of her shirt.

"One week," Ty replied, beaming. "Daniels told me to take some time off, but I wish I could start Monday. I still can't believe I'll be working there." His voice trailed off as he lost himself in the future.

"Your mom's not going to make it tonight?"

"No, she's got her hands full right now, wrapping things up with the farm."

"When will she move to Savannah?" Sam asked, noting the hint of disappointment that flashed across Ty's face.

"She's signing over her holdings to my uncle, so it won't be long. I'm glad she'll be free of it. She can start a whole new life, just like me." He smiled and threw Sam a wink.

The auditorium was humming with anxious chatter as Sam and Ty strolled in. Ty suddenly whirled when he saw his mother and uncle, grinning from across the room. His mother clapped her hands together and gave an excited hop before mother and son rushed forward to embrace. Ty struggled for composure as his mother spilled happy tears, her beauty raging full force now that the funeral was behind her.

"So nice to see you again, Sam, and congratulations to you both," she said, shaking Sam's hand warmly as Ty and his uncle embraced.

"I'm so glad you could make it," Sam replied as the announcement rang out for the cadets to take their seats.

The students shuffled eagerly into formation along the front row, exchanging anxious nudges as the officers took the stage. The instructors marched up the short staircase, gleaming in full dress uniforms. They arranged themselves in order of rank as Daniels approached the podium, clearing his throat and flipping open his binder. A table off to the side held the badges and certificates, lined up neatly in alphabetical order. The ceremony began.

After a brief overview describing their training and the significance of their newly acquired certification, Daniels called Tate onstage to receive the plaque for top honors. Tate leaped from his seat, marched up to the podium, and stood with shoulders back, stomach sucked in, as Daniels extolled his academic achievements. The cadets acknowledged him with hoots and hollers. Tate beamed as he marched back to his seat.

Daniels then summoned each cadet onstage to receive their certificates and have their badges pinned. After each pinning, Daniels gave a firm handshake, congratulating each student on his accomplishment. As Sam approached the podium, she watched Daniels' face. He avoided her eyes, conscious of the audience watching. Finally, they stood face to face as he pinned the badge to her uniform. Sam watched his fingers, flashing back to the night in the tower, the softness of the rope against his calloused hands. Her eyes slid to his face, relishing its closeness, reminding her of that hot afternoon when he inspected her gear, his eyes raking her with their grey intensity. As Daniels finished, their eyes locked, and Sam read each memory reflected in his gaze. He then shook her hand stiffly, congratulated her with a quick smile, and she was gone.

Ty followed, bounding across the stage. Daniels grinned as he pinned Ty's shirt, the two of them sharing the joy of the moment, happy in each other's company. As Daniels went to shake Ty's hand, Ty pushed past it, embracing the commander heartily as the audience laughed. They shook hands and Ty left the stage.

After the ceremony, the cadets exchanged congratulations and huddled up for group photos before filtering out to attend private celebrations.

"Come with us," Ty pleaded as he and Sam stood together, their hands locked. His mother and uncle waited near the exit.

"You go with your family," Sam said with a flick of her head. "I'm sure you and your mother need some time to catch up. We'll have the class party tomorrow night."

"You sure I can't persuade you? I hate to think of you going home alone."

"I'm fine," Sam replied, giving his hands a firm squeeze. She then grabbed hold of him. "Call me tomorrow," she said, her face buried against his neck. She released him and walked quickly away.

Sam was heading for the hallway when Mark yanked her aside with a large hand. "Sam, this is my father. Dad, this is Samantha," Mark said, indicating the older version of himself who stood stiffly near the doorway.

"It's nice to meet you, Mr. Harris. It was great going through the course with Mark," Sam said, craning her neck to read his expression. The man stood well over six feet and shared Mark's imposing build.

"Nice to meet you, Samantha," he replied, his voice resonating through a massive chest as he gave her a crushing handshake. He paused as he glanced at his son. "We're very proud of him," he added, smiling as he looked him over. Mark stared at his father and then dropped his eyes, his face softening into a bashful grin.

Sam smiled, gave Mark's giant arm a pat, threw a nod to his father, and then headed down the hallway. Inside her locker room, she grabbed her meager belongings from her locker, slamming it for the last time. Her thoughts flew back to the first day of class, standing in front of the mirror, marveling at the stranger before her. She dropped her bag to the floor and approached that same mirror, standing stiff-shouldered as she admired her reflection. Her uniform was now a part of her. It represented the person she had become and the future that lay ahead. She smiled to herself, grabbed her bag from the floor, and flicked off the light as she left.

Sam made her way out to the parking lot just as Michaels and Daniels emerged from the far exit. They approached like sentries; their uniforms immaculate as the high lights cut white arcs through the crisp night air.

"Congratulations, Sam," Michaels said warmly, extending a large hand. He flashed back to her practical exam, her determination to finish and the moment they had shared when he removed her mask and helmet. Just as Sam admired Michaels, he had come to respect Sam. They shook hands warmly as Daniels looked on. Suddenly, Michaels turned back toward the building.

"Matt, I forgot one of my files. I'll see you tomorrow night," he said and quickly retreated. But before he left, he caught Daniels' eye, communicating in that silent language the two men shared.

Sam and Daniels stood for a moment, breathing in the cold night air. Sam kicked at a stone with her boot and shifted the bag on her shoulder. Sam's lack of family in attendance had provoked a stab of sadness in Daniels as he watched the cadets rejoice following the ceremony. But aside from her obvious joy at the occasion, she seemed utterly unaware of her isolated status.

"No big plans tonight?" he asked quietly.

"No, I was just going to head home. Ty's mother surprised him, so it seemed more appropriate to let them celebrate together," she said, glancing at the ground.

Her happiness for Ty had quickly turned to disappointment when Sam realized he would be obligated to celebrate with his mother afterwards. Sam had looked forward to a quiet celebration, just the two of them. She had even chilled a bottle of champagne for the occasion. As she was walking out of the academy, she had planned to head home, plop down on the balcony, and scarf the bottle herself.

"Would you like to grab a celebratory cup of coffee?" Daniels asked, smiling.

Sam cocked her head. "I have a better idea."

~

Daniels followed her into her building. On the way over, Sam contemplated how she would handle being alone with the commander now that she was no longer his student. Before, she could hide behind the barriers imposed by their rank structure. Released from such constraints, the barriers fell away. The freedom made her nervous; Sam was more at ease navigating within boundaries.

They entered the dark apartment and Sam smiled as Daniels reached to turn on the small light in the hallway. She excused herself and went into the bedroom to change out of her uniform. When she came out, he had opened the glass door and was staring out into the darkness, his uniform defining his body in crisp angles.

Daniels turned as Sam approached. He noted her change of clothes and glanced down at himself, grinning at the formality of his attire. Sam caught the look and without a word, marched right up to him and slowly began unbuttoning his coat. His hands remained buried in his pockets; he watched her intently as she worked.

Sam slipped his coat off, noting its heft and softness. She folded it neatly and laid it nearby as Daniels hands returned to his pockets. Sam reached for his tie, sliding her finger beneath the knot, and drawing it carefully away from his throat. With the knot loosened, she pulled the tie free. It slid from his neck in a soft swish and she folded it across his coat. Sam unbuttoned his collar and then moved to each of his sleeves, rolling them up to expose his forearms. She could feel his eyes on her, their intensity raising the hairs on the back of her neck. Slowly, she pulled the bottom of his shirt free, her hands grazing his waist, his shirttails hanging loosely at his hips. She eyed him and flashed a quick smile. Daniels now stood as Sam intended: stripped of all authority.

He followed her into the kitchen and Sam pulled the champagne from the fridge and two tall glasses from the cupboard. They headed out onto the balcony where Daniels cracked the bottle, firing the cork into the darkness as they laughed.

They sat for a long time, drinking and talking. Sam noted how he had slipped into his former posture, feet perched on the railing, his body once again a beautiful checkmark. When the bottle was drained, they headed inside, chilled from the night air. Daniels kicked off his shoes and they sat together on the couch until Sam guided his head onto her lap. She thought he might balk at the submissive posture, but he followed with ease, placing his hand casually behind his head as he reclined beneath her.

Their conversation turned to the past and Daniels spoke of his marriage, the accident, and the effect it had had on his life. He discussed the difficulty of returning to shift, the extrication scene that had paralyzed him in his command vehicle, his exodus from the department, and his life-renewing move to the academy. His story unfolded easily. Daniels felt free talking to Sam and the intensity in her face drew him further along. As he spoke, Sam's hand floated to his head, touching his hair, the sensation sending chills down his neck. Her other hand lay lightly on his chest, the reverberations from his voice tingling her fingertips.

Eventually, Daniels fell silent. There was nothing more to tell. He felt unburdened, the grief finally shaken. He closed his eyes and Sam's fingers moved to his face, tracing the arch of his eyebrows, touching the soft bristles above his mouth. She watched as his face relaxed. His brown lashes lay against his cheek and she remembered her dream in the tower when she had watched him work the rope.

Without thinking, she bent down and kissed his mouth. The sensation sent a jolt down his spine; his hand found the back of her head. He noted the boyishness of her short hair, its contrast with the delicate shape of her skull. He pressed her harder as their tongues met for the first time, the warmth of her mouth and the effects of the champagne sending ripples of heat into his core. He felt as if he were falling. After a moment, Sam withdrew, staring down into those clear grey eyes.

~

Ty showed up early the next morning. Sam opened the door to find him smiling and out of breath.

"What are you doing here so early?" Sam griped, as she did an about face and headed back to bed. "I didn't know we had a run scheduled," she said over her shoulder. She dove back into bed, burrowing beneath the covers, hiding her head. Ty plopped down next to her, grabbing at her sides to get her moving. Sam shrieked.

"Get up! Let's go run. You've got OFD to prep for," Ty reminded her as she continued to squirm. That was all it took to get Sam moving. She flipped the covers back with an angry huff, rolled her eyes, and crawled out of bed. Ty sat back against her pillow, hands locked behind his head, grinning as she trudged toward the bathroom.

Sam's burns were healing quickly. The area along her jaw had faded and was barely sore, the skin around her wrists had regained some of its elasticity. The blisters were quickly disappearing, and her shoulders were back to normal. She flipped off the bathroom light and went in search of her tennis shoes.

They headed out on their usual route, through the neighborhoods of downtown. The streets were silent in the predawn darkness, the only sound the lone call of a cardinal from some far-off limb. As she ran, Sam replayed her time with Daniels. He had left shortly after midnight and it had taken her a while to finally fall asleep, her mind churning with their conversation, the intensity of his mouth.

As their run approached an hour, Sam signaled to Ty. They slowed to a walk as the sun made its way through the trees, cutting a sharp angle from the southeast. The air was cold, and the smell of cedars hung heavy. They walked for a while before settling in the grass near one of the small lakes dotting the tree-lined street.

Ty lay back on the grass, legs bent, arms outstretched. Sam sat close to him and placed a light hand on his belly.

"How was it with your mother last night?" she asked through deep breaths.

"It was nice," Ty replied, still breathing hard from the run. "We dropped my uncle off at the hotel and went to dinner. It was strange, you know, talking about our futures, knowing Dad is really gone." Ty's mind drifted out over the lake before floating back to shore. "Everything's almost done, as far as turning the farm over," he added as he picked up Sam's hand and wiped it across his sweaty brow, grinning.

Sam wiped her hand on his shirt and gave him a hearty slap on the belly. "When will she move?"

"I guess within a couple of weeks," Ty replied, his breathing slowing.

"What about all your things? What will she do with your stuff?"

"She's going to take it with her. She'll pack it up with her things and hold it for me."

"Don't you want some of it here?" Sam asked, flashing to Ty's bare apartment. "Now that you have a job lined up, perhaps you might consider moving out of that depressing little hovel you call an apartment," she added, smirking.

"It's not that bad a place."

"Well, it could use some decent furniture, fresh paint, and a thorough scrubbing."

"Maybe I'll look for a new place," Ty replied wistfully. "I'm month-to-month there. Would you help me?" He grinned up at her from the grass.

"Of course," Sam replied, pushing the hair lining his face flat, which she knew annoyed him.

"Hey!" he exclaimed, running his fingers through his hair until it stood on end, damp with sweat.

The silence settled back around them. The neighborhood slept, most of the houses still dark. Ty sat up suddenly and edged in beside her. He took up one of her hands and inspected it.

"What did you do after the ceremony? I felt bad, leaving you."

"I came home," Sam replied, pausing and eyeing him. "Daniels came with me."

Ty was silent. He locked fingers with her before continuing.

"What's going to happen with that?" he asked, quieter.

"I don't know," Sam replied, reaching down to pluck a blade of grass from between her feet. She held the blade between her fingers, noting the faint ridges that lined its length. "I really like being with him. We talked a long time last night. He told me about his marriage and the death of his wife. Did you know he was married?"

Ty stared at the ground between his feet. "Yes, he told me about it one evening after our run. Sorry I didn't tell you. I wasn't sure if he meant for me to keep it to myself or not."

"It was more appropriate coming from him." Sam tossed the blade of grass and brushed her hands together.

"I assume you're going to see more of him?" Ty asked hesitantly, eyeing the sparse traffic on the roadway.

"I'd like to. Will it be strange, now that you'll be working for him?"

Ty paused again. "I think I've worked through most of it." He glanced over at her. "At first, it was a bit weird. We all seem so interconnected, but in different ways. My feelings for you get all mixed up with my feelings for him. Sometimes it's hard to wade through it."

"I feel the same," Sam replied. "The closeness I feel for you is very different from what I feel when I'm around him, but I don't want anything to get in the way of what you and I have." She looked directly into his face. Ty held her gaze and smiled, leaning his shoulder against her.

"Look, I don't care who you see, as long as they know I come first!" Ty exclaimed with a grin, dropping her hand, grabbing her in a headlock, and wrestling her to the ground. The attack made Sam laugh so hard she could barely wiggle free. When he finally let her go, they lay staring up into the early sky, their hands locked once again.

~

Daniels' house was tucked on a tree-lined street in a stylish neighborhood north of downtown. It had an elegant cream exterior and was situated on a vast shaded lot that banked down in back to a lake. Light spilling from the house illuminated the water's surface, glass-like in the still evening. It was a large house; too large, Sam thought, for one person. She wondered what he did with all that room.

Cars lined the street in either direction, all recognizable from the academy. Sam noticed Michaels' pickup parked in the driveway. They entered the foyer, which opened onto a large living room. The lake was visible through a wall of windows lining its far side. A spacious kitchen spread off to the right. The house was done in earth tones and the California influence was apparent. A fire blazed in the fireplace, adding to its warmth and comfort.

"Well, if it isn't the twins!" Tanner exclaimed as he ushered them in. Ty and Sam looked at each other.

"Twins?" Sam replied, staring at the officer. Ty simply shrugged and kept walking. Tanner grabbed him roughly by the shoulders while maintaining his three-foot safety buffer from Sam. He beckoned her with a wave of his big hand.

As Tanner dragged Ty inside using a beefy arm around his neck, Sam hung back, still taking in the room. She was anxious to see Daniels' home. She had pictured something colder, more clinical. She hadn't expected the place to be so inviting. Seeing the rustic comfort of his house made Sam realize how little she knew about the commander, how much there was still to learn.

The noise level in the room was high as the men filtered in and out through French doors, hitting the keg out back and wandering inside for food, which was spread throughout the large kitchen. Sam scanned the room, nodding to Mark and Bill, who were settled in the corner on a large couch. She couldn't spot Daniels. To her left, a room opened and she glimpsed bookshelves lining the walls. She peeled off from the crowd and headed inside.

The den was warmly lit, the furniture in deep browns. A mahogany desk sat beneath wide windows that looked out over the front lawn. The shelves were filled with reference materials on incident command, special operations, and fire administration. There was also a large section on environmental science and coastal habitats, which surprised her; Sam hadn't realized Daniels had an interest in nature. It had never come up in their conversations. She pulled a geology book from the shelf and flipped through it, slipping into the chair behind the desk. Twenty minutes later, that's where he found her.

Sam glanced up with a start to see Daniels standing in the doorway, leaning against the frame with arms crossed, a smile on his face, a bottle of beer in his hand.

"What are you doing?" he asked, grinning. "If you hadn't noticed, there's a party going on." Sam jumped up from the seat.

"I was just flipping through and lost track," she stammered. Sam quickly slammed the book shut and stuffed it back on the shelf. Daniels remained in the doorway, smiling. He seemed to enjoy seeing her flustered. Sam planted her hands on her hips, shot him a perturbed glance, and swung her eyes back to the shelves, pretending to ignore him. Daniels glided over to the shelf.

He pulled out the book she had been reading, glancing at the title. "Geology?"

"I love it," Sam replied, looking down at the book. "It's one of my favorite sciences." She wasn't sure if she should take the book or keep her hands at her sides. She glanced at him sideways, frustrated by her awkwardness.

Daniels slipped the book back onto the shelf and turned to her. "How about something to drink?"

"That'd be great," she replied, relieved to escape the confines of the den.

Sam followed him out and they joined the crowd in the living room. Johnny was well on his way to drunken oblivion, and Sam was happy that for once, he would be able to enjoy himself without worrying about others.

Johnny and Tate caught her as she tried to follow Daniels through the room. Daniels was absorbed by the crowd, so she stayed and chatted. As they talked, Daniels reappeared, slipping her a beer before disappearing. Johnny watched their exchange, catching her eye as Daniels moved on. Sam smiled as she took a long sip.

The party went on for hours and Sam saw little of Ty. The instructors had already taken him in, knowing he would be working among them in a matter of days. Sam enjoyed watching his newfound status take hold. The officers spoke of his upcoming position and the opportunities he would have at the academy. Ty would be initiated by some of the best instructors in the state, taken under their wings to learn the latest techniques in special ops. Daniels was obviously molding him for an exceptional future.

As the evening wore on, the crowd slowly thinned. The students conducted clean-up operations using the same coordinated precision they employed on the field and the house was quickly returned to its original order. Ty had disappeared inside. Michaels was the last to leave. He shook Sam's hand and tossed Daniels a grin as they saw him out.

Suddenly, the house was quiet. The fire had been reduced to embers and there was low music playing in the background, but the sudden absence of voices left a palpable silence in its wake.

"Where's Ty?" Sam asked as Daniels pulled two more beers from the last bit of ice in the sink.

"I haven't seen him," he said, handing her a beer. Daniels moved past her toward the hallway. As he passed the den, he stopped. Sam joined him in the doorway and peered inside. Ty was reclined on the couch, legs splayed out, lost in the depths of slumber.

Daniels handed Sam his beer and returned to the living room, pulling a blanket from the back of one of the couches and returning to the den where he carefully placed it over Ty. Ty gave a bristle of acknowledgment as Daniels stared down at him and once again, Sam was moved by the connection between the two men.

With beers in hand, they headed through the back doors and out onto the expansive lawn. They walked to the water's edge and sat down. The grass was thick and soft, the air around them chilled. The sky was clear, and a heavy quarter moon hung low on the horizon, fading to a burnt orange as it sailed westward.

Sam sat with knees bent, her arms draped as Daniels stretched out beside her. They talked quietly but felt more inclined to silence, the night was that beautiful. After a moment, he pulled her down against him. Sam curled into him as his arms came around her, holding her close. Daniels put his face against her hair and Sam could hear him breathe deeply. Her arm encircled his chest. They lay in silence as the moon was swallowed by the horizon.

As the temperature dropped, Daniels slowly sat up, drawing Sam up with him. They made their way back to the house, pausing before reaching the back doors. Daniels stood before her, outlined by the soft lights from the house. His face was hidden in shadow, but Sam could make out the line of his jaw, its familiar angles. His hand sailed to the back of her head and he pulled her against him, kissing her mouth. The press of his body intensified the experience and Sam was lost in his warmth. She tucked her head on his shoulder, her face against his throat, and she could just make out the faint rhythm of his pulse against her lips. Daniels took her hand and led her into the house.

~

When Ty awoke, it took him a moment to remember where he was. He glanced at his watch, noting the early hour. He rose from the couch on unsteady legs and moved quietly into the living room but found it empty. The back doors were closed, the house silent. He wandered into a hallway, unfamiliar with the layout, but intent on finding Sam.

As he crept down the hall, he came to a door that stood partially open. Faint light bathed the room in a yellow softness, and he could make out a bed in the center of the room.

Sam and Daniels lay curled on top, tucked into each other, a light blanket outlining their legs. Ty stared at Sam's face, how serene she appeared, every angle smoothed by the depth of her sleep. And at Daniels beside her, completely at peace, the lines around his eyes erased by her presence.

Ty stood in the darkness and watched them for a while. He thought about them individually and then together, as they were now, moved by the emotions he felt for both. The affection and understanding he shared with Sam, the respect and admiration he held for Daniels. The bonds they shared surpassed anything he had experienced in his young life.

Ty took one last look, smiled, and pulled the door closed behind him.

Acknowledgments

This book, my first venture into fiction, is the product of many helpful hands. I thank the people at the Florida Historical Society Press, who are so giving with their time and advice. For my friends and family who provided feedback and encouragement, especially Leah - my wonderful sister and ardent supporter. To George McFarland and Chris Gallaway, who painstakingly proofed the manuscript. And finally, to Kirsten Russell, who has mentored me through this process. Her instruction, feedback, and shared knowledge made this book possible, and I thank her from the bottom of my heart.

Thank you for reading *The Mass of Men*. I hope you enjoyed it.

Since reviews are an author's lifeblood, I would sincerely appreciate it if you took a moment to **leave a review** at your place of purchase.

To stay up to date on my books/publications, please go to:

- https://rachelwentzbooks.com/
- Like my Facebook page: https://www.facebook.com/RachelWentzBooks
- Follow me on Twitter: https://twitter.com/RKWentzBooks

For those interested in archaeology, please check out my other books on Amazon:

Life and Death at Windover: Excavations of 7,000-Year-Old Pond Cemetery

Chasing Bones: An Archaeologist's Pursuit of Skeletons

Searching Sand and Surf: The Origins of Archaeology in Florida

And my latest book, *The Body Blog: Explorations in Science and Culture*, Silver Medal winner in the Florida Authors and Publishers Association annual President's Award in Adult Nonfiction.

A sample of the first three essays is provided below.

INTRODUCING THE BODY BLOG

April 3

When I was a child, my class took a field trip to St. Augustine's Fountain of Youth. Immersed in the humid heat of Florida's Atlantic coast, we drifted beneath ancient oaks, their limbs draped in Spanish moss, as our guide, sweating heavily beneath the bulk of his conquistador costume, wove the tales of that historic site. That trip would set a course for my life for it marked the beginning of my obsession with the human skeleton. But it also impacted me in another way: it was the first time I truly contemplated death.

Not that I wasn't already mesmerized by bones or naïve to the concept of death. My first experience with both occurred following the death of our obnoxious parrot, Polly, who finally expired after years of screeching and bad behavior. We buried him with great ceremony beneath a dark umbrella of palm and for days, I contemplated the changes taking place within the shoebox housing his remains, wondering where his annoying little soul was residing, whose hand he was now painfully pecking.

But it was in St. Augustine where I first contemplated my own death. After an exhausting day of trudging through history, our sweaty little group was shuffled into the final exhibit, which back then was an exposed burial ground where Native Americans had been interred some two thousand years before. I stared out over that burial, which held several adults and a few small children, and was shocked to realize that at one time, those pale, dry bones had been animated in life; that the skeletons that lay before me once belonged to living, breathing individuals just like me and that, like them, one day I too would die.

That experience launched my obsession. Suddenly, I viewed my body not merely as a collection of tissues that enabled me to go about my daily business, but as a magical vehicle through which I experienced the world. My body, with all its inner workings, was life itself. And like all of life, it would one day come to an end. I was hooked.

Since then, my careers—as a former firefighter-paramedic and as a bioarchaeologist—have revolved around the human body. As a medic, I dealt with devastating injuries and chronic illness, mitigating both as I frantically worked on patients, piecing together the fragmented remains of high-speed collisions, sending jolts of electricity through hearts ambushed by sudden cardiac arrest, and plugging the holes of those peppered by gunfire amidst the violent streets of Orlando.

As a bioarchaeologist, I examine the bones of the long dead in an attempt to interpret their life experiences: fractures resulting in angulated limbs, infection that settled blanket-like over the skeleton, dental disease that must have sent its host howling, and the creeping grip of arthritis resulting in gnarled and debilitated joints. This book is an extension of my obsession and a means of indulging two of my favorite preoccupations—the inner workings of the human body and how each one of us is impacted by the culture in which we live.

MUSINGS ON AN AUTOPSY

April 4

Let me go back in time, back to when I was a budding paramedic student, before I even knew there was such a field as bioarchaeology. Let me tell you about one of my early experiences with death, one that altered my concept of the "body" and forever changed how I view life.

I was in my first semester of paramedic school, barely twenty-two years old. I had already completed my emergency medical technician certification—a semester of coursework followed by months of fieldwork—and during that time, I had been exposed to the dead. But as an EMT student, I was relegated to the periphery. Suddenly, paramedic school thrust me to the forefront of patient care, where I was forced to make treatment decisions that would correct, stabilize, or kill my patients.

The paramedic curriculum is designed to help students come to grips with this new level of responsibility. The curriculum also forces students to confront death, so that they may develop the emotional callouses necessary for the situations they will invariably face in the field.

The highlight of my first semester was a trip to the county morgue, where we would spend the day observing autopsies. In reality, the visit served two purposes: not only were we forced to confront death in all its cold, antiseptic reality, but the autopsies would provide lessons in anatomy and physiology we simply couldn't get from a textbook or in a lab. This experience would leave a lasting impression on me.

The autopsy room was an assault on my senses. Bright lights glared against steel countertops, the sting of disinfectant penetrated my sinuses, and the sight of sheet-draped bodies made my stomach flip in nervous anticipation. I followed the tech to the nearest table. He slowly removed the sheet, folding it upon itself as he worked his way down the body of a young female. Her jaw lay slack, her eyes closed and sunken. Blood and cerebrospinal fluid seeped from her left ear and her fingers lay curled at her sides. Her fingernails were painted a frosty pink. Her toenails matched.

The tech explained the scenario. A waitress at an all-night café, the girl had been driving home from work early that morning when the driver's door in her pickup gave way. She wasn't wearing a seatbelt and was subsequently dumped onto the pavement where she landed on her head, suffering a fatal skull fracture. The tech reached for the gleaming scalpel and the autopsy began.

He made the typical Y-incision, starting at each collarbone, meeting at the sternum, and then drawing a deep straight line through her abdomen, unzipping her with smooth efficiency. He then peeled back her flesh and proceeded to give me a tour of her anatomy.

It was fascinating. Her glistening organs were neatly tucked within her belly, her heart and lungs nestled beneath her ribs. What captivated me even more than their organization was their stillness. The heart no longer beat, the lungs didn't inflate, her bowels had ceased their churning, and her stomach would never again growl.

He systematically removed each organ. Some were weighed, some were sampled by taking thin sections of tissue, which were deposited into small containers filled with formaldehyde. He squeezed the contents of her stomach into a jar as my own stomach lurched in response. After a few embarrassing dry heaves, I was able to regain my composure and the autopsy continued.

Despite its clinical setting, the procedure was strangely intimate. Her heart fit neatly in the technician's palm as he gently placed it on the scale. He carefully lifted a pale ovary from her pelvis and, with a delicate finger, pointed to the small shiny bulge that indicated she had been ovulating at the time of death.

When he made the large incision across the top of her head and folded her scalp down over her face, tucking it neatly beneath her chin, the woman no longer appeared human. Her body, lacking the animation of life, was but a collection of cells, tissues, and organs. She seemed no longer a person. She was now meat on the slab.

I thought about her often in the following weeks. I still think about her, decades later. That day in the morgue altered my perspective of life, death, and everything in between. An autopsy tears a person down to their foundation. It reduces the individual to his or her once-working parts and what is left is the stillness and silence of a lifeless machine.

But she taught me a valuable lesson. Now, when I peer into an ancient grave or examine the bones of those who lived thousands of years in the past, I force myself beyond their death to what they were in life. I think about their dreams, their fears, and how different those dreams and fears must have been from those we cultivate today. And, although their lives speak of a different time, we share a common thread. We are all descended from those ancient Africans whose bodies, through the slow accumulation of traits, would eventually become us.

We will explore that topic next.

MY COUSIN, THE LIZARD

April 7

Last weekend, a lizard took up residence in my kitchen. On nice days, I throw open the doors and bask in the glorious Florida sunshine. He must have sauntered in, taken a liking to the place, and decided to stay a while.

 All day, we went through the same routine. I would enter the kitchen on silent feet, scanning every surface until I located that small splash of green. There he would sit, spread-eagle on the counter, leering at me with his reptilian gaze. I would lunge for him and he'd hightail it back to the safety of the alcove between fridge and stove. By evening, he was so emboldened that I found him lounging on the kitchen table, taking in the last orange of sunset streaming through the French doors. I made one last attempt as he skittered away, then I clicked off the light in disgust and headed for bed.

I didn't see him for a few days, but I knew he was still around. I found his calling cards: tiny black turds with the telltale white salt deposits. He was mocking me.

It wasn't until Wednesday night, as I was stepping into the shower, that I looked down and, lo and behold, there he was, peering at me like a peeping Tom from the base of the sink. I slammed the bathroom door, blockaded the jamb, threw a towel over the air vent, and gave chase. After a few minutes of awkward naked scrambling, I had him. I clutched his plump little body firmly between finger and thumb and headed for the front door. It was at that moment that I took a good look at him and couldn't help but notice our similarities.

He and I, like all vertebrates, share the same body plan, which evolved some five hundred million years ago during the Ordovician Period. Prior to the evolution of the vertebrates, the sea of life (and by that I literally mean "the sea," since it would require a spine for our ancestors to venture onto dry land) was populated by invertebrates. The spineless had the run of the planet for over two billion years before the vertebrates arose.

The earliest vertebrates were the jawless fishes. You are probably asking yourself, "What the hell is a jawless fish and how does one eat without a jaw?" Well, these strange creatures lacked movable lower jaws and were forced to scrape or suck their prey. The evolution of jaws made for more efficient eating, which led to more efficient hunting; a definite edge when your underwater neighborhood includes arthropods the size of NBA All-Stars. Two other necessities for life on land included lungs and limbs. In order to venture out of the water, it helped if you could breathe the air and get from point A to point B. Thus, the vertebrate body plan.

As vertebrates, we have a front and back and a top and bottom, in contrast to jellyfish, those beautiful, translucent blobs. We have a backbone that encases and protects our spinal cord, with a head at one end containing a brain. We have four limbs: two fore (arms) and two aft (legs), and we exhibit bilateral symmetry—our halves are mirror images of each other (at least on the outside; our guts are another story). These are the basics of the vertebrate body plan. Over millions of years of evolution, our bodies have morphed into what they are today. All the strange and wonderful adaptations we see throughout the phylum Chordata are accents on a basic plan.

What I realized as I carried my little friend through the house was that our similar body plans alluded to a shared history. He is a cousin—many million years removed—but a cousin all the same. Our bodies speak of our common lineage. And with that thought, I released him onto the front porch, and he disappeared into the night.